A
TWIST
in TIME

ALSO BY JULIE McELWAIN

A Murder in Time

A TWIST *in* TIME

A Novel

Julie McElwain

PEGASUS CRIME

NEW YORK LONDON

A TWIST IN TIME

Pegasus Books Ltd.
148 W 37th Street, 13th Floor
New York, NY 10018

First Pegasus Books edition April 2017

Interior design by Maria Fernandez

Library of Congress Cataloging-in-Publication Data is available.

ISBN: 978-1-68177-364-3

10 9 8 7 6 5 4 3 2 1

Printed in the United States of America
Distributed by W. W. Norton & Company

With much love to John and Tammy,
who always have my back.

PROLOGUE

The woman fought a shiver as she scampered down the dark back alley, her footfalls echoing hollowly on the cobblestone. She grimaced, wishing for a more silent approach. But there was no way around it. *Get in, get out*, she reminded herself. Her fingers curled around the collar of her serviceable wool coat, clutching it close to her throat in a vain attempt to ward off the night air. It was uncomfortably moist, thanks to the dirty brown fog that had rolled in earlier from the Thames.

God willing, her brief return would not be noted by her mistress. Soon she'd be back at her sister's flat, safely tucked in the trestle bed with a hot brick to warm her feet for the rest of the night.

As she approached the servants' entrance at the back of the Grosvenor Square town house, she withdrew the heavy iron key from her reticule. From the nearby mews stables, the snuffle and snort and shuffling of horses drifted across the alley. In the distance, a night watchman's voice was a lonely warble as he called out the hour: "Eleven o'clock . . . and all's well."

Squinting—it was so bloody dark here with no torch or lantern to light the way—she inserted the key into the lock, and had to bite back a gasp of surprise when the door immediately creaked inward a few inches. She could've sworn they'd locked the door when they'd been told to leave earlier. She vowed that her mistress would *also* never hear about the shoddy security.

Hurriedly, heart thumping, she slipped into the hall and shut the door behind her. For good measure, she threw the thick bolt. Only then did some of her anxiety ease. Even though it was as dark in the hallway as it had been in the alley, she wasn't concerned. She knew every inch of this place, and so didn't bother to light the tallow candles stored in the mahogany cabinet next to the wall.

She moved quickly now down the shadowed corridor. Only when she reached the foyer, well-lit from the many candles flickering in the two-tiered crystal chandelier, did she pause. The light that dispelled the gloom should have been comforting, but she felt exposed.

If my mistress should see me . . .

Her heart, which had calmed since entering the townhouse, began again to beat painfully against her breastbone.

Get in, get out.

Caution slowed her footsteps as she crept to the bottom of the staircase. There, she stopped and held her breath, straining to hear any noise. *Nothing.* They were most likely already in the bedchamber, she decided. She only needed to be quick about her task. Letting out her breath, she lifted her skirts and scurried up the stairs, no longer afraid about making noise—the thick woven rug that ran the length of the steps would absorb her footfalls.

She hesitated again when she reached the top of the stairs. Like a woodland creature scenting danger, she glanced in the direction of the drawing room. The door was open, allowing amber light to pierce the shadows of the hall.

She pivoted in the opposite direction, toward the narrow stairs that would lead her to the servants' quarters on the third floor. *Get in; get out.*

She would never be able to explain why she didn't go about her business, why the light from the drawing room seemed to beckon her. For a moment, she swayed in indecision, her gaze darting back and forth from the servants' stairs to the drawing room door. If her mistress caught her spying, she'd be dismissed without references for certain. Against her better judgment, she picked up her skirts and stole down the hallway to the doorway.

Silently cursing herself for her foolishness, she held her breath and inched forward. Her heart thudded harder. *Just a quick peek . . .*

The next second, her breath whooshed out of her lungs. She stumbled back, her heel catching on her skirt. As she fell, she was already screaming.

1

Sam Kelly did not consider himself a particularly superstitious man. However, as he sat in the Pig & Sail, a popular tavern with Bow Street Runners such as himself, thanks to its short distance to Bow Street Magistrates Court rather than the quality of its whiskey, the back of his neck prickled with an eerie sense of impending doom.

London Town had always been a brutal city, but tensions had been rising ever higher since England had won the war with Boney, finally exiling the little tyrant to Saint Helena. Sam would've rather seen Napoleon hang—or his head roll from *la guillotine*, like so many French aristocrats had during their bloody revolution twenty years ago. It didn't seem fair that the bastard had been sent to live out the rest of his days on a tropical island, while honorable Brits shivered in late September's cool climate.

In England, it should've been a time of jubilation. But there were too many returning soldiers, and the scarcity of work had put the entire country on edge. The recently passed Corn Laws didn't help matters either, sending the grain price soaring beyond the means of honest, hardworking folk.

Sam stared morosely into the glass of hot whiskey he cupped in his hands, enjoying the warmth from the glass seeping into his fingertips, and ignoring the laughter and talk of those crowded around him in the smoke-filled room. Times were changing, he thought. Every day seemed to introduce some new machinery that could do the work of ten men. He didn't side with the Luddites—a bunch of ruffians, if you asked him, smashing the new power looms and weaving machines, burning down factories, and causing general mayhem—but he sympathized with their plight, with their frustration and fear that the machines were taking away their ability to earn a decent living.

He'd read that some handcrafters had even ended up in the workhouse—if they were lucky. Otherwise, it was debtors' prison. London was a powder keg, he knew, waiting only for a flint spark to set it off. Where would it all lead? How would people survive if machines took over?

"Oy, gov'ner! Are ye Sam Kelly?"

Sam lifted his gaze to the small urchin who'd materialized next to his table. He thought the lad looked familiar, but he couldn't be sure. The city was fair to bursting with smudge-faced urchins. "Who wants ter know?"

"William Drake sent me fer ye. 'E wants ter see ye."

Sam raised his eyebrows. "Will Drake?"

"Aye. 'E's a night watchman."

"I know who he is. What does he want?"

"Yer the thief-taker Sam Kelly?"

"I'm the Bow Street man Sam Kelly," Sam corrected coldly, having always disliked the old-fashioned nickname. It carried the taint of corruption, from the days when a few unscrupulous Runners had been caught working in collusion with the criminal class, assisting thieves to rob the gentry so they could later return the stolen goods for the reward.

The lad sidled closer, almost furtive in his manner, though no one paid him any particular attention. "Mr. Drake wants me ter bring ye ter 'im, if ye don't mind, sir," he said. "Ye see . . . there's been a murder. A Lady. Real vicious-like."

"You saw the body?"

"Nay. Oi was called ter the door. But oi 'eard a mort inside blubberin'. She was carryin' on somethin' awful."

"All right." Sam hastily tossed back his drink—he wasn't about to waste whiskey, even if it came from the Pig & Sail—and pushed himself to his feet, ignoring the twinge in his knees. Shrugging into his greatcoat, he retrieved his Bow Street baton with its distinctive gold tip from the scarred table, and used it to point toward the door. "Let's go."

✤

The Lady had been murdered in Grosvenor Square, which actually wasn't a bad place to cock up your toes, Sam reflected. It was considered one of London's more fashionable neighborhoods, with its stretch of elegant homes, three, four, and sometimes even five stories, house and terraces made of limestone or sandstone.

Not that he could appreciate much of the architecture or the enormous park across the wide street at the moment. At near midnight, the darkness and fog, the latter as thick as porridge, made it impossible to see beyond a dozen paces. Unlike the gas lighting craze sweeping the city, Grosvenor Square residents kept to the tradition of lighting oil lamps, which were legally required to be hung out of each household at night, or risk being fined a shilling.

As uncomfortable as he was about some of the changes he saw happening throughout the country, Sam had to admit that gas lighting on the street would've been helpful. At least he'd be able to do a proper scan of the neighborhood, he thought, as he and the lad scrambled down from the hackney he'd hired to bring them to the address. He dug out a coin and tossed it to the jarvey. The impenetrable blackness beyond the weak yellow glow of the oil lamps was giving him an itchy sensation that he was being watched—not an uncommon feeling in London Town, considering the number of criminals who often lurked in the shadows.

Sam hurried toward the one townhouse that had both an oil lamp burning outside and light spilling from most of the windows. The windows in the adjacent houses were either shuttered or dark, the occupants already in bed or still out for the evening. It almost appeared as though the elegant neighboring buildings disapproved of the unseemly activity taking place at Number 8.

It was a fanciful notion, one which had Sam shaking his head as he approached the two men standing in front of the partially opened door, smoking. He recognized them as members of the Night Watch, Henry Greely and Jack Norton.

"Good evenin'." He nodded at them.

"'Tis evenin'. Nothin' good about it," Jack grumbled and shifted his body so Sam could enter the townhouse. "The devil is surely out and causin' mischief."

Sam merely grunted a response.

"Oy, where'd ye think ye're going?"

Sam glanced over his shoulder to see that Henry had grabbed his young companion by the scruff of his neck, halting his entrance into the townhouse.

The urchin squirmed and glared at the night watchman. "Oi brought the thief-taker, didn't oi? Oi want me bread promised by Mr. Drake!"

"'Ow much did Mr. Drake promise ye?" Jack asked, digging into his pocket.

A crafty gleam came into the child's eyes. "A guinea."

4

Jack snorted. "Do ye take me for a sapscull? Give us the truth, boy, or go hungry!"

"A quid."

"And Oi'm the King of England. Try again!"

With a half smile at the lad's boldness, Sam left the two watchmen to haggle with the scamp. He strode down the long, narrow hall to the stairs, his gaze taking in the black-and-white marble tiles and high ceiling with its white-plaster decorative molding. A chandelier hung in the center, its dozen candles melted down to short stubs, the flames flickering erratically.

Upstairs, another watchman was stationed outside an open door, his attention fixed on whatever activity was going on inside the room. The man started visibly when Sam came up next to him. Without a word, Sam thrust his baton under the young man's nose and moved into the room.

The smell hit him first, that raw meaty odor that signaled fresh death.

Half a dozen men were inside. Sam spotted William Drake immediately. Not only because he'd known him for almost twenty years. But because he was an imposing figure at six-foot-three, easily towering above the other men.

"Drake," Sam said in greeting.

The night watchman glanced around. "Ah, Kelly. Wasn't sure if the lad was going to find you. Told him to look in the Brown Bear or the Pig and Sail. Damn brutal business, this."

"Aye. Murder usually is," Sam remarked, his attention already focusing on the victim.

She'd been left sitting on a sofa designed in the Grecian style, its flowing lines and scrolled feet so popular with the gentry. The velvet upholstery was a soft blue, like a robin's egg, nearly matching the color of the frothy silk and organza gown she wore. Her bosom, revealed by the dress's low, square neckline, looked like it had been tattooed, dark angry wounds puncturing the pale skin. The bodice had also been torn up by the blade, the victim's blood staining the delicate material.

The woman's gently curved white arms, revealed by the tiny cap sleeves of the gown, hung limply at her sides, the small hands resting on the sofa cushions, palms up as though she'd been supplicating her killer. Cuts marred the delicate flesh here, too, he noticed. She'd either tried to fight back, or put up her hands in a futile attempt to protect herself.

Probably fight, he decided, his gaze traveling over the golden blond hair that had tumbled down in wild disarray around her shoulders, hairpins still clinging to the bright strands. Her head had lolled back against the sofa's cushions, her long neck curved like a swan's, her face tilted toward the ceiling. Her eyes were open, and glassy with death.

Distaste tightened Sam's features as he examined the victim's face. It hadn't been enough for the fiend to stab the lass to death—he'd cut her here too. There were two slashes on the right side of her face, one short laceration, no bigger than half an inch, and faint. A scratch, really. The other was a little deeper and longer, running from her outer eye to her mouth.

The left side of her face, however, was far more gruesome. The fiend had actually cut—no, that word implied some skill. The fiend had *hacked* away at the skin, filleting it in a ragged manner so that it flapped down against her jaw, leaving the bloody pulp, bone, and even a few teeth beneath exposed.

Sam's mind immediately flashed to Kendra Donovan, the lass he'd worked with a month ago at Aldridge Castle to solve a series of grisly murders. The American had been a puzzle, both in her behavior and in her peculiar expertise in criminality. What would she make of this?

"I've sent for the sawbones, but the Lady was stabbed, obviously," William said, interrupting Sam's thoughts. "Looks like a dozen times, at least. I only hope to God she was dead before he did that to her face."

Sam asked, "What sawbones?"

"Dr. Munroe. He's the best."

"Aye. That he is." Sam dragged his gaze away from the woman's shocking visage. Immediately his eyes were drawn to the large portrait above the fireplace.

"She was a diamond of the first water, wasn't she?" William said, eyeing the portrait as well.

She'd indeed been a beauty. The artist had painted her fancifully, sitting on a swing in a lush garden setting. Her face was a creamy oval, framed by waves of golden hair. Her eyes, a striking violet shade, stared down at them. The rosebud mouth was curved into a small, provocative smile. A temptress, Sam recognized. Eve in the Garden of Eden. He wondered if that had been the artist's intention, or if he was imagining the connection.

He forced himself to turn away from the painting to survey the room. The décor was too feminine for his tastes, with lots of gilt, ornate moldings, and soft pastel colors. The carpet was woven in blue, purple, and gold. The rest of the furniture matched the sofa in its Grecian style. There was a small writing desk in the corner, a side table that sparkled with decanters and glasses, and a painted pianoforte positioned in front of the Palladian windows.

"What's this?" he asked, moving over to one of the chairs. It held precisely three items: an ivory fan, painted gold and light blue, its spokes broken and bent; an ornate hair comb that glittered with rubies and moonstones; and a heavy roemer.

"We found them under the sofa," William said, coming to stand beside him. "Most likely they fell in the attack and got kicked underfoot."

Sam picked up the roemer, and sniffed it. Whiskey. Frowning, he did another slow scan of the room. Like the entrance hall, the tapers were nearly gone in the chandelier and wall sconces. The log in the carved marble fireplace had been reduced to a pile of fiercely burning embers. But he could imagine how the scene had looked hours earlier, the fire and candles bathing the room in its radiance while the Lady sat facing her killer.

She'd dressed up for him in the low-cut gown, he thought; styled her hair with this jeweled comb. The fan was a tool of flirtation, and he could envisage the woman in the oil painting using it with considerable expertise. Had she also held the glass, sipping the whiskey? Doubtful. It wasn't a lady's drink. So had she prepared it for her killer?

"She had ter have invited the bastard inside. What's the poor lass's name?" Sam asked.

"Lady Dover—Lady Cordelia Dover."

Sam's eyes widened. "The devil, you say!"

"You know her?"

Sam hesitated. "Nay," he finally said. "I've never actually had dealings with her. But she was a guest at the Duke of Aldridge's house party a month ago."

"I heard you did some work for His Grace." William gave Sam a speculative look. "Also heard a tale of a monster on the loose, strangling whores."

"'Tis true enough," Sam remarked. There was a lot more to the story, of course. None of which he could share with the night watchman.

"You caught the fiend then?"

"Aye," Sam replied simply. Kendra Donovan had actually been responsible for catching and killing the bastard, but Sam had promised the Duke to keep quiet about her involvement in the investigation, as well as the identity of the real killer. He was dead. Justice had been done.

Frowning, he glanced at the body of Lady Dover and vowed to get justice for her too.

"Who found the body, and when?" he asked.

"The housekeeper, Mrs. Pierson. She returned an hour ago. When she saw the body, she ran out, screaming for the Watch."

"I guess it was your luck ter be on duty."

"Jack Norton was the one patrolling the area," William said, "but he summoned me."

"Where are the other servants?"

"Lady Dover sent everyone away until the morrow. Mrs. Pierson only returned because she'd forgot her medicine. Thought she'd sneak in—the back door was open—and found her mistress like that."

"The back door was open? This ain't the work of a housebreaker." Sam's gaze drifted back to the mutilated face.

"No," agreed William.

Sam thought he knew the answer, but had to ask anyway. "Why'd Lady Dover send her servants away?"

"She was expecting someone and wanted their meeting to be private."

Sam nodded. It was as he suspected. The room had all the fixings of a romantic rendezvous. "What's his name? The servants must know."

"Aye."

Sam became aware of a certain anxiousness in the other man's manner. "Well? Who is he then?"

"I'd rather you talk to Mrs. Pierson."

Sam frowned. *Now what's this about?* he wondered.

William gestured for Sam to follow him out of the drawing room. They were silent as they descended the two flights of stairs to the kitchen. A night watchman stood inside, and looked visibly relieved at their entrance. Sam suspected that had to do with the woman sitting at the round wooden table, sobbing uncontrollably. She was still wearing her sturdy wool coat and plain bonnet, which partially obscured her face. The rest was concealed by the handkerchief she was sniveling into.

"Oi got Mrs. Pierson a cuppa tea, like ye asked, gov'ner, but she 'asn't 'ad a drop," the young man informed them.

William nodded and moved forward to lay a hand on the woman's shoulder. She jerked slightly and glanced up with watery blue eyes. Sam estimated her to be in her mid-thirties. She might've even been attractive, if her features hadn't been so red and swollen from her crying jag.

William spoke gently. "Mrs. Pierson . . . a Bow Street Runner is here to ask you questions."

The drenched eyes swiveled in Sam's direction. "Oh, it was horrible, sir! I've never seen anything . . . a-anything like it! Her face . . ." The woman shuddered. "Lady Dover was ever so beautiful. Why would he do *that*?"

"Your mistress was meeting a man tonight." Sam decided to get right to the point. "Do you know his name?"

"Oh, aye." Mrs. Pierson blew her nose. "He killed her. He killed her and . . . and b-butchered her face, he did. He's a murderer, but he'll never hang. He's Quality. They're treated different than the rest of us lot." She gave Sam an accusing look, as if he were to blame for England's class system. "You *know* they are."

Sam flicked a look at William, now understanding his odd behavior. The fiend responsible for this heinous crime was a gentleman. Again, he remembered the investigation he'd been involved in last month at Aldridge Castle. Those crimes, too, had been committed by a gentleman. Had all the nobility in England gone mad?

"Gentry or not, he'll hang," Sam promised grimly, catching the housekeeper's eye. "But first you've got ter speak his name. Who was your mistress waiting for tonight, Mrs. Pierson? Who is the fiend who done that ter her?"

She gave him a doubtful look, but whatever she saw in Sam's eyes made her firm her chin with resolve. "He's a marquis, he is," she whispered. "A duke's nephew. The Marquis of Sutcliffe—he's the murderer."

2

I believe I have a solution to your dilemma, my dear."

Kendra Donovan was sitting in the Duke of Aldridge's study. The early-morning sunlight that slanted into the room from the windows hurt her eyes, which were gritty from lack of sleep. She wondered if that had also affected her hearing.

"You've figured out how I can go home?" she asked, incredulous.

Aldridge frowned. He was a man in his mid-fifties with a longish face and rather bold nose. His pale blue-gray eyes stared out at the world with the kind of gentle regard that Kendra had rarely seen in her lifetime. Yet she knew that gentleness should never be mistaken for weakness. In his own way, Albert Rutherford, the seventh Duke of Aldridge, was one of the strongest men Kendra had ever known.

He admitted, "Well, no . . ."

Kendra wasn't surprised. The Duke was a brilliant man, but she seriously doubted that he'd found a solution to her problem. After all, her dilemma was being here at Aldridge Castle, in the early nineteenth century.

Which wouldn't be a problem at all if I'd been born in the freaking nineteenth century. Or, more accurately, since she was twenty-six years old and it was currently 1815, in the latter half of the eighteenth century. But since she'd been born a couple of centuries later . . . well, it was hard to imagine a dilemma that would be harder to solve.

Kendra shifted her gaze to the ancient tapestry that decorated the wall behind the Duke's desk. The heavy material concealed a secret panel that opened to reveal the stairwell that led to the room that Aldridge used as his laboratory. In the castle's long and bloody history, the passage had been used by the fortress's occupants to flee from religious prosecution and invading armies. A month ago, she'd made use of those stairs, fleeing from an assassin in the twenty-first century. She didn't know exactly what had happened then, except, physically, it had been a nightmare. Later, she could only assume she'd gone through some sort of wormhole or closed time-like curve, which had essentially transported her from her own era to this one.

And how crazy is that?

Of course, that's what she'd thought initially: that she'd gone insane. Even now, she had to suppress a shudder at the memory of the icy terror that her mind had somehow shattered.

It hadn't been easy for her to accept the truth, but she'd finally adjusted to her bizarre circumstance. Adjusted, but not fit in. She didn't belong here. Her one hope of returning to her own time line had been entering the passageway during the next full moon—a month from the time she'd entered the stairwell and arrived in the early nineteenth century. She'd wanted to believe that there was a link between the full moon and its gravitational pull on the wormhole, similar to the effect that the moon had on the earth's tides, and that the vortex would open again.

It had been a long shot. But she hadn't been willing to accept what the fates, the universe, or God had thrown at her.

So last night, she'd tried.

She'd taken the spiral stairs to the halfway point and sat down to wait. She'd waited for the unnatural darkness to wrap itself around her like wet wool, for the temperature to plunge and the nauseating vertigo to hit. She'd braced herself for all that, as well as the pain—excruciating, unimaginable, like she was being dissolved in a vat of acid, shot through an endless tube, and then reformed in another location.

She'd waited. And waited. And . . .

Nothing.

There'd been no vortex. No wormhole. No paranormal activity. She'd sat on the clammy stone steps until her ass had grown cold and numb. She'd sat for hours, until the Duke had finally come and coaxed her back down to the study. He'd pushed her gently down on the sofa and pressed a glass of brandy in her hands. His blue-gray eyes had been alight with sympathy. Much like now.

She wanted to scream.

"Your explanation of a space-time vortex is fascinating, but I am at a loss as to how to create one," the Duke continued.

"Damn it. I have to go *home*." Frustration knotted her stomach and drove her to her feet. She crossed her arms and paced the room.

Aldridge gave her a helpless look. "My dear, you do not appear to have any choice in the matter. You have no recourse but to accept this as your home—at least for the foreseeable future."

For how long? Kendra wondered. *How long will I be forced to stay here?*

That was followed instantly by the question every human being has probably asked themselves during a dark time in their lives: *Why me?*

A month ago, she thought she'd known the answer to that question, when a young girl had been found floating in a nearby lake, butchered by a serial killer. In the twenty-first century, she was the youngest FBI criminal profiler at Quantico, so it had seemed that fate—or whatever—had brought her here to apply those skills. When the murderer had eventually perished at her hand, she'd believed that she'd done her job.

I should be able to go home.

Kendra met the Duke's sympathetic gaze. He understood, she knew. She'd finally confessed her unusual situation to him, and though the Duke considered himself a Man of Science, she hadn't been entirely sure how he'd handle such a revelation. He could've easily considered her insane and had her locked up in a mental hospital, a thought that made her shudder. It had been a risk to tell him, but given her status at the castle as neither servant nor nobility, she really had no choice.

She'd gotten lucky—if you could call being stranded in a different era lucky. The Duke of Aldridge was one of those Renaissance men written about in history, like da Vinci or Voltaire, a philosopher and a scientist rolled into one. A nimble thinker, he'd happily embraced the unknown, and spent hours engaging in theoretical discussions on time travel, even as he probed for answers to scientific, political, and moral questions that he hoped had been resolved in the twenty-first century.

What to say, what *not* to say? Time travel was only a theory in the twenty-first century's scientific community, but there was no shortage of dire warnings about the unintended consequences of changing the future. She was forced to treat every discussion that they'd had with extreme delicacy.

"Which dilemma are you referring to, then, if not mine?" Kendra said, bringing them back to the Duke's earlier pronouncement.

Aldridge picked the pipe up off his desk and studied it like a new plant species he'd found growing in the woods. "I was considering the situation of your being an unchaperoned female living under my roof, Miss Donovan."

Ah. If there was one thing she'd learned about Regency England, it was that there were *rules.* Lots and lots of rules. Most of them, she thought, ridiculous. And most of them targeted at women.

"You have a lot of unchaperoned females living under your roof," she pointed out drily.

Aldridge Castle was, quite frankly, enormous. The main section dated back to William the Conqueror, and as the Duke of Aldridge's ancestors became more affluent and powerful, they'd built wings onto the central tower—and then wings onto those wings. And because the Industrial Revolution was only beginning in the north of England, vast numbers of men and women were required to maintain the ancient fortress, keeping it from tumbling into a pile of rubble.

"My dear, you are well aware that I am not referring to the staff," the Duke replied. "You are not a servant, Miss Donovan. Nor are you a relative." His gaze flitted to the oil painting of a woman and child that held a position of honor above the fireplace.

Kendra followed his gaze to the portrait. The dark-haired, dark-eyed beauty was Aldridge's late wife, and the young girl she held his late daughter. Both had died tragically in a boating accident twenty years before. While the Duke had recovered his wife's body, his little girl had never been found.

His eyes were shadowed when he finally shifted his attention back to Kendra. "I would not want your reputation to suffer unduly, Miss Donovan."

"There are hundreds of rooms in the castle. We could live here together for a year without even seeing each other."

"That is not how such things are judged." He gave a slight smile, well aware that Kendra Donovan came from a time when social mores were much more lax. Women had not only gained the right to vote, but Great Britain had even had a female prime minister—it had fascinated him when they'd spoken of it. "You are not living in your future, my dear; you are living in my present. You must fully adapt to the customs and expectations here—for your own sake."

Kendra was already considered an eccentric around the castle because of what many deemed her brazen behavior. Even her looks had caused comment when she'd first arrived, with her raven hair cut short in a pudding-basin style reminiscent of a medieval page. The style, while odd, was becoming on her, emphasizing her long-lashed, onyx eyes that glowed with intelligence. Yet in matters of fashion, the Duke's opinion mattered naught, and someone—perhaps his goddaughter, Lady Rebecca—had convinced her to grow out her hair and pin it up in the style that was the custom of ladies.

All for the best, he supposed. It was one thing to be considered an Original, and another to be regarded as an oddity and ostracized completely.

He tapped his pipe bowl with his forefinger. "However, as I mentioned, I believe I have come upon the solution."

"Great. You're going to rewrite the antiquated rules of society?"

He smiled, his blue-gray eyes twinkling. "I would if I could, Miss Donovan. Rather than take on such a formidable task, I shall do something much simpler—I shall make you my ward."

Kendra stared at him, puzzled. "I don't understand. You'd be my legal guardian?"

"You would be under my protection, yes."

"I'm too old to be anyone's ward."

"It is slightly unconventional, but I have given this a great deal of thought. We shall put it out that you are, in fact, the daughter of an old friend, who immigrated to America before you were born. Arrangements were made that I would become your legal guardian should anything happen to your parents. When they perished, and you found yourself alone on these shores, I fulfilled my duty, and took you in." He grinned at her, clearly delighted by the tale he'd spun. "By proxy, you would be my daughter."

As cover stories went, it was inventive. Still . . .

She shook her head. "It won't work. Everyone here will know it's not true."

"The staff will take their direction from me."

"It's not just the staff. Everyone who attended the house party knows that I was working as a servant before Lady Rebecca hired me to be her companion."

"My dear, I am the Duke of Aldridge. No one who attended the house party would have the temerity to question my account."

She raised her eyebrows. "Do you really have that kind of power?"

Kendra knew that the Duke lived in the top echelons of this world of rank and privilege, and few people would want to make an enemy out of him. Yet it was difficult to believe that he could simply rewrite history by putting out another version of that history.

Then again, people did it all the time in her own era, she thought. It was called public relations. *Spin.*

The Duke smiled at her. "Let us just say that I could make life uncomfortable for anyone who disputed my claim. Do not fret, my dear. 'Tis a mere formality. I do not want you to be gossiped about while you are living under my roof."

It was too late for that, Kendra knew. The servants had been gossiping about her since the moment she'd arrived.

But she thought of something—or, rather, someone—else. "It's not the servants you'll have to convince. Lady Atwood is not going to like your idea at all."

"Nonsense! My sister will not only like it, but she will *approve*," he said confidently. "If there is one thing Caro does best, it's adhering to the proprieties."

The Countess shared the same coloring as her brother—blue-gray eyes and blond hair that, now that they were both past fifty, had taken on a silvery sheen. And, in the Duke's case, thinning considerably on top.

"'Tis madness, Aldridge."

"Caro, be reasonable—"

"*Reasonable?* How in heaven's name is making Kendra Donovan your ward *reasonable*? It was outrageous enough when Lady Rebecca hired her as a companion! And why the devil didn't Lady Rebecca take the creature with her when she returned to her home?"

Kendra pressed her lips together to keep herself from arguing in her own defense. Lady Atwood paced agitated circles into the study's rug, and she wouldn't want to hear it. The fact that the woman had actually said "devil" showed her distress—it was a vulgar curse word in this era, which should never be uttered by a lady or in the presence of one.

"She has bewitched you, Aldridge, to even consider such a . . . such a cracked-brained notion!" Lady Atwood continued furiously. "Think of your title, our family's lineage!"

"My dear—"

The Countess spun around to glare at Kendra. "Miss Donovan, it is past time that we had frank words. Pray tell, how did you put this ridiculous idea into my brother's head?"

The Duke sighed. "'Tis *my* idea, Caro."

"I tell you, she has cast some sort of spell upon you."

"Do not be stupid. There is no such thing as spells or any other such nonsense. Miss Donovan's presence at the castle is bound to cause talk. This shall stop any more vicious gossip before it begins."

"Packing her off ought to accomplish the same thing. Send her to one of your other proprieties. Or put her back on staff."

"I've need of Miss Donovan's assistance in my laboratory, and I do not wish her reputation to be in tatters. Now, enough of this discussion." A rare note of steel came into the Duke's voice, reminding Kendra yet again of the strength that he often kept hidden. "I have made my decision."

Lady Atwood slid another glaring look at Kendra. Then she gave a put-upon sigh. "You always were an eccentric, Bertie."

"And you are gracious, as always, my dear."

The Countess ignored his sarcasm. "If you insist on turning this . . . this *American* into a family connection, I shall do what I can to assist."

That roused Kendra enough to break her silence. "What do you mean?"

"What I *mean*, Miss Donovan, is that I can no longer overlook your shocking lack of social graces. I shall do my duty to my family by giving you Town polish. In fact, I shall polish you until you shine. Do you even know how to dance? I do not recall seeing you on the dance floor during the house party."

Kendra thought of the intricate steps required of dancers during this time, the elegantly formed configurations, bows, and curtseys. "No, but—"

"Then you shall learn. I will engage a dancing master for you."

"Oh, my God—"

"And you shall stop this profanity at once. Do not think I have failed to notice your blasphemy—and your *utter* lack of decorum!"

"I'm not Eliza Doolittle," Kendra snapped, and shot a desperate look at the Duke. But he wasn't looking at her; he was studying his pipe again with abnormal interest.

Panic sent her pulse racing. She refused, absolutely *refused*, to be shaped, molded, pushed, or pummeled into someone she didn't want to be. Christ, hadn't she already been through that with her parents? Dr. Carl Donovan and Dr. Eleanor Jahnke had essentially conceived her only to advance their own philosophy of positive eugenics. The first fourteen years of her life had been a carefully choreographed routine of instruction, education, and testing. She had an excellent memory—not quite eidetic, but close—that allowed her to score well when it came to tests, but she'd fallen short of the level of genius, her parents' goal. She'd managed to get into college at fourteen, but in a rare burst of courage, she'd told her parents that she wanted more independence and a chance to pursue her own interests, rather than their narrow ambition for her.

It had been a shock when they'd responded by cutting her loose and walking away.

The memory of how easily they'd abandoned her still knotted her stomach. It was a good reminder that she really only had herself to rely on.

"Who, pray tell, is Eliza Doolittle?" Lady Atwood gave her a suspicious look. "Another American?"

Kendra pinched the bridge of her nose in frustration. There was no way she could explain that Eliza Doolittle was a character in a play that would be written almost a century from now. "I don't want to be here," she muttered, more to herself than anyone else.

"Bertie, the creature wants to return to America," the Countess said. "Book her passage on one of your ships, and be done with this madness."

"Caro—"

Aldridge broke off, looking relieved when the door opened and the butler, Harding, approached with formal dignity, carrying a silver salver that held a single envelope.

He said, "Forgive me, Your Grace, but this letter was delivered with some urgency."

"Thank you, Harding." Aldridge picked up the creamy envelope. Frowning thoughtfully, he broke the crimson seal as the servant gave an abbreviated bow and left the study as silently as he'd entered.

"Good God." Aldridge sat up a little straighter as he scanned, and then rescanned, the letter.

"What is it, Bertie?" his sister demanded.

He looked up at them, horror darkening his gaze. "We must leave for London at once."

"What? Why? What's happened?" Kendra asked, taking a step closer.

"Lady Dover was murdered last night."

The Countess put a hand to her throat. "Dear heaven. How?"

"It does not say."

His sister's thin eyebrows pulled together as she eyed him in confusion. "'Tis terrible, of course . . . but what does this have to do with you, Bertie? You scarcely knew the creature."

"I didn't, no." He hesitated, and his gaze shifted to meet Kendra's. "But Alec did . . . and he's been accused of her murder."

3

Aldridge Castle was a place of constant movement, but the announcement that they'd be traveling to London sent the entire household into an uproar. Lady Atwood took charge of organizing the servants who would be accompanying them, packing trunks with clothes and fresh linens and traveling cases with other necessities. Unwilling to wait for those tasks to be completed, the Duke called for his carriage so he and Kendra might set out for London immediately, to be followed later by his sister and staff.

The announcement didn't sit well with the Countess, who pointed out the impropriety of her brother traveling alone in a carriage with an unmarried female.

"Tis a good thing that Miss Donovan is now my ward then," the Duke responded.

"That arrangement has not yet been made official, Bertie—"

"For God's sake, I'm hardly likely to molest a young lady in a carriage on our journey to London," he snapped, as he paced his study. The Duke's uncharacteristic anger revealed his worry for Alec—Alexander Morgan, the Marquis of Sutcliffe, and, perhaps more important, his nephew and heir more than anything else.

The Duke's anger effectively ended the argument between the siblings. Half an hour later, Kendra found herself holding onto the thin leather strap near the door as her body swayed back and forth like the tick of a metronome, as the carriage barreled down the country road. At six miles an hour, the journey to London would take approximately four hours, plus time to rest and water the horses, or to rent four more to take them the remainder of the way into the city. A month ago, the same journey had taken her less than thirty minutes in traffic in her rented Volkswagen Golf. Everything in this era was so damn *slow*.

"You must have patience, Miss Donovan."

Surprised, Kendra wondered if she'd spoken out loud. Then she realized she was strumming her fingers impatiently on her knee. She forced herself to stop the telltale movement, her hand curling into a fist.

"Sorry."

"Do not apologize. I, too, am anxious." He leaned back against the cushioned seat and regarded her with interest. "Tell me, how do you travel in your time?"

"We're a little beyond the horse-and-buggy stage."

His eyes brightened. "There's talk of building a contraption that uses steam, much like the newer ships."

"That sounds promising."

He gave her a vaguely disgruntled look, piqued as always by what she knew he considered her overly cautious nature. "Miss Donovan, this is a long journey. Surely you can tell me how you would accomplish the same journey in the future?"

Kendra lowered her eyes as she considered the matter. Finally, she said, "Well . . . I suppose I can tell you . . ."

He leaned forward eagerly. "Yes?"

She lifted her gaze. "We use a machine called a disintegrator-integrator. Basically it breaks down our atoms so we can be zapped from one place to another."

His eyes widened. "You can *instantly* transport yourself to your destination? How extraordinary!"

"Yes, but you have to be careful not to have any flies in the chamber with you. You see, there have been instances where the atoms have mixed, and people have become a human-fly."

"Good God! What do you do . . ." The blue-gray eyes narrowed suddenly. "Are you having sport with me, Miss Donovan?"

Kendra had to laugh. "Sorry, yes. But . . . oh, my God, you should see your face!"

"Hmm. Human-fly, indeed."

"It was a good movie."

"Movie—ah, yes, moving pictures." Telling the Duke how people entertained themselves in the twenty-first century had seemed innocuous enough to Kendra.

"Come, Miss Donovan," he continued, spreading his hands in an imploring gesture. "I understand your fear of changing the course of history, but surely no harm can come from discussing transportation?"

She gave him an ironic look. He was too intelligent not to understand that a nation's progress and prosperity correlated directly to its transportation. History buffs liked to say the American West was won by the gun, but it was developed—economically, socially, politically—by the railroad. A nation that has the ability to move goods faster and more efficiently would always hold the advantage over a country that still operated by donkey and cart.

"The concept of traveling by machine is hardly new," he continued. "When I was a boy, French inventor Nicolas-Joseph Cugnot designed a steam-driven vehicle to carry passengers. Why, only a few years ago, Richard Trevithick built his Puffing Devil that carried six men!"

"Hmm. Since we're traveling in a horse-drawn carriage, I guess it wasn't successful."

"Unfortunately, no. The machine broke down several days later when it hit a ravine. And then burned up completely. Something to do with the water boiling out while it was left unattended, or some such nonsense. Despite these setbacks, I believe we are on the advent of new methods of transportation, much like the steam ships that are now replacing sail. Am I wrong?"

Kendra couldn't resist the pleading look he gave her. "You're not wrong. Mankind will see great advances in transportation."

"And shall that include flight?"

Kendra had to smile. Did every generation dream of flying? "To the moon, and beyond."

"My God." Aldridge looked dazzled. "You are traveling to the moon? Has it been colonized?"

"No. And trips to the moon have been infrequent. More commonly, astronauts travel to the space station . . ." Realizing how easily information slipped out, Kendra pressed her lips together and shook her head.

"Space station? My God, what I wouldn't give to see this future of yours, Miss Donovan. Tell me, what has mankind discovered about the planets? Are there other intelligent beings in the universe? Have we made contact? Can I not persuade you to tell me more, my dear?"

It was tempting. The Duke's enthusiasm made Kendra feel like her own era was a beautifully carved sculpture, something to be held in awe, admired, and cherished. She'd taken so many things for granted.

She knew the Duke would be thrilled with the Internet, especially, and the speed at which information could travel. He corresponded with like-minded men of science and philosophy throughout Europe, sharing ideas and discussing theories, and she'd watched him dip his quill in ink and write long missives to be posted. It could take weeks, maybe even months, for a return letter. *Slow*, she thought again. For him to be able to pick up the phone, log on to Skype, or send an email, would seem wondrous, magical—even for a Man of Science.

"Miss Donovan?" he pressed, giving her a wheedling smile. "Surely no harm would come if you took me into your confidence?"

Jesus Christ. How did she know? "Can a butterfly flapping its wings in one part of the world cause a hurricane in another part of the world?"

Aldridge frowned. "I don't see how that's possible."

"It's a theory—the butterfly effect, also known as chaos theory. It purports that one seemingly inconsequential act can ripple out and create devastating consequences. Do you understand? I don't know what your fellow scientists are working on. What if you shared something that I told you, and that information was the missing piece to a puzzle that one of your friends was working on? A puzzle that shouldn't be solved for another decade or century? I could change history's timeline."

"But what if you shared something that would change the world for the better? Have you considered that, my dear?"

Kendra was silent for a long moment, then expelled a breath. "Fritz Haber," she said.

"Pardon? Who is Fritz Haber?"

"He was a man who wanted to make lives better too." She recalled an image of the man—balding, mustachioed, and round-faced, wearing Teddy Roosevelt–styled spectacles.

"And did he?"

"Yes. In the beginning. He invented a fertilizer that boosted crop production. He probably saved thousands from starvation."

"That is extraordinary."

"It was . . . until war broke out and his invention was weaponized."

Kendra thought of the poisonous gas that the scientist had utilized for Germany during World War I, which had earned

Fritz Haber a new moniker: the father of chemical warfare. In World War II, the Nazis would use his invention in their newly created gas chambers to kill millions of Jews, including some of Haber's own relatives.

"I can't predict how any knowledge that I share would affect history," she said, "and mankind has enough problems without me messing around with it."

Aldridge looked like he wanted to argue. Instead, he sighed. "Is everyone from the future so pessimistic?"

A laugh escaped her. "If you read the news, yeah. We're a pretty doom-and-gloom group. And you know what I do—*did*." She sobered. "I'm not pessimistic. I'm *realistic*."

"Yes . . . I do know what you do." He gazed at her thoughtfully. "Your butterfly theory suggests that random events, no matter how inconsequential, are connected. Have you considered that this may be, too?"

"What do you mean?"

"A month ago, I believed there was a purpose for your presence here," the Duke reminded her. "You hunt society's monsters. Don't you see, my dear? My nephew did not kill Lady Dover. I know it—and now you must prove it. It would seem that we still have need of your services."

❊

By the time the carriage rolled into London, around three P.M., the sinking sun cast the entire city in a sepia-toned haze. At least, that was Kendra's first thought as she stared out the window. Then she realized that what she was actually seeing was nineteenth-century air pollution, a brownish miasma that hung low in the sky, the result of millions of coal- and wood-burning fireplaces, plus the flecks of drying manure that floated into the atmosphere.

As they moved into the city limits, Kendra was assaulted by the smell—like rotten eggs—and the noise—the clip-clop of horseshoes and the thunder of wagon wheels over the cobble-stone streets, the cries of peddlers (*Hot pies! Posies! Fresh oysters and cockles!*) pitched above the rumble of voices punctuated with laughter and angry shouts, and an odd hammering and shrill clanging. People streamed along buildings, darted across busy thoroughfares, and spilled from skinny, winding walkways. Not unlike the hordes of pedestrians that went about their business in modern-day London, Kendra reflected, except these were no sophisticated urbanites.

Kendra observed beggars huddled in doorways and children dressed in rags running around—and, if she wasn't mistaken, stealing whenever they got the chance from peddlers' carts. There were workers of all stripes, some dirty and unkempt, others tidy in their homespun clothing. And it was, she realized with some surprise, an international mix. The majority were white, but there were also black, Asian, Middle Eastern, and Mediterranean faces in the crowd.

The countryside landscape fell away to reveal row after row of narrow, soot-stained, attached single- and multiple-story build-ings. In the distance, she saw the familiar dome of St. Paul's Cathe-dral and the spires of Parliament, but those landmarks were soon lost as they traveled along the narrow streets, the Duke's coachman expertly weaving the carriage through traffic. The streets were con-gested with individuals on horseback, cattle being herded, hired hackneys, public and private coaches, and the never-ending queue of pedestrians. The sheer humanity was overwhelming.

The Duke was also affected. "'Tis worse than I remembered," he murmured.

Kendra dragged her gaze away from the window. "When was the last time you were in London?"

"Three, perhaps four years ago. My family makes use of my residence here. Speaking of which, it will not yet be habitable. Caro will manage it with the servants, but since they are some hours behind us, we shall call upon Alec immediately."

"He doesn't stay at your place, then?"

"No, he has his own residence."

Kendra barely heard him. Her eyes were once again drawn to the passing scenery. More than a month ago, she'd driven through this bright and vibrant city with its melding of ancient structures and modern skyscrapers. Understandably, those shiny steel-and-glass buildings had vanished, but a surprising number of the early edifices still stood.

Of course, many of the structures that she'd regarded as old in her era didn't exist yet in this time. Victorian-styled pubs and iconic images, like Big Ben, were missing. In twenty years, fire would sweep through the halls of Westminster, destroying much of the palace. The famous clock tower would be part of its redesign, completed in 1858.

It was weird to be in a London without Big Ben. It felt *wrong*.

As the carriage rolled on, the streets became wider, the buildings on either side more elegant. The streams of traffic and people thinned to trickles, and vanished in some sections altogether. It was almost as though they were back in the country, with enormous swathes of greenery and woods breaking up the stone and pavement.

The carriage slowed and navigated a variety of turns, enough to make her lose her sense of direction. Her stomach contracted uncomfortably when they eventually came to a stop outside an elegant Georgian townhouse. The coachman leaped off his high perch and came around to unfold the steps and open the door.

Aldridge stepped down and turned to offer his hand. When she hesitated, he gave her an encouraging smile.

"Come, Miss Donovan. Alec will be delighted to see you again."

Kendra didn't say anything but slowly put her hand in the Duke's, allowing him to help her down. Her nerves skittered as she thought about the last time she'd seen Alec, just yesterday morning.

The Duke seemed to think that she was fated to save Alec. But she knew differently. In fact, if she'd have given him a different answer to the question he'd asked her, he would never have left Aldridge Castle. He would never have made the journey to London. He wouldn't, at this very moment, be accused of murdering his former mistress.

Kendra knew she wasn't Alec's savior. She was the one responsible for putting him into this situation in the first place.

4

The Duke didn't bother with the calling card ritual—presenting one's card to determine if someone was receiving visitors—much to the chagrin of his coachman, who, Kendra knew, always took great pride in the duty. Seemingly oblivious to his servant's crestfallen expression, Aldridge ushered Kendra up the short flight of stairs to the gleaming green door and gave the snarling brass lion's head knocker three loud raps. He was about to give it another when the door swung open suddenly.

A tall, burly man with hair the color of wheat and stormy blue eyes surveyed them with a frown. "Yes?"

"I am the Duke of Aldridge. I'm here to see my nephew, the Marquis of Sutcliffe," Aldridge said, and there was something in his normally affable tone that demanded deference.

Kendra wasn't surprised when he got it. The man blinked and then nodded, shifting quickly to the side to let them enter. "Of course, sir, Your Grace . . . Miss. If you'll come with me, please. I am William Drake, by the by."

"And your connection to my nephew would be . . . ?" Aldridge asked as they followed the big man into the shadowy foyer. It was long and narrow, the walls divided starkly between the dark paneled wainscoting below and white plaster above. Ornately framed portraits hung from golden rods hooked near the crown molding. Kendra wondered if the faces staring back at her were blue-blooded ancestors of Alec and the Duke.

"Oh. I was called to the scene, sir," William explained. "I'm a night watchman. Sam Kelly is with His Lordship in the morning room."

"Sam Kelly is investigating?" the Duke asked, surprised, and exchanged a glance with Kendra.

"Aye. I believe you are acquainted with him?"

"Yes, we had dealings with each other a month ago. He is an excellent Bow Street Runner."

They passed the stairs and continued down the corridor to a pair of double doors, one of which was open. Respectfully, William stood to the side so they could precede him into the room. The Duke made a similar gesture to Kendra.

For just a moment, she hung back and wished the Duke wasn't so damned chivalrous. She didn't want to be the first person to enter the room. But a moment later, her cowardice shamed her, and she squared her shoulders. Ignoring the nerves fluttering in her stomach, she swept through the doorway. *Never let them see you sweat.*

It was a large room, done in masculine hues: browns, greens, golds. Beige canvas dust covers had been tossed on the floor, obviously having recently been draped across the furniture. Four enormous windows took up the wall opposite the neoclassical fireplace where a fire burned, the flames gnawing through the wood and offering a small bit of warmth.

She noticed this only vaguely, almost as if it were part of her peripheral vision, because her attention fixed immediately on the man sprawled lazily in one of the chairs. He held a stout glass in his hand, filled with whiskey or brandy, Kendra suspected. Her Georgian counterparts, she'd discovered, could drink Dionysus under the table.

He'd been gazing into the flames, but at their entrance, he looked around—just a cursory glance, as though used to unwanted guests entering the morning room. His eyes, deep forest green with flecks of gold around the pupil, were cool and distant between his spiky black lashes. But they blazed suddenly, and the detachment fell away when he saw her. The hand holding the heavy glass gave a tiny jerk and then, in a lithe movement, he was on his feet.

The Marquis of Sutcliffe was as dark as his uncle was fair, his olive skin and chiseled good looks inherited from his late mother, an Italian Countess who'd married into the English aristocracy. At six feet, he was tall for this era, and athletic (*not unusual for this era*). Still, exhaustion and worry had taken its toll. Shadows she didn't remember were stamped beneath those staring eyes. A day's growth of dark stubble gave him a rakish appearance.

"Miss Donovan! Your Grace!" That greeting came from Sam Kelly.

With some relief, Kendra looked away from Alec, pivoting to the familiar figure hurrying across the room toward them. The Bow Street Runner was a short, muscular man with elfin features, reddish-brown curls, and graying sideburns. His eyes were light brown, almost gold, like a Spanish doubloon. Right now, his smile reached those eyes, but Kendra knew from personal experience how quickly they could turn into "cop eyes"—expressionless and penetrating. They'd taken on that inscrutable look more than a few times a month ago, when she'd caught him studying her over the course of their hunt for a serial killer.

Initially, they hadn't trusted each other. Kendra had dismissed him as a nineteenth-century detective with little forensic knowledge, while Sam had viewed her unusual proficiency in crime detection with a great deal of suspicion and skepticism. It didn't help that he'd known she'd lied about her arrival in England. She could hardly tell him the truth; only Alec and the Duke were privy to her secret. But she'd come to trust Sam as a fellow investigator. As it turned out, basic police work was as much a part of this era as it was in her time, even if there was no true police force in England but rather a loose network of constables, magistrates, sheriffs, bailiffs, Bow Street Runners, and watchmen, like William Drake.

"'Tis good ter see you, Your Grace." Sam gave a little bow. He turned to Kendra and grinned. "And Miss Donovan. You're in fine looks, lass. Much better than the last time I laid me peepers on you."

"Thank you." Kendra had to smile. The last time she'd seen the Runner, she'd been stabbed and beaten. "I'm feeling a lot better too."

"You chose not to leave, after all?" Alec cut in, his tone brusque.

She tensed, and glanced back at the Marquis. "It wasn't my choice."

"I see."

Kendra heard the cold contempt in those two words and felt a rush of anger. How dare he take that tone with her? Like he was judging her for not accepting his proposal yesterday morning?

"Stay. Marry me."

The words came back to her, along with the thrill and giddy fear. Damn him, he had no idea what he was asking of her, no idea what he was asking her to give up. The future, *her* future, was far from perfect, but at least she had the right to vote.

"Where is Lady Rebecca?" Sam asked suddenly, looking around him as though the Duke's goddaughter would materialize next to the sofa.

"Lady Rebecca has returned to her family's estates," the Duke responded carefully. "Of course, as my ward, Miss Donovan does not require Lady Rebecca to act as a chaperone."

Kendra had to give Sam credit for barely reacting. He gave only a quick bob of his eyebrows and then nodded. "I understand, sir."

"Always a surprise, Miss Donovan," Alec murmured in a low, mocking voice, in response to the Duke's comment. Of course, he couldn't yet know about the Duke's plan to make Kendra his ward, and this was some way for him to find out.

Alec pivoted, sauntering toward the table that held a half a dozen cut-crystal decanters. "Forgive me. I'm being a poor host. Duke, would you and your *ward* like something to drink? Unfortunately, I cannot offer coffee or tea, as I am temporarily without servants. Would you care for some brandy? Madeira or sherry?"

"Brandy, thank you," Aldridge accepted. "Miss Donovan?"

"Sure. And pen and paper—I'd like to take notes about the murder. That's why we're here," she reminded the room, and winced a little at the nasty edge in her tone. But her nerves were scraped raw. It didn't help when she caught the expression of surprise on William Drake's face as he shot her a look.

Aldridge must have seen the night watchman's expression as well, because he said, "I am here to investigate this crime that my nephew has been wrongly accused of, Mr. Drake. My ward shall be assisting me in my endeavor."

William raised his eyebrows. "Your ward assists you in such matters?"

"Yes, much like Caroline Herschel aids her brother Sir William in his work with astronomy."

The watchman considered that, then nodded. "She has helped Sir William discover several comets, hasn't she?"

"Actually, Caroline Herschel discovered several comets by herself," Kendra remarked drily, and gave the Duke a sidelong glance. She knew he was trying to protect her reputation, but it rankled to have her contributions reduced in such a way. She was now second chair in the string orchestra, not because of her talent, but because of her sex.

She turned to Sam. "Mr. Kelly, why don't you tell . . . *the Duke* about the murder while I take notes?"

"Oh. Aye." He coughed, and to Kendra's ears, it sounded suspiciously like he was masking a laugh. The gleam in his eyes was definitely amused.

The levity vanished when he told her, "Her Ladyship was stuc—er, stabbed. And . . . cut . . ." He paused as Aldridge rifled through a nearby desk, producing foolscap and a graphite stick, which he handed to Kendra.

"Go on," Kendra encouraged as she sat down at the desk.

"Her housekeeper, Mrs. Pierson, discovered her last night. Mr. Drake here was brought ter the scene, and sent for me. I arrived about ten minutes before midnight."

"What time did the housekeeper find her?" she asked.

Sam raised a brow at the night watchman. "What time, would you say, Mr. Drake?"

"Eleven, or thereabouts. I arrived about fifteen minutes later."

Kendra wrote that down. "The servants didn't hear anything, see anyone?"

"Ah, well, no . . . Lady Dover sent her staff away for the evening," said William.

"Why?"

William looked like his cravat had suddenly shrunk a size, choking him. "Ah, um. Well, as to that . . ."

"It looked like she was expectin' someone," Sam supplied slowly.

"I see." And Kendra did. She shot Alec a cool look. "You?"

"No." Alec met her gaze as he brought her the brandy-filled goblet.

"Then why are you a suspect?" she asked, keeping her eyes on his as she accepted the glass.

"A misunderstanding."

"Aren't they all?" Kendra murmured. Her throat was dry, so she indulged in one tiny sip before setting the brandy aside. She looked at Sam. "Why do you think Lady Dover was expecting Lord Sutcliffe?"

"Mrs. Pierson. She believed . . . she was under the impression . . ." Sam stuttered to a halt and glanced at Alec.

Kendra turned back to the Marquis. "I know you were involved with Lady Dover," she said bluntly. "I'm assuming the house-keeper knew about your relationship?"

"Lady Dover and I had a special friendship," he acknowledged dispassionately. "But our liaison was finished more than a month ago. Shall I tell you why?"

"No." She knew why. It made her feel . . . she didn't know what it made her feel. She cleared her throat. "If you broke up a month ago, why did Lady Dover's housekeeper think you were the person she was meeting last night?"

"Broke up?" Alec looked briefly amused, his green eyes brightening. "A unique way to phrase it, implying something was shattered."

"*Was* something shattered? Lady Dover's heart, for instance?"

His mouth twisted into a small, humorless smile. "No. Cordelia's heart had no room for anyone other than herself. She wasn't in love with me. She was, however, a proud and beautiful woman. She refused to accept that our relationship was over. Or, perhaps, more accurately, that I was the one who ended it. She wrote me several letters, expressing a desire that we continue our . . . friendship."

"I see."

"Do you? Lady Dover was not an innocent maid, nor was our relationship what you would describe as exclusive."

"Are you saying that she was involved with other men?"

"As I said, she was a beautiful woman. She collected admirers like other women collected fripperies."

Kendra remembered the Lady from the house party, when the only admirer she seemed to want to collect was Alec. "Do you have the names of her other admirers?"

"No. Cordelia did not discuss her friendships with me."

Given her romantic interest in Alec, her silence on the subject made sense. Kendra glanced at Sam, who gave a nod, anticipating her question. "'Tis something we've been askin' in the course of our inquiry, Miss."

"Any names come up?"

The Runner shook his head. "Nay, not yet. But sometimes it takes a bit of time ter get folks talking, especially when what they're talking about has ter do with their betters."

Kendra understood. Nothing silenced the general population like fear of reprisal from the wealthy and powerful, even in her era. "What time did she send her servants away?" she asked.

"Eight o'clock."

"So she was alive at eight. Who was the last person to see her?"

"Mrs. Pierson and the butler, Mr. Sayers. They left together after seeing ter their mistress's comfort. It was only later, when Mrs. Pierson realized she'd forgotten her medicine, that she returned and found her mistress dead."

"She didn't see anyone or hear anything?"

"Nay. But the back door was open."

"You think the killer came in from the back door?"

Sam hesitated. "Maybe. Or he came in the front door and left by the back. Mrs. Pierson said the back door was ajar."

Kendra stared at the Bow Street Runner. "Was the front door open as well?"

William Drake answered, "It was closed but unlocked."

"Okay." She decided to let that line of inquiry go for now. She'd get a better sense of it when she was actually at the crime scene, walking the perimeter. "What about the neighbors? Did they hear anything? See anyone around the house?"

"Nay."

Kendra consulted her notes. "You said that she was cut. That wasn't part of the stabbing?"

Sam shook his head. "She was cut on the face," he said slowly. "It was . . . peculiar. I think it was done after she was stabbed. Leastwise, I hope so. Dr. Munroe will most likely be able ter tell us."

Kendra raised her eyebrows. "Dr. Munroe is doing the autopsy?"

"Aye."

"It would seem that we are coming together once again," murmured the Duke, shooting Kendra a pointed look.

She ignored him, not wanting to contemplate just now if their reunion had a deeper meaning. It was too distracting. She shifted her gaze to Alec. "You know, it would really help if you had an alibi for last night, between eight and eleven."

Alec's mouth twitched, but Kendra couldn't be sure if it was from amusement or annoyance. "I am aware of that, Miss Donovan. Unfortunately, I don't have one, as Mr. Kelly and Mr. Drake can already attest. And my staff is not with me. Not even my valet. When I left Aldridge Castle yesterday morning, I rode to London—alone."

"And came directly here?"

"I believe I had some vague notion of going to my club. When I arrived here, I decided to stay. I polished off an excellent comet vintage. I can show you the empty bottle."

Aldridge eyed his nephew. "Brooding, Alec?"

The Marquis shrugged and said nothing.

Kendra caught the speculative look in Sam's eyes and was annoyed when she felt her face heat up. *This can't be personal.*

"Did Lady Dover try to contact you when you arrived in London?" she asked abruptly.

"Not that I am aware. I do not believe she even knew I was in Town."

"Are you sure?"

"My journey here was impulsive. No one in Town knew I was arriving. And, as I said, I spent the evening alone."

Kendra frowned, turning to Sam. "The housekeeper didn't see the killer, and it's only her belief that Lord Sutcliffe was the man Lady Dover was waiting for. That's pretty flimsy evidence on which to charge the Marquis with murder."

Sam raised his eyebrows, astonished. "His Lordship ain't been charged with murder, lass. That would require an indictment by the House of Lords. Only they can charge the nobility with a crime."

Kendra stared at the Bow Street Runner, not sure she'd heard him correctly. She'd known there was a class system here, but two *justice* systems?

"Don't look so bloody appalled, Miss Donovan. With luck, mayhap I'll be sent to Newgate once the House of Lords convenes," Alec said sarcastically.

"That's not the point," she snapped, irritated. "It's not about you. It's about justice, regardless of class, gender, or race."

"A noble sentiment, but we're not in your America."

She glared at him. "You don't have to tell me *that*."

Of course, if she were absolutely honest with herself, Kendra had to admit than even in her America, justice wasn't always blind to race, gender, the political elite, or privilege. How many times did a celebrity get away with a crime because their face was known to millions? How many times did an average citizen get prosecuted for an offense that a politician walked away from, untouched?

"Alec may not be clapped in irons, Miss Donovan, but his future is by no means secure," Aldridge intervened calmly. "If there is enough sentiment against him in the House of Lords, he could still find himself swinging or transported. We must find the real murderer."

The familiar weight of responsibility settled on her shoulders. She met the Duke's gaze and nodded. "Yes, sir. I'll need to see the crime scene and the body myself."

Aldridge frowned, uncertain. "The crime scene perhaps—"

"And the body," she repeated firmly, and fixed her eyes on him. Damn the proprieties of this century. She wouldn't back down on this, not if they wanted her to do her job properly.

"I don't think Dr. Munroe will object, sir," Sam put in carefully.

"'Tis not Dr. Munroe that I am concerned about," the Duke said ruefully. "Oh, very well. Is it too late in the day, Mr. Kelly, to pay the doctor a visit?"

"Not at all. I shall bring you ter him, sir, Miss."

As she rose, Kendra saw that William Drake was eyeing her oddly again. She hadn't done a very good job pretending to be the Duke's assistant. She decided not to worry about it.

"You can't come to the morgue," she told Alec when he stood as well.

"I understand that, Miss Donovan. I have no wish to see Cordelia in such a state," he said quietly. "Regardless of our relationship, she didn't deserve what was done to her."

"I know. I understand." Responding to his bleak gaze, Kendra reached over and gave his hand what she hoped was a reassuring squeeze. She'd known Lady Dover slightly, during Lady Atwood's house party. She hadn't liked her, but the woman was now a victim of a violent crime. She deserved justice.

"I'll do my best," she told him. That was all she could promise.

5

C ovent Garden, where Dr. Munroe's medical school was located, had once been a trading town called Lundenwic in the days when the Roman Empire had conquered half the world. It was still a trading center, but its commerce was slightly different from the time centuries before when farmers and merchants bartered over pigs and bags of barley. Since the eighteenth century, the largest trade in the area was prostitution. Kendra could easily pick out the working girls. They strolled the area boldly, their faces enhanced with rouge, powder, and lipstick, and wearing brightly colored gowns with plunging necklines that revealed more than they concealed, their skirts rucked above the knees or cut into slits to reveal a seductive flash of thigh.

Once again Kendra was struck by the sheer number of people as their carriage rolled past Tudor-style taverns, shops, and a slew of crowded coffeehouses. Starbucks, apparently, wasn't a new concept.

The Royal Opera House loomed over Covent Garden. It wasn't the same building that existed in her timeline, she knew. This one, like its predecessor, would eventually be destroyed by fire and rebuilt. As she scanned the narrow wooden buildings on either side of the street, Kendra wasn't really surprised that London had been and would continue to be razed by fire. Considering the vast number of candles, oil lamps, and coal- and wood-burning fireplaces that existed in each dwelling, she only marveled that the city hadn't burned down more often.

The carriage drew to a jerky halt in front of a wide, three-story brick building. There was no sign outside to indicate its purpose. Kendra supposed that was deliberate. Although some of the antiquated rules against dissection had been lifted, the role of a medical examiner was still a dubious one. Only cadavers from executed criminals could be used in anatomy schools like Dr. Munroe's, which meant a constant shortage. As Prohibition had given birth to bootleggers, this governmental regulation led to new criminals, as well—the resurrectionists, or body snatchers, who filled the void by robbing graves to deliver fresh specimens. Sometimes a little too fresh, Kendra knew, with a few impatient and unscrupulous resurrectionists resorting to murder to fill their quota.

The coachman opened the door and unfolded the steps so they could descend. Kendra noticed how the man's eyes darted around the vicinity, his hand resting on the butt of his blunderbuss, which was tucked into his belt. It occurred to Kendra that the man wasn't only the Duke's driver. He was also his bodyguard.

"Come, my dear." The Duke took her arm and they followed Sam up the short flight of steps to the door. Inside, oil lamps hissed, revealing a darkly paneled foyer. At the end of the foyer was a hallway that split to the right and left. Straight ahead was a pair of open double doors. Curious, Kendra paused long enough to peer inside. The room was as dark as a witch's cauldron, but she got the sense of space. She could just make out the stage area with a table slab set in the center, circled by wooden bleachers.

"'Tis where Dr. Munroe gives his instruction," Sam said, glancing back at her.

Kendra nodded, and they continued down the shadowy hall to the right. They passed several more closed doors before Sam stopped in front of the last one and knocked. There was a muffled response, then the Bow Street Runner was pushing open the door, and gesturing them inside.

"Good evening, Dr. Munroe. I—"

"A moment, if you please, Mr. Kelly." The doctor didn't look up at the Runner's greeting. Instead, he continued to scribble furiously at his desk.

He wasn't alone. A thin young man with wispy blond hair and a weak chin had been seated in front of the desk but now stood politely at their entrance.

As they waited, Kendra studied the cluttered office. Its walls were lined with shelves that held an assortment of books, instruments, several brass microscopes, and large glass jars. Some of the jars were empty. And some were filled with a murky liquid that offered glimpses of pale floating objects. She allowed her gaze to drift to the full skeleton that had been strung together and hung on a T-stand in the corner, its wired jaw slightly agape as if was offering a crooked smile to the room's occupants.

"Now then, Mr. Kelly, I've only— Your Grace! Miss Donovan!" The note of exasperation in Dr. Munroe's voice vanished as soon as he realized the Bow Street Runner hadn't come alone. He threw down his quill pen and surged to his feet, coming around the desk with a smile, his hands outstretched to take Kendra's. "Miss Donovan, I am delighted to see you in such exceptional health."

He was a big, distinguished-looking man in his early fifties, with a thick silver mane he wore in a ponytail. In contrast, his eyebrows were dark, set above shrewd gray eyes that viewed the world from behind round spectacles, which were pinched into place on a hawkish nose.

Kendra smiled back at him. She remembered only too well how he'd ministered to her after she'd nearly been killed fighting a madman. "I have you to thank for that, Dr. Munroe. Your poultices worked."

"Splendid." He let go of her hands, his gaze moving to the Duke and Sam. "But I suspect this is not a social call. You are here to discuss Lady Dover's murder?"

"More than discuss—I want to view the body," Kendra told him bluntly.

Munroe raised his eyebrows at the Duke. "Would that be wise, sir? We are not at Aldridge Castle."

Kendra stiffened, annoyed that the doctor seemed more concerned by the propriety of her viewing the body than in making use of her skills. And he wasn't even asking *her*; he was asking the Duke, like she was a child.

"Why wouldn't it be wise?" she demanded to know.

Aldridge laid a calming hand on her arm. "I understand your concern, Dr. Munroe, but my nephew is under suspicion for Lady Dover's murder."

"I am aware of that, sir."

"I believe Miss Donovan's help in this matter will be invaluable. Of course, I would not wish for any undue prejudice against my ward. I would not want word to spread about her involvement in this matter, other than the fact that she is assisting me."

"Your ward? Oh." Munroe gave Kendra a startled look. "I see. I shall not mention it."

"You have always been discreet, Dr. Munroe. However . . ." Aldridge looked pointedly at the young man.

"Forgive my manners—this is my apprentice, Mr. Barts," Munroe introduced. "Mr. Barts, this is the Duke of Aldridge and Miss Donovan . . . His Grace's ward. You know Mr. Kelly."

"Your Grace, Miss Donovan." Barts gave an awkward bow.

"Well, Mr. Barts?" the Duke prodded. "Can I rely on your discretion in this matter?"

Barts stared at him. "This matter, sir?"

"My ward will be accompanying us into the dissection room. I would not want Miss Donovan's name besmirched in any way."

The apprentice glanced at Kendra, wide-eyed, then jerked his gaze away almost instantly. "I understand, sir. I shall not speak of it, sir."

"There is no cause for alarm, Your Grace," Munroe assured. "We anatomists know how to keep secrets. The ill-informed are always trying to halt the progress of science and will pounce on any morsel of gossip to use against us. Is that not so, Mr. Barts?"

Barts nodded vigorously. "Yes. Quite so."

Munroe moved toward the door. "The matter is decided then. If you will follow me?"

They retraced their footsteps back down the hall, and then followed the corridor to the left of the foyer, which ended in a long flight of steps that plunged downward. It made sense that the bodies were kept in the basement, Kendra reflected, where it was naturally colder. Still, there would be no way bodies could stack up here to await dissection like in modern morgues. Without the embalming process or refrigeration, the corpse would break down rapidly—a couple of days at most, before bodily gases began to rip open the flesh, rendering any examination useless. And the odor would become unbearable.

"Did Mr. Kelly explain to you what was done to Lady Dover's face?" inquired Dr. Munroe.

Kendra nodded. "He told me that she'd been cut. And it was peculiar."

"Most peculiar," Sam agreed as they entered a dark room that carried the stench of decay.

"I'll be interested to see what you have to say about this particular act of barbarism," Dr. Munroe commented, as he and Barts spent the next few minutes lighting wall sconces and candles.

The mottled light revealed cupboards and shelves, more old-fashioned microscopes, and jars like in Dr. Munroe's office, filled with cloudy liquid, with pale, amoeba-like shapes that seemed to stare back at Kendra through the opaque mixture.

She shivered from the chill in the underground room—or so she told herself. She wasn't normally squeamish, but found herself turning her attention to the more mundane items around the room to remain grounded: wooden buckets filled with red-tinged water; sponges; metal tools; a bundle of clothing; a pair of shoes. It was better than the icehouse that had become their makeshift morgue at Aldridge Castle, she supposed, but not by much. Kendra never thought she'd miss the sterile autopsy rooms of the twenty-first century, with their harsh florescent lights and smell of chemicals, but she did.

Especially the chemicals. Nothing could eliminate the stink of death, but the chemicals helped distract from it. Here, the odor of death was overpowering. She could taste it, like an acrid troche caught in the back of her throat.

There were three empty tables. Above each table was an iron contraption that resembled a wagon wheel, attached to the ceiling by a heavy iron chain. On the outside of the wheel were hooks. Munroe and Mr. Barts began attaching lanterns to the hooks, creating a circle of light directly over the table.

"My own invention," Munroe explained. "It eliminates the risk of contaminating the body with dripping candle wax."

"Ingenious."

"Thank you."

He and Barts disappeared through another door. A minute later, they reemerged, carrying a stretcher that held a figure draped in a cotton sheet. After setting the stretcher down on the middle table, Munroe adjusted his spectacles and looked at Kendra. "Now then. I realize that you are not a fainthearted female, Miss Donovan, but I would feel remiss not to warn you that this is grisly business."

"Duly noted." She strived to keep the bite out of her voice, but she was getting damned tired of being treated so carefully. If women were such feeble creatures as these gentlemen seemed to think, mankind would've died out a millennium ago.

"Mr. Barts, please help me roll the sheet up. We'll keep her face covered, for the moment. I want everyone to concentrate on the injuries that killed her."

As they exposed the body from toes to throat, Kendra saw that Dr. Munroe had already performed the autopsy. She ignored the standard Y-incision and poorly done stitches—MEs didn't have to have the delicate touch of a cosmetic surgeon—and focused instead on the wicked lacerations marring Lady Dover's chest.

"I counted forty-three stab wounds," said Munroe. "Angled downward."

"So the unsub was taller than the victim."

Munroe peered across the body at her. "Or she was sitting down when he attacked her."

Sam said, "She was found sitting down in the upstairs drawing room. 'Course, she could've fallen back onto the sofa when the attack happened."

"Regardless, she died while sitting," Munroe said. "She had lividity in her buttocks and the backs of her thighs."

Kendra moved closer. "Do you have a magnifying glass?"

"Certainly. Mr. Barts?"

The apprentice retrieved a magnifying glass from one of the cupboards. He gave Kendra a strange look as he handed it to her. Ignoring him, she bent over the body and angled the glass to give her the best view.

"Definitely stabbed, as opposed to being cut," she agreed softly, frowning. "But these are more like punctures. What kind of knife did this? The width looks narrow but the penetration appears quite deep." *Larger than an ice pick*, she thought. *But similar.*

"The blade was seven inches long, half an inch wide. It also has a unique contour. Triangle in shape. The tip is sharp, but not the blade, making it ill-suited for cutting."

Something stirred in the back of Kendra's mind. Another case that she'd worked on . . . "Could the weapon have been a stiletto?"

Dr. Munroe looked surprised, then pleased. "Yes! Well done, Miss Donovan."

"Stilettos are not a common weapon," Aldridge remarked, intrigued. "Knights would often use them in the battlefield as their secondary weapon. They became known as a *miséricorde*. Do you know why?"

"Mercy," Kendra translated easily. She had a gift for languages and was fluent in several, including French.

"Yes, Miss Donovan. A stiletto was thin enough to slip through the chain mail worn in the battlefield. Knights would often use it to finish off their wounded opponent. It was actually an act of mercy—hence the name." The lantern's light fell across the Duke's face in such a way that it turned his eye sockets into grim, shadowy pools. "No mercy was shown Lady Dover."

"No," Kendra agreed softly, disturbed as always by mankind's capacity for violence against one another.

"The stiletto was also an assassin's tool," Sam pointed out. "Quick and deadly-like. Easy ter hide in your clothing."

"That brings up a good point," said Kendra. "Was there a collection of ancient weapons in the room where Lady Dover was discovered?"

The Bow Street Runner looked puzzled. "Nay. Why?"

"Process of elimination. We're not dealing with a crime of impulse. They weren't engaged in a heated argument, where he grabbed a nearby weapon and killed her in a frenzied rage. He must have brought the weapon with him, which means the crime was premeditated."

Frowning, Kendra scanned the lacerations tattooing the torso. *Too many.*

"He may have planned to kill her, but he's not an assassin," she continued slowly. "He lost control, became enraged while he was stabbing her."

Munroe nodded. "I concur. There is a certain, as you say, *frenzy* about the wounds."

"He must have had control at some point, though," Kendra added.

The Duke frowned. "Why do you say that?"

"Assuming the killer used the front door for his arrival, Lady Dover would have had to let him in. She wasn't stupid—and you'd have to be stupid to invite a man in an uncontrollable rage into your house."

"True, but as Alec said, Lady Dover was a beautiful woman, and confident in her beauty," pointed out Aldridge. "Perhaps if he was enraged, she believed she could use her feminine wiles to calm him?"

Kendra conceded, "That's possible, I suppose."

She returned her attention to the body, and the gashes on the hands and arms. "He attacked her, but she wasn't passive. She fought back, or at least tried to defend herself by raising her arms to protect herself. See? These are defensive wounds."

"Yes," agreed Munroe. "I believe the assault was quick and overwhelming—less than two minutes. She went into shock and collapsed—or was already seated. Unfortunately, her death wasn't so quick. Because the knife was thrust in a downward motion, it struck bone as many times as it struck vital organs. Her ribs had several scrapes caused by the blade striking them. The bleeding was mostly internal, into her stomach cavity and lungs."

"Aye," Sam agreed, nodding. "There was very little blood at the scene given the number of injuries."

Munroe said, "There wouldn't be with this type of puncture wound."

Kendra studied the injuries. "The killer is right-handed."

Sam lifted his eyebrows. "How do—"

"Most of the wounds are angled to the left side of Lady Dover's torso," Kendra said, cutting off the Bow Street Runner. "And the majority of the victim's defensive wounds are on her left hand and arm. If someone was holding a weapon with their right hand, they'd bring it down in a natural arc to the left." She turned to the Duke, since he was the nearest, and pantomimed a knife attack with the magnifying glass. "If I were holding a knife, Your Grace, you'd lift your arms and hands to shield yourself from attack and—"

"You would be striking my left arm and hand, since that's the natural trajectory. Yes, I see what you're saying. Fascinating."

"Also, since the punctures are quite deep, we know that the unsub used considerable force. If the killer used his non-dominant hand, the wounds would be shallower."

"A remarkable observation, Miss Donovan, and one with which I concur." Munroe smiled at her. He then crossed the room to the worktable, picking up the material she'd noticed earlier and shaking it out to reveal a powdery blue, silk evening gown. The bodice was cut low and sparkled with seed pearls and embroidered flowers.

Pretty, Kendra supposed, if you ignored the stain of blood and the tears made by the knife.

Munroe said, "I matched the bodily injuries to the slits in the material."

"So she was dressed when she was attacked," concluded Kendra.

"Yes. And she sustained no sexual injuries."

Kendra walked to the table to scan the other items: a nude colored chemise and stays; matching hose; lacy garters. There were shoes that were little more than slippers, designed in pale blue silk, and decorated like the bodice, with embroidery and beads. They were ridiculously tiny, like a child's.

"She definitely dressed up for someone," she murmured.

"It certainly appears that way, yes." Munroe walked back to the autopsy table. "Now I shall remove the material from her face. Miss Donovan, I am interested to hear your theories about this." Without further delay, he removed the cloth and handed it to his apprentice.

Kendra was no stranger to death. As an FBI criminal profiler, she'd seen it in person and studied all manner of it in photographs. Yet her heart gave a queer jolt when she saw Lady Dover lying on a slab beneath the flickering light from the oil lanterns in such a state.

They hadn't been friends. In fact, they'd barely spoken to each other. But Kendra remembered the other woman's exquisite beauty, her golden hair and clear, ivory skin, paired with large blue, almost violet, eyes set below delicately arched, dark brown eyebrows. The Grace Kelly perfection had been a perfect foil for Alec's dark good looks. At the time, Kendra had acknowledged that they'd made a striking couple, even though it had annoyed her to see them together.

Any lingering irritation fell away now. Lady Dover's eyes were closed and her mouth was slightly open, but she would never be mistaken for sleeping. The killer had made two shallow cuts on the right side of her face. On the left, he'd slashed and gouged until the skin flapped down against the jaw, looking like an upside down U. In the raw pulp, Kendra caught the glimmer of white bone, possibly teeth.

"Good God," breathed the Duke. Two words only, but they were filled with horror.

Kendra was silent for a long moment, letting her own horror wash through her. *Acknowledge it, compartmentalize it, and move on.* It was a trick she'd learned when she'd begun her training at Quantico.

"This was *not* done in a frenzy," Kendra finally said. She pointed to the first two marks. "Those appear to be hesitation marks. Superficial. Like he tried to start something and couldn't go through with it."

Dr. Munroe eyed her curiously. "And the left side of her face?"

"He was obviously a lot more determined to complete the task. Was she alive when he did this?"

"No."

"Thank God," muttered Aldridge.

"The same weapon—the stiletto—was used here," said Dr. Munroe. "'Tis why the edges of the injury are so ragged. Stilettos are excellent for thrusting, but they make poor cutters. He had to have spent some time to fillet the skin like that. If he'd used a better knife, he could have done this in a matter of seconds. Instead, I estimate that the injury took minutes—maybe even as long as five minutes to complete."

"Why'd the bastard do it?" Sam asked, and everyone, including Barts, looked at Kendra. This reaction was, she supposed, some kind of validation.

"It's not unheard of for a man to kill and disfigure a woman who's trying to break off a relationship. But that kind of violence is usually done in the heat of the moment." She considered past crime scenes, where the woman's face had been obliterated, either by fists or a bullet. "He was already stabbing her in rage. He should have done the same to the face."

She frowned as she examined the gruesome disfigurement. "This was calculated. It has a purpose. She was already dead. He could have walked away. Why didn't he?"

"Pray tell, Miss Donovan, are we dealing with the same kind of monster that we dealt with before?" asked Aldridge. "Will more women turn up dead?"

Kendra dragged her gaze away from the damaged face to look at the Duke. She saw the fear in his eyes, and understood. The monster they'd dealt with a month ago had been a serial killer.

"No. No, I don't think so." She shook her head, and then her eyes returned to Lady Dover, scanning the puncture wounds piercing her chest and the grisly cut on her face. "Everything about this is . . . *personal*. He didn't choose her because she fit his pattern. She wasn't a stranger to him. She was involved with him, but something set him off."

"I may have a theory . . ." Munroe hesitated.

Kendra looked over at him and saw something in his eyes that made her stomach clench and sent an icy shiver dancing down her spine. The moment seemed to hang suspended like Munroe's lighting contraption. Kendra had an overwhelming, completely irrational desire to stop him from saying anything more.

Then it was too late.

"Lady Dover was pregnant," he said slowly. "At least three months. I think such news may very well have set the killer off."

6

Kendra, Aldridge, and Sam Kelly were seated in the Duke's carriage, again rumbling down the street, taking them away from Covent Garden. The curtains had been drawn tight, a barrier against the night and, she suspected, the more unsavory elements that existed outside in that darkness.

"Alec was *not* the father of Lady Dover's child," the Duke insisted.

"You don't know that," Kendra said, and her voice, to her ears, sounded distant and hollow, like she was hearing it from the other side of a long tunnel. The news of Lady Dover's pregnancy had shaken her more than she cared to admit. "We can't ignore the possibility," she forced herself to say. "The timing works out. He was involved with her—by his own admission—during that period."

Inside the carriage, a small brass lantern had been lit, and in its feeble glow, she could see Aldridge's quick frown, although he didn't try to contradict her.

But then how could he? Unfortunately, there was no way to determine the paternity of the child in this era. Blood testing, an inaccurate method at best, wouldn't even be available for another hundred years, DNA testing obviously much later.

Sam stirred in his seat. He had on his cop face, impassive with a thousand-yard stare. "If Lady Dover was playing fast and loose with her charms, as we suspect, there are likely other men who could've fathered the babe," he offered.

Kendra made an effort to shake free of the strange sense of malaise that gripped her. She needed to *focus*. "Yes. We're looking at anyone Lady Dover may have been involved with in the last three months. As Dr. Munroe said, learning about the pregnancy could've been the trigger that set off the killer."

It was, in fact, the number one reason pregnant women wound up dead in her own time, Kendra knew. *The dark side of the twenty-first century.*

"Miss Donovan, surely you don't believe that my nephew . . . that *Alec* is capable of that barbarism—"

"No. You misunderstand. Sutcliffe could have fathered Lady Dover's child, but I don't believe for a minute that he killed her." She'd seen Alec run hot and cold. He could kill, she was certain. She'd heard that he had been involved with the war effort against Napoleon, even if the details were ambiguous. And war tended to push people over lines that they never thought they'd cross. So maybe Alec had killed, just as *she* had killed. But not in the manner that had been done to Lady Dover. Never like that.

Aldridge relaxed, and nodded. "Excellent. Then we are in accord."

Kendra wondered how long that would last during the course of the investigation. Alec's involvement made it too personal. Emotions were already running high. Disagreements were inevitable.

She shifted her gaze to Sam. "I still need to go to the crime scene."

"Aye. I can bring you ter the house tomorrow morning, when it's light."

Kendra flicked another look at the curtained windows. She didn't like waiting, but she understood that without electricity, she'd have a hell of a time seeing anything. Candlelight couldn't compete with a lightbulb. Even in the bright light of morning, what would she really find? Trace evidence like fiber and fingerprints was rendered useless here, with no state-of-the-art laboratories filled with shiny, taxpayer-funded equipment to process it.

Still, it was procedure. Both her instinct and her training compelled her to follow it.

"Is the house secure?" she asked.

Sam gave a shrug. "'Tis secure enough. We only had a few folks coming through this morning ter look around, but—"

"Wait. *What?*" Kendra stared at the Bow Street Runner, not sure she heard correctly. "Folks. What do you mean, *folks?*"

Sam frowned. "Curiosity seekers. The usual lot. It seemed like half of London Town tramped through the Marrs' household after those murders. I don't hold with the practice meself," he added defensively. "But it ain't against the law."

Kendra pinched the bridge of her nose in amazement. Was she really trapped in an age where people—*civilians*—were allowed to walk through crime scenes for fun? *So much for procedure.*

"My dear, things are done differently here," Aldridge reminded her gently.

"I'm aware," she retorted, and had to bite back a more scathing reply.

"We didn't have near as many people come through Lady Dover's residence," Sam offered in a tone that was meant to soothe. "Her returning staff, servants from neighboring houses, a few merchants. Mostly common folk and urchins who'd got word about the crime."

"*Children?*" Again Kendra couldn't control her shock. "You're telling me that children walked through the crime scene?"

"Aye. Bloodthirsty, the lot of them. But Dr. Munroe already got hold of the body, so no one saw nothin'. They'll learn more from the broadsides, if they can read."

Broadsides were oversized single sheets of paper printed with the news of the day. The Declaration of Independence had even been published on a broadside and posted in a public square. While some broadsides contained news, the majority could give twenty-first-century tabloids a run for their money, with their lurid headlines, salacious gossip, and crime reporting.

"The premises are locked," Sam added. "I've got a few Charlies . . . er, night watchmen keepin' an eye on the place tonight."

Kendra acknowledged his words with an unhappy nod. It wasn't like she could do anything about it. "Tell me about the staff," she said instead. "How many, and who are they?"

"Mrs. Pierson, as you know, is the housekeeper. Then there's Mr. Sayers. He's the butler. Her Ladyship employed a cook, Mrs. Mason, and two footmen—one who served as her coachman—and two maids. Her personal maid's Miss Marat."

"And they have alibis?"

"Aye, we checked them out and got their stories verified by others."

"They didn't mention any of Lady Dover's other admirers besides Lord Sutcliffe?"

"Nay. Like I said, folks know how ter keep their silence about such things when it's about the gentry. But I think they really do believe it was His Lordship that their mistress was waiting for last evenin'. He'd been a frequent guest, and they all knew that Lady Dover had set her cap for him." He paused, then scratched his nose as he eyed her. "Maybe you should talk ter Miss Marat, Miss. Ladies share secrets with their personal maids, don't they?"

"It depends on the secret, I suppose."

"Maybe you'd get more outta her, being you're a woman, and all."

"Finally an advantage to being a woman here," Kendra muttered.

Aldridge smiled, then said to Sam, "Miss Donovan is being sorely tested by the restrictions of Town. Would you be able to arrange to bring Miss Marat to my residence tomorrow? It might be easier for Miss Donovan to conduct the interview there."

"Aye. If you'd give me your address, sir, I'll make arrangements."

"Grosvenor Square, Number 29."

Sam gave them a startled look. "Is that right? 'Twould appear that Lady Dover was your neighbor, sir. She was murdered in Grosvenor Square. Number 8."

Aldridge's eyebrows rose, equally startled. "But that is an excellent neighborhood! I cannot believe she was attacked there . . ." The Duke's voice trailed off as he apparently recognized the foolishness of his own statement. A month ago, he'd learned that evil wasn't restricted to the lower classes, or the undesirable neighborhoods. Safety was an illusion.

He knew that now. Unfortunately, Lady Dover had found that out too late.

❖

They dropped Sam Kelly off at the Bow Street Magistrates' Office at Number 4 Bow Street, not far from Covent Garden, before proceeding on to Grosvenor Square. It didn't surprise Kendra that the Duke of Aldridge's residence was one of the largest in the area, set slightly off the street, featuring a mammoth buff-colored edifice with imposing pale columns that stretched four stories of the five-story building. A wrought-iron balcony stretched across the second floor. The façade was stucco, which had become fashionable in this era thanks to the famous architect John Nash. Parapets circled the roof, hiding the slanted peaks. Light spilled from tall, skinny Georgian sash windows. An oil lantern hung outside the crimson door. Similar lamps flickered like tiny golden dots from the neighboring houses.

The street seemed unnaturally hushed after the clamor they'd encountered in London's busier thoroughfares. The only sound was the clip-clop of the horses' hooves on the cobblestone and the turn of wheels as the carriage departed after depositing them at the front entrance. From one of the nearby houses, Kendra heard the faint high notes of a harpsichord being played. She imagined the daughter of an aristocrat dutifully sitting in front of the instrument, supplying the evening's entertainment for her family. God knew, Kendra had been treated to enough evenings with that type of entertainment last month at Lady Atwood's house party.

They climbed the front steps of the house, where Aldridge paused and pointed. "Lady Dover's townhouse is located in that section of the square."

Kendra turned to look, but their line of sight was obstructed by a vast wooded area. Despite the moon, she could barely make out the details of trees and shrubs. It was like staring into an abyss.

"We'll need a map of London," she said.

"Of course. And I shall procure a slate board, as well as any other tools you may require."

The Duke's butler, Harding, materialized as soon as the Duke had opened the door and they'd stepped into the foyer. The general layout was similar to Alec's townhome, with a chandelier suspended from the center of the decorative plastered ceiling and stairs at the rear of the house,. The scale, though, was much larger, the style more grand. The floor was a polished pink and gray marble and the walls were plastered and painted white. Gilt-framed mirrors made the foyer seem even larger.

"Good evening, Your Grace, Miss Donovan." The butler gave a slight bow, his feet whispering across the marble tile as he took the Duke's hat and gloves. "Lady Atwood and the Marquis of Sutcliffe are upstairs in the drawing room."

"Excellent. How was the journey, Harding?"

"It went very well, sir. We encountered no difficulties."

"And the household is settling in?"

"Yes. Lady Atwood is most proficient, sir. She and Mrs. Danbury have things well in hand. The Countess has insisted His Lordship stay until his own household is in order. She's issued a menu to Monsieur Anton and requested that dinner be served at half past nine—Town hours, sir."

"Ah. Very good. Thank you, Harding."

Kendra accompanied the Duke to the second floor—or, rather, the first floor, by English standards. The drawing room they entered had damask wallpaper in yellow and white stripes and bucolic John Constable landscapes. Candles had been lit throughout the room while flames devoured the logs in the elegantly carved white marble fireplace. Two sofas, an assortment of chairs, and gleaming cherrywood side tables were positioned around the room for comfort and convenience.

Lady Atwood was sitting on one of the sofas, sipping sherry. She'd changed into an evening gown, Kendra noticed, an olive green satin with long sleeves. The neckline was square, the bodice decorated with satin ribbons and intricate beadwork, which twinkled in the candlelight. Her hair had been swept into a fashionable top-knot, anchored by a Spanish comb designed with eye-catching emeralds. Alec was standing in front of the fireplace in a contemplative pose, his hands shoved in his pockets, his gaze fixed broodingly on the orange and gold flames in the hearth. Like Lady Atwood, he'd changed for dinner, looking outrageously handsome in a simple white cravat, black coat, and snug trousers. When he glanced around at their entrance, Kendra saw that he'd also shaved.

She felt bedraggled in comparison. It had been a long day— hell, it had been a long *year*.

"Good evening, my dear." Aldridge went forward and pressed a kiss on his sister's forehead. "You've done an excellent job with the household."

The Countess waved the compliment away. "What's happening, Bertie? Pray tell, did you get these ridiculous charges against Alec dropped?"

"Alec hasn't been charged," he reminded her and moved to the credenza, which held a gleaming array of decanters and crystal glasses. "Sherry, Miss Donovan?"

"Sure. Thanks."

"You know what I'm referring to," Lady Atwood snapped impatiently. "Our nephew is under a dreadful cloud of suspicion. It's outrageous, and it must be lifted!"

"We are working toward that goal, Caro," the Duke responded mildly, handing Kendra the glass of sherry.

"What did you learn from Dr. Munroe?" Alec asked.

Aldridge hesitated, flicking a glance at his sister. "This isn't an appropriate discussion for the drawing room, Alec. Perhaps later, in my study—"

"Nonsense!" Lady Atwood cut him off. A bit more softly, she conceded, "Normally, this would not be a discussion for the drawing room. But I'm not a green girl or a shatter-brained female, likely to swoon or go into the vapors. You and I have always spoken freely with each other, Bertie. You appear to have no difficulty speaking freely with *her*."

Kendra stiffened as the Countess shifted to glare in her direction.

Aldridge held up a hand, as though declaring peace. "Very well, my dear. I shall speak freely." Still, he took a fortifying swallow from his wineglass before continuing. "Lady Dover was stabbed most viciously with what looks to be a stiletto."

"Good heavens," Lady Atwood said faintly.

"A stiletto?" Alec frowned. "That's an uncommon weapon in this modern era. Italian assassins were famous for using them. My mother's family has many on display at their palazzo in Venice."

Kendra eyed him over her wineglass. "Are the weapons still with your mother's family?"

"Naturally."

"Then you might want to keep quiet about that," she advised. "You're already under suspicion of Lady Dover's murder. The authorities don't need to know that the Italian side of your family collects the same weapon that was used to kill her."

"I hardly went to Venice to borrow one. What else did you learn?"

"Based on the number of wounds, this was personal," Kendra said. "The killer also cut her face postmortem." She frowned as she summoned up a mental image of Lady Dover's savaged face. The injury had been a mark—not the teeth marks that serial killers enjoyed placing on their victims, like the monster from a month ago, who'd scored his victim's flesh with a single bite mark to the breast. But the cutting had been a mark, neverthe-less. It meant something. *What?*

"The facial damage was not done in the heat of the moment," she continued quietly. And because her throat had grown dry, she took another sip of sherry. "But I think it was impulsive."

Aldridge eyed her with surprise. "How can it be both calcu-lating and impulsive?"

"The unsub—the killer," Kendra identified, for Lady Atwood's benefit, "didn't plan to cut her face in such a manner. He only thought of it after she was dead."

"How do you know that?" the Countess demanded. "How can you possibly know what was in the fiend's mind?"

"It's a calculated deduction based on what we know," Kendra told her. "We know the killer used a stiletto, which he brought with him. That shows premeditation. He was either going to kill her or use it to threaten her. Yet if he intended to kill her and then cut her face like he did, why didn't he bring a better knife? One better suited to that purpose?"

The room fell silent as they considered that.

"Mayhap the attacker was unfamiliar with knives, and there-fore unaware that a stiletto is a tool used to stab rather than cut?" Aldridge offered finally.

"Possible," Kendra conceded. She'd remained standing. Having spent so much time sitting in the carriage, she now wanted to move, which she did as she spoke. "But the cutting wasn't done in the heat of anger. Lady Dover was dead by that point. I feel like the mutilation was a statement."

Lady Atwood gave a delicate shiver. "Regarding what?"

"I don't know. But we need to figure it out, because I think it's key. It certainly was important enough for the killer to take the time, possibly risking exposure, to do it." She paused and sipped her sherry as she turned over several possibilities in her mind. "Maybe he did it to show his vengeance. Tit for tat. He'd ruin her beauty just as she was trying to ruin him."

Lady Atwood frowned. "Ruin him? Pray tell, how would she do such a thing?"

Kendra froze, realizing too late how sensitive the next topic would be.

Alec's eyes narrowed. "Miss Donovan?" he prodded when she remained silent. "I, too, would like an answer to that question. What power did Cordelia hold over her killer?"

She exchanged a glance with the Duke. There was no easy way to deliver this news, no way to cushion it.

"Lady Dover was pregnant," she said simply.

"Good heavens!" Lady Atwood gasped.

Alec's face went blank in his shock. "Pardon?"

"I'm sorry," Kendra said. "Dr. Munroe said that she was about three months pregnant. You didn't know?"

"Good God, no. How can you think . . . no." He stared at Kendra for a second. Then he turned around abruptly, went to the side table, and selected a stout glass. He bypassed the more placid sherry and went for the whiskey. Kendra didn't blame him. Splashing a generous three fingers into the glass, he tossed it back like it was medicine, and then refilled his glass.

"Alec, my boy . . ." the Duke began uncertainly.

"She sent me letters, asking me . . . begging me to meet her. What if it was to tell me about the child?"

Tricky area, Kendra thought. "What would you have done?"

"Christ, I don't know."

The blasphemy, more than anything, told Kendra how shaken Alec was by the news. Gentlemen were never supposed to curse in the drawing room, in the presence of ladies. She discounted herself from that particular category of delicate sensibilities, but there was still his aunt to consider.

"Our affair had run its course," Alec continued, "and I'm not such a fool as to take Cordelia's word that the child was mine."

"You might not have had any choice if she had created a scandal-broth by claiming you were the father of her child, Alec," Lady Atwood said sharply. "You would have been forced to marry her."

"Her own reputation would have been in tatters," countered Aldridge.

"Pshaw!" Surprisingly, the Countess was the one who issued the rude sound. "What is that measured against becoming a marchioness and eventually a duchess? Men have no understanding of what some women will do to achieve their ambitions."

Kendra moved to the window as she considered the matter. The street and park below were as dark as pitch, any light from the moon scuttled by clouds and probably fog. She could feel the moist, cold air seeping through the windowpanes. Shivering slightly, she turned back to look at Alec. "If, as you say, Lady Dover was involved with other men, then you might not be the only one she sent letters to. Ambitious women—and men, for that matter—usually have more than one game plan."

Lady Atwood's blue eyes took on a steely glint. "You are quite right, Miss Donovan. If she failed to bring my nephew up to scratch, the brazen creature may very well have had someone else in mind." She sniffed, then tilted her head to study Kendra. "Tomorrow, you and I shall pay a morning call to an old friend of mine—Lady St. James. We had our first season together."

"What?" Kendra was taken aback at the non sequitur. "No, I can't. Mr. Kelly is bringing us to the crime scene tomorrow morning."

The Countess gave her an exasperated look. "Don't be stupid. Morning calls are *not* done in the morning—certainly never before eleven. Do Americans know *nothing* of social etiquette? We shall time our visit to half past three, since Lady St. James and I have a close connection. I trust you will be finished with your business by then. It will also give me time to engage the services of a lady's maid for you."

Kendra's head began to spin, and it wasn't because of the sherry. "I don't need a lady's maid. I already have Molly helping me."

"Nonsense. You are the ward of a duke! You shall require a proper lady's maid. Which reminds me, we must visit my London modiste. You will need new gowns."

"I already have gowns." Morning gowns, walking gowns, afternoon gowns, evening gowns; Christ, she had gowns coming out of her ears.

"We are not in the country anymore, Miss Donovan. We are in London."

"We are in London to investigate a murder."

"You can investigate and still be fashionable."

Kendra's temper began to rise. The woman was insane. "Being fashionable is the least of my concerns!"

"*That* is quite obvious—"

"Half past three will be plenty of time for us to pursue our inquiries," interrupted the Duke, clearly recognizing the stubborn glint in both his sister's and Kendra's eyes. "But I must ask, my dear, why you insist on paying a call tomorrow to Lady St. James? We do have other priorities."

The smile the Countess bestowed on them was smug. "You want to know who Lady Dover may have been involved with, do you not? Lady St. James is not only one of my oldest friends, but she is one of the most notorious gossips in all of London. If

Alec did not father Lady Dover's babe, she ought to be able to tell us who did."

❖

In the park below, the huddled figure watched as the woman came to stand in front of the upstairs window. Though he knew she couldn't see him in the darkness, he found himself sidling closer to the trees, using the foliage as cover. He couldn't see her clearly, either, as the mist that had crept in off the Thames made her features indistinct. Her face was a pale cameo, warmed by the glow of the candles positioned around her. And she only looked out for a moment. Then she turned away, appearing to talk to someone. She moved out of his line of sight.

The woman didn't return to the window, nor did anyone else, but he remained where he was, burrowing deeper into his coat and scarf in an attempt to keep warm. *Watching.*

7

One day down. Fifty years to go.

Or maybe less. What was the life span of a woman in this era?

Kendra refused to think about it as she rolled out of the big four-poster bed with its cream silk canopy and feather tick mattress to begin the morning rituals common to the early nineteenth century. She relieved herself in the chamber pot tucked discreetly inside a wooden washstand in the small alcove and brushed her teeth using a tooth powder mixture of soda, chalk, and salt (courtesy of Mrs. Tobin, who ran the stillroom at Aldridge Castle). And after stripping off her nightdress and donning undergarments—a simple chemise and stays—Kendra went through her own morning ritual: bending, stretching, and twisting in a series of yoga positions.

"Mornin', Miss."

Kendra glanced over from the side-plank position as Molly, a young maid called a tweeny, came into the room carrying a tray with a coffeepot, sugar bowl, and cup and saucer. In addition to helping the other staff with their duties, Molly had become Kendra's de facto lady's maid, since it was nearly impossible for a woman to dress in this era without some assistance.

"Thought ye'd be awake doin' . . . wot'ever it is ye do." Molly no longer watched in fascination as Kendra went through the rest of her exercise routine. She'd become used to what she regarded as Kendra's eccentricities, believing yoga to be something every American did before they ate their breakfast.

Funny how the strange becomes familiar, Kendra mused. *Like pissing into a chamber pot.* She no longer thought twice about it. And that frightened her more than anything.

So don't think about it.

Molly poured coffee into the cup, sweetening it with a lump of sugar. She brought it over to Kendra as she pushed herself to her feet. "Ain't London Town grand, Miss? Oi've never seen the like. Never been outside of Aldridge Village. It's ever so excitin'— Oh!" Her pale, freckled face scrunched in consternation. "'Course, 'tis a terrible thing about 'Is Lordship. Pay me no mind. Oi'm babbling like a brook, as me ma says."

"It's perfectly natural for you to be excited about being in a new environment, Molly." Kendra smiled at the tweeny as Molly bustled around the bed, straightening the sheets and fluffing the pillows.

"Aye, Miss." Molly moved to the enormous wardrobe to inspect the gowns inside. She shot Kendra a quick glance. "Mrs. Danbury reckons the Countess'll be 'iring ye a proper lady's maid."

"You're proper enough for me."

It probably wasn't much of a compliment, Kendra decided wryly, given that everyone at the castle thought she was a freak. But Molly flashed her a quick smile and pulled out a green cotton muslin, which she laid on the bed. She left the bedchamber, returning ten minutes later with a pitcher of lavender-scented water and a bowl of lemon wedges.

Last night, the servants had hauled up a copper tub and steaming buckets of water so she could bathe. This morning, Kendra settled for a quick sponge bath from the porcelain bowl that Molly poured the scented water. She tried not to think of the quick morning shower she indulged in before going to work in the twenty-first century. She also tried not to think about the hundreds of convenient antiperspirant sticks that were available in her time.

As she swabbed her armpits with the slices of lemon, which acted as a natural deodorant, she wondered what Molly would think if she walked into a modern store and saw the entire aisles devoted to the countless brands of deodorant that promised to stop the stink, stop the sweat, stop the stains. For men, for women, even for teens, as if a sixteen-year-old's perspiration was somehow biologically different from a twenty-five-year-old's. Would Molly be enthralled? Or would she think the greatest fear in the twenty-first century was unpleasant odors?

"W'ot?" Molly asked.

Only then did Kendra realize that she'd given a small laugh. She shook her head. "Nothing. I was just thinking how different my life was before arriving in England."

"Ooh, Oi'd love ter hear about America. It's ever so far."

Kendra smiled slightly as she pulled on the dress the maid had selected. "It is far."

After Molly buttoned her up, Kendra sat down at the mirrored vanity. Fifteen minutes later, the tweeny had managed to coil Kendra's dark hair into some kind of twisty chignon, anchored with silver combs and long hairpins.

Kendra left the bedroom. In the hallway, a couple of maids were already sweeping the carpet with sturdy whisk brooms and polishing the side tables with beeswax that carried the faintest odor of honey. They gave her quick curtsies, which surprised

Kendra. Then she realized that they must have heard that she was now the Duke's ward, an elevation in status that required their deference, at least outwardly. Given their carefully blank faces, Kendra had a feeling that they thought something else entirely. Servants in grand households like the Duke's were notoriously snobbish.

She found the Duke and Sam Kelly in the dining room, halfway through the English breakfast that had been set up on the buffet.

"Good morning, Miss Donovan," Aldridge greeted her. "I hope you slept well."

"Yes, thanks. I was out like a light." Only when she caught Sam's perplexed stare did Kendra realize that the idiom made virtually no sense in an age without electricity.

Aldridge looked only amused. "Um. Yes, indeed. Anyhow, Mr. Kelly has informed me that Lady Dover's maid, Miss Marat, has agreed to meet with us later this morning."

"Aye. She'll be here at eleven."

"Good." Kendra filled a plate with eggs, sausage, and stewed tomatoes, poured another cup of coffee and added sugar, and brought it over to the table.

"I've ordered a slate board and supplies brought to my study." The Duke picked up his teacup, and surveyed them over the rim. "We shall use that room to discuss sensitive matters. It's imperative that we resolve this investigation quickly." He paused, then added, "I've learned that the House of Lords will convene soon to decide my nephew's fate."

Kendra glanced up from her eggs, surprised. "How do you know that?"

"Though I do not sit in Parliament, I am a member of the House of Lords, Miss Donovan. And I am not without resources."

"Of course not." A man as wealthy and powerful as the Duke of Aldridge wouldn't be. "When will this happen?"

"Ah, as to that . . . I do not know. It is currently being discussed. However, a fortnight, perhaps."

A fortnight. Derived from Old English—*fēowertyne niht*. Fourteen nights.

"Okay." Kendra took a couple more bites before pushing her plate away. "Let's go see the crime scene."

❖

They decided to walk to Lady Dover's residence on the other side of the square. In truth, it wasn't a square at all, but a large oval, with a three hundred-acre park at its center. And "park" was also a misnomer. That implied meticulously groomed lawns, tidy shrubs, and trees. What Kendra saw through the black iron gate was a wilderness bisected with a series of paths designed for horse riders and pedestrians. For just a moment, she thought she caught a movement in the dense foliage, and her neck prickled with the sensation of watching eyes. Whether those eyes were human or animal, though, she didn't know.

She switched her gaze to the neighborhood. The residences were a mixture of mansions, like the Duke's, and terraces, which were essentially elegant brownstones.

"You said that you canvassed the area. The neighbors didn't hear anything?" Kendra asked of Sam, scanning the surrounding buildings. Most of the windows were still shuttered. Nine in the morning was like the crack of dawn for London's aristocracy. But while they might still be in bed, she knew the servants had been awake for hours, preparing for the day belowstairs.

"Based on the defensive wounds on her hands and arms," she mused, "Lady Dover fought back. I'd think she would've screamed."

Sam shrugged. "The only screams they heard was done by Mrs. Pierson."

"And no one saw Lady Dover's visitor either?"

"Nay."

It took ten minutes at a leisurely pace to loop around to the other side of the park. Kendra didn't need to see the address to know which home belonged to Lady Dover. She spotted two men in an intense conversation standing on the front steps of a townhouse.

"All's well?" Sam called out as they approached, and the night watchmen jerked to attention. Even at a distance, Kendra could read the dismay on their faces, and her stomach tightened. *Something's wrong . . .*

"Ah . . . hmm, gov' . . . well, we patrolled the area just like ye told us," said the taller man.

"Aye. Not a peep around 'ere," supplied the other watchman. "But, ye see, well . . ."

Sam's eyebrows had pulled together, and now he snapped, "Out with it!"

The taller man said, "We went in, just ter look around, mind ye . . . and, ah . . . it's been tumbled."

Sam stared at him. "What?"

"It's been robbed, sir," the other man clarified. "The door was locked, but a clever cracksman got in."

"*What?*" Sam's face reddened. "You sodding simpletons! God's teeth, I gave you one bloody order. *One!* Ter watch the house. *Watch the bloody house!*" His voice echoed loudly on the silent street. Kendra had never seen the Runner so angry.

"We did, gov'ner! God as my witness," said the taller watchman. "We patrolled the area, jest like ye told us ter do. Kept our peepers on the house. It was quiet-like, I swear. We never saw nothin'."

"Damn it!" Sam spat on the sidewalk, then shot a stricken glance at Kendra. "Beggin' your pardon, Miss." He turned back to glower at the night watchmen. "Send a crew around ter check the flash houses and rookeries, see if you can get a line on the thieves that done it. This kinda job, this kinda neighborhood, word's gonna go around."

"Aye, sir!"

They both hurried down the sidewalk, obviously eager to get away from Sam's baleful glare.

Kendra shook her head in disbelief. "Does this thing happen often here? Crimes scenes robbed?"

Sam shuffled his feet, looking embarrassed. "I wouldn't say often, nay. But it's been known ter happen. That's why I had it locked and watched, ter *prevent* a bloody robbery." He pressed his lips together as though to contain a string of curses that he wanted to let loose. Then he expelled an angry breath. "Ah, well. Nothing ter do about it now but to see the damage."

They went up the steps. The night watchmen hadn't locked up again, so the door swung open easily. The morning sunlight spilled inside the black-and-white-tiled foyer.

"The silver candleholders are missing from that table, there," Sam pointed out, sounding aggrieved again. He stomped through the narrow hall. Silently, Kendra and the Duke followed him upstairs to the drawing room. At first glance, it looked untouched, no overturned furniture or anything obviously rifled through. Then Kendra realized that every surface was devoid of ornaments.

"Bugger it!" Sam stormed across the room to glare at the empty desk, hands on hips. "The rogues even stole the bloody glass!"

"Glass?" Kendra echoed.

"A goblet. It smelled of whiskey. I think she gave it ter the killer. We found the glass under the sofa with a fan and a fancy jeweled comb that lasses wear in their hair."

They turned to the sofa in question. Kendra eyed the dark stains on the cushions. Not much blood, really, given the number of times Lady Dover had been stabbed. But Kendra recalled what Dr. Munroe said, that a stiletto did most of its damage internally.

"She was a beautiful woman," the Duke murmured. Kendra glanced around to see him staring at the enormous oil painting of Lady Dover positioned above the fireplace.

"Yes," she agreed simply. The artist hadn't used his skill to flatter his subject like so many portrait painters did during this era, the nineteenth-century version of Photoshop. Women who looked like Lady Dover didn't need to be altered.

"I did not know her, really. When we chanced to meet socially, she was always entertaining and pleasant. What was done to her . . ." Aldridge shook his head, remembering the horrors that had been revealed when Dr. Munroe had pulled back the shroud.

Kendra said nothing. Instead, she turned to survey the room again, trying to imagine what it had been like that night. A fire would have been burning in the grate, candles lit. In the twenty-first century, that would be the makings of a romantic evening. Here, it could've been an evening like any other.

But it wasn't an evening like any other.

"Okay, let's assume the killer came through the front door. He could have murdered Lady Dover as soon as he was inside the door, in the hall," she said slowly. "They were alone. She obviously answered the door, since she sent her servants away. But he didn't strike then. He bided his time, followed her up the stairs, into this room."

"That's not a lot of time. Two minutes," countered Sam.

"Two minutes can feel like eons if you have murder on your mind. What does that tell us?"

"Lady Dover didn't regard him as a threat," Aldridge supplied.

Kendra nodded. "He didn't do anything to alarm her, to make her afraid of him. He was not in a rage—or he hid his rage well."

"Or, as we discussed last night, she felt confident enough to appease his anger." The Duke's gaze strayed to the portrait again.

"Yes, but the point is the killer didn't take out the stiletto and stab her immediately. The rage that took over during the stabbing was absent while they were downstairs." Kendra looked at Sam. "There was only one glass of whiskey?"

"Aye."

"I wonder if she made the drink for him, or for herself?" It was a rhetorical question, but Sam answered anyway.

"It was for him, I reckon." He caught her look and shrugged. "Whiskey ain't a lady's usual drink."

"Hmm." Kendra decided to let that bias go. "Whoever the drink was for, Lady Dover must have been holding it when he attacked her."

Sam raised his eyebrows. "How'dya know that?"

"Because the killer needed his hands free. We have to assume his weapon was concealed somewhere on him." Kendra positioned herself in front of the bloodstained sofa, imagining Lady Dover facing her killer. Holding the glass in one hand, the fan in another. "If the drink was hers, she could have been sitting. If she'd made the drink for him, she could have been standing here, offering it to him. The killer needed to retrieve the stiletto. He then moved forward, bringing up his hand with the weapon . . ."

Kendra began counting as she went through the motions. Putting her hand in her pocket—"One"—pulling out the imaginary knife—"two"—lunging forward toward the sofa and raising her fist—"three"—bringing down her hand in a slashing motion—"four."

She straightened, glancing at the Duke and Sam. "If the killer had been holding the glass, he'd have had to put it down, most likely on the side table there. It wouldn't have been kicked under the sofa."

"Yes." Aldridge nodded. "Yes, that is an excellent deduction, my dear."

Kendra changed positions, putting herself where Lady Dover was during the attack. "Most of Lady Dover's wounds were on the left side, but they were frontal lacerations. She was facing her attacker. Holding the drink. Let's say she was standing . . ." Kendra pretended to hold a glass. "He brought the knife out." She opened her closed hand, and brought her arms up to her face, as though to ward off an attack. "She dropped the glass, and tried to protect herself—protect her face. That's what she cared about the most. Unfortunately, it left her chest exposed. Dr. Munroe said it only took two seconds. By the time she collapsed on the sofa, she'd already been stabbed multiple times."

"Jesus." Sam's gaze sharpened in horror, clearly visualizing the scene.

"When he came at her, he could've kicked the glass, and it rolled under the sofa. Or she did it herself."

"The fan and her hair frippery also fell ter the floor during the struggle," added the Bow Street Runner.

Kendra had to pause to shake herself free of the dark imaginings. She circled the room, then came back to the sofa. "As far as I can tell, the blood spatter is contained to the sofa. Another indication that she didn't have a chance to run or crawl away. Even though she'd collapsed, he kept stabbing her, a frenzy brought on by adrenaline and rage. After it was over, he would've been shaking, burning through adrenaline like that."

"But he still took the time to mutilate her face," Aldridge pointed out.

Kendra's gaze was thoughtful. "Yes. That means he stayed to calm down before he disfigured her."

"Cold bastard," Sam muttered.

"Yes—and no." Kendra considered the crime, and shook her head. "It's an anomaly. The rage that drove the attack was hot. But what was done to her face . . . It's not easy to carve up a human being's face. That's why the right side of her face had those two slashes—hesitation marks. It took him two tries before he got himself under control, and succeeded. Again, that takes time."

Sam scowled. "But why, Miss? Why'd he feel like he had ter keep trying?"

Kendra realized Sam hadn't been around for their discussion last night. "I don't know. It might have been a form of retaliation, a final insult. She prized her beauty, so the killer wanted to mutilate her. It's something we need to figure out."

Kendra looked around and tried not to think about all microscopic evidence that she was leaving behind. But even if she had the ability to collect and process it, the crime scene had been compromised—they'd had fucking civilians walk through it, like it was some sort of exhibit. And that wasn't even to mention the robbers.

"Okay, I'm done here," she said. "Let's go through the rest of the house."

⁂

In particular, Kendra wanted to go through Lady Dover's bedroom. It was the most personal of all the rooms and had the potential to yield the best evidence, like a memento a lover had given her, a diary in which she'd written, or letters she may have kept.

Every century, every decade, people left bits and pieces of themselves behind in some sort of paper trail. In the twenty-first century, the paper had become figurative, but the trail was still there—Twitter, Instagram, Facebook. Hell, Facebook was her timeline's version of a diary, where people spilled their thoughts and desires, both bright and dark, for public consumption. These were digital bread crumbs people left behind for investigators like herself to sift through.

How many times had she collected evidence against murderers who'd first begun their plan with the assistance of Google? Visiting websites to give them instruction on how to commit or hide their offenses? She'd only needed time and resources to pull back the layers.

Unfortunately, the layers had already been peeled back in Lady Dover's bedroom. The thieves had made their way through here, too—the vanity had been picked clean. No combs or brushes or jewelry boxes remained. Not even a goddamn real breadcrumb had been left behind. If Lady Dover had letters tied together with a ribbon or a diary where she'd penned her thoughts, they were gone too.

But there was still something to learn here. Like the drawing room, the bedroom was ultrafeminine in its décor. Lady Dover had favored pastels, Kendra knew, as they'd complimented her golden beauty. She was the jewel, and this was her setting.

"Professional gang, for sure, that robbed the place," Sam sounded disgusted when he returned to the bedroom door. "Novices would've ripped the place apart, left a right mess. Taken even more stuff, like Her Ladyship's handkerchiefs."

Kendra was sorting through the gowns hanging on hooks in the big wardrobe, but now she laughed. "Right. I suppose there's a crime wave on hankies?"

The Runner gave her a strange look. "Aye, Miss. There are plenty of Billy Buzmans around."

She had to ask. "Billy Buzman?"

"Pickpockets who specialize in silk handkerchiefs," supplied the Duke.

"We caught plenty of fences that made a fine living outta selling purloined handkerchiefs. We even nabbed a shopkeeper that had a secret room filled with 'em. She used ter remove the owners' marks from the silk and then sell the handkerchiefs in her shop below. Real canny operation, when you think of it."

Kendra was silent, absorbing the information with varying degrees of surprise, amusement, and resignation. She recalled reading an article on how human hair had become a lucrative target in beauty supply store smash-and-grabs in Atlanta and Chicago. If hair was popular to steal in her era, then why not hankies during this time?

She put the subject from her mind and said, "I want to see the back entrance."

The back door was at the end of a long hallway, with only a small window lightening the shadows. Kendra slid back the dead bolt and stepped out into a back alley. On the other side of the cobblestone street were the stable mews. Even now, Kendra could hear the movement of horses inside and smell the hay and manure. Her gaze lifted to the rooms above the stables, where the grooms and stable boys sometimes slept. In another two centuries, those horses would be gone and these buildings would be turned into swanky dwellings for wealthy urbanites. The upper class living in stables—what would Sam think about that?

"Mrs. Pierson said the door was open," Sam reminded them.

"Why come in the front door and leave from the back?" Kendra wondered.

The Duke scanned the alley. "'Tis certainly more private here."

"Aye. Maybe someone was on the street when the fiend was leavin'."

"That's possible," Kendra agreed. "The killer must have been familiar with Lady Dover's townhouse to use the back door."

Aldridge shook his head. "Not necessarily. Most of the terraces and houses in the area have the same floorplan. Every house has a servants' entrance. It would not require any great imagination for the villain to find his way here."

They filed back inside, with Sam throwing the deadbolt. *It's a little late for that*, Kendra thought cynically, but kept quiet.

They were approaching the foyer when the front door opened and a man came inside. For a startled moment, they stopped and stared at one another. The stranger spoke first.

"Who the devil are you?" he demanded, raising his lion-headed walking stick like a weapon.

"Who are *you*?" Sam shot back as he hurried forward. "What're you doin' coming into Lady Dover's residence?"

"'Tis *my* residence." The man drew himself up. He wasn't tall, but he was taller than the Bow Street Runner. Even if he hadn't been, Kendra suspected he would've still been able to look down his nose at Sam. He had that kind of demeanor.

"*I* am Lord Dover," the man replied. "Now, I insist that you tell me who you are before I have you arrested for housebreaking."

8

The newcomer regarded them with arctic blue eyes. He had a lean face that reminded Kendra of a greyhound, and a nearly lipless mouth that looked like it hadn't smiled in at least a decade. His hair was sandy blond. Kendra thought he was the type to be dealing with male pattern baldness, though that view was obscured by the black, curled-brim top hat that he wore, fashionable for everyday outdoor use now and only acceptable for magic shows in her own era.

Sam frowned. "I thought Lord Dover was dead."

The man replied, "Don't be ridiculous. *I* am Lord Dover. And this is my property. You are trespassing."

"I seem to recall Lord Dover had a son from a previous marriage." Aldridge eyed the other man. "You are Lady Dover's stepson, are you not? I don't recollect your name, sir?"

"Why should I answer you? Who the devil are you people?"

Sam brought out his gold-tipped baton. "My name is Sam Kelly, and I am the Bow Street Runner investigating your step-mother's murder. You're aware that she was murdered, ain't you?"

"Of course." He didn't seem too impressed with Sam's credentials, merely giving it a passing glance. "My club has spoken of little else since it happened." His lips twisted. "Cordelia always knew how to set tongues wagging."

Kendra wasn't sure whether it was irony or bitterness she heard in his voice. Clearly there was no love lost between Lord Dover and his stepmother. "You don't seem too upset over your stepmother's death."

He looked surprised that she'd addressed him. "Whatever I feel—or do not feel—has nothing to do with you, madam."

"When did you last speak to Lady Dover?" she asked, ignoring his tone.

"Who—"

"I am the Duke of Aldridge," Aldridge interrupted, his own tone becoming imperious, "and this is my ward, Miss Donovan."

The other man responded instantly, the aggression going out of his shoulders as he lowered his walking stick. The hostility was replaced with confusion. "I don't understand, Your Grace. What are you doing here?"

"As Mr. Kelly said, we are investigating the murder of your stepmother."

"She was murdered upstairs," Kendra added.

"I am cognizant of that fact . . . but . . ." Lord Dover shook his head. Then, understanding lit the frosty blue eyes. "Ah. I have heard that Lord Sutcliffe is a suspect in my stepmother's murder. Your nephew, is he not?"

"Yes. Naturally, he did not murder Lady Dover."

Lord Dover opened his mouth as though to dispute that statement. But he seemed to reconsider and pressed his thin lips together instead, saying nothing.

"When did you last see your stepmother?" Kendra asked again.

"What? Oh." He shot her a distracted glance. "I'm not certain . . . Lady Gray's ball last week. Or Hyde Park? I forget. Cordelia enjoyed being the center of attention. She attended most festivities."

"I take it you two weren't close?"

"No."

"So you don't know who she may have been involved with?"

She had his full attention now. His lips twisted again, and he shot a sideways glance at the Duke. "Other than Lord Sutcliffe, do you mean?"

"Yes. Somebody who might have wanted her dead?"

"Anyone she may have provoked, I would imagine."

"You make it sound like she provoked a lot of people."

He gave a shrug. "My father was blinded by Cordelia's beauty, but I saw the creature for what she really was—a mushroom. She had no pedigree, no personal fortune. Nothing to recommend her except for her comely figure, which she artfully used to seduce an old man still grieving his late wife. My father went to his grave regretting his impulsive decision, I think."

"That must have been difficult for you, having this stranger take advantage of your father."

"I found it . . . distasteful."

"I can imagine." Kendra nodded and then fixed her eyes on his. "Where were you on Monday night, between eight and eleven, Lord Dover?"

He frowned. "What does . . ." He gave a gasp of outrage. "Good God, you don't think . . . ? *I* did not *murder* her!"

Sam spoke up. "Then you shouldn't have any difficulty in telling us your whereabouts during that time, milord."

He gave the Runner a sharp look. "I *do* not have any difficulty. I do find it insulting."

"Rise above it," Kendra suggested.

Lord Dover glared at her, but, after his gaze flitted to the Duke, he appeared to swallow whatever angry rebuke sprang to his lips.

"I spent the evening at my club," he offered grudgingly.

Kendra asked, "All night, from eight until eleven?"

"Don't be absurd. I left around ten or half past ten. I don't remember the exact time."

"What's the name of your club, sir?" wondered Sam.

"White's."

Kendra took up the next question. "And where do you live?"

"Upper Brook Street."

"Your specific address, sir?" Sam put in.

Lord Dover's mouth knotted, but he answered, "Number 52."

"What time did you arrive at your home?" Kendra asked.

"I don't know. Eleven, I suppose."

Sam had on his flat cop face. "How did you travel?"

"I hailed a hackney."

"The jarvey will verify your whereabouts?" persisted the Bow Street Runner.

Lord Dover gave a sniff. "If you can find him, I would assume so. I hardly made the acquaintance of a hackney driver!"

Kendra prodded, "But he brought you home?"

He shot her a bewildered look. "Of course. Where else would I go?"

Kendra ignored his question, asking instead, "Your staff will confirm that you returned at eleven?"

"I imagine so." He seemed to have reached the end of his patience and abruptly pivoted away from Kendra and Sam to face the Duke. "Sir, I hope this unorthodox interrogation isn't a way to divert suspicion away from your nephew."

Aldridge stiffened. "Certainly not. This is about finding justice for your stepmother. I assume you do want justice?"

"In truth, I can't say I care one way or the other. I realize this shocks you, Your Grace, but Cordelia's behavior was brazen, an embarrassment to my family's good name." Lord Dover's voice was as cold as his eyes. "We dealt with each other by going our separate ways, both during her marriage to my father and afterward. If I did not murder the wretched woman during the years my father took her as his bride, why the devil would I do so now?"

"Maybe because your stepmother was pregnant," Kendra told him bluntly, and watched his reaction carefully. His eyes widened with what looked to be shock. It only lasted for a second, though. Then his face tightened in disgust.

"I did not know about her . . . condition."

Kendra waited. When he didn't elaborate, she asked, "Do you have any idea who the father could have been?"

Dover shot a pointed look at Aldridge. "I'd rather not speculate, but this does not bode well for your nephew, Your Grace."

"Why'd you come here today, if you don't mind me askin'?" Sam wondered, drawing Lord Dover's attention back to him.

"Because this townhouse was my father's and now it is mine. I shall need to take inventory."

That announcement made Sam shift uncomfortably. He scratched the side of his nose and said, "Ah, as ter that . . . I'm sorry ter say a housebreaker got in last night. The rogues made off with the silver, jewelry, and a variety of personal items."

"Damnation!" Lord Dover's demeanor changed in an instant. He looked about him wildly, as though the thieves were still lurking in the shadowy corners of the foyer. Then he spun toward Sam, thrusting his walking stick forward to poke at the Runner's chest. "What are you doing about it? The valuables stolen are family heirlooms! *My* family heirlooms. They must be returned!"

"You seem more concerned with thieves taking a few things than your stepmother's murder," Kendra commented sarcastically.

He whipped around to glare at her. "I told you, I did not kill Cordelia. I don't believe any highborn gentleman is your killer, regardless of the rumors. You should look in the stews for your fiend."

Kendra raised her eyebrows. "Why? Because the upper classes *never* commit crimes?"

Lord Dover's eyes narrowed. "No. Because I believe Cordelia was part of the criminal underworld. And I think her sordid past finally caught up with her."

Aldridge frowned. "That is a bold claim, sir."

"I do not make it lightly, Your Grace. I told you, Cordelia was without pedigree. She claimed to have come from Cornwall, a daughter of a poor vicar—Cordelia Stewart. But I had her investigated after my father took her to wife. Not that he'd listen to a word against her." Lord Dover's thin lips twisted in a knot of bitterness. "Her tale was rubbish. No Cordelia Stewart ever lived in Cornwall. Cordelia Stewart never existed before my father made her a Countess."

9

So . . . Lady Dover wasn't Lady Dover," Sam remarked slowly as they walked back to the Duke's house.

The square was beginning to wake up around them. Two gentlemen on horseback trotted in the opposite direction down the street. As Kendra watched, one of the horses lifted its tail and dumped a pile of dung in its wake. That probably accounted for the vague stench of manure that seemed to permeate the city, despite an army of street sweepers—the two-legged kind—working nonstop to clean the feces left behind. In the second story of a nearby townhouse, she glimpsed the pale face of a footman as he folded back the wooden shutters from a tall, skinny window. A quicksilver movement out of the corner of her eye made her turn toward the dense green foliage of the park. A squirrel or a rabbit, maybe. Still, she couldn't shake the sensation of being watched.

"No," she finally said. "She was Lady Dover. We just don't know who she was *before* she became Lady Dover."

"Sounds damn fishy ter me, ter change your identity like that."

Kendra caught the Duke's eye. She knew they were both thinking about the background he'd fabricated for her yesterday morning. "Maybe she wanted a better life."

The Bow Street Runner frowned. "Well, she got that. Not everybody would've been pleased ter see her go above her station, though. Maybe His Lordship is right. Maybe somebody from her past found out and killed her."

"It's possible, but it seems more likely that the situation would be reversed—Lady Dover would've been the one motivated to kill in order to keep her past a secret," Kendra countered. "How long has Lady Dover been a Countess? Lady Rebecca once told me that she'd been a widow for five years."

"I'm not certain," admitted Aldridge. "We shall have to ask Alec."

"You said the crime was personal, Miss. If Lady Dover left a beau behind when she bettered herself by marrying the Earl . . . well, that's personal. Mighta made someone angry."

"It's a long time to be angry, if it was somebody from her past. There had to have been a recent trigger."

"England's a big place, Miss. Maybe the bloke she'd left behind only just saw her," Sam suggested.

He had a point. Kendra recalled how Molly had never been outside Aldridge Village until now. Granted, the tweeny was only fifteen, but Kendra imagined that her situation was the norm for a great percentage of the country's population, especially for those in the lower socioeconomic levels. Their mobility was probably limited to a five-mile radius of the town in which they'd been born.

Unless a person was like Lady Dover and saw opportunity in London, a place teeming with immigrants and outsiders, where she, with her beauty, might reinvent herself.

"There's something else to consider," she said as they approached the front steps of the Duke's mansion. "Lord Dover is the one casting suspicion on his stepmother's background. And I don't think he's one of her admirers."

"No love lost betwixt them," agreed Sam. "I'll be going ter his club this afternoon ter check out his alibi." He paused, giving Kendra a shrewd look. "He didn't seem ter know about the babe, though."

"Or he's a good liar."

"Aye, there's that. No shortage of those in Town."

Kendra said, "He seems to care a lot about his family's good name. If he found out that his stepmother was pregnant, I doubt he would've been fine with it. Considering her husband's been dead for five years, Lady Dover's pregnancy is either a hell of a miracle or a major scandal."

Sam laughed. "Ain't no miracle, I can tell you that."

"Right. Major scandal, it is. And by a mushroom. What exactly is a mushroom, anyway?"

Aldridge was the one who answered. "'Tis slang for a social climber. Like a fungus that appears overnight, a person who appears suddenly in society's upper circles."

It occurred to Kendra that she'd be considered a mushroom. As far as anyone knew, she'd begun her life as a servant at Aldridge Castle before Lady Rebecca had hired her as her companion. Now she was the Duke's ward.

Hell, she was a mushroom on steroids.

In the foyer, Harding was supervising two footmen who were carrying an enormous rectangular object wrapped in burlap and blankets up the staircase.

"Your slate board has arrived, sir," the butler informed them. "Lord Sutcliffe departed for his own residence ten minutes ago. And Lady Atwood is in the morning room, with a lady's maid— Watch it!" He had snapped at one of the footmen, as the man nearly tripped and the slate board teetered precariously.

Kendra glanced at the Duke. "Lady Dover's maid. She's early."

They found Lady Atwood seated opposite a woman who looked to be in her late twenties, her dark hair swept into a neat coil. She was a stranger, but Kendra had the oddest sense of recognition. Déjà vu. It took her a moment to understand why. The woman was wearing a dark eggplant-hued gown, similar to the one Kendra had donned to disguise herself as a lady's maid to attend the fancy dress ball at Aldridge Castle.

A month ago—and two hundred years in the future.

She pushed aside the disconcerting feeling as she strode briskly into the room. "Miss Marat. I'm Kendra Donovan," she introduced herself. "We didn't expect you un—"

"Ah, Miss—" Sam began.

"You are mistaken, Miss Donovan," Lady Atwood cut in coolly. "This is Eva Cooper. The agency sent her—she will be your new lady's maid. Miss Cooper, this is Miss Donovan, who you shall be required to assist. And my brother, the Duke of Aldridge." She flicked a look at Sam, but didn't introduce him.

The woman rose and dropped into a deep, graceful curtsy. "Your Grace. I am eager to begin my services in your household," she intoned with a smile. The smile, Kendra thought, curled a little with condescension when Miss Cooper turned to look in her direction. She could only imagine what Lady Atwood had been telling the woman.

"Miss Donovan, I shall endeavor to guide you in the proper etiquette."

Kendra's jaw clenched at the schoolmarm tone, and the way Miss Cooper's eyebrows arched as she exchanged a knowing glance with the Countess.

"Thanks," she replied, "but I'm old enough to guide myself."

"Miss Cooper comes with exceptional credentials," Lady Atwood put in smoothly, and gave the servant an encouraging smile. "You are fortunate to have someone of Miss Cooper's character assisting you, Miss Donovan."

"I am certain Miss Cooper shall be an excellent addition to the household," the Duke said hurriedly, no doubt recognizing the combative gleam in the eyes of both Kendra and his sister. "As usual, my dear, you have everything well in hand."

"Thank you, Bertie." Lady Atwood regarded Kendra. "First, Miss Cooper shall settle into her bedchamber. Then she will assist you in dressing for our morning call to Lady St. James."

"Very good." The Duke nodded before Kendra could say anything. "That ought to give us time to collect our thoughts in the study before Miss Marat arrives. Come, my dear." He reached for Kendra's arm to usher her out of the morning room. "Mr. Kelly, if you will follow me."

"I don't need a lady's maid, or lessons in etiquette," Kendra all but exploded as soon as they were out in the hall.

The Duke hesitated, then said lightly, "Your American customs *are* different than our English ones, Miss Donovan. It might benefit you to have a lady's maid who would help guide you."

She knew he wasn't talking about the difference in countries. Still, she shook her head. "You know that she'll be reporting everything I say or do back to Lady Atwood. I'll be under a microscope." *Again*, she thought. It gave her the creeps.

Aldridge and Sam both wore the carefully blank expression that men sometimes donned when they didn't want to get involved in a conflict between two women. It only added to Kendra's irritation.

"And why do I need to change my clothes again? What's wrong with what I have on now?" she complained as they ascended the stairs. "Christ, she acts like we've got an appointment with the Queen."

Sam gave a snort. "Better than a meetin' with the King, Miss. Poor mad bloke."

Kendra swallowed hard. As always, it made her stomach twist to remember that the head of the British monarchy during this time was King George III. Although, technically, she supposed his son, George IV, was Great Britain's ruler now. He'd become Prince Regent a couple of years ago, when his father succumbed either to mental illness or a blood disease called porphyria. Experts in the twenty-first century were still debating that one.

Because such thoughts always gave her a headache, she turned her focus back to the investigation as they entered the study. It was a smaller, brighter version of the Duke's retreat at Aldridge Castle.

The light maple bookcases were filled mostly with books, plus a handful of knickknacks—Chinese figurines, carved in ivory and bamboo, mixed with classic white-and-blue Wedgwood trinket boxes and Greek vases. A large desk was positioned in one corner, the fireplace in another. A trio of windows allowed the sunlight to spill across two tufted, damask sofas with scrolled armrests and stout legs carved into a griffin's talons. Three similarly styled chairs completed the grouping.

Harding had set up the slate board next to the rosewood table and chairs. There was a box on the floor. Inside the box was a map of London, sheets of foolscap, and a smaller container filled with pastels and pieces of slate. Not exactly the high-tech world she was used to, but it worked—surprisingly well, in fact.

They unrolled the large map with its intricate network of streets on the table. Aldridge put four heavy brass candlesticks on each corner to keep it from curling.

"There—that's Lady Dover's residence." Sam jabbed his finger on the spot.

Kendra had to squint to read the spidery printing. "Okay." She selected a red pastel, and marked the location. "Where's Lord Dover's club?"

"I believe it's in this vicinity," said the Duke, circling an area with his finger.

It took a few minutes to find. When they located it, Kendra marked it in blue.

"What about Upper Brook Street, Number 52?" she wondered, and Aldridge pointed it out.

"Not far from Lady Dover's townhouse," Kendra observed, tracing the line with her finger. "Still, his window of opportunity is pretty tight. I'm not sure he would've had the time to kill his stepmother between leaving his club at ten and arriving home at eleven—assuming he's telling us the truth about those times."

"I'll send me men ter look for the hackney driver, but I would be careful about puttin' ter much hope there," Sam said. "Picking up gentlemen near their clubs and dropping them off at home is what they do every evenin'."

"Excuse me, Your Grace." Harding had slipped silently into the study. "Miss Marat has arrived. I have put her in the drawing room, and await your instructions."

"Thank you, Harding. We shall be there shortly," Aldridge told the butler, and then glanced at Kendra and Sam. "Let us hope that Miss Marat will be able to provide the answers we are seeking about Lady Dover's background."

⁂

Miss Marat was a pale, slender woman, with Viking blond hair she'd arranged with one section up in a top knot and the rest dangling in fat sausage curls that framed her plain, narrow face. Blue eyes peered out at them from between very long, very fair lashes, which she fluttered in a manner that was far too coquettish for a lady's maid. Kendra had learned a month ago that the prerequisite for being a good servant was to blend in with the furniture. She'd failed miserably in that role.

Kendra thought those lashes would be Miss Marat's most memorable characteristic, until the woman opened her mouth and spoke with the most atrocious fake French accent that Kendra had ever heard. Nails-on-a-chalkboard bad. So bad that Kendra couldn't bear listening to the woman massacre one more vowel with her exaggerated pronunciation.

She interrupted the maid in the middle of thanking the Duke for sending his coach to retrieve her, which apparently had caused some excitement at the inn she was currently staying, by saying, *"Merci de nous avoir ruçus, Mlle Marat. Voulez vous continuer en Français? Ou ferions nous mieux d'arrêter de faire semblant que vous maîtrisex cette langue et passer à l'Anglais à la place?"*

Miss Marat froze.

Aldridge's lips twitched, but he managed to keep a straight face. "I believe what Miss Donovan is trying to say is that we are aware that French lady's maids are highly sought after by the Ton, but we would prefer a more candid interview. You are not French, are you, Miss Marat?"

Miss Marat looked at him, and whatever she saw in his eyes had her slowly relaxing. Kendra had to give the Duke points for diplomacy. He'd have made an excellent good cop in an interview, soothing the frazzled nerves of witnesses or lulling criminals into a false sense of security.

"Lady Dover set great store in having a proper lady's maid," she admitted. "But Oi'm originally from Twickenham, sir."

"You fooled Lady Dover into thinking you were French?" Kendra asked in amazement. Had the woman been deaf?

"Ack, no. Lady Dover knew Oi weren't no froggy. They were too hoity-toity for her tastes, she said. She only liked me to pretend because it's fashionable, like you said, Your Grace."

Kendra suspected that the pretense included Miss Marat's last name, but let it go. Miss Marat's background wasn't the one she was interested in.

"How long did you work for Lady Dover?" she asked.

"Ever since her husband, His Lordship, cocked up his toes. She got in all new staff, she did. Didn't much care for the old ones that His Lordship had. She said that they were very high on the instep."

Which was another way of saying hoity-toity, Kendra supposed. "Do you know how long Lady Dover and his wife were married?"

Miss Marat frowned. "No. Can't say Oi ever thought about it. Why?"

"Did Lady Dover talk about her past? What she did, where she lived before she met her husband? Her family?"

"No."

"Her family never came to visit her?"

"No. Never," Miss Marat said slowly, and in such a way that Kendra suspected it was just occurring to her that this might be odd.

"How'd she get along with Lord Dover—her stepson?"

"Oh, that one! Lady Dover didn't like him at all. He was a stuffed shirt, she said. But Oi thought—" She stopped abruptly.

"You thought what?"

"Nothin'." Her eyes flicked to Sam.

"Whatever you say shall go no further than this room," promised Aldridge. "And it may help us find whoever hurt your mistress."

The maid hesitated, then gave a small nod. "'Tis nothin', really. Just . . . well, Lady Dover was lovely. Better than lovely, she was. She wasn't used to any gentleman that didn't fall for her charms, if ye know what Oi mean."

Kendra eyed the other woman with renewed interest. Maybe she was more astute than she looked. "Do you know if their relationship had changed recently?"

Miss Marat frowned. "What do you mean?"

"Did their dislike for each other intensify in any way? Did Lady Dover ever feel threatened by her stepson?"

"Not really. But they got into a right vicious fight the other week. We heard them shouting all the way to the kitchen from the drawing room, we did. His Lordship more than Lady Dover. But she was in a spiteful mood when he left."

Kendra asked, "Did you hear what they argued about?"

"Somethin' about her making a spectacle outta herself at the theater. Put him into a fine rage, it did."

"Did she talk to you later about the argument?"

"She talked about *him*, called him a lockeram-jawed bastard, she did—beggin' your pardon, Your Grace, sir, but those were her words, not mine. She didn't say nothing about the words they had with each other."

"Lockeram-jawed means Lord Dover has a thin face," Aldridge clarified for Kendra's benefit.

"An accurate description," Kendra conceded with a faint smile. She returned her attention to the lady's maid. "What was Lady Dover like to work for?"

Miss Marat frowned as she thought about it. "Fine, Oi guess. Better than some Oi'd worked for. Probably better than some Oi'll be working for."

The long lashes fluttered and Kendra caught the bleak gleam in the other woman's eyes. The future was far from certain for a woman from Twickenham who was pretending to be a French lady's maid.

"She never confided in you about personal things?"

"She liked to gossip about the Ton. She had a wicked tongue on her, she did." A slight smile curled Miss Marat's lips, probably an appreciation of that side of her employer. "But mostly we talked about fashion. Lady Dover was most particular about her appearance.

"After Lord Dover died, she had to wear the proper mourning colors, of course. She hated the lack of style. She burned all her gowns when the mourning period was over. She set them on fire right there in the fireplace in her bedchamber. Oi watched her do it."

"Well, that certainly is a statement," Kendra said. She decided to get to the heart of the interview. "We were told Lady Dover had plenty of admirers. Do you know who they were?"

"Lord Sutcliffe, of course," Miss Marat said immediately. "He cuts a dashing figure. She went to a house party last month, hoping that she'd bring him up to scratch. It didn't work, and she came home in a vile temper. Said some whey-faced chit had turned his head. Oi can tell ye that didn't sit well with Her Ladyship! She ain't used to being thrown over for another lady."

It suddenly occurred to Kendra that if Miss Marat had accompanied Lady Dover to the house party, they'd have met each other during the first breakfast held for upper servants. By lunch, of course, she'd been demoted.

"Why didn't you go with Lady Dover to the house party?" she asked now.

Miss Marat's gaze slid away. "She said that the Countess who was having the house party would provide abigails. She didn't need my services."

Kendra thought Lady Dover probably hadn't wanted to inflict Miss Marat's hideously fake French accent on anyone else. Or, more likely, she was concerned about having her lady's maid exposed as a fraud. It seemed Lady Dover knew how to keep her secrets.

"Mrs. Pierson thinks that Lord Sutcliffe killed Lady Dover," Miss Marat continued, apparently unaware of the Duke's connection to the Marquis. "But Oi don't believe it. He's a gentleman. Oi don't mean he's gentry. I mean, when he came around, he was always discreet-like. He never stayed the entire night, even though he wasn't leg-shackled. He was respectful of my mistress's reputation, even if she didn't care."

"Were other men as respectful?" Kendra asked carefully. "We've heard that Lord Sutcliffe wasn't the only man in her life."

"Oh, she had other callers, but none like Lord Sutcliffe. But . . ."

"But . . . what?" Kendra prodded when the lady's maid fell silent.

Miss Marat bit her lip. "Well . . . Oi think she might've had another house. For privacy, you see. More privacy than she'd get at Grosvenor Square."

Kendra lifted a brow, surprised. "Why do you think that?"

"She kept a key in her jewelry box. It was a house key, Oi could tell. But it wasn't for her house. And there were times that Oi'd help her dress, fancy-like, but Oi knew she weren't going to no ball. And in the beginning, she used to hire a hackney to go off into the night."

Sam leaned forward, his golden eyes taking on a gleam of interest. "You think she was meetin' a gentleman at another house?"

The sausage curls bounced as Miss Marat nodded. "Yes. Mr. George would know for certain."

"Mr. George is—*was* Lady's Dover's whip and senior footman," Sam told them. He frowned at the servant. "I talked ter him. He didn't mention any other residence."

"No, and he wouldn't, would he?" Miss Marat gave him a knowing look. "He wouldn't peach on Her Ladyship. 'Tisn't respectful."

"'Tisn't respectful ter lie ter an officer of the law," snapped the Bow Street Runner.

Miss Marat set her jaw defiantly. "He didn't lie, did he? He just didn't speak out of turn. They'll probably all think Oi'm leaky if they know everythin' Oi've been saying to you."

"We appreciate everything you've told us, Miss Marat," Aldridge said. "I shall make certain you are justly compensated."

The servant visibly brightened.

Kendra eyed her. "You said that she would take a hackney in the beginning. Her behavior changed?"

"Yes. She began using her own carriage a month ago, after she got back from the house party."

Kendra wondered if the change was significant. But that was something to ponder later. Now she asked, "Do you know who Lady Dover might have been meeting at this other house?"

"No, ma'am."

"Anyone you might have thought it was? Maybe she talked about any other men, or a particular man?"

"No, Oi haven't the faintest. Truly."

"What about the other evening, when she sent you away? What happened that night?"

"What do you mean? Oi left like everyone else."

"Before you left. What was her demeanor like? Was she upset? Happy?"

Miss Marat thought for a minute. "Maybe excited," she finally said. "She was very precise on what she wanted to wear. Oi helped her dress. Then she sent us away."

"Why do you think she did that?"

"Oi expect she wanted privacy because she was meetin' someone."

"And you don't know who that someone is?"

"Oi thought it was Lord Sutcliffe like the rest of the staff, but . . . Oi can't imagine him doing what was done to her. Mrs. Pierson said that her face was cut horribly. Is that true?"

Kendra said, "We can't talk about the details of the crime."

Miss Marat gave her a strange look. The standard line probably did sound crazy in a time when civilians could stroll through crime scenes.

Kendra changed tactics. "Did you know Lady Dover was pregnant?"

Miss Marat's fair eyelashes lowered, veiling her eyes for a second. Then she nodded. "Oi suspected. She didn't confide in me about the child, but you can't be a lady's maid without knowing these things, if you take my meaning."

Kendra thought of the intimate duties of a lady's maid, and understood. It was the reason she didn't want Miss Cooper invading her space. She was more comfortable with Molly.

"I know what you mean. How do you think Lady Dover felt about the pregnancy?"

"Oi don't know. She didn't seem any different, really, which was odd, since she wasn't married and her husband was long dead. It would've set a lot of tongues waggin', Oi can tell you that. Maybe that was why Lord Dover was so angry."

"Do you think he knew about the child?"

Miss Marat gave a shrug. "Secrets of that sort come out eventually, don't they?"

"Yes, they do." Kendra stood up. "Thank you, Miss Marat. You've been very helpful."

"Oi have?"

"Absolutely. But if you think of anything else, please let us know."

Aldridge fished in his pocket for a silver case. He opened it and gave her his calling card. "Here—this way you won't forget."

Miss Marat stared at the card for a moment, then she lifted her gaze to the aristocrat. She grinned suddenly. "Oi ain't likely to forget, Your Grace. Even working for Lady Dover, it ain't every day a girl from Twickenham gets to talk to a Duke."

10

S tanding in front of the slate board a short time later, Kendra mused, "Why would Lady Dover need another residence in London?"

Aldridge eyed her. Sam Kelly had left to hunt down Lady Dover's former coachman/senior footman, while they'd retreated to his study.

"We already addressed this, my dear," the Duke said. "Lady Dover required more privacy. Clearly it was a rendezvous point for her and her lover."

"But she's a widow. I thought the rules in this era were more relaxed for married women and widows."

"Relaxed, but not dispensed with," he responded, absently picking up his pipe. "She would have been ostracized from the Polite World if rumors circulated that gentlemen callers were staying overnight in her home."

"What about the gentlemen? Would they have been ostracized, too?"

He apparently heard the critical note in her voice, as his tone was distinctly apologetic. "Miss Donovan—"

"Never mind." She cut him off with a wave of her hand. "What about the separate residence? She entertained Alec in her home. And even if he didn't spend the night, I doubt they were playing chess."

"Yes, well . . ." Aldridge's lips twitched at her dry innuendo. "There is another possibility. Gentlemen of the Ton have been known to set up separate residences for their mistresses in Town."

Kendra jiggled the slate as she thought about it. "So you don't think Lady Dover set up the residence, but her lover?"

"It's a possibility."

"Then why didn't she meet him there? Why go through the trouble of sending the servants away? It seems pretty inconvenient."

"Only for the servants. And I rather doubt Lady Dover was the kind of woman who spent too much time thinking about the convenience of her staff. Still, you make a good point, Miss Donovan. Why rendezvous with him at her home when there was a more private house at their disposal?"

"Home-court advantage? Maybe she thought it gave her some semblance of control. Holding the meeting on her own turf makes a more powerful statement."

"Rather dramatic."

Kendra had to smile. "Please. This is a woman who burned her gowns after she was finished mourning her dead husband. Dramatic, I think, is what Lady Dover did." She paused and gave him a look. "You know that Lord Dover lied to us, right?"

"I am cognizant of the fact that he failed to mention that he'd visited his stepmother a week ago."

"Not only visited—they had an argument loud enough to draw the attention of the staff. He hated her. She'd been an embarrassment since the day his father married her. And if he learned she was pregnant . . ."

"He would have been displeased."

"Yeah, as in royally pissed."

That improper and bizarre comment drew a laugh from him. "I'm assuming you are not referring to urination by a member of the royal family."

"No." She gave him a quick smile, but the smile faded quickly. "Lord Dover had motive—his family's reputation. Sort of like your sister being terrified that I'm going to be a stain on your family tree."

He sidestepped the reference. "By all accounts their dislike was mutual. I cannot credit that Lady Dover would have dismissed her staff for an assignation with him."

"No," Kendra admitted, and scowled. "I can't see her doing that, either. But we may be coalescing two different scenarios. The person she was meeting and the killer. They may not be one and the same; she may not have invited the killer inside. Lord Dover is familiar with the house. He may even have a key, which is why the locks were not tampered with."

There was the lightest of knocks on the door, and then Harding stepped into the room. "Your Grace, ma'am. Lady Atwood instructed me to inform you that a light meal will be served shortly en famille. Lord Sutcliffe is expected to join you."

"Thank you, Harding." Aldridge nodded at the butler, who bowed and retreated.

With a sigh, he pushed himself to his feet, his gaze traveling to the slate board, which held only one name in the suspect column. "I sincerely hope Lady St. James lives up to her reputation. We could use another name besides Lord Dover's on the slate board."

"I agree, Your Grace." Kendra tossed the piece of slate on the desk and sighed. "Otherwise, this will be a nightmare."

He eyed her with some surprise. "We've only just begun our inquiries, Miss Donovan. Do not be discouraged. I'm confident we will save Alec before he is brought before the House of Lords."

"I wasn't talking about the investigation, sir. I was actually referring to spending the afternoon with your sister."

❖

Kendra was only half joking. The prospect of spending any time with the Duke's sister was enough to twist her stomach into painful knots. Her mood wasn't helped when she found Miss Cooper already inside her bedchamber, shuffling through the clothes hanging on hooks inside the giant wardrobe. She closed the bedroom door behind her more sharply than she'd intended. It was irrational, she knew, for her to feel like her space was being invaded.

Miss Cooper merely gave her an assessing look. "Miss Donovan. Do you have a preference on what you wish to wear for your morning call on Lady St. James?"

"No." Kendra crossed the room to the washbasin. She caught the curl of Miss Cooper's lip out of the corner of her eye. She'd only just met the woman, but she was beginning to have an intense dislike for that small gesture.

"Yes, Her Ladyship indicated that you have little interest in fashion."

"I'm not running around naked, you know," Kendra muttered.

"I should hope not."

Kendra lifted the porcelain pitcher and poured water into the bowl. That done, she paused, regarding the lady's maid. "You're not related to Mrs. Danbury, are you?"

Miss Cooper blinked, startled. "Mrs. Danbury—the Duke's housekeeper?"

"Yeah. You have the same look about the eyes." Certainly the same disdain that the housekeeper had bestowed on her during her first days at the castle. Kendra set the pitcher aside and reached for a lump of lavender-scented soap, washing the chalk dust from her hands.

"I have no connection to Mrs. Danbury," the maid said flatly.

Kendra shrugged as she finished washing her hands.

Miss Cooper returned to the wardrobe, pulling out a mint-green poplin gown, designed with delicate lace trimming the neckline and long sleeves that were scrunched and puffed near the shoulder. "Since you have no interest in fashion, I have taken the liberty of selecting your afternoon dress. Is this acceptable?"

"Sure."

"Now as far as dressing your hair . . ." She eyed Kendra critically. "'Tis shorter than what is considered fashionable. Mayhap a hairpiece?"

"It's longer than what it was." Kendra knew she sounded defensive, and hated feeling like she needed to explain herself to justify her choices. Miss Cooper's censorious gaze reminded her too much of her father, when he'd looked at her and found her wanting. Damn it, she was an adult. She *should* be beyond all the hurts, inadequacies, and anxieties that had tormented her as a child. She knew better than to let it affect her. And yet . . .

She drew in a breath, and let it out slowly. "And I'm gonna say no to a hairpiece."

Miss Cooper sniffed. "We shall make do, if we must."

Kendra bit back a snarky reply. She didn't like the woman, but she didn't envy her the duties of a lady's maid. It was still something of a shock to remember that she'd been a colossal failure at it, being demoted to a downstairs maid within a day. *My first-ever demotion.*

She turned her back on the servant's disapproval, moving to the window as she dried her hands. The park below seemed to glisten as green as emeralds in the sunlight. On the street, a dangerous-looking contraption—an open carriage with a high perch—was being drawn by two matching horses at a fast clip, its driver expertly flicking the reins. Further along, four horseback riders trotted past a handful of strolling maids.

"Lady Atwood has made an appointment with her modiste for a new wardrobe for you," Miss Cooper said from behind her.

The maid's words barely registered. Kendra's eyes narrowed as she scanned the park, having caught a glimmer of light in the trees. It took her a moment, but she finally traced the quick flash to a figure almost hidden behind leafy branches. He was wearing brown and green, perfect camouflage against the woods. In fact, if he hadn't moved, she doubted she would've seen him at all.

"Do you have jewelry, Miss Donovan?" asked Miss Cooper.

Kendra leaned forward. The figure had on a cap, which he'd pulled low in an effort to shield his face. Still, his head was angled in such a way that Kendra knew he was watching the Duke's residence. Not just idle curiosity. Kendra's gut tightened. *Surveillance.*

"Miss Donovan . . . ?"

Kendra turned abruptly away from the window. She didn't stop to consider what she was doing. She picked up her skirts and bolted for the door.

"Miss Donovan . . . !"

Miss Cooper's astonished gasp barely registered as Kendra ran headlong from the room. She nearly crashed into a footman, who'd come out of another bedchamber carrying an empty silver basket. At the last minute, she skidded to the side to avoid the collision, then kept running down the stairs to the foyer. Out of the corner of her eye, she saw Harding emerge from a door, his mouth falling open in astonishment, but she darted past him and yanked open the door.

Outside, the sun warmed her face as she leaped down the short flight of steps. She dashed across the wide street, instinctively avoiding the piles of manure that had been left by the departing horses. There was a roar of adrenaline in her ears, but she thought she heard her name being called. She ignored it as she plunged into the woods, in the direction of where she'd seen the loitering figure.

She wasn't sure how long she ran, but her lungs were burning, and there was a stitch in her side by the time she finally came to a stop.

Shit.

Her chest heaved as she drew in great gulps of air and scanned the now-empty area. He'd been standing here, damn it. *Right here!* He must have seen her coming . . .

She tensed at the snap of twigs ahead of her. She started forward again, weaving between trees and shrubs. rewarded a second later when she spotted the man about a hundred yards ahead, a small shadow that scurried deeper into the forest. Though her lungs continued to burn, she renewed her efforts to catch up to him. She thought she was gaining, but by the next break in the trees, he'd vanished again.

"Fuck," she gasped, stumbling to a stop. Her breath came in ragged pants and she became aware that her feet hurt. The thin-soled slippers that ladies were forced to wear were not meant to race in, probably because women were not meant to run.

Kendra put her hands on her hips and bent over, in an effort to draw more air into her starving lungs. Her heart beat so loudly that she thought it would thump right out of her chest. The roar in her ears was like a freight train.

Which was why she never heard him come up behind her.

11

A re you mad, woman?"

The hand that clamped down on her shoulder sent a bolt of adrenaline shooting through her. Instantly, she spun with hands up to launch a counterattack. She only checked the movement when her gaze locked on Alec.

"What are you doing racing around London like a bloody hoyden?" he demanded, the flecks of gold in his green eyes burning with temper beneath slanting black eyebrows.

She put her hand on her chest instead of into his throat, as she'd almost done. "Jesus Christ, Alec. You shouldn't sneak up on people like that. I could've hurt you!"

"Miss Donovan, you cannot wander about Town unchaperoned. Hell and damnation, Kendra! This is London—not the country."

Kendra found her own temper rising. "I'm aware of our location, Alec. Someone was watching the Duke's house."

That gave him pause. "Someone out for a stroll, surely. Mayhap he—"

"No. Goddamn it, I know surveillance when I see it! I've had the feeling since yesterday that someone was watching us, but today I saw him. I couldn't see his face. He wore a cap. But he was definitely watching the Duke's house."

He stared at her in amazement. If he was angry before, now he looked livid. "And you thought you'd confront the villain? *Alone?*" He swore rather colorfully in Italian. "You bloody fool! What if he was Cordelia's killer?"

Her jaw tensed. "Then we'd be able to wrap up the investigation damn fast."

He grasped her arms, his fingers digging into her flesh. "Or you'd be dead. Have you no sense?"

"I'm not that easy to kill."

It was partly bravado, a flippant response meant to diffuse the tension. But she *had* been trained in self-defense, including the more brutal hand-to-hand combat of Krav Maga. She wasn't the defenseless woman of this era.

His hands around her upper arms convulsed. "Devil take it. That is that kind of arrogance that gets men killed on the battlefield."

He had a point. But she refused to give ground, twisting out of his grasp and meeting his glare with one of her own. "Stop it! Stop telling me what to do, Alec! Stop lecturing me. Stop trying to fucking protect me! I'm not an idiot. I can take care of myself. I've taken care of myself for a very long time."

"Kendra—"

"I was the youngest recruit at Quantico. You *know* that. I'm damn good at what I do . . . did. *Shit.*" Her breath hitched unexpectedly. She felt like a piece of driftwood caught on a tidal wave that was taking her further out to sea, away from everything that had been familiar. She'd never considered herself an emotional person. She'd prided herself on using her brains and cold logic to keep her world sane. It had been her survival mechanism since she was fourteen years old, cut adrift then as well. Yet it had all gone to hell since she'd ended up in the nineteenth century. Not only was she in the wrong time, she felt as though she were in the wrong skin. The tears that pricked her eyes now left her aghast.

"I don't belong here, Alec," she whispered.

He'd been watching her carefully and now reached for her, this time not in anger but comfort. "Why are any of us here?"

She gave a watery laugh, and rested her forehead against his chest. She could hear the strong beat of his heart. "Don't you dare get philosophical on me, Alec."

"Maybe Duke is correct, and your purpose here is to save me."

"He thinks we're all linked on some cosmic level."

"Normally I would leave such romantic ideals to poets like Byron," he murmured and gathered her closer, allowing his hands to caress the line of her spine. "However, you cannot deny there is something between us, Kendra. I have never felt this way before."

"Temporary insanity."

"Love and lunacy have been linked, but I don't think there is anything temporary about how I feel."

"Don't." Kendra pulled away to regard him with dark, somber eyes. She didn't know if she was telling him or pleading with him. "Don't, Alec. I can't think of . . . of that right now."

He gave her a crooked smile and lifted his hands to cup her face. "What are you so afraid of?"

"I'm not afraid." But she was. She was terrified.

"I promise not to hurt you."

"I still plan to go home."

"How do you propose to do that? Are you going to go into the stairwell at Aldridge Castle every month when there's a full moon and hope your wormhole magically appears?"

Put like that, it sounded stupid.

"I don't know," she replied. "It shouldn't have appeared in the first place!"

"Is your life so perfect in the twenty-first century, Kendra? You have told me that you are estranged from your family, that you have no husband."

Kendra had to laugh. "Believe it or not, where I come from, women aren't always looking out for a husband."

"I only meant that you are free . . ."

Free to leave the twenty-first-century behind, perhaps. *But I'm not free here.* She wanted to remind him of that, to make him understand everything he was asking her to give up. But her thoughts scattered when she met his gaze, and she read the intention in his eyes even before he leaned closer.

She knew it was a mistake, but she didn't move away. Instead, she leaned forward to meet his kiss.

"Oh, ho! It looks like we're interruptin' somethin', lads!"

The booming voice made Kendra and Alec jerk away from each other. For the second time in less than twenty minutes, Kendra found herself adopting a defensive stance as she turned to meet the three approaching figures.

"A lord and his doxy, by the look of it," one of the men said. "Ain't that right, Ned?"

"Aye, that it is, Tom. That it is," Ned replied.

Alec took a step forward, positioning himself in front of her, which would have annoyed the hell out of her if she hadn't been so intensely focused on the three strangers. Two were men, average height, possibly late thirties, but they could have been younger, their hard lives adding phantom years to their faces. The one called Ned had sandy hair and a wiry build. The other one—Tom—was darker and more muscular, except for the slight paunch hanging over his belt.

Thugs. That's what they were, Kendra recognized. Not because of the rough, filthy clothes they wore, but because of the flat, mean expression in their eyes.

Her gaze cut to the other person in the trio. She knew from his clothes and cap that he was the one who'd been spying on the Duke's residence. But with a start of surprise, she realized he was only a boy. The angle and distance when she'd spotted him from her upstairs window had distorted her perception. Now, as she regarded his round freckled face beneath the wool cap he wore, she estimated him to be about ten years old.

"I'm not carrying a purse," Alec said in a low, cold voice. "You shall have to look elsewhere for your gold."

"Ack. Ye insult me, m'lord," Tom said, and spat a large wad of tobacco on the ground. "He thinks we're footpads, Ned."

"Yeah." Ned grinned, revealing teeth that had never seen a dentist, crooked and stained. "Damn insulting, ye are."

"We ain't no footpads, Lord Sutcliffe."

Alec's expression became shuttered and Kendra fought to keep her own face impassive. Their knowledge of Alec's identity meant this was no random attack, no crime of opportunity. The child hadn't been keeping an eye on the Duke's residence to rob it; he'd obviously been assigned to watch for Alec.

"Nay, we ain't 'ere ter rob you," Tom continued. He and Ned brought up the flintlock pistols that they'd been holding. Now they aimed them right at Kendra and Alec's heads. "We're 'ere ter get justice."

12

The park suddenly seemed as desolate as the moon. The men forced Kendra and Alec to walk ahead of them, along the twisting path that cut through trees and shrubs. *We are being kidnapped in broad daylight,* she thought in disbelief. *Can no one see us?*

But how many times had she leafed through manila folders thick with crime scene photos that had begun with an abduction similar to this, the kidnappers eschewing the darkness for a bold attack in the middle of the day? She wondered if those victims had felt the same incredulity as she was feeling now.

They came out of the woods on the street farthest from the Duke's mansion. A dusty black carriage was waiting against the curb like a fat beetle.

Kendra shot a wild glance up and down the wide lane. Here, there were people. A young maid was sweeping off the steps of a terrace house only two hundred yards away. Farther down the street, three women were walking and talking. Beyond that group were two men on horseback, who'd stopped to converse as well. The shutters were off all the windows. Surely someone was looking out? Didn't anyone see their captors behind them, holding guns?

Kendra didn't think she slowed her pace, but she felt a sharp pain as Tom dug the muzzle into her lower spine.

"Don't even think about doin' anythin' stupid," he growled.

"Leave her be, damn you," Alec snapped. "You have me. You don't need her. You can leave her behind."

Tom ignored him and ordered, "Snake, get the door."

The kid sprinted forward. From his perch, the coachman shot them a testy look. "'Urry up, will ye? The damn Watch'll be making the rounds soon."

Tom shoved Kendra forward. "The mort gets in first. Get up with ye, bitch, and be quick about it!"

Alec moved forward, but Ned pushed him back.

Tom brought up his flintlock to Kendra's temple, the steel cold against her flesh. "Ye don't wanna do anything rash, gov'ner, or the mort'll be 'avin' an extra 'ole in 'er 'ead."

Alec tensed. "Let her go and I promise to go with you peaceably."

Ned gave an ugly laugh. "Ye'll be goin' with us, peaceable or not."

"Stop it, Alec," Kendra said quietly, although her heart began hammering in her chest. The pressure of the muzzle against her temple made her feel vaguely ill. "I told you, I don't need you to protect me."

"She's a right plucky one, ain't she?" Tom said. "But ye're right, me lord—we don't need 'er. We can end 'er right now if ye don't move yer arse!"

A muscle leaped in Alec's jaw. Kendra ended the standoff by climbing into the carriage, which reeked of sweat and smoke. As she settled against a leather seat cracked with age, she thought she saw the servant girl pause in her sweeping, giving them a curious look. Kendra tried to make eye contact—*help us*—but then her view was obstructed when Tom came up behind her, followed by Snake, Alec, and finally Ned, who slammed the door shut. He rapped his knuckles on the trapdoor on the ceiling, keeping his gun and eyes trained on Alec.

"Move!"

The carriage lurched forward. Inside, the space was tight, with Tom and Alec sharing one seat and Kendra squished next to Ned and the boy named Snake, making it impossible to fight back. Threadbare curtains hung over the windows, darkening the interior and making her feel slightly claustrophobic.

"Who are you?" she demanded, and was pleased that her voice revealed none of her inner turmoil. *Show no fear.*

"Oi'm Tom, and that there's Ned. And Snake."

Kendra glanced at the kid. "Snake?"

The boy grinned and pulled out a silver flask from his coat. Kendra realized that had probably caused the flash of light that she'd seen from her bedroom window.

"Aye, Oi'm a little snakesman," he said, and unscrewed the top. She caught the strong, sharp smell of whiskey, and couldn't control her shock as she watched him take a swallow. Underage drinking and drugs weren't exactly unknown in her era, but still . . .

"He's a thief," Alec clarified, drawing her attention. "Young children are often used by housebreakers. They're small enough to wiggle through tight areas—down chimneys or through sink-holes. When they get into the house, they unlock the doors and let their . . . accomplices inside."

"Snake 'ere is the best in the business—if'n 'e lays off ol' Greta's pies," Tom said, earning a sheepish grin from the boy.

Kendra asked, "Were you the ones who broke into Lady Dover's house?"

Tom, who appeared to be the spokesperson of the trio, scowled. "Nay. But we'll find them that did."

Uneasily, Kendra met Alec's gaze. She didn't like that their captors hadn't made any attempt to mask themselves and gave their names so easily. That was never a good sign. There were only two reasons a criminal didn't bother to conceal their identities: they were idiots, or they knew their victims wouldn't be able to identify them because they had no intention of leaving them alive.

She didn't think these men were idiots.

"What do you want with us?" she asked again.

Tom's eyes glittered at her like those of a malicious rat. "Not ye. Snake 'ere watched the gov'ner's house for 'Is Lordship 'ere. When he left this mornin', we'd known he'd be comin' back, so we waited for 'im. But ye . . . ye're an unexpected surprise. Ain't she, Ned?"

In answer, Ned gave a nasty laugh. "She's a tasty morsel."

Alec gave them a cold look. "This woman is the Duke of Aldridge's ward. Do you understand what that means? If she is harmed in any way, you'll be swinging at Newgate—or, if you're lucky, sent to Botany Bay. The Duke shall offer a reward that will turn your friends into enemies. You won't be able to trust anyone. Not your mother. Not your father. Not your goddamn doxy." He let his words hang in the air for a moment. "If you don't let this woman go, you shall be dead by nightfall."

There was a brief silence. Then Tom snorted. "What, d'ya take me for? A singleton? No ward of a duke would be out walkin' alone with ye in the park. Ye're jest tryin' ter protect yer light skirt. Ye're the Marquis of Sutcliffe. Ye're the Duke of Aldridge's nephew. Ye're the one 'Is Grace'll be wantin' back. Ain't that right, Ned?"

"Aye, but we're not gonna oblige 'im. Someone else wants ye more."

"Who wants him?" Kendra demanded.

"Bear wants 'im," the boy piped up from beside her.

Bear, Snake. What is it with the animal nicknames? Kendra wondered. She looked at Alec. "Is that slang for another criminal activity?"

"None that I've heard."

"Guy's 'is name," Snake continued, "but 'e fought a bear, 'e did, and—"

"Shut it," Tom growled at the kid.

"The Duke shall pay you handsomely for Miss Donovan's release," Alec put in. "I'm the one you say you want. You have no reason to keep her."

"Oh, Oi wouldn't say *no* reason." Tom's laugh made Kendra's skin crawl. "Oi can think of at least *one* reason ter keep 'er."

Alec's expression hardened and his jaw clenched. "The Duke of Aldridge would not want Miss Donovan harmed in any way."

Kendra had to give Alec points for trying. In his world, the mere mention of the Duke's name was enough to evoke respect, even fear. But their captors were clearly from the underbelly of London, far away from the so-called Polite World with its rules and restrictions.

"Oo's talkin' 'arm," Ned said with a chuckle, and reached over to squeeze Kendra's thigh. "Oi'm thinkin' me and the lass'll 'ave a bit o' fun."

Kendra stiffened. She had to stop herself from reacting to the unwanted hand clamped around her thigh. It was too dangerous to fight back in the carriage's confined space, with two guns pointed at them. She looked at Alec, worried that he might attempt something. He was staring at the man who was touching her, and she had to suppress a shiver at his expression. She'd seen him furious before—often at her—but this was something more. This was lethal.

Ned laughed again, but the sound was forced and uneasy. When he withdrew his hand, Kendra knew it was a victory. Unfortunately, it would be a short-lived one. Because she knew that whoever was waiting for them at the end of the carriage ride had no intention of letting them go.

13

T ime really was relative. The carriage ride seemed to go on forever, oppressive in its silence. And yet when the vehicle finally rolled to a jerky stop, the journey had suddenly been too short.

Kendra found herself holding her breath when the coachman opened the door. Snake hopped down with the nimble grace of a child, followed by Ned, who turned and pointed the gun at Kendra. She hesitated but realized that even if the thug was close enough for her to make a grab for his weapon, there was still Tom, who was aiming his flintlock at Alec.

Exhaling, she climbed out of the old carriage and looked around, a little surprised to find herself on a busy thoroughfare, people streaming around them. Men dressed in similar fashion to their kidnappers brushed past them, balancing wooden barrels or bags of grain or milled flour on their wide shoulders. Others pushed wheelbarrows filled with an assortment of cockles and fish. There were women and children running to and fro, as well, carrying baskets of produce, flowers, and laundry. Horses clopped down the street, either with single riders on their backs or harnessed to wagons, hauling everything from dead carcasses to crates with squawking chickens inside. A scraggly herd of cows moved down the center of the street, prodded by two farmers carrying sticks.

A mishmash of businesses and tenements rose up on either side of the street. The stink of manure, rotting animal flesh—at least she hoped it was the four-legged, fish, or fowl kind—and hundreds of unwashed bodies had Kendra swallowing hard to prevent her gag reflex from kicking in.

They were still in London, she knew, but it was hard to imagine that this was the same city occupied by the elegant streets and stately homes of Grosvenor Square. They were probably only a couple of miles away, but she felt like she'd landed on a planet in a distant galaxy.

Don't you see us? Kendra wanted to shout as the flood of humanity swirled past them.

But she knew that they did. She could see their plight reflected in their quickly averted faces, their darting eyes. They could see them. They just wouldn't help them.

"Keep yer mouth shut if'n yer thinkin' of screamin'. No'ne 'ere will care," Tom said. "Go on now. *Move!*"

The ruffian herded them forward much like the farmers prodding their cows to market. *To slaughter,* Kendra corrected, and had to suppress a shudder.

They were directed into a long, skinny alley. As they walked, Kendra's mind raced with possible escape scenarios. Unfortunately, their captors were clever in keeping her and Alec separated, with Snake between them and Ned and Tom coming up the rear. Kendra couldn't envision a situation where either she or Alec wouldn't get a bullet in their back if they tried to escape.

They emerged in a large outdoor area, about the size of a basketball court, surrounded by the rear end of attached and semi-attached two- and three-story buildings. The exteriors were either brick or stucco, darkened with coal soot, chipped and cracked. The ground was mostly dirt, with a few clumps of spindly blades of grass poking through. Wooden barrels and empty crates were stacked against the buildings. Flies buzzed in dense hordes around abandoned glass bottles and earthenware jugs, as well as a shallow pit that had been dug in the middle of the clearing.

"Cockfighting pit," Alec identified softly.

Tom heard him and laughed. "Aye, but terday it won't be birds. It'll be a different kinda *cock* fight. Eh, Ned?"

"Aye, Tom," Ned agreed, laughing.

Kendra didn't hear anything, but it was as though a signal had rung. Doors slammed open and men began streaming out of the narrow alleyways between the buildings, two dozen, at least, hard men with pitiless eyes. Their gazes locked on Alec and Kendra as they formed a circle around the pit. About half of them were silent and hostile. The rest were jovial, talking to each other and laughing. The air was suddenly ripe with more than body odor. A testosterone-induced lust for violence seemed to blaze. Kendra could see it in their body language, in their fisted hands and feral gazes.

They want blood.

Kendra could feel Alec tense beside her, angling his body in such a way as to shield her. *Impossible.* Even though some unseen force was keeping these men on a leash, she knew that even if she or Alec could figure out a way to escape, they'd be torn to bits by the mob.

She struggled to stay calm as she scanned the ground, looking for something, *anything*, that she could use as a weapon. A heavy stick or lead pipe. Maybe if she could tear off the slats to one of the crates . . .

"I am *Bear*!"

120

The voice was so loud that Kendra could've sworn it rattled a few of the glass windowpanes in the nearby buildings. Her mouth went dry with fear at the sight of the man who sauntered out of one of the alleys and into the clearing. He had to be about six-foot-seven, with a neck the size of a tree trunk that spread out into massive shoulders and a barrel chest. Kendra gauged him to be at least three *X*s beyond extra large, but none of the weight he carried appeared to be from fat.

Even though he looked to be in his mid-thirties, he was already going bald. He'd compensated the lack of hair on his scalp by growing bushy brown sideburns that angled down to his square jaw. A scar knotted the flesh near his left eye. Gold winked in one earlobe. He carried no weapon—but he didn't need to, Kendra thought. He *was* the weapon.

"Ye murdering bastard." His eyes were mud brown and expressionless as he fixed his gaze on Alec. "Ye killed me Cordi, ye son of a whore. I'm gonna mill yer glaze." Slowly, he began to roll up his sleeves, revealing muscular forearms dusted with hair and marked with tattoos.

Kendra didn't understand the words, but she recognized his intent. *Fight Club.* She knew with a chill that froze the marrow in her bones that he was going to beat Alec to death in this makeshift boxing ring, right before her eyes. She surged forward in a panic, but Tom caught her arm.

"Wait. Stop! *You can't do this*," she shouted.

Bear yanked his eyes away from Alec to look at her. "Who's the bitch?"

"'Is 'arlot." Tom pointed his pistol at Alec.

Bear's eyes narrowed into malevolent slits. "Is that right? Ye'll be mine after I trounce this popinjay. Spoils of war. Right, lads?"

A wild cheer went up around the ring.

"But I'm no cheeseparing fellow," he told the men, lifting his muscular arms as he circled, like a gladiator revving up the crowd. "I'll share the lightskirt."

Another cheer, even louder, seemed to shake the ground.

Alec stared at the giant with icy disdain. "She's the Duke of Aldridge's ward. Let her go and you may yet save your worthless neck."

"'E's tellin' a clanker," Ned protested. "They'd snuck away ter the park together. No Lady would do that!"

Alec kept his eyes trained on the giant. "I'll willingly fight you, but only if she's safe."

"I'm not going anywhere," Kendra said through her teeth.

"Goddamn it, Kendra—"

"No. I'm not fucking leaving you, Alec," she shot back, equally angry. She'd never be able to live with herself if she left. Of course, she probably wouldn't live if she stayed. An impossible choice, which was really no choice at all.

"Ho, she ain't no Lady!" Bear's raucous laughter was immediately mirrored by the other men in the circle, coupled with a few wolf whistles.

Kendra clenched her hands together to keep them from trembling as she pinned her gaze on Bear. "No, I'm not a Lady. I'm the person who will find the man responsible for Lady Dover's death. That's what this is about, isn't it?"

The laughter died instantly. Kendra found herself transfixed by the giant's shark-like gaze.

"I *know* who killed me Cordi. That nobby bastard did the deed. But because he's *gentry*"—he spat on the ground when he said the word—"he'll never pay. Right, lads?" Once again, he turned to the crowd, which answered him with a chorus of nays and curses. "When has one of our betters ever paid, eh?" He swiveled back to Kendra. "But *I'm* gonna make him pay."

The mob's chorus changed to ayes, loud and vicious. She could see the bloodlust transforming their faces into harsh angles and planes.

"You'll be making the wrong man pay!" Kendra had to shout to be heard over the noise of the crowd. "The real murderer will go free! Do you want justice? Then let me do my fucking job!"

Bear regarded her like she was strange object that had fallen from the sky. "Yer *job*? Next ye'll be tellin' me that yer a Bow Street Runner."

That statement brought more gales of laughter from the onlookers.

Alec caught Kendra's eye, and she recognized in his gaze the kind of fury born of gut-churning fear. "Kendra—" he began, but she deliberately turned away, ignoring him.

"How did you know Lady Dover?" she asked of Bear. *I just need to keep him talking.* As long as he was talking, he wasn't pounding Alec into dust.

For the first time, the cold eyes warmed with real grief. "She was the most beautiful lass in the world. Better'n Cheapside. Better'n that bleeding Lord she got herself leg-shackled to. Cordi was a queen, she was. She deserved better than being gutted."

"Yes, she did," Kendra agreed. "She deserves justice. I promise to get that for her. For *you*." Again, Kendra held her breath, willing Bear to take her offer. It was a long shot.

She knew it hadn't worked when his eyes narrowed, his expression hardening.

"I'll be gettin' justice for meself. And for Cordi. 'Cause the sodding magistrates won't be doin' it. Not when it involves the likes of him." He looked over at Alec and brought his fists up in a boxer's stance. "C'mon, dandy. 'Tis time to pay the piper fer what ye did!"

Alec's face revealed nothing as the crowd roared and whistled. Then he shrugged out of his coat and untied his cravat. He handed them to Kendra. For a long moment, he looked at her. Then he leaned close, brushing his lips against hers.

"When you get the chance, run," he whispered.

"Alec—"

But he was already moving away.

Kendra stared helplessly from the sidelines as both men began to circle each other. Alec was tall and athletic, but he was dwarfed next to the mountainous Bear. She made an instinctive movement forward, but was checked by Tom, who stood on her right. Ned was on her left. Snake, she noticed, had clamored to the top of a stack of crates for a better view. He was only ten, but he eagerly joined the spectators, offering his own colorful curses and invectives.

It was as though the men had shed their humanity, and only their most primitive selves remained. She'd seen such things happen before—mob mentality.

Bear was the first to throw a punch. It looked like it could've put a crater in a cinder block. Kendra didn't want to imagine what it would do to Alec's face. Thankfully, the Marquis dodged the blow, dancing nimbly to the side before countering with his own lightning-fast jab. Although that connected squarely with Bear's stomach, the giant only grunted before swinging out again. Alec easily evaded.

"If that's the best you can do, no wonder Cordelia left you for an old man," Alec taunted, his green eyes fixed on his opponent. "Maybe it wasn't riches she was after, but a better performance."

Kendra stared at Alec in disbelief. What the hell was he doing? Then, with sickening clarity, she understood. He wanted everyone's attention on him. He wanted to whip them into a frenzy so she would be able to escape.

He was going to sacrifice his life for hers.

Bear roared and lunged. But instead of punching, he kicked Alec mid-thigh, causing Alec to stumble. Fear rose up and nearly choked Kendra as she watched, transfixed, as Bear swung out his enormous fist. She was certain that it would break Alec's jaw. But at the very last second, Alec righted himself, dodged the uppercut, and deftly danced backward, unscathed.

For the moment.

The two men continued to circle each other like they were connected by an invisible tether. She'd already known that this wasn't going to be a gentleman's sport of boxing. There would be no Marquess of Queensbury Rules of conduct. This would be a bare-knuckled fight to the death. And while Alec had surprised her, both by his speed and skill, she had very little doubt that in the end, Bear would be the victor, and Alec would be a bloody stump on the ground.

"I'm shocked Lord Dover would marry a woman so far beneath his touch," Alec continued. He wasn't exactly panting, but his breathing was becoming more labored as he ducked and wove. "Beauty doesn't equal class."

"Mind yer bleeding tongue. Or I'll cut it out of ye and wrap it around your throat like a fucking cravat," growled Bear. He grunted again when Alec zipped in and nailed him in the nose, hard enough to spill blood.

"Ooh, 'e drew yer cork, Bear!" someone yelled.

"C'mon, Bear! Thrash the dandy!"

"Aye—kill the fucker!"

The goliath rushed forward and embraced Alec in a parody of a hug. Alec brought his hands up to box his opponent's ears. Bear responded by slamming him to the ground, and then kicking Alec solidly in the ribs.

Alec groaned as he rolled away. Bear swung his foot forward for another kick, but Alec's hands whipped out, grabbing the man's boot. In a deft maneuver, he jerked upward, sending Bear toppling like a giant oak into the dust. Awkwardly, Alec scrambled to his feet, holding his side.

"Crack 'is napper, Bear!"

Bear leaped to his feet and rushed Alec again. As he did so, he threw out a hurried punch. The blow glanced off Alec's cheekbone with enough force to snap his head back. Another punch grazed Alec's jaw. The crowd roared their approval over Bear's attack. Alec staggered backward.

Kendra forced herself to look away from the fight. *Think.* Goddamn it, she needed to *think*!

Everyone's attention was focused on the fighters. Alec had wanted her to use the distraction to slip away, but Kendra had no intention of doing that. Beside her, Tom was still holding his pistol, but it was almost an afterthought. He no longer pointed it at her. Like everyone else, he appeared to have forgotten she was there.

An idea began to take shape. Kendra shot a quick look at her other captor. Ned had even gone so far as to tuck his pistol into his belt, in order to use his hands to cup his mouth and yell, "Clout the devil!" His attention was completely focused on Bear as the man delivered another stunning blow to Alec.

It's now or never. She sucked in a deep breath and pretended to stumble into Ned.

"Eh, 'ere now. Watch it!" he snarled, and shoved her back, not bothering to look at her. Not feeling the weight of the pistol sliding off him . . .

Deliberately, Kendra went with the momentum of the shove, which took her toward Tom. He glanced at her, irritated, but it was already too late. She dropped Alec's coat and cravat, whipping up the pistol that she'd taken off Ned. She slammed it into Tom's temple with as much force as she could muster. As his knees gave out from under him, she snatched the gun out of his slack hand, and jumped back.

"*Freeze!*" she yelled, but her voice was drowned out by the whoops and hollers of the men surrounding the fighters.

Ned was the only one who'd noticed her action. He stared at her in open-mouthed shock. "What the devil—?"

"*Stop!*" She tried to pitch her voice over the noise of the crowd. "Goddamn it! I *said*—"

She lifted one of the weapons. They were two-barreled flintlocks, which meant they held exactly four balls of lead between them. She'd have three balls left if she fired one. But if she didn't, Alec was as good as dead.

Kendra squeezed the trigger. The explosion that followed made her ears ring and the recoil made the weapon buck like a live animal in her hands.

"—*stop!*" Her voice sounded abnormally loud as silence descended abruptly on the clearing. Heart pounding, she steadied her grip on both weapons and leveled them at the mob, which turned like a single organism to gape at her.

"I want to see your goddamn hands up," she ordered. "Walk backward to the wall."

"Ye only got three balls in them barking irons," one man snarled. "Ye can't kill us all."

"Congratulations, you're a fucking mathematician. I can still take out three of you assholes, beginning with you. So unless you want to die today . . . *get back.*"

She cocked both hammers, earning nervous glances from the men. She prayed no one was going to challenge her. She had no compunction about following through on her threat. She could take out three men—but then she and Alec would be toast.

Son of a bitch.

"Yer only a woman," someone muttered.

Kendra leveled a stare at the man. "Correction, asshole. I'm an excellent shot. Of course, at this distance, it would be damn near impossible to miss. So unless one of you wants to serve as an example of what happens when you don't obey instructions . . ."

Slowly, mumbling beneath their breath, the men shifted until they were lined up against the far wall.

"You, too, Snake," she told the child, who was still sitting on top of the wall of crates.

The boy gawked at her. Then he scrabbled down like a monkey from his perch and headed for the wall.

Kendra's gaze cut to Bear and Alec. Neither had moved. Unfortunately, Bear was the one standing. Alec had fallen to his knees. She could see blood spatter on the ground beneath him.

"Step away from the Marquis," she ordered Bear. When he didn't move, she pointed the flintlock at his head, careful that she was far enough away from the massive reach of his arms. "Are you deaf? Get the hell away from him."

Bear's eyes remained flat and unafraid. "I'm not lettin' this murdering bastard get away."

"He didn't kill your girlfriend. And I'm going to prove it. Step back, unless you want a bullet destroying what little brain cells you have inside that place you call a head."

Bear didn't move. *Crap.* If she didn't do something fast, the other men would assume she didn't have the nerve to shoot and they'd be on her like a pack of ravenous wolves.

Very slowly she lowered the weapon. Her line of sight went to his heart. Lower still until the gun pointed at his abdomen. Lower still . . .

And watched the giant go pale.

"If I shoot, there's a good chance you'll live . . . assuming you'd *want* to live, that is." She summoned a smile. She could almost hear the clicks of two dozen Adam's apples, as the men lined up against the wall swallowed simultaneously. Amazing—none of them blinked at a gun pointed at a man's head, but they looked ready to faint when she pointed the weapon at his groin.

"Your choice, Bear," she continued. "Put your hands up and walk backward to your friends. Or take your chance that I'm bluffing." They stared at each other. "The way I see it, I have nothing to lose."

That statement seemed to register with the giant. He raised his enormous fists and slowly backed away to join the other men. He kept his gaze trained on her.

She spared Alec a quick glance, sucking in her breath when she saw his bruised and bloody face. His lip was split and swollen. "Are you all right, Alec? Can you walk?"

"Christ," Alec groaned, but he managed to get to his feet. "I can walk."

Kendra now regarded Bear steadily over the flintlocks. "Okay, listen up. We're leaving. But I'm going to tell you this one last time: Alec isn't your guy. He didn't murder Lady Dover."

Bear said nothing.

"I'm going to prove it, but I need time. And I don't want to be looking over my shoulder, worried about you."

The giant eyed her like she was insane. "Who the bloody hell are ye?"

"The person who's going to find Lady Dover's killer."

"You're a woman."

"What's your point?"

Bear seemed flummoxed by the question. Then he scowled and spat on the ground. "Why should I believe this here bastard ain't me Cordi's killer?"

"You don't need to believe me. I just need time to prove to you that he didn't do it."

"Do ye take me for a fucking fool? Ye want time for ye and yer lover to flee. Ye're American. Ye'll go home and take him with ye."

"No, I won't. I don't have a home anymore. I give you my word of honor that I won't leave. I want your word of honor that you'll back off until I've completed my investigation."

"Ye'd take the word of a man like me?"

"I would. Of course, if you don't keep your word, the Duke of Aldridge will hunt you down, and I will personally carve out that part of your anatomy that you seem to prize so much."

He stared at her. "God's teeth, woman, ye're a bloodthirsty wench."

"Do we have a deal?"

"How much time?"

"A month."

"Nay. A week."

"I'm not a damn magician. Three weeks."

"Two. The nobby bastard has two weeks to live before I come for him."

"On your word of honor?" She'd never found the axiom "honor among thieves" to be true, but she was hoping it might hold more weight in this era.

"Aye."

"Okay. If you break it, everyone here will know that your honor means nothing." She glanced at Alec. "I'm going to start walking backward. You'll need to guide me to make sure we get into the alley." She kept the pistols aimed at Bear as Alec snatched up his coat and cravat. "I want everyone to start counting," she called back to the assembled men. "When you reach one hundred, you can leave. If you leave before that number, you might get the surprise of your life."

They gaped at her.

"I said *count*."

"One," someone muttered, and the throng shifted and joined in. The counting grew louder. Bear stayed silent, his gaze locked on her.

Once they were in the alley, Alec demanded through clenched teeth, "What the bloody hell are you doing?"

Kendra looped an arm around Alec's waist to hurry him through the narrow passageway and shot him a grin.

"Why, I thought that was obvious, m'lord. I'm saving your ass."

14

They drew a lot more stares exiting the alley than when they'd gone in at gunpoint, Kendra noticed. But still, no one seemed inclined to help them.

Of course, that could've been the influence of the two pistols that she was now carrying. Certainly the hackney driver that they approached eyed her with alarm. He only became agreeable when Alec tossed him a guinea and promised him another if he drove them to Grosvenor Square.

Kendra waited for the carriage to move before she dropped the pistols on the seat and reached for Alec's torn, bloody shirt. Agitation made her fingers clumsy as she wrestled with the buttons. His face was ghastly with cuts and bruises, but nothing appeared broken. She was more concerned with his ribs. Broken bones had the potential of splintering off and piercing internal organs.

"I always imagined this differently," Alec drawled.

"What?"

"Being undressed by you."

She fumbled on a button, and her gaze flew up to meet his. He gave her a crooked smile and his eyes brightened with wicked amusement.

"This isn't funny, Alec." Still, she had to quell the urge for a humorous response. "You could have broken ribs—" She gasped as his shirt fell away to reveal flesh that had already turned purple. Definitely broken ribs. "We've got to get you to a hospital."

"No."

"You've just had the shit beat out of you by the Incredible Hulk. You need a doctor."

"The incredible hulk? That's an apt description."

"Never mind. Alec, you need medical attention."

"I'm bruised, but nothing is broken."

She glared at him. "Where did you get your medical degree?"

Kendra regarded him closely, her earlier panic subsiding. His breathing was more shallow than normal, but not labored. She wasn't a doctor, but from personal experience, she knew that burst blood vessels would begin to clot almost immediately after an injury, one of the body's remarkable self-healing properties.

"I didn't realize you cared."

Her throat tightened and her gaze fell on the button she was unconsciously fiddling with.

"I care," she whispered finally. "But that doesn't mean I belong here."

"I think you belong where you *want* to belong," he countered softly.

"You really need a doctor to examine you." It was a retreat, she knew. But he made her feel too exposed.

Alec gave a sigh—a small one, since his ribs ached. "I'll send for a doctor, if it will ease your mind, when we return to Grosvenor Square."

"Good." She sat back and watched as he buttoned up his shirt. His fingers were long and agile, but his knuckles were swollen and flecked with dried blood.

"And Kendra?"

"Yes?"

"The next time I tell you to run, I expect you to run."

That surprised her enough to bring her eyes up to meet his. "Are you serious?"

"Quite."

"Did you fail to notice how I got us out of there, Your Lordship? Without me, you'd probably already be buried in a shallow grave somewhere."

"Doubtful. The only gravedigging those ruffians would do would be to rob a grave of its corpse or haul a body to a surgeon for dissection. Most likely they would have tossed me into the Thames. Much more efficient."

She glared at him. "This isn't a joke, Alec."

"No, it damn well isn't." Beneath the bruise on his jaw, a muscle ticked. "Do you have any idea, woman, what those men planned to do to you after they had dispatched me?"

"I don't even have to use my imagination; Bear let everyone know that he was a generous guy."

"Precisely. They would have used you viciously. Afterward, if you were lucky, they might have slit your throat. If you were unlucky, you'd have ended up in a brothel somewhere, catering to cutthroats and ruffians of the worst sort."

"Are you trying to shock me?"

"I'm trying to make you see sense!"

"Would you have left me?"

He scowled. "Don't be ridiculous."

Anger flooded her bloodstream. "Why is that ridiculous? Because you're a man and I'm a woman?"

"Hell and damnation, Kendra, this isn't about women's rights—"

"No, it's about integrity and honor. Women have both of those, too, you know. Do you really think I'd have been able to leave you to be beaten to death while I ran away like a coward? You don't know me at all."

"Christ. Most women would be having a fit of vapors." He hissed out a sigh as he leaned back against the seat, his hand resting lightly against his ribs. He regarded her quizzically. "I was trying to protect you, you know. And if you think that I shan't try to protect you now or in the future . . . well, then you don't know me at all, either."

An impasse. "I need you to respect me, Alec," she said finally.

"This is not about respect." He picked up her hand, and studied it for a long moment. Small and soft, yet less than fifteen minutes ago, it had been rock-steady as she'd aimed the flintlocks at the group of cutthroats. "I respect you, Kendra. And I believe in you. I know you shall find the fiend who killed Cordelia."

Her chest tightened and she hoped she didn't sound as worried as she felt when she spoke. "I've got two weeks. Then the House of Lords will convene and Bear will come after you—assuming he'll honor our deal."

"Bear or the hangman's noose. I'm not certain which would be a worse fate."

"Let's hope you won't have to decide."

❖

Their arrival at Number 29 Grosvenor Square caused a commotion. Footmen in the foyer stopped what they were doing and stared in shock. Even Harding lost his composure, to the point where he actually raised his voice.

"Your Lordship! Miss Donovan!"

Several more servants came into the foyer to investigate the butler's rare shout.

"Send for a doctor!" Kendra yelled. "And someone help me carry Lord Sutcliffe to a bedroom."

"I can bloody well walk," Alec muttered irritably. "I walked in here, didn't I?"

"You need to lie down and take deep breaths."

"What I need is brandy. Harding, a bottle, if you please."

The butler had regained his equanimity. "Yes, m'lord. The Red bedchamber is still available, sir. Ah . . ." He hesitated, eyeing Kendra. "Shall I relieve you of your pistols, Miss?"

"What? Oh." She'd forgotten about the guns. She handed them over to the butler. "Thanks."

"Good God! *Alec!*" The Duke stood on the upstairs landing, gaping down at them.

His shout drew another audience. Lady Atwood appeared next to her brother, followed by a man and woman. Another figure squeezed through the two strangers to grasp the railing. Kendra felt a dart of surprise and affection go through her as she identified the familiar face of Lady Rebecca Blackburn.

She'd met the younger woman a month ago, when Rebecca had attended Lady Atwood's house party while her parents were touring their Barbados sugar plantation. Rebecca hadn't been part of any of the cliquey groups that had formed—her face, which had been scarred since surviving childhood smallpox, made her an outsider, an ugly duckling drifting on the fringes of the beautiful debutantes that had gathered at Aldridge Castle.

Kendra had liked her immediately. Or maybe she'd recognized a fellow outlier—and a more modern spirit in the follower of the early feminist Mary Wollstonecraft.

"Good heavens, Sutcliffe. You look as though you've gone several rounds with Gentleman Jackson himself," Rebecca declared. "Who planted you a facer?"

"Rebecca!" admonished the woman standing next to her. Given that the older woman's hair matched Lady Rebecca's dark auburn shade exactly, Kendra guessed her to be Rebecca's mother.

She could only assume that the man beside them was Lord Blackburn.

Rebecca was unabashed. "It's not like we can ignore Sutcliffe's face, Mama. It's right there in front of our noses!"

"Contain your curiosity until Lord Sutcliffe is made comfortable," her mother replied.

Unlike Rebecca's cornflower blue eyes, Lady Blackburn's eyes were a deep caramel brown. Yet the keen intelligence Kendra saw in them made her think that she shared more with her daughter than the color of their hair.

"Neville, Duke, perhaps you could assist—Miss Donovan, is it?—in bringing the Marquis upstairs," Lady Blackburn said. "Has a doctor been sent for?"

"It shall be done, m'lady," said Harding.

"I'm not an invalid," Alec muttered when his uncle and Lord Blackburn came down the steps. "Or a child."

"Then stop acting like one," Aldridge reprimanded. Still, he preserved Alec's dignity by only drawing Alec's arm around his shoulder and then putting his arm around his nephew's waist to haul him up the stairs. Rebecca waited until they passed her on the landing. Then she flew down the stairs and gave Kendra a surprisingly strong hug.

"'Tis good to see you again, Miss Donovan!"

"You too." With some surprise, she realized she meant it. In her own time, she hadn't developed many friendships. Colleagues at the Bureau, yes, but no real friends. Yet by the time Rebecca had left Aldridge Castle, Kendra had come to regard her as a friend.

"We came to London as soon as we heard Sutcliffe was under suspicion. Utterly preposterous! What happened to him, anyway? Does it have anything to do with Lady Dover's murder?"

"You could say that. I know you didn't like Lady Dover, but what do you know about her before she married her husband?"

"Well, I . . ." Rebecca frowned thoughtfully. "Now that I consider the matter, I have to admit that I know very little. I only made Lady Dover's acquaintance after her husband had expired. In truth, I never thought to inquire about her connections before she became Lady Dover. Why? What have you learned?"

"Her stepson checked into her background and discovered that she was not who she claimed."

"She was an impostor?"

"She's not the vicar's daughter that she purported to be," Kendra replied wryly.

"Who is she, then?"

"I don't know, but I think we just met someone from her past."

"The man Sutcliffe fought?"

"Yes."

"Alec is an excellent pugilist. I hope he soundly thrashed the other man."

"Alec held his own, but the other guy was bigger than a house. And Bear was—"

"Bear?"

"Rumor has it that he once fought a bear. After seeing him, I'm inclined to believe the story."

"Dear heaven. How did you manage to escape?"

Kendra smiled. "You might say that I reminded Bear of what he holds most dear. But it was clear Lady Dover was a close second."

"Are you saying this criminal and Lady Dover were involved?"

"They had a history. He still loves her, I think. And he believes Alec murdered her. He wants justice."

"What utter rot! Sutcliffe would never harm a woman." Rebecca gave her one of her piercing stares. "That is why you are here, is it not? To find the person who really murdered the woman?"

"Yes."

Rebecca gave her a smug look. "I suspected as much." She glanced around, and though the foyer was currently deserted, she lowered her voice to a conspiratorial whisper. "The Countess told us that you are now the Duke's ward. 'Tis a clever strategy to protect your reputation."

"I think Lady Atwood is more concerned about the Duke's reputation."

Rebecca grinned at Kendra's dry tone and then reached over to link her arm through Kendra's and steer her toward the stairs. "You know, Miss Donovan, after your refusal to continue as my companion, I assumed you would sail back to America."

"My plan was to return home," Kendra admitted. "It didn't work out."

"I, for one, am happy you remained." Rebecca glanced at Kendra from the corner of her eye as they began ascending the stairs. "Duke said that Sam Kelly and Dr. Munroe are also investigating. Do you not find that interesting?"

"Interesting is one word for it."

"*Rota Fortunae.* It would appear the goddess Fortuna has spun her wheel and fated us to be together again."

Kendra didn't say anything. Having that particular deity controlling her fate wasn't exactly comforting. The goddess was often depicted blindfolded as she spun the wheel of fortune.

Fortuna was also considered quite insane.

15

Two and a half hours later, Kendra reflected that a crazy goddess was as good as any other explanation for her current situation, standing half-naked in her bed-chamber while Rebecca sat on the bed, watching Miss Cooper help her into a mint-green afternoon dress.

"Lady Atwood was most distressed when you left the residence without a chaperone," said the maid, managing to sound both injured and critical. Consequently, Kendra felt both guilty and irritated. "'Tis my duty to accompany you when you go outside, Miss Donovan," Miss Cooper reminded her, as she began buttoning up the gown.

Kendra clenched her jaw. Then, deliberately, she relaxed it. "I'm not a child." *So says the woman who needs to be dressed.*

"No, you are the Duke of Aldridge's ward, and you must behave accordingly," admonished the lady's maid. "Lady Atwood employed me to assist you in that endeavor. A lady's reputation is not something to be taken lightly, Miss Donovan. You must never leave the premises again without a proper chaperone."

"I didn't go out for a stroll, you know. I saw someone watching the house."

"If you were alarmed, you ought to have sent word to Mr. Harding."

"And what exactly would the butler have done about it?" Kendra didn't bother to hide her sarcasm.

Miss Cooper seemed to consider the question seriously. "Why, Mr. Harding would then have shared your concerns with His Grace."

"I am certain Miss Donovan will be more careful in the future, Miss Cooper," Rebecca interceded, apparently recognizing the battle light in the American's dark eyes. She'd persuaded her mother to let her accompany Kendra and Lady Atwood on their morning call to Lady St. James. Now, she smiled brightly, ignoring the scowl on Kendra's face. "You look charming, Miss Donovan."

Miss Cooper said, "I must redress her hair. I do wish you would reconsider a hairpiece, Miss Donovan."

"No," Kendra replied staunchly to the hairpiece. But she allowed the maid to steer her to the velvet-tufted stool in front of the vanity table. She caught Rebecca's amused gaze in the mirror as the maid plucked the hairpins from the coil. Even though she couldn't say she liked the woman, Kendra had to admire how Miss Cooper wielded a brush and comb. It took less than a minute for the maid to conquer the silky strands and then recoil them into a tight chignon.

Miss Cooper surveyed the hairstyle critically. "Mayhap a few ribbons . . . no, the rosettes, I think."

Kendra suppressed an impatient sigh. In the twenty-first century, before she'd been wounded, she'd always worn her hair long, pulled back into a ponytail, and had cycled through a wardrobe that was more functional than fashionable. She wasn't used to this level of absorption in her appearance, where every detail was scrutinized.

She leaned forward, scooping a handful of rosettes out of the open silver container on the vanity. But when she tried to hand them to Miss Cooper, she was waved away.

"Those are red, Miss Donovan," she chided gently. "I shall need the green ones. The *lighter* green to match your gown." She didn't wait, but reached across Kendra to select the adornments herself. Another couple of minutes of fiddling, and finally the maid stepped back. "There, Miss Donovan," she pronounced, clearly satisfied with the results. "I shall retrieve your cloak."

Kendra waited until Miss Cooper fetched the velvet, green-hooded cloak. It was a relief to finally be able to escape the maid's censorious stare.

"You really shouldn't be too cross with her, you know," Rebecca whispered when they were walking down the hall. "She has your best interests at heart."

"I think she has Lady Atwood's best interests at heart."

"Well, yes. Can you blame her? The Countess hired her, and Miss Cooper's position in this household is incumbent upon making certain you are above reproach with your dress and how you comport yourself."

Kendra wanted to point out to Rebecca that she wasn't ten years old, that she'd been taking care of herself for a very long time. But that would only open the door to more questions about her family and background.

She expelled a breath, some of her resentment against the maid beginning to fade. Unfortunately that left the guilt. It wasn't Miss Cooper's fault that the rules governing a woman's behavior in this era were irrational and archaic.

Oh, God.

Her stomach flipped as she considered a future filled with such rules and restriction. She hadn't really been free in her own timeline either—hell, she'd worked for the FBI. You couldn't set foot in that bureaucracy without getting tangled up in red tape. But at least she hadn't needed permission to walk down the street by herself.

How can I live like this? she wondered. *How can I live in a constant state of being treated like a child?*

Then came the equally bleak thought: *Do I have a choice?*

❖

The ride to Lady St. James's townhouse took approximately twenty minutes, mainly because of the heavy congestion in the streets, which included several wagons carrying containers of coal, drums filled with salted meat, and kegs of ale. Then came another eight minutes of waiting, as Lady Atwood gave her calling card to her coachman, who in turn presented it to Lady St. James's butler. The card had Lady Atwood's name and title glazed elegantly on it, along with information regarding her own "At Home" days—dates and times when Lady Atwood would be available to receive visitors at the Duke's residence.

Mentally, Kendra followed the card's journey as the butler disappeared into the house. The servant would carefully place it on a silver salver, which he then would carry to wherever Lady St. James was located—most likely a drawing room—where she would read it and send back her response.

No one was surprised when word came back that Lady St. James was at home and would be delighted to receive them.

Inside the entrance hall, Lady Atwood paused long enough to peer into a crystal dish that held more than a dozen calling cards. Then she smiled and swept ahead.

Kendra shot Rebecca an inquiring look.

"The staff is always instructed to put the day's most important visitor's calling card on top, in full view." Rebecca explained softly. "'Tis a way to impress others who may come calling. Lady Atwood's card is obviously the one on top."

It was silly, of course. But no more silly than buying a bigger car, house, diamond ring, or rare painting to show off one's status to neighbors, friends, and family. Human beings had been trying to outdo each other since they'd begun etching their drawings onto cave walls.

The butler escorted them into a drawing room that Kendra could only describe as fussy. It was as though Lady St. James couldn't decide which of the era's popular trends that she liked, so she'd included them all—a mélange of Chinese and Indian motifs, with Dutch chintz. The furniture reflected Grecian, Egyptian, Roman, and more Chinese influences.

The overdone, over-the-top fashion applied to the woman herself, who appeared never to have met a ruffle that she didn't like. Kendra counted at least four flounces edging the hem of her bright, yellow-and-orange-striped skirt, two ruffle tiers on her sleeve, and one flopping around her square neckline. The large lace cap that she wore over graying brown curls struck Kendra as one giant ruffle.

Introductions were made, and then tea and small butter cakes were brought in while Lady St. James regaled them with the tale of how she and Lady Atwood had been diamonds of the first water during their debut season twenty-five years earlier. Between bites of cake and small sips of tea, the aristocrat waxed nostalgic on their successful matches. Lord St. James had passed away three years ago, but her union had produced eight children.

"All successfully married, thank heavens," Lady St. James finished, offering them a smug smile.

Kendra listened, still bemused by the concept of having such a large family. It was the norm in this era, though so, too, were children who never survived infancy or childhood. There were also methods of birth control, she knew. She'd read about an excavation at England's Dudley Castle that had unearthed a sewer filled with condoms made from animal membranes that dated back to the seventeenth century. Most likely, men wore them to protect themselves against venereal diseases, which, in this pre-antibiotic time, could lead to insanity or death. She doubted they were worn as a consideration to women to prevent pregnancy. And she imagined that married couples didn't give any thought to them at all.

What about Lady Dover? Kendra wondered. She'd been married and then a widow for five years, during which time she'd taken lovers. But she hadn't become pregnant until three months ago. For the first time, Kendra considered the timing. Had Lady Dover deliberately gotten pregnant to use the child as leverage against her lover, to try to force him into marriage?

"I do not recall the Duke of Aldridge having a ward," Lady St. James was saying, and eyed Kendra as though she was another slice of butter cake. "You must be . . . what? Four and twenty?"

"Actually, twenty-six," Kendra said, picking up her teacup.

"'Twas a pact made by my brother and Miss Donovan's father years ago, before he immigrated to America," Lady Atwood lied smoothly. "Aldridge could hardly turn his back on Miss Donovan when she showed up at his door."

"No, no. Certainly not. And with the Duke's name lending Miss Donovan support, she ought to make an admirable match—despite her advanced age."

Kendra had just taken a swallow of tea and promptly choked on it. "Excuse me?"

"Do not fret, my dear. You may not be fresh out of the school-room, but I dare say Lady Atwood shall find an appropriate husband for you."

It took Kendra a moment to find her voice. "Thanks, but I'm not looking for a husband."

Lady St. James laughed as though Kendra had just told a joke. "My dear . . . of course, you are."

"No, I—"

"What Miss Donovan is trying to say is that our stay in London has been overshadowed by this ugliness with my nephew," Lady Atwood cut in. "I'm certain you're cognizant of the unpleasantness?"

"Yes, I had heard. Perfectly outrageous, of course." Lady St. James's mouth pursed in sympathy, but she couldn't quite conceal the gleam in her eye. Kendra had no doubt that whatever was said here would be making the rounds when Lady St. James met with her friends later, and most likely with a few embellishments. "Pray tell, how *is* the Marquis handling everything?"

"As well as can be expected, given the falsehood."

"Lord Sutcliffe is only a suspect because of his previous friendship with Lady Dover," Rebecca said carefully, setting down her teacup. "But as we all know, Lady Dover had many other friendships."

Lady St. James took the bait. "Heavens, *yes*. And she was *quite* brazen about them too. Why, less than a fortnight ago, the creature made a spectacle of herself at the theater. I was there when it happened. I'd gone to watch Mr. Edmund Kean's performance. He was said to be utterly brilliant as Shylock in *The Merchant of Venice*. But poor Mr. Kean was quite overshadowed by the theatrics offstage."

Kendra perked up. Now they were getting somewhere. "What happened?"

"Lady Dover had the utter audacity to come to the theater wearing jewels that have been in the Weston family for generations!"

"Well, how did she . . . *no!*" Lady Atwood set her teacup down with a rattle.

"*Yes.* Five strands of pearls interspersed with pink diamonds. Supposedly it had been part of King Louis XIV royal household, but that is only conjecture, no doubt advanced by the Weston family. Still, the necklace is quite unmistakable."

"We are speaking of Lord Henry Weston, the Earl of Dewsbury, are we not?" asked Lady Atwood.

Lady St. James gave her a significant look. "Yes."

"Dear heaven," Lady Atwood breathed, shocked. "What possessed the foolish man to bestow a family heirloom on Lady Dover? Even if she was his paramour—"

"Oh, I think there can be no doubt about *that*, my dear," Lady St. James murmured slyly. "I'd heard he was dazzled by her. Lady Dover is—*was* a remarkable beauty. I have to allow her that. One can only imagine how she seduced him into handing over such a valuable piece of property."

"Disgraceful." Lady Atwood pressed her lips together. "One does not hand over an heirloom to an inamorata."

"But that is not the most shocking thing, my dear." Lady St. James leaned forward, her gaze darting between her guests as though she wanted to absorb every expression that flickered across their faces. "The entire Weston family was at the theater the evening that Lady Dover flaunted the necklace!"

Both Lady Atwood and Rebecca gasped.

The Countess asked, "Lady Weston?"

"*Yes.*"

"Dear heaven. The utter humiliation."

"I agree. The Earl should be horsewhipped for bringing such disgrace upon his family." Having imparted what she considered the most shocking aspect of the story, Lady St. James leaned back, her gaze drifting to the cakes on the tray beside her. She selected another wedge, popped the bite-sized morsel into her mouth, chewed, and swallowed before continuing. "I heard that Weston's son, Viscount Dawson, visited Lady Dover the next morning to demand that she return the jewels."

Rebecca asked, "Did she?"

"She refused, and the *on dit* is that she laughed at the young puppy. Can you imagine? Really, the woman was quite shameless."

The image of Lady Dover's body lying on the table in the morgue came to Kendra's mind. The frenzied, furious stabbing indicating an uncontrollable rage.

"Who is Lord Weston?" asked Kendra.

"He is the seventh Earl of Dewsbury, my dear." Lady St. James gave her a pitying look. "Americans have done away with titles and rank, have they not? I really don't know how you manage. It seems so . . . undisciplined."

Easy to say when you're born into the part of society that holds titles and a pampered position, Kendra thought.

"I seem to recall that Lord Weston has three daughters, as well as their son," Rebecca said. "Lady Isabella—"

"Yes, and Lady Louisa and Lady Frances," Lady St. James rushed in, obviously disliking having her own story usurped. "Naturally, the Viscount is the heir, although I'd heard there is not much left of the family estate in Dewsbury. Lord Weston had several bad investments, you know. The family lives in London most of the year. Dawson will no doubt be on the hunt for an heiress soon."

"Yes, I'd imagine," murmured Lady Atwood.

"Thankfully, Lady Weston managed to successfully marry off two of her daughters. My sympathies lie with the middle chit, Lady Louisa. The poor dear failed to bring any suitor up to scratch during the last *three* seasons. She must be approaching two and twenty now."

"Oh, dear."

"It wasn't as much of an issue when the eldest daughter wed. A mere Mister, but he works in the government; I can't recall which cabinet. However, the youngest chit recently wed the Honorable Mr. Cecil Roberts, who is in line for an earldom when his grand-father expires. An excellent match, but it must have created quite a bit of consternation for Lady Louisa, I'd imagine."

Kendra asked, "Why would that be a problem?"

Lady St. James regarded her with surprise. "Why, because she married *before* Lady Louisa, who is older and has yet to secure a match. 'Tis mortifying. There has been talk that Lord Ludlow has shown an interest in the poor wretch, but unfortunately, the man is known to be a high stickler. This scandal with Lady Dover could very well frighten him off. More tea?" She lifted the pot, and cups rattled as tea was replenished.

"Pray tell, did Lord Weston ever retrieve the necklace?" Lady Atwood inquired, stirring milk and sugar into her tea.

"Not that I'd heard. Though the silly man should never have given it to the creature in the first place, of course."

"I fancy he's now suffering for his foolishness."

"The entire family is suffering. Lady Weston hasn't shown her face in public since that night at the theater. Taken to her bed, I've heard, and dosing herself with laudanum."

Rebecca said, "Poor woman!"

"Yes, indeed," agreed Lady St. James. "I must admit that I applaud Lady Frances's fortitude. She carried on with the ball she'd had on the calendar . . . although I dare say it would've caused even more gossip to call it off."

"When was that?" Kendra asked.

"Monday evening."

Kendra stated the obvious. "The night Lady Dover was murdered. Do you know who attended the ball?"

"Most of London attended. *I* attended. It was a dreadful crush. I'm certain that the Ton was hoping to witness another scene like the night of the theater," Lady St. James confided with a knowing smile.

Kendra had a feeling Lady St. James fell into that category. "So the entire Weston family was there?"

"Yes—well, *no.* Not Lady Weston. As I mentioned, the humiliation has forced her to her bedchamber."

Rebecca's mouth tightened. "Lord Weston should be the humiliated one. He is responsible for the scandal."

Lady St. James lifted her eyebrows. "If only that was how society worked, my dear. But men will be men, you know."

"And women will suffer," Rebecca muttered beneath her breath.

Kendra put down her teacup. "What about Lord Dover—Lady Dover's stepson?"

"I do not know if he attended the ball. I have only the slightest acquaintance with him, but I did not see him. In the horde of people, though, he could easily have been missed."

"No, I meant . . . I heard that he and Lady Dover had a contentious relationship," Kendra said carefully.

Lady St. James's eyes brightened. "Oh, yes. Gossip is that he never forgave his father for marrying the woman. They had rows about it, which led to an estrangement. He never gave Lady Dover the cut direct, of course, but there was talk that he'd given her the cut sublime *and* the cut indirect a time or two."

A month ago, Kendra had learned that the cut direct was looking someone dead in the eye before ignoring them. The cut indirect was pretending not to see the other person in the first place.

But she had to ask: "What's the cut sublime?"

"You don't have the cut sublime in America?" Lady St. James gave her a pitying look. "Well, 'tis simple, really, my dear: if you wish not to speak to a person who is approaching you, you raise your eyes until the offending person is gone."

Kendra frowned. "But isn't that the same thing as the cut indirect? Pretending not to see someone?"

"Oh, goodness, no. The cut indirect is when you keep your eyes on the same level as the offending party, but you pretend you do not see them. Much more offensive. The cut sublime is when you *raise* your eyes to the *heavens*." She demonstrated by flicking her gaze melodramatically toward the ceiling. She lowered her eyes back to Kendra. "Do you comprehend the difference, my dear? There is also the cut infernal, where you lower your gaze to the floor. It's much more effective with gentleman than ladies, though, since they can pretend to brush a smudge from their boots. Quite impossible for a lady to do with any decorum."

Kendra stared at the other woman, and again thought how ridiculous humans could be at times.

Lady St. James said, "I *had* heard that Lady Frances gave Lady Dover the cut direct. I did not witness the insult myself, mind you. Still, I have no reason to doubt it. And I was told that Lady Dover was livid. Absolutely *livid*."

"Was this after the theater incident?" asked Kendra.

"I'm not entirely certain, but I believe so. It certainly would make sense, would it not?"

Lady Atwood murmured, "Indeed, it would."

They were silent for a moment. Then Kendra asked, "Was Lord Dover more angry than usual with his stepmother? Did something happen to cause even more friction between them?"

"No, not that I am aware . . . except, Lord Dover *was* at the theater on the night of the incident as well. And he has a reputation for being a prig. I can imagine that he was displeased by his stepmother's shameful behavior."

And he'd recently had a violent quarrel with Lady Dover—loud enough to draw the attention of her staff. This was interesting news.

"Had Lady Dover been involved with anyone else, besides Lord Weston?" Kendra asked.

"Oh, the woman always had young swains dancing attendance on her. Young Henry Dutton—Lord Ellery's son—made a cake of himself by asking her to dance two sets at the Hamilton Ball. Can you imagine? I will credit Lady Dover for very properly declining the second one." She pursed her lips as she considered the matter. "But as far as more serious dalliances go, the only men linked to her recently were Lord Weston and . . . well, Lord Sutcliffe, of course."

"My nephew did not murder the creature," Lady Atwood said stiffly.

"No, of course, not. Such a thing is too preposterous to even consider," Lady St. James assured her hurriedly.

But Kendra noticed how their hostess's gaze slid away. She might not know about the different ways someone could ignore a person in this society, but she understood that reaction. In the minds of the Ton, Alec had already been convicted.

16

Cordelia and Weston? Are you certain?" Alec asked.

With the exception of Sam, they'd assembled in the Duke's study—Aldridge behind his desk, Rebecca sitting on the sofa, and Alec sprawled in one of the chairs. Kendra had taken up a position before the slate board, and now eyed the Marquis with some concern. Earlier, the doctor had diagnosed him with bruised ribs, advising bed rest and offering him laudanum to ease his discomfort. Alec had refused both, and now his hand was wrapped around his own medicinal treatment: a glass of brandy.

Still, Kendra thought Alec's olive complexion had a sickly gray tinge to it. "Are you sure you're up for this?"

He lifted his glass in a sardonic gesture. "I'm quite well, thank you."

Rebecca brought the conversation back to the investigation. "I'd say the theater incident all but confirms the two were involved, Sutcliffe," she said. "Lady Dover's decision to wear the Weston jewels in public was tantamount to declaring war."

Alec inclined his head. "It was outrageous, even for Cordelia."

"Outrageous, and mayhap a clever stratagem to bring Lord Weston to heel."

Alec shot her an irritated look. "Becca, you make her sound as though she were Wellington campaigning to defeat Napoleon."

Rebecca returned his gaze with a pitying one of her own. "Men have little comprehension in such matters. I may be unwed, but I know that a woman on the hunt for a husband could out-strategize even Wellington."

"And yet that is the crux of the matter, my dear," the Duke pointed out mildly. "Lord Weston is already married. Lady Dover couldn't honestly believe he'd divorce his wife and marry her?"

"How difficult would that be?" Kendra asked. She liked to think she wasn't cynical enough to believe that people in the twenty-first century entered into marriage lightly or callously. However, if it didn't work out then, there was little social stigma to prevent divorce. This century's societal mores were different; she just wasn't entirely sure how different.

"It would create an enormous scandal," Aldridge said. "And it would be expensive. Lord Weston would have to sue the church and take the matter into court—and that would be *before* petitioning Parliament. I'm not certain what grounds Weston would even have to pursue such a course of action. He'd have to prove that his wife had committed adultery. Better to simply petition for legal separation."

"Not better for the wife." Rebecca's eyes narrowed. "A wife who's no longer living legally under the same roof as her husband is ostracized from society, while a man continues to be invited to soirees and balls. *His* life continues. *Hers* is finished."

Aldridge acknowledged the hypocrisy with a nod. "True. However, Lady Dover wouldn't fare much better than Lady

Weston. Why would she even attempt such a thing? She would have to be mad."

"Cordelia was not mad. She obviously thought she could bring Weston up to scratch. Such things do happen." Alec looked at his uncle. "Only consider Lord Bentinck and Lady Abdy."

The Duke frowned. "Caro informed me of their conduct." He caught Kendra's eye and explained, "Lord Charles Bentinck ran off earlier this month with Lady Anne Wellesley. They are married—unfortunately, not to each other."

"There is talk that Lady Abdy is with child," Alec said quietly. Kendra watched his green eyes become flat and faraway, and knew he was thinking about Lady Dover and her unborn child.

"'Tis still shocking, and requires a great amount of audacity," said Aldridge.

"I'd say that fits Lady Dover's personality." Kendra shifted her gaze to the slate board, under the Victimology column. "Think about it. She invented a new background for herself and pulled herself out of Cheapside, didn't she?"

"God, *Cheapside*." Alec's mouth twisted. "One would hope so."

"And it takes a lot of . . ." Kendra wanted to say *balls*, but knew that wasn't the right word for this time period. ". . . *audacity* to wear jewelry in public that belongs to the woman whose husband you're sleeping with."

The door opened and a footman stepped in to announce Sam's arrival. It seemed a bit redundant, considering the Bow Street Runner was already halfway into the room.

"Your Grace . . ." Sam began, then stopped when he spotted Rebecca. "M'lady, this is a wondrous surprise." He sketched a quick bow and smiled. But his smile slipped and his eyes widened when they fell on Alec. "Bloody hell. M'lord! What happened ter you? It looks like you've been in a mill!"

"Sutcliffe fought a ruffian named Bear," Rebecca told him. "Good evening, Mr. Kelly. I'm delighted to see you as well. It

would seem fate has drawn us together again—*Rota Fortunae.*"
She shot Kendra a smug smile. Kendra rolled her eyes.

Sam didn't notice the byplay. "Bear? Did you say, *Bear? The Bear?*"

"Yes." Rebecca raised her eyebrows, her turn to be surprised. "Are you are acquainted with the man, Mr. Kelly?"

"I know *of* him. His Christian name is Guy Ackerman, but everyone calls him Bear. They say he once fought a—"

"Bear," Kendra supplied. "Yeah, we heard. God knows, he's big enough for that rumor to be true. Who is he?"

"You encountered the rogue as well, Miss?"

"I was with Lord Sutcliffe at the time."

That brought him up short. "You were?"

"Yes. What do you know about him?"

He regarded her closely, probably checking for bruises or post-traumatic stress. When he didn't see either, he said, "Bear's a crime lord, Miss. Keeps mostly ter the flash houses in Cheapside." He looked back to Alec. "How'd you tangle with him, if you don't mind me askin', sir? He's a cutthroat, ter be sure, but it isn't like him ter take on the nobility with his fists."

"He's not exactly adverse to it, either," Alec muttered, sipping his brandy.

Sam's eyes widened. "Never say you fought with Bear and *won.*"

Alec scowled. "I'm not a fop, Mr. Kelly. I spar on a regular basis with Gentleman John Jackson himself."

"Oh. Aye, sir. It's just that Bear weighs at least twenty-one stone. He . . . ah . . ." Sam hesitated, then apparently realized there was no way he could extract himself from the insult he'd unintentionally delivered. He asked instead, "Do you want ter press charges? I can round up me men and go after him."

Alec sighed. "No, we've reached an understanding for now. I may reconsider the matter in two weeks."

"Two weeks, sir?"

Aldridge answered. "That's the length of time the criminal gave us to prove my nephew is innocent in Lady Dover's murder, before he attempts to dispense his own brand of justice." He pushed himself to his feet. "Would you like a drink, Mr. Kelly?"

Sam visibly perked up. "Aye, sir. Thank you."

"Whiskey?"

"If it's no trouble." Sam eyed the amber liquid with appreciation as the Duke splashed a generous four fingers into a stout glass. "I don't understand. Why would a man like Bear concern himself with Lady Dover's murder?"

"It would seem that they were acquainted when she lived in Cheapside," Kendra said. "More than acquainted, really. He appears to have been in love with her."

"But . . . Lady Dover's from *Cheapside*?"

Alec lifted his glass in a mocking toast. "My sentiments exactly. The horror."

Kendra ignored him. "It looks that way. Did you locate Lady Dover's coachman?"

"Aye, I did." He smiled as the Duke handed him the glass of whiskey. "For the last month, he's been deliverin' his mistress ter a cottage in St. Margaret's every Wednesday evening, half past nine. He then picked her up some time in the early morning hours."

"Who did Lady Dover meet?" Kendra asked.

"His duty was ter leave her off. He never saw the man." Sam paused to take a swallow of whiskey before continuing. "I made inquiries around the neighborhood. The cottage was purchased five months ago, but nobody's seen the owner."

"Obviously it was purchased for the purpose of being a place to rendezvous with Lady Dover," said Rebecca.

"Aye. I was given the address of a local widow who'd been hired ter clean the cottage and have a hot meal waitin', the fires and candles lit."

"Excellent." Aldridge smiled. "Who did she say hired her?"

"I don't know. The widow—Mrs. Frost—appears ter have disappeared."

The Duke asked, "What do you mean, she's disappeared?"

Sam shrugged. "She's gone. She was seen getting into a hackney, so I think she's still in London Town, unless she later got on a stagecoach ter take her elsewhere. I've got me men on it. We'll find her."

"'Tis too convenient. Why vanish now?" Rebecca shook her head. "Lord Weston must have bribed the woman into leaving, to avoid having his name become linked with Lady Dover's in such an intimate way."

"Lord Weston's name was linked with Lady Dover the moment she appeared in public wearing the Weston jewels," Aldridge pointed out.

Sam eyed the slate board. "Lord Weston—that's the cove that you think Lady Dover was having an affair with?"

"It looks that way," Kendra said.

Rebecca frowned. "I would agree that Lord Weston is a likely suspect, given his relationship with Lady Dover. Except for one thing—he was at the ball that his daughter, Lady Frances, threw on Monday night. Lady St. James said that the entire family attended, with the exception, of course, of Lady Weston."

"Lady St. James also said that most of London was at the ball," Kendra pointed out. "The bigger the crowd, the easier it is to slip away unnoticed. The real problem would be getting from Point A to Point B without being seen. Where was the ball held?"

"Presumably, the home of Lady Frances and her husband, Mr. Roberts," Rebecca replied.

Kendra went to study the map of London. "We need a location, and we can work from there." She looked at the Bow Street Runner. "Did you check with Lord Dover's club to see if he was there as he claimed?"

"I spoke with the porter and he told the same story as Lord Dover. His Lordship left the club at ten. The porter offered ter hail a hackney for the Earl, but Lord Dover declined the service, said he'd do it himself."

Kendra frowned. "Why would he do that?"

"I asked if Lord Dover was in the habit of hailing his own hackneys; the porter said His Lordship did it on occasion. Sometimes gentlemen who imbibe too much like ter walk a bit ter clear their heads before getting a hackney."

"And had Lord Dover imbibed too much?"

"The porter couldn't say. Or wouldn't." Sam shrugged. "I went ter Lord Dover's residence and interviewed the staff. They confirmed that His Lordship arrived home at eleven o'clock; the housekeeper was certain she'd heard the Watch yell out the time. Lord Dover's butler was also positive, as he'd been counting the household silver, a duty he says he performs before retiring, precisely at eleven."

Kendra heard the skeptical note in Sam's voice. "You don't believe them?"

His shoulders twitched in another shrug. "I don't know, just a feeling. They were both very certain, and in my experience, folks are never that certain. But can't say I blame them. Both the housekeeper and butler are older; they might worry about findin' another job if they lost their current positions. Either way, I'd like ter find the hackney driver that His Lordship hailed ter see what he says. I've got me men on it."

Kendra said, "Lady Dover was killed after eight and before eleven. If Lord Dover left at ten, that's not much time to get to his stepmother's to kill her before returning home. Of course, that's assuming the porter at his club got the time right. Have you learned anything more about Lady Dover's townhouse being robbed?"

"Nay. Me men are still making the rounds. Why?"

"I want to know if the Weston necklace was stolen, or if the unsub took it."

"The Weston necklace?"

Of course, Sam hadn't been in the room earlier. After Kendra had updated him about Lady Dover wearing the Weston family jewels to the theater, he nearly gave a low whistle, but caught himself from the vulgar act.

"It sounds like Lord Weston had a very good reason ter kill his mistress," he said instead.

Kendra jiggled the slate, her eyes drifting back to the slate board. "I'd say the whole damn family had a reason to want the woman dead."

17

J eans. Sneakers. Zippers. God, *chocolate*—the kind that you didn't just drink, but was poured over nuts and nougat and molded into candy bars to be savored later. PMS-suffering women would have to wait at least another three decades for their chocolate bar fix.

Kendra missed all of those things. But, most of all, she missed her FBI badge, and the status it brought her. Here, she had to rely on the Duke of Aldridge's power. But even he couldn't knock on a fellow peer of the realm's door at nine P.M. so his ward could interview him about his mistress's murder. Apparently, investigations in London that involved so-called polite society required a lot more finesse than those in the vicinity of Aldridge Castle, where the Duke was the largest landowner and thus held more clout. Here, they'd need a strategy.

It was actually Lady Atwood who came up with one when they—all but Sam—sat down for dinner. The Bow Street Runner had left to pursue his inquiries, or so he'd said. Kendra suspected that he'd left because the Countess intimidated him. She couldn't blame him for that. Hell, she wished she'd gone with him.

"The Digby Ball," Lady Atwood said, and gave a definitive nod.

The Duke paused in the act of spearing a tender asparagus stalk with his fork and peered across the candlelit, darkly paneled dining room at his sister. "Pardon? What's this about a Digby Ball, Caro?"

"I have been sorting the invitations we have received since our arrival in town. One is from Lord and Lady Digby, who are having a ball tomorrow evening. The *on dit* is that they will be announcing the engagement of their daughter to Sir Basil Radcliffe. I am certain most everyone in Town shall be attending." She gave them a meaningful look. "Lord Weston most likely will be in attendance."

"Ah." Aldridge gave a nod. "I have not made the acquaintance of Lord Weston, but this shall be an excellent way to make my introduction."

"Will the rest of the Weston family be there?" Kendra asked, slicing into the filet of beef and sauce Périgueux that the Duke's temperamental French chef, Monsieur Anton, had prepared. Having worked in the kitchens, Kendra knew the chef was high-strung and hostile toward the other servants—especially since he didn't classify himself as such—but when the savory steak almost melted on her tongue, she knew why the Duke kept the Frenchman on staff. He was a wizard in the kitchen.

"I'm not certain of the two married daughters, as they have their own households," Lady Atwood replied. "But the middle child, certainly. And most likely the Viscount, if he is looking for a bride. Lady Weston . . ." She gave a dainty shrug. "She has to come out of her bedchamber eventually. Lady Digby would be over the boughs if the woman used her fete to make her first appearance in society since that embarrassing incident at the theater."

Alec had brought a poultice to the table and was now pressing it against his swollen eye. Amusement gleamed in his good eye. "If you think cockfighting is a bloody sport, Miss Donovan, you haven't seen the Ton's tabbies circling some hapless victim," he drawled. "Never let their polite manners fool you."

"I never do."

"Obviously we do not have enough time to engage a dancing master for you, Miss Donovan," the Countess put in.

"Thank God," Kendra muttered, picking up her wineglass.

Lady Atwood's eyes narrowed. "We shall have to figure out some excuse as to why you do not know how to dance."

"How about: I can't dance?"

"Don't be stupid. *Everyone* knows how to dance, even scullery maids."

Rebecca looked at her. "You truly don't know how to dance, Miss Donovan?"

Kendra gave a small shrug. "I know how to waltz." That, at least, hadn't changed. Had it?

Alec gave her a crooked smile. "Put my name on your dance card, Miss Donovan."

"You shall not be accompanying us to the ball, Alec. You look like a ruffian yourself." Lady Atwood shot her nephew a stern look, but her gaze softened as she regarded his bruised face. "Are you in pain, dear?"

"I can manage to stand on the sidelines of a ballroom."

"You shall *not*. We'd be inundated with questions on your health all evening. Your association with this creature named Bear would set tongues wagging. You shall remain at home tomorrow evening, recuperating." Having made that announcement, the Countess turned to glare at Kendra. "And, of course, *you* would know the most scandalous dance in England."

Kendra raised her eyebrows. *The waltz—scandalous?*

"It was scandalous two years ago, Your Ladyship, but it *is* becoming more acceptable," Rebecca countered.

"Even a scapegrace like Lord Byron has condemned it as disgraceful." Lady Atwood sniffed. "One cannot have unmarried young ladies being *embraced* by gentlemen on the dance floor. 'Tis improper. I rather doubt Lady Digby will allow the waltz to be played at her ball."

Kendra wondered what Lady Atwood would think about dancing in the twenty-first century, the twitching and grinding that often caused consternation and controversy. Then she wondered about society further in the future. Would people in the twenty-second century eventually regard twerking as demure as she considered the waltz? That was hard to imagine.

Lady Atwood lifted her wineglass and viewed Kendra critically over the rim. "You shall have to wear one of your old evening gowns tomorrow. I've made an appointment with my modiste, but it isn't for a few more days."

Kendra felt the familiar panic rise within her. "I already told you, I don't need any more dresses."

"And I told you, as the Duke of Aldridge's ward, you shall dress appropriately."

"I can afford a new wardrobe for you, my dear," the Duke cut in with a smile. "Do not distress yourself."

Kendra's throat tightened unexpectedly, like a hand had closed around it, and she could only shake her head. She knew her anxiety was illogical. She couldn't explain, even to herself, why every new gown she was given made her feel that her present circumstance was becoming more permanent. Until Aldridge mentioned it, she hadn't thought about the expense. Now it added a fresh layer to her unease.

She looked across the table at the Duke. He knew about her true origins, but he still didn't understand. No one in this room, shifting with shadows and dancing candle flames, would possibly understand her disquiet. Lady Atwood, as a widow, was fairly independent, but only because she lived on the largesse of her late husband. The Countess had spent most of her life relying on someone else for the roof over her head, the clothes on her back, the food she ate at the table. Even Rebecca, for all her talk of women's rights, was completely dependent on her parents for her livelihood.

Kendra had once relied on her parents to take care of her, too—then they'd abandoned her. A cold sweat broke out on her palms even now when she remembered the mind-numbing terror that had come with the awareness that she was completely alone in the world. Thinking back, she supposed there were things to be grateful for. Plenty of children were tossed out of their families like trash, forced to do whatever they could to survive on the streets. She'd at least had a small trust fund to pay for school, and the computer skills to get a part-time job as a programmer.

The first year had been the worst. She'd focused with single-minded determination on her studies, on becoming self-reliant. By the time the FBI had sparked her interest, she'd built up her defenses—and her bank account. Money meant independence. The Bureau meant structure and discipline. She'd never realized how important both had been to her during that time of her life. She'd only known that she'd never wanted to be placed in the position again where she was completely dependent on another person for support.

Like I am now.

She didn't know how to operate in this strange class system. A washerwoman could at least earn her keep, as little as it was, while women in the upper echelon of society were kept by the men in their lives, whether they were father, husband, son—or guardian. She couldn't even buy herself a new gown without approval. How was she ever going to get home? And how could she ever accept *this* life? To rely so heavily on people, even someone as kind as the Duke, after she'd spent years becoming self-reliant, made her feel slightly nauseous.

She became aware that everyone was looking at her, waiting for a response to the Duke's generosity. She cleared her throat, and finally murmured, "Thank you, Your Grace." Really, what else could she say?

The conversation shifted into more trivial subjects. Kendra remained silent, and her mind drifted back to the investigation.

Two weeks. Bear's threat seemed even more dire than the possibility of the House of Lords charging Alec with murder. She knew with absolute certainty that the criminal would make good on his promise to exact justice. And his fury would no longer be hot as it had been today. It would be ice-cold and hardened into vengeance. That would make him even more dangerous. In two weeks, nothing would stop him.

I just need to focus; I just need to do my job. This survival tactic had worked well for her in the past. Only now, it wasn't her survival that hung in the balance. An icy shiver snaked down her spine.

She needed to find Lady Dover's murderer. Alec's life depended on it.

18

Kendra got her first look at Lord Weston when he moved past her on the dance floor at the Digby Ball. He cut a trim figure in his dark blue superfine jacket, taupe knee breeches, and white stockings. Late forties; average height of about five-ten. He still had a full head of light brown hair, tinged with silver, that shimmered in the glow of the candles and wall lamps. He was attractive in a distinguished way, but sporting shadows under his eyes that Kendra could see from across the room.

Was he having trouble sleeping because his mistress had been murdered? Or because he was the one who'd murdered her?

At least two hundred people had crowded into the Digby mansion. The music from the five-piece orchestra blended with the low murmur of conversation. The ballroom was large but stuffy. The day had taken a turn for the worse, with clouds and a light rain arriving along with the evening, forcing the Digbys to close all their doors. A liberal use of perfume and cologne permeated the mansion in an attempt to mask everyone's body odor.

Lemon wedges and lavender water went only so far.

Kendra allowed her gaze to drift to the woman gliding next to Lord Weston—*Lady Weston*. She was at least a head shorter than her husband and a few years younger, with dark brown hair pulled to the top of her head. Nice figure; pleasant-looking, but nowhere near Lady Dover's stunning beauty.

How did that feel? Kendra wondered. Looking across a crowded theater, and seeing your husband's younger and more beautiful mistress wearing jewels that were rightfully yours? To know that he had given them to her?

"Poor woman," Rebecca whispered next to her. "This is Lady Weston's first public appearance since the scandal at the theater."

"I guess Lady St. James was right—most of London seems to have come out to see her." Kendra considered the woman for a moment more, then said, "We'll need to get Lady Weston's alibi confirmed."

"She was in seclusion at home."

"Was she?"

"But you can't possibly think . . . *Lady* Weston . . . ?"

They were standing in the corner of the ballroom and even though everyone around them seemed preoccupied in their own conversations, Kendra was careful to keep her voice low. "Lady Dover was killed by a stiletto. She was taken by surprise, not overpowered. None of that requires any great strength. And don't forget, we're dealing with an enraged killer. And rage is exactly what Lady Weston must've been feeling toward Lady Dover."

She studied the woman's blank face, her gaze fixed at some undefined point in front of her as the Westons surged forward in their dance steps. *Rage is probably what she's still feeling*, Kendra amended silently. Hell, how could she not?

Lord Weston, she noticed, wasn't looking at his wife, either. Their arms were raised, their hands linked, but there could've been a million miles between them.

"I need to talk to both of them," Kendra said.

"That will require some finesse, Miss Donovan. You can hardly quiz Lord Weston—or Lady Weston, for that matter—in the middle of the dance floor. And this particular set takes nearly half an hour to complete."

"Half an hour? For *one* dance?"

Rebecca merely smiled. "Come along, Miss Donovan. If I'm not mistaken, Lord Weston's eldest daughter, Lady Isabella, is standing near the painting of King George. I have a brief acquaintance with her, so we do not require an introduction."

They wound their way through knots of people. The Duke and Lady Atwood were in the same set as the Westons. Kendra glimpsed Lady St. James on the other side of the room, seated in the middle of a clique of women. She was wearing a mustard-colored evening gown, as frilly and flouncy as the gown she'd worn earlier. She'd exchanged her lace cap for a silk yellow turban with a large white ostrich feather that bounced back and forth as she undoubtedly told her seatmates about their visit the previous afternoon, Kendra thought.

Finally, they came to a halt in front of two women. Rebecca smiled at the taller of the two, who was wearing a deep crimson gown. She was attractive with sharp features and dark brown hair styled in the familiar topknot, held in place by a diamond comb. More diamonds circled her throat. Her eyes were hazel and cool as they regarded Rebecca.

"Lady Isabella. Pray, forgive my boldness, but I wanted to renew our acquaintance." Rebecca gave a small curtsy. "We met last fall at Mrs. Ashworth's salon. I am Lady Rebecca. My father is Lord Blackburn?"

Lady Isabella's eyes didn't warm, but her thin lips curved in a practiced smile and she offered her own curtsy. "Of course,

I remember, my lady. How do you do? This is my sister, Lady Louisa." She indicated the woman standing next to her, who wore a gauzy gown in pale pink.

Like Isabella, Louisa had dark brown hair and hazel eyes. Unfortunately, that's where their resemblance ended. Loose side curls framed a pale, plain face dominated by a beak-like nose and receding chin.

"Good evening, Lady Louisa," Rebecca said. "And may I introduce Miss Donovan. She is from America . . . and she is the ward of the Duke of Aldridge."

Both pairs of hazel eyes swung around to inspect Kendra like she was an exotic animal at a petting zoo.

"An American," Lady Isabella said. "How very interesting. How long have you been in England, Miss Donovan?"

Despite her misgivings, Kendra gave an abbreviated version of the cover story that the Duke had invented. Lady Isabella and Lady Louisa accepted it without even blinking.

"You are fortunate to have the Duke of Aldridge as your benefactor," Lady Isabella said.

Lady Louisa asked, "Will you never return to America then?"

I wish I knew the answer to that, Kendra thought. "I'm here for now."

"My husband, Mr. Sedwick, is interested in foreign affairs." Lady Isabella gave them a smile that veered toward smug. "He works for Lord Sidmouth, the Home Secretary."

Rebecca didn't appear impressed. "Tell me, is our former prime minister still rabidly against Catholic emancipation?"

Lady Isabella raised her eyebrows, surprised. "Certainly. Lady Rebecca, surely you cannot side with the position of the younger Mr. Pitt, who would actually allow the papists to hold positions of power? Their allegiance will always be to the pope, not the crown. Mr. Sedwick says that if we ever were to allow Catholics to own land or to have a voice in government, we would find ourselves in middle of a civil war." She gave a shiver. "Only look at what Ireland has endured with their rebellion."

"I'm inclined to look at what the Irish have been forced to endure because of British rule."

"Surely you jest? Mr. Sedwick says that the Irish do not have the fortitude to govern themselves. You cannot deny that they are a drunken, crude lot. Mr. Sedwick says that we are being good Christians by guiding them with a firm hand."

"Whatever would they do without us?"

"Yes, indeed." Lady Isabella didn't seem to hear the sarcasm in Rebecca's voice. "Now, enough talk of such matters. Politics, as Mr. Sedwick says, is a man's concern. Women simply do not have the head for it." She turned to Kendra. "What brings His Grace to London even before the season begins?"

"Lady Dover's murder."

There were a million more diplomatic ways to broach the subject, but Kendra wanted to shake them up and observe their reaction. The sisters stared at her in shock, and something else, something that Kendra thought might be fear.

Lady Louisa put a hand to her throat, her eyes like saucers. "Whatever do you mean, Miss Donovan? Why would His Grace come to London for such a thing?"

Rebecca had appeared nonplussed by her blunt introduction to the subject as well. But she took her cue from Kendra, and said, "You must have heard that the Duke's nephew, the Marquis of Sutcliffe, has come under suspicion for Lady Dover's terrible death. 'Tis ridiculous, of course. The Duke and Miss Donovan shall find the fiend who truly committed this monstrous act."

Lady Isabella stared at Rebecca. "The Duke of Aldridge is a gentleman, my lady. A peer of the realm." Her diamond comb twinkled like stars as she shook her head in denial. "He would hardly soil his hands in something so vulgar as murder. And Miss Donovan . . . pray, take no offense, Miss Donovan, but you are a woman."

Kendra recognized the militant light that flared in Rebecca's eyes. "I think women are vastly underestimated in the world,"

Rebecca said hotly. "Only look at the aeronaut Sophie Blanchard. Until she took to the skies, everyone thought women had no place air ballooning." Her upper-class accent had become sharp enough to cut glass, a good indicator, Kendra had learned, of her irritation.

"Miss Donovan is a woman who happens to have an expertise in criminal investigation," she continued. "In fact, her deductive reasoning is quite singular. Only last month, Miss Donovan was responsible for solving several ghastly murders around Aldridge Castle. 'Tis why the Duke brought her to London with him."

The statement didn't have the expected reaction. Lady Isabella laughed. "You are telling a Banbury tale, Your Ladyship!"

"I can assure you I am not," Rebecca replied, insulted. "You must have heard about the villain murdering Unfortunate Women near Aldridge Village. It was Miss Donovan's investigation that uncovered the monster. She has a peculiar talent for solving crime. I have no doubt that she will find Lady Dover's murderer as well."

Once again the sisters regarded Kendra like she had 666 carved into her forehead.

"You speak as though Miss Donovan is a Bow Street Runner," Lady Louisa said finally. "'Tis absurd—"

"The Duke is a Man of Science," Rebecca interrupted, "hardly a nodcock. He had the foresight to utilize Miss Donovan's unique skills last month. London Town will be able to rest easy; the fiend who murdered Lady Dover shall be caught."

Lady Isabella and Lady Louisa didn't seem to know what to say to that pronouncement. Their stares made Kendra's neck prickle. She wasn't sure if Rebecca's strong advocacy had done her any favors, but decided to roll with it.

"I heard that you were at a ball on the night Lady Dover was murdered. Is that true?" Kendra asked, and waited out the awkward silence.

"The ball was hosted by our sister, Lady Frances, and her husband, Mr. Roberts," Lady Isabella said with cool condescension. "It was a lovely evening."

"Not for Lady Dover," Kendra remarked drily.

Lady Louisa frowned. "We were not well acquainted with Lady Dover."

"Really? What did you know of her?"

Lady Isabella flushed, her jaw tightening. "Everyone knew the creature was practically a lightskirt."

"I met her, you know—a month ago, at Lady Atwood's house party," Kendra said. "She wasn't a very nice woman."

"No, she was not," Lady Louisa agreed curtly. She looked like she was going to say something else, but a tall, thin man, carrying two glasses of lemonade, squeezed his way through the crowd to stand before them.

"I apologize for the delay, madam, but 'tis bedlam." He offered Lady Isabella and Lady Louisa the glasses of lemonade, and then glanced curiously at Rebecca and Kendra. "Forgive me for interrupting. Will you introduce me to your friends, my dear?"

Lady Isabella's mouth flattened into a tight, thin line. For a moment, Kendra thought she'd refuse, and wondered if they'd just invented a whole new category of getting the cut. But then she grudgingly performed the duty.

"Mr. Sedwick, this is Lady Rebecca and Miss Donovan. Lady Rebecca is Lord Blackburn's daughter, and Miss Donovan is the Duke of Aldridge's ward. This is my husband, Mr. Sedwick."

"Good evening, ladies." He wore the same practiced smile that his wife had given them earlier, the kind of smile that politicians used when they were holding babies and flashbulbs went off. It reminded Kendra instantly that the man worked for the government.

He was in his early thirties, Kendra surmised, with mouse-brown hair cut into the popular windswept Brutus style. Unfortunately, the heat of the ballroom had the curls sticking to the sweat on his forehead. The heat had also wilted his intricately tied cravat, which had probably begun the evening starched and perfectly folded.

"Would you care for some lemonade?" he asked.

"No, thank you."

"Are you certain, Miss Donovan?" Lady Isabella asked, her gaze challenging. "Being a Bow Street Runner must leave you thirsty."

Sedwick shot his wife a puzzled look.

"Goodness—'tis warm in here!"

That laughing declaration came from a young, dark-haired woman who sailed into their group. She wore a gorgeous gown of ice green silk with a train long enough to require her to hold it in one small hand. Her other hand was tucked into the crook of an arm of a much older gentleman. She shot them all a dazzling smile that revealed even white teeth and two dimples. "The Digbys ought to crack open a door to the veranda before someone faints."

Introductions were made once more, and Kendra learned that the woman was the third Weston sister, Lady Frances, and her escort was one Lord Ludlow. Talk turned back to the ball, and Lady Frances took a breath and fluttered her lashes at her escort, who was at least five decades her senior. "Lord Ludlow was good enough to escort me out of the mayhem. I swear my feet are ready to fall off, I've danced so much this evening!"

"My pleasure, Lady Frances." The older man gave a stiff bow.

Kendra could've sworn she heard his bones creaking. He was dressed in the same jacket, shirt, cravat, breeches, and silk hose that the rest of the men in the ballroom wore, but he'd covered his head with a powdered periwig, an accessory that Kendra had come to learn had been abandoned by most men during this timeline, except for liveried footmen or those serving in a court of law. He could've been bald, Kendra supposed, and vain enough in his seventh decade to try to hide it. Yet she sensed that it wasn't lack of hair, but a dogged commitment to dress in the style of his youth, that had him continuing to don the wig, like the sexagenarians in her era who insisted on wearing leopard-print leggings and tube tops long after they should've retired them.

"Lord Ludlow." Lady Louisa stepped forward, and offered a smile that made her weak chin vanish altogether. "You are looking in excellent health. I . . . I have not seen you at recent routs."

Lord Ludlow turned slowly—maybe it was the only way he could move, Kendra thought—to regard Lady Louisa with rheumy eyes.

"I have been busy with my estates, Lady Louisa."

That statement resulted in a weird silence, thrumming with expectation. *Lord Ludlow.* The name rang a bell. Then Kendra remembered: he was the aristocrat that Lady St. James had said Lady Louisa was hoping to marry.

Holy crap.

"My sisters have abominable manners." Lady Frances turned, and smiled at Rebecca and Kendra. "We have not been introduced. I am Lady Frances."

As Rebecca responded, Kendra considered the oddity of genetics. Lady Frances had inherited the same dark hair and hazel eyes as her sisters, but she'd received the bounty of looks in the family. Her skin, even filmed with sweat from the overheated ballroom, was flawless. Her eyes were more green than brown. And the features in her heart-shaped face were arranged in such a way to turn heads.

"Mr. Sedwick, would you be a dear and get me a glass of lemonade?" She gave her brother-in-law a dimpled smile. "Baron Faust requested the next dance, but I'll collapse if I don't have something to drink!"

"We cannot have that, my lady." He smiled and dutifully plunged back into the crowd to fight his way to the refreshment room.

"Perhaps you ought to sit out a few sets, my dear, to recover," Lady Isabella suggested, in such a way as to make Kendra wonder if she resented Lady Frances using her husband as a servant.

"For shame, sister. I cannot disappoint Baron Faust." Lady Frances fluttered her fan. "I do wish Lady Digby would play the waltz, though. 'Tis a glorious dance. I vow I shall introduce it at my next ball."

Apparently, Lady Isabella shared Lady Atwood's disapproval of the dance, because she said, "Don't be stupid, Frances. Such indecency shall never be accepted in England."

Lady Frances gave her sister a sharp, almost feline smile. "It's already being accepted, dear. The courts of Vienna have been dancing the waltz for years, and I have even attended assemblies here in London that have included it. Mr. Roberts and I have danced it. The Countess de Lieven is an admirer of it, and I hear that she is petitioning to bring it to Almack's."

"I do not believe it."

"When did you become such a prig, my dear?" Lady Frances laughed, and turned to Rebecca and Kendra. "You would not credit it, but when we were children, Isabella persuaded Louisa and I to sneak out of our schoolroom by climbing down the tree in the backyard so we could feed sugar lumps and apples to the horses in the stables. We were very naughty, but it was a grand adventure."

Ludlow frowned. "It sounds quite dangerous."

Lady Frances gave the old man a playful tap with her fan. "Oh, it was, I assure you. Which is why it was such fun."

Lady Louisa forced a laugh that sounded too shrill. "Do not tell Lord Ludlow such fairytales, Frances. I would never have behaved in such an ill-mannered way. You are misremembering the incident."

"I remember it exactly, sister dear. In fact, you were first out the window. A regular hoyden."

Kendra observed the sisters' interaction with interest. She'd never known her half siblings—from her father's second marriage—but she'd seen similar rivalries when she'd gone to college. It had been awkward to be so much younger than her classmates, but it had allowed her to observe them as they jockeyed for positions in the social hierarchy, to witness what she'd always thought was a shocking amount of pettiness.

Lady Frances might have been the youngest of the three girls, but Kendra suspected that her natural beauty had given her a great deal of confidence. Her more advantageous match—with her husband in line for an earldom—had apparently increased her self-assurance.

Her snide comment made Lady Louisa turn red. She looked quickly to Lord Ludlow and assured him, "Lady Frances is teasing, sir."

"Ah, yes . . ." His gaze barely touched Lady Louisa's before drifting off. "I must take my leave." He offered another creaking bow, then made a quick retreat into the crowd—well, as quick a retreat as a man his age could manage.

Lady Louisa looked stricken. Then she glared at her younger sister. "How could you say such a thing, Frances? You know His Lordship is a high stickler when it comes to propriety!"

"Calm down, darling. You are turning into the ape leader you so fear. We were children. Oh, Mr. Sedwick," she purred, as her brother-in-law returned with her lemonade. "You are a godsend, sir. I swear, one more minute, I'd have sipped from the Thames itself."

"Where is Mr. Roberts this evening?" Lady Isabella asked abruptly.

"Heaven knows." Frances gave a shrug before sipping her lemonade. "He mentioned spending time at his club. He may come here later." She took another swallow of her drink, then handed the glass back to her brother-in-law. "Now, I do believe the dance has finally come to an end. I really ought to find Baron Faust. It was lovely to meet you, Lady Rebecca, Miss Donovan." She gathered up her train again and as gracefully as she'd sailed into the group, she sailed out again.

Sedwick collected the empty glasses and waved down one of the circulating footmen to deposit them on his tray. Returning, he offered his arm to his wife. "I have been remiss in my duties— would you care to dance, madam?"

"Thank you, sir." Lady Isabella gave a distant nod to Rebecca and Kendra. "Good evening."

Kendra glanced at the sister who'd been left behind and felt an unexpected surge of sympathy for Lady Louisa. There was something forlorn about the woman as she stood with her gaze fixed on the parade of men and women gliding by on the dance floor.

Rebecca must have felt it too. She gave the other woman a kind smile. "Do not be distressed by your sister's story, my lady. Personally, I'm of the mind that children ought to get into mischief once in awhile, otherwise they'll become spineless adults."

Lady Louisa stiffened. "My sister spins tales. I have never been so unladylike, so ill-bred. I . . . I need to go to the withdrawing room. If you'll pardon me . . ." She dipped into a quick curtsy and hurried away without meeting either Kendra's or Rebecca's eyes.

Kendra expelled the breath she hadn't even realized she'd been holding, and shot Rebecca a look filled with irony. "Well, my lady . . . I guess we both need to work on our finesse."

19

Rebecca had the grace to look sheepish after Lady Louisa's hasty exit. "I don't know what I was thinking through that entire discussion. When Lady Isabella was admiring that idiot Sidmouth, it became clear that she didn't have a thought in her head except what was put there by Mr. Sedwick. I was annoyed."

"And you thought you'd be less annoyed if you told them that I was investigating Lady Dover's murder? That my deductive reasoning is quite singular? That I had an expertise in criminal investigation?"

"Did I say that?"

"You did."

"Well, I have complete faith in you, Miss Donovan."

Kendra gave her a wry look. "So much for flying under the radar."

"What does that even mean?" Rebecca's eyebrows pulled together in a perplexed frown, but as she had apparently grown accustomed to the American's odd expressions, she waved away the question almost immediately. "Never mind. I confess that I let my temper get the better of me, Miss Donovan. 'Tis sad that the spirit Lady Isabella and Lady Louisa displayed as children has been diminished."

"Lady Frances seems to have enough spirit for all of them."

"Yes, I saw that. Though she was unkind to Lady Louisa with her comment about being an ape leader."

"Yeah, what exactly is that?"

"'Tis a spinster, Miss Donovan. You must know the expression. Women who fail to be fruitful and multiply are punished in the afterlife by leading apes into hell."

"I think I'd prefer that to being married to Lord Ludlow. He isn't exactly a prize. Unless there's another Lord Ludlow, maybe a century younger?"

Rebecca's lips twitched. "Keep your voice down, Miss Donovan. And, no, that is the only Lord Ludlow."

"He's older than Methuselah. His bones creaked."

Rebecca laughed. "Those were his stays. Some men wear them, like the Prince Regent. The device helps with their . . . form." She paused. "Poor Lady Louisa. From what we witnessed, her efforts are for naught. Lord Ludlow's interest has faded."

"She should be celebrating."

"Really, Miss Donovan? Being on the shelf, unwanted and disregarded? Society doesn't look kindly upon women who fail to secure a marriage by the time they're twenty-one."

"You don't seem to be doing so badly." Kendra said it with a smile and expected Rebecca to agree. She was surprised when Rebecca turned solemn.

She said softly, "I'm fortunate to have a family sympathetic to my circumstance. Look at me, Miss Donovan." Rebecca deliberately thrust her chin up so the golden light played across the pitted skin. "Do you know what I've been called behind my back? Do you think that any man desires to have someone who looks like me as a bride?"

Kendra didn't know what to say. It had never occurred to her that Rebecca might dream of marriage and motherhood. It wasn't just her talk of the early feminist Mary Wollstonecraft; it was her air of confidence and contentment.

But maybe she'd projected her own unconventional views onto Rebecca. And the thing was, Kendra had never discounted marriage and motherhood for herself, either. It just hadn't been something she'd thought much about. In western civilization, in the modern era, women had a vast array of choices. You didn't regard yourself as a shriveled-up spinster at the age of twenty-six. Hell, you didn't view yourself that way at ninety-six.

"Do not look at me with pity, Miss Donovan," Rebecca warned, her eyes narrowing.

Did she pity Rebecca? Kendra gave the matter serious thought. The answer surprised her.

"I don't pity you."

Rebecca seemed skeptical. "No?"

"No," she said unequivocally. "Look, I'm sorry you were teased and ostracized when you were a child. Believe me, I know what it feels like to be an outsider. But I like who you are now. If you hadn't had smallpox, you might have had a more traditional upbringing. You would have had your season." And from what she could determine, the sole purpose of a season was pairing debutantes with potential husbands. It was *The Bachelor* without the TV cameras.

"You might have turned out exactly like Lady Isabella and her sisters," Kendra concluded.

"Good heavens. Put like that, Miss Donovan, you make me grateful that I had smallpox and nearly cocked up my toes." Rebecca's grin came back. "My parents may have indulged me, encouraging my more intellectual pursuits as there is little chance of me securing a husband. But I do know married women who are admirers of Mary Wollstonecraft. I also know single women who have not had smallpox, but are concerned with the lack of rights for English women."

"It was just a thought."

"Yes, and a very interesting one. Along that same vein, what of you, Miss Donovan?"

"Me?"

"Yes, you. You are a most unusual female—and that is a compliment. I would like to hear about your life in America. Your background. Your family."

Where do I start? Kendra thought, but shook her head. "It's a long story."

Rebecca smiled, but her eyes remained sharp. "I'm not asking you tell it in the middle of the Digby ball. But someday, when you are ready to confide in me, Miss Donovan, I shall be ready to listen."

❖

It was nearly midnight by the time Kendra finally got her chance to talk to Lord Weston. She'd kept him under surveillance for hours. For most of the evening, he'd spent his time on the dance floor, though not with his wife. After that first obligatory dance, they seemed to avoid each other. Back in the twenty-first century, the couple would have had their high-priced divorce lawyers on speed-dial, trying to figure out ways to stick it to each other in court, or hiding their assets in the Cayman Islands. Here, they danced and stayed out of each other's way. Very civilized. Kendra didn't trust it.

Beneath someone's civilized smile existed a violent rage that had propelled them to drive a stiletto into Lady Dover's soft flesh forty-three times. And after she lay dead, when their fury should have been spent, the killer had then been compelled to mutilate the woman's face. That aspect of the crime remained the most troubling.

Kendra touched the Duke's arm lightly when she saw Weston moving toward the arched doorway that opened to the hallway. Rebecca was, at that moment, on the dance floor, engaged in a quadrille, which to Kendra's eyes seemed to be more or less a sedate version of the square dance. Lady Atwood had joined Lady St. James in the area staked out by society's matrons, their sharp eyes watching everything.

Aldridge gave a slight nod to let her know that he understood. "Shall we stroll, Miss Donovan?"

They discarded their glasses and wove their way through the press of warm bodies, Kendra making good use of the Japanese fan that dangled from her wrist as they went. Earlier, when Miss Cooper had given it to her, she'd regarded it as nothing more than a silly fashion accessory. But it was proving a useful tool to combat the oppressive heat caused by two hundred plus people packed into a relatively small space. As she fanned herself, she could feel the beads of moisture evaporating from her brow. Unfortunately, it did nothing to stop the thin line of perspiration from wiggling down her spine or between her breasts.

More people were loitering in the hallway, drinking lemonade or wine, engaged in idle conversation. Kendra and the Duke caught up to Lord Weston before he entered the library, which had been converted into a game room for the evening.

"Lord Weston . . . good evening," Aldridge called out, causing the man to stop and turn.

Recognition registered in Weston's brown eyes. "Your Grace, good evening." He bowed.

"May I introduce my ward, Miss Donovan?"

Another bow. "How do you do?"

"We should speak in private." Aldridge scanned the hallway with a frown, then ushered them farther down toward a shadowy alcove. It wasn't really private, but if they kept their voices low, they wouldn't be overheard.

"What is this about, sir?" Weston gave them a quizzical smile.

Kendra said, "We understand that you attended your daughter's ball on Monday evening. Do you remember what time you arrived?"

Weston frowned. "The ball began at nine. I arrived not long after. Why?"

"Did you come alone?"

"No. My daughter Louisa accompanied me. What's this about?"

"What time did you leave?"

He was silent for a long moment. "I don't recall precisely," he said finally, and then glanced at the Duke. "Sir, I really must insist that you tell me what these questions are about."

"I am in London to investigate the murder of Lady Dover," Aldridge told him.

Weston inhaled sharply at that pronouncement. Kendra watched him carefully, saw something flicker in his eyes and then was gone.

"You were involved with her," Kendra added. She'd deliberately made it a statement, not a question, to see how Weston would react. In her experience, married men who were confronted with their infidelity usually had one of two kneejerk responses: flat-out denial (*Who, me? I would never cheat on my wife.*) or outrage (*How dare you? I'm a happily married man!*)

Weston displayed neither. His eyes darted quickly up and down the hall, searching for potential eavesdroppers. Then he edged closer. "Are you trying to embarrass me, Miss Donovan? My family has suffered enough because of . . ." He paused and pressed his lips together in a tight line for a second, then he cleared his throat and continued, "Because of my association with Lady Dover."

"We know about the incident at the theater. Did you manage to retrieve your family's necklace?"

He hesitated. "No."

"But you did *try* to retrieve it, didn't you?"

His eyes widened. "What are you talking about?"

"We have witnesses that saw you with Lady Dover after the incident."

Weston went very still. "Well, yes, of course," he admitted. "I met with Cordelia the next morning. I requested that she return the jewels. I hardly think that is unusual."

"What was her response?"

The brown eyes narrowed, and Kendra thought she saw the first stirrings of real anger. "I think you are aware of her response, Miss Donovan," he snapped.

"Not to you. However, we heard that she laughed at your son when he met with her to make the same request."

Weston flushed and said nothing. He was sweating, Kendra observed. But then so was everyone at the ball. She couldn't use that as a barometer to gauge his nerves.

"You must have been very angry with Lady Dover for putting you and your family in this position." She waited a beat. "When was the last time you saw her?"

"I already told you: the day after the theater incident."

"You didn't meet with her again? Maybe at the cottage in St. Margaret's?"

"I don't know what you're talking about."

Kendra leveled a long look at him. "We know about the cottage, my lord. We know you purchased it for her about five months ago." They actually didn't know that, but Weston couldn't know she was lying.

He tore his gaze away from hers and threw a beseeching glance at the Duke. "This is not the time or place for this sort of discussion, Your Grace."

Aldridge's face fell into solemn lines and he suddenly looked every inch his title. "I apologize, my lord, but this discussion must be had. You realize that, do you not?"

"But not here, sir."

Kendra pressed, "Then when?"

Weston licked his lips, scanning the hallway again. "Tomorrow. I have an appointment at noon, but I shall be available in the morning."

"We shall call upon you at eleven," said the Duke.

Weston gave a sharp bow and walked away—not into the gaming room, which had been his original destination, Kendra noticed. Instead, he retraced his footsteps down the hall, disappearing back into the crowds of the ballroom.

"Something tells me that the Westons will be leaving shortly," she murmured.

"Yes, I believe we may have spoiled the evening for Lord Weston." Aldridge lifted a brow as he fixed his gray-blue eyes on her. "My memory may be faulty, but I don't seem to recall a witness who saw Weston with Lady Dover after the theater incident."

Kendra feigned confusion. "Really? My mistake."

Aldridge laughed. "Very clever, my dear."

"Weston had no intention of telling us that he'd visited Lady Dover the morning after the theater to demand the necklace back," she replied, serious again.

"Yes, well, very few men would admit to the humiliation, if she refused him."

"He also lied about the cottage at St. Margaret's. And, yes, I know, a married man might not want to admit that either, but a lie here and a lie there . . . it makes me wonder what else His Lordship is lying about."

20

Sam Kelly stepped into the Blind Duck. He paused for a moment, just to appreciate the pub's warmth against the fog and cold at his back. Though it was long past midnight, the taproom was crowded, and noisy with talk and raucous laughter. Smoke from the coals burning in the fireplace, tallow candles and oil lamps, as well as the pipes and cigars lit by the tavern's many patrons hung gray in the air, thick enough to make his eyes sting.

He blinked a few times, then scanned the room. He spotted his quarry at the corner table, just as his informant had said. Keeping a wary eye out for trouble, Sam forced himself to walk slow and steady to the table.

The woman was surrounded by three men, two seated beside her, one draped over her shoulder. She was somewhere in her late forties, he thought, with her reddish-brown curls, streaked with silver, tucked into a linen mop cap. She wore a serviceable brown wool gown, with a white fichu tucked in the neckline. As Sam approached, the man standing behind her leaned down, his hand stretched to grab a plump breast.

"C'mon, Abby, me love, let's have a go," he wheedled.

Rather than take offense, she laughed, and lightly swatted the splayed hand. "Ack, yer a familiar one, y'are, Mr. Hobbs. Ye behave yerself!" She picked up her stout glass and tossed back the whiskey like a woman who'd had practice.

"Mrs. Frost?" Sam inquired.

She lowered the empty glass. "Who wants ter know?"

Sam brought out his baton, flashing its distinctive gold tip. "Sam Kelly—Bow Street Runner."

"What's a thief-taker want with the likes of her?" asked the man whose hand was still on Mrs. Frost's breast.

"Only a few questions, nothing more," Sam replied, and brought out a couple of coins, which he laid on the table. "Maybe you fellows would like ter get a drink at the tap while Mrs. Frost and me have words."

The men didn't need more persuading. The coins disappeared and the two men who'd been sitting departed quickly. Mr. Hobbs lingered long enough to give Mrs. Frost another squeeze.

"I'll be back, love." He grinned, before following his friends to the tap.

Sam signaled the barmaid and took a seat. "You tended a cottage in St. Margaret's."

"Aye." Her hand went to the center of her chest, in an automatic, protective gesture.

Sam kept his expression neutral, but he thought this was telling. He knew lasses sometimes kept their money in pouches, tucked in their chemise. He suspected Mrs. Frost had a pouch of money hidden in just that spot. And because her instinctive action seemed prompted by the mention of St. Margaret's, it didn't require any great imagination to suspect that the two were linked.

"Two whiskeys," he told the barmaid who came around and gave her two coins. There was no reason he shouldn't take advantage of being in the Blind Duck as well.

"Who paid you ter tend the cottage?" he asked, eyeing the widow.

"A man-of-affairs. Called himself Mr. Kent. I was ter clean the cottage, wash the linens, have supper waitin' every Wednesday night. Fancy French food." Her nose wrinkled. "I can cook anythin' with a pot and fire, but give me a proper English pigeon pie, I say. Not Froggy food."

"Who made use of the cottage, Mrs. Frost?"

"It weren't Mr. Kent, I can tell ye that." She gave a snort. "I dunno who I was cookin' and cleanin' for, but they were gentry." Her eyes gleamed with sly amusement. "Or at least the man was. Dunno about the woman."

"How'd you know that they were gentry, if you never saw them?"

"They left things about, fripperies and the like. And I can't complain about me wages. He weren't clutch-fisted."

"How'd you get your wages?"

"Mr. Kent sometimes would come 'round, or he'd send a boy with me wages and instructions. Every fortnight." She paused when the barmaid circled back to deliver the whiskeys.

"Where can I find Mr. Kent?" Sam asked once the maid had left.

"I told ye, he came ter me."

"How long did you take care of the cottage?"

"Five or six months, or thereabouts. It was a tidy business." She took a swallow of the whiskey, then let out a deep sigh. "I'm gonna miss it."

"I was in St. Margaret's. Your neighbors said you'd cleared off."

Again, she touched the spot between her breasts. "Aye. No point in stickin' around, is there?"

"Not when you were told ter go."

She gave him a belligerent stare. "Who says I was told ter go? Me brothers live around these parts. No law against me visitin' them."

"Don't lie, Mrs. Frost." He matched her stare with one of his own. "You have no cause ter protect anyone. You did your duty, and are well out of it. Did Mr. Kent send you packing?"

She considered his words, then shrugged. "Aye. He paid me a nice sum and told me ter leave for a while. I got the feelin' he didn't want trouble for his master or mistress, whoever owned the cottage."

"You don't know the owner's identity?"

"Old Man Fenn used ter own it, but he sold it around the time I was hired. Probably ter Mr. Kent, or his master. I suppose they'll either sell it or rent it out. Plenty of London coves wantin' their privacy, if ye take me meaning."

"Are you sure you can't give me Mr. Kent's address?" Sam stared hard at the woman, but she moved her plump shoulders again.

"Nay. I'm telling ye the truth, God's witness. Mr. Kent's a wily one, ain't he?"

Sam tried a different tack. "Did you ever hear the name Lord Weston mentioned?"

She frowned, apparently thinking back. "Nay," she said finally.

"You said the couple left things about. Like what?"

She blinked several times, then her gaze slid away. "Oh, I dunno. Things."

Sam's gut tightened. Deliberately, he moved the baton he'd laid on the table. Her eyes flicked toward the gold tip apprehensively.

"When was the last time you were in the cottage, Mrs. Frost?"

"I cleaned it after Mr. Kent told me I should visit me brothers. Seemed like the Christian thing ter do. Couldn't very well leave it fer the next tenants, could I?"

Sam gave her a skeptical look. He doubted she'd been a good Christian woman when she'd performed her housekeeping duties for the last time. More like a mudlark, the folks who descended on the banks of the Thames during low tide to search for anything of value left behind that they could sell later.

"What'd you take, Mrs. Frost?"

Her chin rounded in a defensive manner. "Who says I took anythin'?"

Again Sam twisted the baton so that the gold tip glinted in the tavern's candlelight. "You were done with your housekeeping duties and given money ter go away for a bit. I wouldn't blame you for pilfering anything that had been left behind in the cottage. Not like the cove was gonna come back for it, right?"

"Aye." Mrs. Frost's gaze suddenly turned suspicious. "What's all these questions fer, anyways? Why'd ye wanna know who used the cottage?"

Sam had wondered how long it would take the housekeeper to ask him that. There was no reason she'd know that one of the people she'd set a table for and cleaned up after had turned up dead. And he doubted if anyone living in St. Margaret's would've connected the temporary occupant in the cottage to a murder of a Lady in Grosvenor Square.

"The woman who used ter come ter the cottage was murdered, real vicious-like," he said, hoping to shock her. It might loosen her tongue.

She looked surprised. "Truly? How? Who did it?"

"That's what I'm tryin' ter figure out. I need ter know what you took."

She gave him an uncertain look. "If I did pinch somethin'—and I'm not sayin' I did—how's that gonna help ye find the murderer?"

Sam thought of Kendra Donovan's insistence that every detail, no matter how small, mattered during an investigation. "You never know. Tell me what you found."

Mrs. Frost hesitated and seemed to weigh all the angles. Then she heaved a sigh. "Ack, very well. Not like I can make use of it meself since I've never taken up the habit, but I thought it would've been a nice little trinket for Mr. Hobbs . . ."

She lifted a tattered looking reticule off her lap and placed it on the table. Her hand dipped inside and she brought out a diminutive silver tabatière, the lid inlaid with ivory, which had a bucolic landscape hand-painted on it.

Sam seriously doubted Mrs. Frost had planned to give it to Mr. Hobbs, unless he could fence it for her. But he didn't press the matter. Instead, he took the box from Mrs. Frost's palm and used his thumbnail to flick open the lid. He inhaled the scent of vanilla and orange from the remaining finely ground snuff inside. He found himself smiling. He'd never been one to take snuff himself, but he knew that he would be able to trace the owner of this particular brand. The tobacco shop owners prided themselves on their proprietary blends for their clients.

Still, he said, "Maybe it's Mr. Kent's."

"That one! Ha! Not bloody likely. I found it on the floor in the bedroom, next ter the bed." The gaze she leveled at him was filled with bawdy amusement. "Mr. Kent didn't look like the sort ter have even a bit of fun. Very stiff sort of gent."

Sam gave a grunt and closed the lid.

"Do ye think this will help ye find yer murderer?" Mrs. Frost wondered.

"At the very least, it should make one particular lord very uncomfortable." Sam grinned suddenly, and shoved the box deep into his pocket. His gaze fell on his untouched whiskey glass. He picked up the glass, gave the widow sitting across from him a silent toast, tossed back the spirits in one gulp—and nearly died. The back of his throat burned as though it had caught on fire. His chest seized as the fireball descended, evaporating all air. His eyes watered. He choked and gasped.

"Me brother supplies the Blind Duck with its whiskey. He makes it himself, ye know," Mrs. Frost told him with a smile.

"Holy . . . hell . . ." Sam finally managed to say, sucking in air. "Now I know how that damn duck went blind."

21

The Westons lived in a charming four-story Georgian townhouse in Portman Square, made no less charming by the pewter gray clouds boiling overhead, spitting out a steady downpour of rain. It was eleven A.M., but the foul weather had darkened the city into a premature twilight.

Kendra yanked up the hood of her green velvet cloak to protect herself from the rain, even though the Duke carried an umbrella. They dashed down the path to the front steps and up the short flight of stairs. The Westons' butler was holding open the door for them, as the coachman who'd delivered the Duke's calling card had alerted him of their arrival, but despite the umbrella, the hooded cloak, and the open door, both Kendra and the Duke were damp by the time they were inside the foyer.

The butler pushed the door shut and turned to face them. "His Lordship is expecting you, Your Grace. May I take your hat, coat, and umbrella, sir? Your cloak, Miss? I shall put them by the fire to dry."

As they divested themselves of their outerwear so the butler could hand them off to a nearby footman, Kendra glanced around. It took a moment for her eyes to adjust to the gloomy interior. No one had lit the chandelier or wall sconces, relying on the fan window over the front door for light. Given the dreary day, the hall remained heavily shadowed.

And freezing, Kendra thought. The thin blue-and-white sprigged muslin walking dress that Miss Cooper had selected for her, even with its long sleeves and modest neckline, did little to shield her from the chill.

They followed the butler down the narrow hall and up the stairs, then turned right at the landing. The manservant gave the door at the end of the corridor a brief rap with his knuckles before entering.

"The Duke of Aldridge and Miss Donovan," he intoned, and then departed, shutting the door on his way out.

Lord Weston was standing, his hands clasped behind his back, gazing into the flames in the hearth. The room was lit by a few wall sconces, and the gray daylight that streamed through the tall, skinny windows. The fire added a little warmth, but not much. At their entrance, Weston pivoted to greet them. Kendra doubted that he was happy to see them, but he kept his emotions in check behind a mask of cool politeness.

"Good day, sir, Miss Donovan. Please have a seat." He gestured to the wingback chairs in front of the large desk, then moved behind the desk and sat down. It was a position of distance and dominance, an attempt to gain the upper hand. Kendra had every intention of shaking that up, though the Duke began the interview on a cordial note.

"Thank you for seeing us," Aldridge said as they settled into the chairs. Weston regarded them solemnly. For a few seconds, the only noise was the popping of logs in the fireplace, the ticking of the wooden bracket clock on a corner table, and the soft tapping of the rain against the window. Then the Earl sighed.

"I could hardly refuse you, Your Grace," he said, as he picked up the silver penknife on his desk and began to fiddle with it. "I really don't know what more I can tell you, though."

"Let's begin with you telling us about Lady Dover, since you were in a position to really know her," Kendra said. "What was she like?"

"I don't like to gossip, even if the person is dead."

"This isn't gossip, sir. We're trying to understand who would have cause to kill her—if it wasn't you. Help me get an accurate picture of the kind of woman she was."

Weston's mouth tightened. "You are very blunt, Miss Donovan."

"If I need to be."

He was quiet for a moment. Then he said slowly, "She was beautiful, of course. Intelligent. Well-read. Witty." His eyes darkened, and Kendra thought she saw genuine sorrow there, but it was gone in a moment. "I can't imagine what kind of monster could do . . . do what was done to her."

He swallowed hard and looked away.

"It was terrible," Kendra agreed. She waited, but when he didn't elaborate, she asked, "Exactly how long did you know Lady Dover?"

"Years. I met Cordelia for the first time when Dover—the late Earl—brought her home as his bride."

"You began an affair?" Kendra asked.

"No! Not then." Weston shifted uncomfortably. "There may have been a flirtation. She was a vivacious woman. Our acquaintance became . . . *intimate* only last February."

"So seven months ago," Aldridge murmured.

Kendra asked Weston, "Did you know that she was seeing other men while she was with you?"

The Earl pressed his lips together and shot the Duke a knowing glance. "I was aware that Cordelia had an intimate connection with your nephew, Your Grace. That is the reason you are investigating the murder, is it not?"

"I have involved myself in the investigation because I find murder abhorrent," the Duke replied carefully. "There is no place for it in a civilized society. I imagine you'd want Lady Dover's killer caught as well."

Weston's gaze flickered, but he answered readily enough, "Of course."

Kendra repeated, "Did it bother you that she was dating other men?"

"Dating?" That earned a quizzical frown. "I don't comprehend."

"Romantically involved with," she clarified.

"I could scarcely make demands of the widow."

"Did she begin to make demands of you?"

"No."

"Really? Not even asking if she could wear jewelry more appropriately worn by your wife?"

Weston's brown eyes sparked with anger, then he lowered his eyes to the penknife he was twisting in his fingers. "That was . . . different."

"Did she want more of a commitment from you? Maybe marriage?"

He kept his gaze on the penknife. "That would have been impossible. I already have a wife and a family."

"It's amazing how the impossible becomes possible, if you want something enough. Did your wife know about your affair with Lady Dover—before the theater incident, that is?"

"I certainly never discussed it with her." He lifted his gaze to meet Kendra's and gave a dismissive shrug. "Lady Weston and I have a marriage typical of our social sphere, Miss Donovan. Once our nursery was set, we were free to indulge in our amusements elsewhere."

Kendra had to think about that. "You mean you have an open marriage?"

"I'm not familiar with the term, but Lady Weston and I have never lived in each other's pockets."

Aldridge shifted in his seat. "As you say, sir, your arrangement with your wife is often typical of the Ton. However, the rule is discretion. Lady Dover broke that by wearing your family's jewels to the theater, humiliating your wife *and* your family. I can't imagine that you weren't enraged by your mistress's behavior."

Weston was quiet for a long moment, as though debating what he should say. At last, he said, "It was distressing, but you can't believe that I would resort to murder to express my displeasure? I would never do that, never do what was done to Cordelia. Never." He sounded adamant.

"When did you give the necklace to her?" Kendra asked.

For the first time since they'd begun the interview, Weston flushed. "It wasn't a gift. She asked if . . . well, it was only supposed to be temporary."

"Okay, so she asked to wear them—"

"Privately," Weston insisted. "I would never have allowed such a public display. I had no idea that was her intent."

That brought up a very good point. "Why do you think she did it?"

"I don't know."

"To punish you?"

"I don't know."

Kendra eyed him. She found it curious that he didn't ask, *Punish me for what?* But maybe he didn't ask because he already knew the answer. If the beautiful Lady Dover had been pressuring him to leave his wife and he was resistant, Kendra could see Lady Dover retaliating by demanding the necklace. She could have then worn it in public to embarrass his entire family. It was outrageous and vindictive. Unfortunately, Kendra felt a growing certainty that it had also been the trigger for her murder.

"When did she ask you for them?" she asked.

"I don't recall the exact date."

"How long before the theater?"

He frowned. "A week or two. I'm not certain. Why is that important?"

"I'm curious how long she'd been planning to make your relationship public. It wasn't impulse that made her put on that necklace that night."

Weston's flush had subsided, leaving him pale. "I hadn't thought about it."

Kendra waited a beat and then changed tack. "You must have been furious when you saw her the next morning to ask for the necklace back."

Weston hesitated. "I was upset," he allowed warily.

"What was her mood like? Apologetic, or perhaps regretful? Or did she taunt you, like she'd taunted your son?"

Weston's eyes lit with something indefinable, but angry. "My son has nothing to do with this. He was at his sister's ball the night of the murder—as was I."

"Lady Frances's ball was even more crowded than the one last night," Kendra countered. "It wouldn't be too difficult to leave unnoticed."

"That's absurd."

But Weston was becoming increasingly agitated. The silver flashed as he twisted the penknife. Kendra stared at the man's elegant hands and could easily envision those long, tapered fingers curled around another knife, its blade narrower and more deadly.

She lifted her gaze to his. "Where does Lady Frances live?"

"Mount Street," he replied with a weary tone.

Somewhere down the hall, the ethereal notes of a harp rose up. Kendra glanced at the door, listening for a moment, then looked back at Weston. "Nice," she commented.

"My daughter Louisa. She's rehearsing for Mrs. Biddle's salon next week." He said it grudgingly, almost as if he didn't want to give her any information, even something as benign as his daughter's recital.

Weston put the penknife to the side and looked at Aldridge. "I don't mean to be rude, sir, but I have other business to attend to yet this morning. Are we done here? I don't know what else I can add."

Kendra smiled. It never failed to amaze her how she could conduct most of the interview, and yet the Duke was still the one called upon to end it. Was it because his title gave him the position of power? Or because he was a man?

She rose but kept her gaze on Weston. "Do you have any idea who might have killed Lady Dover? Did she ever mention being afraid of someone?"

Weston frowned as he pushed himself to his feet as well. "Never. I'm convinced it was a housebreaker. I heard her house was robbed after the murder."

"No, what was done to Lady Dover was very personal."

Aldridge reached for Kendra's arm. "Thank you, my lord. I realize this is unpleasant business, but it is necessary. Please, stay. We can show ourselves out."

Weston looked relieved.

The Duke exited first, with Kendra following. Pausing deliberately on the threshold, she swung around to look Weston in the eye once more. "Did Lady Dover tell you her secret, milord?"

He froze. "Pray tell, what secret is that?"

Kendra kept her gaze on his face for a long moment. Then she said, "I'm sorry, I'm not at liberty to say."

She stepped out into the hall and closed the door—but not before she saw Weston's hand tremble as he lifted it rub his jaw.

In the hall, Aldridge said softly, "I suspect he knows what Lady Dover's secret was."

Kendra smiled without humor. "Oh, he most definitely knows."

The sound of the harp still filled the hall. Kendra tugged the Duke farther down the hall, toward the sound, and they studied the domestic scene beyond the drawing room's open door. Lady Louisa, wearing a charming ivory Indian sprigged muslin day dress, sat on a stool, her arms outstretched gracefully as her fingers plucked and strummed an enchanting melody from the beautifully carved instrument. On the gold-and-brown paisley fringed sofa, Lady Weston and Lady Isabella sat together, their heads covered in lacy mop caps, eyebrows furrowed in concentration as they pushed their needles and colorful silk floss through the material stretched tight across embroidery hoops.

Kendra didn't think they'd made a sound, but suddenly Lady Louisa's gaze shot toward them. Her hands dropped from the harp like pale birds falling in midair. The only sound left in the room was the hiss and pop from the coal fire in the grate.

Lady Weston glanced up. "What is it, Louisa?"

"We have company, Mama." Her voice was colorless as she nodded toward Kendra and the Duke hovering in the doorway.

Lady Weston gave an inelegant squeak when she saw their guests. "Dear heavens." She pushed herself to her feet in a flurry of skirts. "Your Grace! It is you, is it not?"

"It is I. Please, forgive the intrusion," Aldridge said, unable to stop the ladies from offering curtsies. "My ward and I were simply swept away by your daughter's playing. It is enchanting."

"You are most gracious, sir. Let me introduce you to my daughters Lady Louisa and Lady Isabella. Lady Isabella is married to Mr. Sedwick, who works for the Home Office."

"Good day, my lady. And this is my ward, Miss Donovan."

"We are already acquainted with Miss Donovan, Your Grace," Lady Louisa said, regarding Kendra with a veiled expression. "We met at the Digby Ball last night."

"I see." Lady Weston offered a polite smile. "Sir, will you and your ward sit? I shall ring for tea."

"Do not trouble yourself, Your Ladyship. We only came to call on Lord Weston and were in the process of leaving." He gave Kendra a questioning look. "Is that not so, my dear?"

She nodded, then smiled at the assembled ladies. "Perhaps we'll see each other at Mrs. Biddle's salon."

Lady Isabella frowned. "You will be in attendance?"

"Absolutely." *And why don't you look pleased about that, Lady Isabella?* she wondered. "Maybe we can talk then."

After making their farewells, the Duke waited until they were descending the stairs to ask quietly, "What was that about?"

"I wanted to meet Lady Weston. Now we don't need to be introduced, right? I can talk to her whenever I see her?"

"Yes, you no longer need a formal introduction."

The butler met them at the bottom of the stairs. He handed them their dry outer garments, which now smelled faintly of smoke. Outside, the rain had stopped and the clouds overheard had thinned to a dove gray, but the wind had picked up. Shivering, Kendra raised her hood for protection against the wind.

Aldridge gave her a sideways look. "Why do I get the impression that you are hoping to make the Westons nervous, my dear?"

"Possibly because that was the idea. Nervous people tend to make mistakes."

As they walked down the path to the street, Kendra got a prickly sensation between her shoulder blades. She held the hood of the green cloak in place as she turned to look behind her. The sky's muted light bounced off the windowpanes of the Weston home, transforming them into mirrors. But she detected movement behind the reflective surface, and she thought she saw a pale glimmer, a face staring down at them. Then it was gone, but Kendra's twitchy feeling remained.

Maybe I've already made someone nervous.

22

Kendra paused as the Duke helped her into the carriage following their meeting with Lord Weston. "Do you feel up for another visit?"

"Certainly." The Duke eyed her questioningly. "Where do you wish to go?"

"I'd like to pay a call on Lady Frances. She *did* invite me."

"Ah, so that is why you asked for her address from Lord Weston." The Duke gave the instructions to his coachman, then climbed in after Kendra. "It's not exactly a fashionable hour to make a morning call."

"I'm not really interested in being fashionable."

Aldridge smiled. "I assume Lady Frances is another person you hope to make nervous?"

"From what I observed last night, that might be difficult. She has nerves of steel."

The wet day had kept most of the gentry indoors, but not the servants who continued to go about their business, scurrying across the wet cobblestone streets and darting into buildings. When the carriage turned onto Mount Street, the coachman had to stop to ask for the Roberts' exact address from a young maid carrying a basket of vegetables. Then the carriage jerked forward again, and two minutes later, they once again dispatched the Duke's calling card into one of the larger houses, its stucco exterior designed to look like gray brick. Five minutes later, they were escorted through the entrance foyer and up the sweeping stairs.

When they reached the top of the stairs, both Kendra and the Duke stumbled to a stop and stared around them in amazement.

"Holy crap," Kendra whispered.

The butler paused, looking back at them when he realized they were no longer walking with him. "Is something amiss?"

Both Kendra and the Duke stood transfixed by the medieval weapons that covered almost every square inch of the white plaster walls. Kendra moved to one of the long, narrow wood-and-glass cases that lined the wall, displaying assorted knives and swords.

"This is quite a collection," she murmured, and exchanged a significant glance with the Duke. "I see several stilettos."

"Yes, Miss," said the butler. "The Earl is quite a collector."

Kendra studied the glass case closely. There was no lock, she noticed. The lid could be lifted easily. And on the night Lady Dover had been mortally attacked, nearly three hundred people had assembled here at Lady Frances's ball . . .

She lifted her gaze to the Duke's and gave him a significant look. They may have just found the original home of their murder weapon.

❖

Lady Frances and her husband, the Honorable Cecil Roberts, were waiting for them in a large drawing room lined in delicate red silk wallpaper and filled with polished cherrywood furniture. A spinet and a harp—apparently Lady Louisa wasn't the only Weston daughter who played—were tucked in a corner, near the arched windows that overlooked the back gardens. Lady Frances was seated in front of the fire on an amber paisley sofa, looking beautiful with her dark hair caught up in a bandeau decorated with daisies and wearing a long-sleeved coppery-brown day dress. At their entrance, she immediately stood and offered the Duke a graceful curtsy.

"Your Grace, this is an honor." She gave him a dimpled smile before turning to Kendra. "Miss Donovan, I am so delighted you took me up on my invitation to call." Still, she shot a pointed glance at the ormolu clock on the mantel.

"Your Grace, Miss Donovan." Roberts smiled and bowed.

Lady Frances hadn't been forced to marry a man who wore a corset and was at least five decades her senior. Her husband was handsome, with light reddish-brown hair, cut short and combed forward, with long sideburns. He stood tall and trim, which he showed to good advantage by wearing a fashionable blue coat over a silk blue-and-white-striped double-breasted waistcoat, paired with buff-colored pantaloons tucked into gleaming black Hessian boots. His cravat was elaborately tied and high enough to touch his chin. Catching his bright blue eyes, Kendra had a feeling that he, like his wife, wasn't oblivious to his own appeal.

"Please, shall we be seated?" Lady Frances said, and returned to her former spot on the sofa.

As they were sitting, a maid wearing a traditional mop cap and apron wheeled in a tea cart, which she parked next to her mistress.

Lady Frances smiled. "I took the liberty of calling for tea. 'Tis such a dreary day." She reached for the creamer, pouring a little into her teacup before she filled it with tea. "How do you take your tea, Miss Donovan?"

"Black, two sugars," she replied, and waited for Lady Frances to pour. She glanced at Roberts. "You've got quite a collection in the hall."

"Actually, my grandfather is the collector. He has a passion for the medieval times," he explained. "I thought it quite blood-thirsty of him when I was a boy—and loved every ghoulish artifact." He grinned. "I don't share his passion to collect such ancient weaponry, but I would be pleased to show it to you, Miss Donovan, or you, Your Grace."

"Your grandfather . . . I'd heard the Earl has retreated to his estates in the north," Aldridge said.

"Ah, yes. Near Yorkshire. My grandfather claims the London air is not fit for man nor beast. Unfortunately, the air in the country doesn't seem to have helped him much, either."

"Your grandfather is ailing?"

Roberts shrugged. "He hasn't been well since my grandmother expired. He gave me this house for my use, as my father and mother are content with their home in Hanover Square."

Once the tea had been distributed, Kendra said, "I heard that a lot of people came to your ball on Monday night."

"Yes," Lady Frances said with a smile. "It seemed that all of London was in attendance."

"All of your family members attended?" Kendra asked. "Even your mother?" She kept her gaze on the younger woman, deeply interested in what she'd say.

Lady Frances's smile faltered. "Oh . . . well, no. My mother was indisposed that night." She tilted her head and regarded Kendra. "What my sisters told me must be true. You *are* playing the Bow Street Runner."

Lady Frances appeared amused. But Kendra sensed there was much more beneath the surface than the beautiful façade would suggest.

"We are investigating Lady Dover's murder," Aldridge cut in, lifting his teacup to his lips and taking a swallow. He set the cup down on its saucer, then gazed calmly at Lady Frances. "You were acquainted with Lady Dover, correct?"

"Of course. We traveled the same circles as the Countess," she said, unruffled. "But we were not, nor had ever been, friends."

"You must have formed an impression," Kendra pressed.

Lady Frances appeared to consider the matter as she took a sip of her tea. "I do not like to speak ill of the dead . . . but I considered the Countess ill-bred and dreadfully vain. She did her best to monopolize the attention of those around her."

Kendra kept her gaze on the younger woman. "Men, you mean?"

"Yes. She had little use for her own sex. She preferred the company of men. Is that not so, love?" Lady Frances glanced at her husband from the corner of her eye.

"She was a flirt," Roberts acknowledge carefully.

And did she flirt with you? It suddenly occurred to Kendra that while Lady Frances had managed to avoid marrying someone like Lord Ludlow, a good-looking, younger man might have a different set of problems.

"I heard that you gave Lady Dover the cut direct," she said.

"It's possible, I suppose." Lady Frances moved her shoulders in a dainty shrug. "I had little use for the creature."

"Were you at the theater the night when Lady Dover wore your family's necklace?"

For the first time, Lady Frances's composure cracked: she went rigid, her hazel eyes blazed, and then she dropped her gaze to her teacup, her eyelashes concealing her expression. "Yes, Mr. Roberts and I were in attendance. As I said, ill-bred."

"Were you aware before the incident that your father was involved with her?"

Roberts frowned. "You cannot think that Lord Weston had anything to do with the Countess's murder. 'Tis impossible. He was here the night of the ball."

"He never left?" Kendra shifted her gaze to him. "You had him in your sights the whole evening?"

204

"Well, no, of course not. But you can hardly think the Earl would have committed murder between dance sets!"

Kendra said, "We're looking into all leads right now. Do you know anyone else Lady Dover may have been involved with?"

Roberts looked aghast. "How would *I* know such a thing? I scarcely knew the woman!"

His adamant declaration struck Kendra as a little too forceful. She gave him a long look before offering an enigmatic shrug. Let him make of that what he would. "People talk."

"She was involved with the Marquis of Sutcliffe," Lady Frances supplied. Her smile was back, but this time it didn't bring out her dimples or reach her eyes. "She was quite taken with him. I'd even heard that she hoped to become his Marchioness. Although in that, I can scarcely blame her. He's a handsome devil. And your heir, is he not, Your Grace?"

"He is."

Lady Frances let that hang in the air for a moment. Then she gave a light laugh. "Of course, there is the Dutton boy. He was besotted with her, even asked her to dance twice at the Hamilton Ball."

"He's a puppy," Roberts said. "Lady Dover wouldn't have offered him a second look."

"Indeed?" Lady Frances shot her husband a veiled glance. "I don't think she was too discriminating as to who she took to her bed, darling." She turned back to Kendra. "Unfortunately, you will be forced to interview most of the male population in London if you want to find the fiend who murdered the poor wretch."

Lady Frances gave a shudder that Kendra couldn't determine genuine or fake. "Personally, I believe it was someone from the stews. I simply cannot credit that a gentleman would use a dagger against a lady. It's too barbaric."

Kendra put down her teacup and stared at the other woman. "How do you know that a knife was used, Lady Frances?"

Lady Frances smiled. "As you say . . . people talk."

23

Lady Frances does not have a nervous disposition," Aldridge murmured after they'd left the Roberts' residence, walking down the winding flagstone path to the street. "Her comment about the dagger was interesting. It almost appeared as if she were baiting you, Miss Donovan."

Kendra remembered how Lady Frances had teased her sister about becoming an ape leader. "I think baiting people is what Lady Frances does." She paused to draw the cloak's hood up again, glancing up at the sky. "It stopped raining. Why don't we walk back to your place?"

Although Aldridge shot an uncertain look toward the heavens, he nodded. "You are conducting an experiment, to determine how long it will take us to walk to Lady Dover's residence."

"And I'm going to say that it's pretty good odds that our killer stole one of those stilettos from the Roberts' residence and used the party as a cover to murder Lady Dover."

"That theory eliminates Lord Dover. He was at his club, then home."

"I'm not eliminating him. I don't like that he never mentioned arguing with his stepmother after the theater incident, and I want to do a follow-up interview to ask him about that. But he drops down on the list."

The Duke told his coachman to drive home without them, then he offered his arm, which Kendra accepted. They strolled down the sidewalk together, in the direction of Grosvenor Square.

"I realize that Lord Weston is our most obvious perpetrator," Aldridge began, "but I believe he genuinely cared for Lady Dover. 'Tis hard to conceive of him mutilating her face as the fiend did."

"'You know that when I hate you, it is because I love you to a point of passion that unhinges my soul,'" Kendra quoted softly. "Jeanne Julie Éléonore de Lespinasse wrote that about one of her tragic love affairs. Maybe our killer felt the same unhinged passion for Lady Dover."

Aldridge regarded her with genuine surprise. "You are familiar with the work of Mlle de Lespinasse?"

"In college, I took a course on women in the Enlightenment period. She was one of the women we studied."

"She died nearly forty years ago. I find it fascinating that her memory and her work continue to influence society so far into the future. Then again, I continue to be influenced by the likes of John Locke and Jean-Jacques Rousseau, Aristotle and Plato," he mused, his blue-gray eyes taking on a faraway gleam. "We must live in the present, even as we attempt to build something that will last into the future. However, we can never be certain of our legacy, if it's strong enough to be sustained or if it will simply fade away, a memory forgotten." He brought his gaze back to her. "You know, though."

Kendra tensed, uncertain what to say, so she said nothing.

"You were in Aldridge Castle when you went through your wormhole," the Duke continued. "'Tis good to know that my home still stands in the future. So many Norman strongholds survive only as ruins. I know you prefer not to have these discussions, but if I may ask . . . is it well cared for?"

"It's magnificent," she whispered, and her throat felt oddly tight. Beneath her fingertips, through several layers of greatcoat, coat and shirt, the Duke's arm felt solid. Real. *Alive.* Yet the first time that she'd walked through the doors of Aldridge Castle, the Duke of Aldridge or, at least, this particular Duke had been buried for centuries in his family crypt, his flesh having decayed into dust, leaving only moldering bones.

If she managed to return to her own timeline, this man walking beside her, so vital and strong—and Alec and Rebecca, too—would be long dead. The thought left an ache in her heart. She didn't belong here, she knew that, but she couldn't bear to think of these people rotting in their graves in the twenty-first century.

"You worry too much, Miss Donovan," the Duke said quietly.

Kendra realized that the Duke's intelligent blue gaze was fixed on her, a funny smile curving his mouth. "None of us are immortal, my dear. But ideas, inventions, discoveries, even buildings can all be a form of immortality. Not everyone is in the position of leaving a legacy, or is aware of the responsibility such a legacy requires. Aldridge Castle is part of my heritage and it is heartening to know that it endures."

Yet he didn't ask *who* cared for the castle. Maybe there were some things that the Duke didn't want to know either.

They stepped back from the curb to avoid a spray of dirty water when the wheels of a wagon loaded with wooden barrels hit a puddle. It broke the musing mood of their talk, so Kendra returned to her earlier point as they resumed walking. "Weston may have loved Lady Dover, but that doesn't mean he didn't kill her in a rage."

"But her face . . ."

"The mutilation was more calculated. If Weston is our killer, maybe he did it to throw everyone off, because it *is* hard to imagine a man carving up the face of the woman he loved. It fits with the hesitation marks on the other side of her face—the unsub obviously had to work himself up to the gruesome injury."

She frowned as she recalled their conversation with the Earl. "I can't help but think about what he said: 'I can't imagine what kind of monster could do what was done to her.' It was almost like he knew the details."

"He could have heard about the disfigurement. Gossip flows through this city like the River Thames. I'd say his horror is understandable, especially given their intimate relationship."

"Maybe." But Kendra couldn't help but feel there was something more. The look of revulsion that had blazed in Weston's eyes had seemed too strong for someone who had simply heard about the mutilation secondhand. "He became pretty defensive when I mentioned his son."

"Also an understandable reaction. In fact, I think it would have been unnatural for a father not to leap to his son's defense if he felt suspicion of murder was being cast upon him. I've found myself defending Alec in much the same manner."

"There's something else—Weston didn't deny that Lady Dover was pressuring him for a commitment."

"He did deny it. He said—" Aldridge frowned as he recalled the conversation. "He said that he was already married . . . ah, I see your point. He didn't say no, precisely."

"No, he didn't. So let's assume that evasive answer means we're on the right track and Lady Dover was pressuring him to divorce his wife and marry her. I think Rebecca was right: wearing the Weston necklace publicly was Lady Dover's declaration of war."

"I'm not sure it would have accomplished her objective. The only thing it did was expose their affair and humiliate the entire Weston family."

"You need to turn up the heat if you want a pot of water to boil."

Aldridge smiled. "That is a unique way of phrasing it."

They stopped as they reached the end of the lane. Ahead of them was Grosvenor Square. Kendra could see Lady Dover's townhouse.

"Ten minutes—and we were strolling," she said. "Someone walking fast could've made it in five. Five minutes to get here; ten, maybe fifteen to stab and mutilate Lady Dover; another five to return to Lady Frances's ball . . ."

Kendra could picture it in her head: the killer slipping through the darkness, knocking on Lady Dover's door. Pleasantries exchanged. Then she'd invited the killer up to her drawing room.

Her gaze refocused, meeting the Duke's. "Half an hour. That was all the unsub needed. He could have killed Lady Dover in less time than it takes for one dance."

24

Good—you've returned, Miss Donovan. No, don't take off your cloak," Lady Atwood ordered as soon as Kendra and the Duke stepped into the foyer. The long skirt of the older woman's navy blue pelisse billowed out as she swept down the stairs. She was tying the ribbons of her bonnet below her chin, and her eyes zeroed in on Kendra. "We must leave for our appointment with Madame Gaudet. We are already late."

The dress designer, Kendra remembered. So much for her intention to update the slate board and organize her notes. Most likely recognizing her irritation, the Duke gave her a reassuring pat on the arm.

"Cheer up, my dear. I'm told it doesn't hurt a bit."

"Well, really." The Countess eyed them both with exasperation. "It's not as though I'm dragging the creature off to the workhouse."

"Miss Donovan, good day!" At the top of the stairs, Rebecca came into view, followed by Alec. "I'd come for a visit, and Lady Atwood has graciously invited me along to Madame Gaudet's establishment."

She picked up her skirts and practically flew down the stairs, earning an admonishing frown from Lady Atwood.

"Ladies do not race down staircases."

Rebecca gave an unabashed grin, skittering to a stop next to Kendra. Harding emerged, holding her caped redingote and hat.

"Thank you, Harding." Rebecca gave Kendra a significant look as she shrugged into the coat, then said, "You know, Madame Gaudet is excellent with the needle. I believe many ladies of the Beau Monde patronize her. I would not be surprised if Lady Dover had been a client."

"Becca is correct," Alec said, and descended the stairs without his usual grace. He kept one hand on his ribs. "I can attest that Lady Dover patronized Madame Gaudet's establishment. What did you learn from Weston?"

Lady Atwood made a sweeping gesture to Kendra and Rebecca like she was shooing chickens. "There is no time to discuss that now. We must leave. Come along."

Behind them, the Duke clapped Alec lightly on the shoulder. "While the ladies are at the modiste, I shall tell you what transpired, my boy. Let's go to my study. We might as well be comfortable."

❖

Madam Gaudet's establishment was located on Bond Street, which was as ultra fashionable in this year as it was in Kendra's own. The building itself was a three-story, cream-colored sandstone with wide windows on the ground floor, skinny rectangular windows on the next level, and bricked up windows at the top—a clever way to get around the much-despised window tax that the Crown had imposed on its people more than a century before.

Above the slanted roof peaks, the sky had become dark again, the clouds pregnant with rain yet to come. Still, the dismal weather wasn't a deterrent to shoppers. Bond Street was bustling, the thoroughfare loud with the clatter of wheels from fashionable carriages, public coaches, and large service wagons hauling goods. The steady clop of horses' hooves rang against the cobblestones. All tiers of society—Kendra was beginning to recognize the different classes based on their dress—walked up and down the sidewalks.

The coachman unfolded the steps, and they'd just descended to the ground when a loud commotion drew their attention to the street. Two horses pulling a cart suddenly reared up, whinnying. The cart lurched dangerously to the side and its driver let out a fierce yell.

"Blast ye! Oi almost got ye, ye bleeding twat!"

The young man who'd run across the wide street and nearly gotten clipped by the horses and cart responded with a rude gesture that spanned centuries.

"London," sniffed Lady Atwood, her mouth thinning with disapproval. "'Tis constant mayhem."

She marched toward the dressmaker's shop. A bell attached to the door jingled when they entered the room, the air heavy with the scent of lilac and gardenia. Long oak worktables were positioned in front of shelves laden with round barrels tipped sideways, allowing an assortment of luxurious fabrics to spill out in a decorative display. There was a low table, several chairs, and a sofa angled in front of an elegantly carved marble fireplace. A homey fire burned in the grate.

On sunnier days, Madame Gaudet probably relied on the natural light from the enormous multipaned windows facing the street to brighten the shop's interior, Kendra thought. Today, oil lamps had been lit around the room.

"Bonjour! Bienvenue!"

A woman emerged from the yellow silk curtain stretched across a doorway on the other side of the shop, sending the fabric fluttering behind her. Madame Gaudet was a petite, attractive brunette of indeterminate age. At first glance, Kendra probably would've pegged her at thirty-five, but on closer inspection, she revised that to at least ten years older. No matter her age, the dressmaker was her own best advertisement, wearing a simple apricot-hued gown that she carried off with the kind of sophistication that seemed embedded into the genetic code of the French.

"Lady Atwood." Smiling, Madame Gaudet clasped the Countess's hands and gave both of her cheeks an air kiss, a shocking amount of familiarity in this day and age. She spoke with a French accent that had been softened by her years in London. *"Vous êtes magnifique! Toujours aussi ravissante. Vous éclipsez toutes les autres femmes!* You must confess your secret to me, *oui*? I am becoming haggard in my old age, whereas you only become more youthful."

Flattery never goes out of style, Kendra thought wryly as she watched Lady Atwood beam.

"You are too kind, madame. May I introduce Lady Rebecca, goddaughter to the Duke of Aldridge, and Miss Donovan, my brother's ward. Miss Donovan needs an entirely new wardrobe, one befitting her station."

Madame Gaudet's gaze was shrewd as it slid over Kendra. Then she clapped her hands and called for a young maid to take their cloaks and parasols, and sat her clients at the table to warm themselves in front of the fire.

"You will have tea or a small sherry, *oui*? To take the chill out of this wicked day?"

"Tea would be lovely, thank you," accepted the Countess.

Again the modiste clapped her hands for the harried young maid to fetch a tray. While they waited, Madame Gaudet distributed fashion plates and magazines for them to examine, explaining the trends coming out of Paris now that the war was over.

"Notice the V-neckline, so *parfait* to show off a woman's décolletage, *oui*? And see how the waistline is higher, and the skirt is fuller? I will need to take Miss Donovan's measurements . . . Giselle!"

A pretty young girl of perhaps seventeen floated through the yellow silk curtain. "Yes, madame?"

"Bring more fashion plates for Her Ladyship. *Merci*." She turned to Kendra. "If you will follow me, mademoiselle?"

The little Frenchwoman ushered Kendra through the yellow silk curtain. On the other side was a room with half a dozen young girls industriously stitching gowns by hand. The room had only one window and a scattering of oil lamps. Kendra predicted that every seamstress in the room would need glasses or be out of their job by the time they hit forty.

Madame Gaudet led Kendra into another small room cluttered with stiff patterns and headless dressmaker's dummies, with bolts of material stacked haphazardly in a corner. She wasted no time, immediately undoing the buttons on Kendra's dress.

Kendra decided not to waste time, either. "I heard Lady Dover was a client of yours."

The Frenchwoman's fingers stilled, but continued to slip the buttons through the buttonholes in a moment. "*Oui*. Such a terrible tragedy."

"What was she like?"

Madame Gaudet paused again, but Kendra didn't think it was her question that had caused the dressmaker's hesitancy. She'd pushed the gown off Kendra's shoulders and had probably seen the scars puckering Kendra's flesh, souvenirs she'd picked up in the twenty-first century.

But Madame Gaudet didn't make any reference to the old wounds. After a moment, she continued in her task. "Lady Dover was one of my best clients," she finally said. "She was a woman of great style and discerning tastes. And so lovely—that golden hair, her skin, those eyes! And her figure . . . ah, perfect! A beautiful woman such as she deserved the best of fashion." She whipped out her measuring tape from the pockets she apparently wore under her skirts. "Please stand straight, mademoiselle. Lift your arms. *Merci.*"

"When was the last time you saw her?"

"Her Ladyship had an appointment here only a week ago. To think that would be the last time we should speak . . ." She sighed and shook her head. "Life can change so quickly, *oui?*"

"You don't know the half of it."

"Pardon?"

"*Oui*—life can change very quickly. But tell me about Lady Dover's last appointment. Did she want one new gown, or did she need a new wardrobe?"

The dressmaker said cautiously, "She requested new gowns, *oui.*"

Kendra looked at the other woman. "I think you know what I'm asking, madame. Did she tell you about her pregnancy?"

The dark eyes studied her. "This is not idle gossip, mademoiselle."

"The Duke of Aldridge and I are investigating Lady Dover's murder."

"A nobleman such as the Duke of Aldridge conducting an investigation into murder? And you—a woman? I have never heard of such a thing."

"There's a first time for everything."

The Frenchwoman continued to stare at her. "I know Lord Sutcliffe is a suspect in the crime. I suppose their connection explains His Grace's interest . . . but I do not think it would be good business to gossip about my patrons."

"That's too bad." Kendra let out a long sigh. "The Duke told me that I could order whatever gowns I wanted. But I'm not sure if I'm in the mood anymore . . ."

Madame Gaudet apparently came to the decision that satisfying a live customer was much more lucrative than keeping the secrets of a dead one. "Lady Dover had many lovers over the years," she said slowly.

"And recently?"

The modiste concentrated on Kendra's measurements. "She was enchanted by Lord Sutcliffe—that may not help you."

"I already know they were involved. I want to know who else she was involved with."

"The father of her child in particular, *oui*? In that, I cannot help you. We did not discuss . . . her condition. But I was aware. There can be no secrets of that sort between a lady and her modiste." Her gaze drifted pointedly to Kendra's scars before returning to meet her eyes.

Kendra gave a faint smile. "How about if I throw out a name? Lord Weston?"

Madame Gaudet gave Kendra a sly look. "The entire Beau Monde is aware of their love affair, since Lady Dover wore the Weston family jewels to the theater."

"Yes, I heard that it caused quite an uproar."

"The English, they do not understand passion like the French. They hide their feelings and smile at the world as though their lives are perfect behind their proper iron fences."

"But the Westons' lives were not perfect."

"Is anyone's? *Non*. Lady Weston and her daughters are also my patrons. Lady Weston is not a happy woman, I think."

"I can't say I'd be too happy either if my husband's mistress paraded around in jewels that were supposed to be around my neck for everyone to see," Kendra said. "Did Lady Weston say anything to you about that night?"

"Me? Oh, *non*, I haven't seen her for over a month, well before that night at the theater. Her daughters have been in, though, and they spoke of it. Not to me—only to each other. As if I don't have ears."

"Which daughters?"

"The older one and the sow-faced one."

Lady Isabella and Lady Louisa, Kendra noted. "What did they say?"

Madame Gaudet motioned with her hand. "Ah, what did they not say? They spoke of their disgrace, their mother's humiliation, and Lady Dover's wickedness. They were distraught. They bought a dozen new gowns." She smiled with the craftiness of a businesswoman. "Distraught women are my best customers."

"Retail therapy is a time-honored tradition," agreed Kendra.

Madam Gaudet's smile faded after a moment, and a certain grimness stole over her face. "They also said they wished Lady Dover was dead. And then she *was* dead." She paused, appearing to be entirely absorbed in her work for a few beats. "Maybe they hired someone to kill their father's mistress. It's been known to happen."

Kendra thought of the frenzied stabbing, the mutilation. A hit man wouldn't have been so personally invested as to cause such damage. "What about Lord Dover?" Kendra pressed. "Her stepson? Did she ever mention him?"

"*Oui.* He could put her into a fine temper. She despised him." Madame Gaudet rolled up her measuring tape and tucked it into her pocket. She picked up Kendra's discarded gown and helped her back into it. "You think he may have murdered her?"

"Do you?"

She frowned. "They loathed each other for a very long time, I think. Why would he kill her now?"

Kendra thought about the unborn child, and Lady Dover pressuring Weston to leave his wife. Would Lord Dover kill his beautiful stepmother if he thought she was bringing disgrace to his family name, a nineteenth-century honor killing?

"Who do you think might have done it, then?" Kendra asked.

Madame Gaudet considered the question for a long time. "Lord Weston, I think."

"Why? Because of the necklace?"

She hesitated. "*Non* . . . because I think Lady Dover took another lover."

Kendra stared at her, surprised. "Why do you think that?"

The dressmaker gave a shrug. "I do not know how to explain. Her demeanor had changed. For a while, she was happier, in the way a fresh romance makes a woman happy."

"When exactly did she change?"

"A little less than a month ago."

So not the father of her child. "Any idea who he was?"

"*Non*, she didn't speak a name. But if Lord Weston found out she was playing him false . . ." Madame Gaudet let that idea hang in the air.

"He knew about Sutcliffe, and he seemed to accept that relationship."

"Ah, but the Marquis and Lady Dover were involved before she began her affair with Lord Weston."

"What difference does that make?"

"It makes all the difference in matters of the heart. And her affair with the Marquis had run its course." She waved her hand in a dismissive gesture. "Perhaps it is my imagination."

"You said she was happier 'for a while'. What do you mean?"

A small line formed between Madame Gaudet's eyebrows. "The last time I saw her, a week ago, she was . . . *songeuse*. How do you say?"

"Thoughtful."

"*Oui.*"

"Not worried or scared?"

"Lady Dover was not a mouse, cowering in the corner. She was a lion; she knew her power."

Kendra regarded the dressmaker. "If she was trying to get Weston to leave his wife and marry her, why would she risk becoming involved with another man?"

The Frenchwoman's lips curved in a knowing smile. "Jealousy can be an effective tool, *oui*? If it is used correctly, your lover will do anything to be in your arms. But if you miscalculate . . ."

"So she might have taken another lover to make Weston jealous, and . . . what? It didn't go according to plan?"

"She is dead, is she not?"

Kendra couldn't argue with that.

They turned together to walk back through the curtain, but something new occurred to Kendra. She reached out to stop the other woman, noting, "You don't seem surprised that Lord Weston or someone from the Beau Monde may be responsible for Lady Dover's murder."

"*Non,*" the Frenchwoman replied, and was quiet for so long that Kendra thought that was all she was going to say. But then she continued, her voice a dry whisper.

"I was a young woman in Vendée during the Revolution, you understand. I witnessed greater atrocity than one woman's murder. Educated men, peasants, clergy, women, children—their blood ran down the street gutters. There was no mercy on either side. It was madness; I had never thought to see such a thing. Never thought to see people—friends, neighbors—behave with such . . . such barbarism."

She gave a small shrug, and her eyes darkened with past horrors. "But once you do, you realize madness can seize anyone. So, *non,* I am not surprised. I know what people—*all* people—are capable of."

25

By the time they left the shop two hours later, the haunted look in Madame Gaudet's eyes had been replaced by the happy glow of commerce, thanks to the small fortune Lady Atwood had dropped for Kendra's new wardrobe. The Countess and Lady Rebecca hadn't been immune to the siren call of satin and silks, buying several new gowns for themselves in addition to the new wardrobe they'd ordered for Kendra. Kendra could only shake her head, a little baffled by their fascination with shopping.

Most of the orders would be stitched together in increments and delivered over the next few weeks, but they hadn't left the store empty-handed. They carried boxes filled with hair accessories, beaded and embroidered evening reticules, ivory and feathered fans, three shawls, and a beautiful velvet hooded cloak of midnight blue with a silver satin lining. Madame Gaudet had said an unfortunate merchant's daughter had changed her mind about purchasing this last piece, but Kendra had to wonder if the woman had changed her mind or simply run out of funds.

"Now I can give you back your cloak," Kendra said as she and Rebecca walked into her bedchamber with their packages. She'd almost forgotten that more than a month ago, Rebecca had been the one to loan her the green cloak for a funeral. She'd never returned it.

"Do not concern yourself, Miss Donovan." Rebecca deposited the packages she was carrying on the bed. "Why don't you give it to your lady's maid? That is what is usually done, you know. I often give my old dresses to my maid. Of course, Mary has to alter them considerably since she is shorter than I, but she's a skillful seamstress."

Miss Cooper wouldn't even have to alter the cloak, Kendra realized when the lady's maid arrived a short time later to help unpack the boxes. They were pretty much the same height. But Kendra was taken aback at Miss Cooper's reaction when she offered her the cloak.

The habitually stern lines of her face fell away in an onslaught of surprised pleasure. "Thank you, Miss Donovan," Miss Cooper breathed, reaching out to take the garment and stroke the soft material with reverent fingers. "'Tis lovely. I shall treasure it."

The maid's gratefulness made Kendra feel awkward, and once again she was reminded of the vast gulf that existed in this era between the classes. She—or, rather, Lady Atwood—had just spent the afternoon ordering dresses that could probably fill up three rooms, and yet a castoff cloak was precious in the eyes of Miss Cooper.

Kendra was relieved when she and Rebecca left the bed-chamber for the study.

"Does making someone else happy always give you a sour stomach, Miss Donovan?" Rebecca asked her lightly. "Miss Cooper was grateful for the gift of the cloak. Why do you look as though you just ate some bad fish?"

"I don't want her gratitude."

"You'd rather have her annoyed with you?"

"No, of course, not." How could she explain the guilt that she was feeling? "Doesn't it bother you how reliant a servant is on the people who employ them?"

Rebecca frowned. "The role of a lady's maid is a coveted one, and Miss Cooper appears to enjoy her status."

"Who can enjoy that?" *Spending her life in servitude*, Kendra thought. *Thrilled to receive any hand-me-downs.*

"My maid is quite content. And Miss Cooper appears an educated woman. If she's unhappy, she can hire herself out as a governess. Or she can marry."

Kendra sighed heavily. "Those shouldn't be her only choices. And even if Miss Cooper married, what then? She'd be indebted to a husband. And what happens if her husband dies? She's forced back into servitude, like Mrs. Danbury."

Rebecca regarded her with surprise. "Who told you Mrs. Danbury was married?"

"No one. I assumed—well, she is *Mrs.* Danbury. She's never been married?"

"No. 'Tis an honorary title—a sign of respect for her position as housekeeper."

"Oh, for God's sake—this is what I'm talking about. Why would being married make her *more* respectable, give her *more* honor?"

"Why do you think?" Rebecca shot her an exasperated look. "What do you think I have been railing against, Miss Donovan? Women hold little value in this society unless they are attached to a man, even a fictitious husband. I have come to believe that our sex must be given the parliamentary right to vote if we ever hope to achieve anything of significance with our lives."

It struck Kendra that she wasn't the only one in the wrong time. Rebecca may have been born in this era, but she was an outlier. The women's suffragist movement wouldn't be formed for another half a century. And even then, it would be decades before a woman was given the right to cast a ballot. Rebecca would never live to see it.

The thought chilled her, and she determinedly pushed it away as they entered the study.

The Duke, Alec, and Sam Kelly were already there, sitting around a table that held platters and plates filled with cold cuts, chunks of cheese, and brown bread. The men rose at their entrance.

"How was the shopping expedition?" Aldridge asked.

"Successful." Rebecca gave him an impish smile. "Your purse is considerably lighter now, Your Grace."

"I think I can withstand the assault. Would you like tea or coffee? Or a glass of sherry?"

"Coffee," Kendra said, and went to the sideboard to get it herself. As she sat down next to Alec, she noticed that Sam was holding a glass of his favored whiskey. It occurred to her that as often as she saw him drink, she'd actually never saw him drunk. The man was a medical marvel.

"I shall have tea. And I'm famished," Rebecca declared, reaching for a thick slice of brown bread. "Mr. Kelly, do you have anything new to report? Have you learned about Lady Dover's background yet?"

"Me men are still checking into that, and her connection ter Bear. But as I was just telling His Grace, I found the housekeeper, Mrs. Frost."

"Is there a Mr. Frost?" wondered Kendra. "Or is he a figment of everyone's imagination?"

The Runner blinked. "Pardon?"

Rebecca paused in layering her bread with almost transparent cuts of roast beef. "Do not concern yourself, Mr. Kelly. Miss Donovan is only teasing. Did Mrs. Frost offer new information?"

"She never saw the couple that she'd been commissioned ter cook and clean for. She only dealt with a man-of-affairs named Mr. Kent. Still, she knew the man was gentry. He left that behind." He pointed to a small silver container on the table.

"What is it?" Kendra asked.

Aldridge picked up the box and handed it to her. "'Tis a tabatière—a snuffbox."

Sam said, "Mrs. Frost took it from the bedchamber after she'd been told ter clear out."

"Well, obviously it must be Weston's," Rebecca said.

"Maybe." Kendra studied the bucolic landscape painted on the inlaid enamel. "Or maybe it belonged to the new man in Lady Dover's life."

Sam's eyebrows shot up. "There was a new man? How'd you know?"

"Madame Gaudet." Kendra put the snuffbox down and picked up a plate, filling it with bread, meat, and cheese. "Lady Dover never actually confided in her, but she got the impression that the Countess had become involved with someone else."

Alec raised a skeptical brow. "An impression? You are relying on the sensitivities of a dressmaker?"

"Yes." Kendra went about the business of making herself a sandwich. Bread, baked fresh from scratch, had become one of her greatest culinary pleasures while living here. "Madame Gaudet makes her living by being sensitive to her clients' needs and being able to gauge their emotions. She said that she noticed a change in Lady Dover's demeanor several weeks ago. I'm inclined to believe her."

Aldridge said, "So this man could not be the father of Lady Dover's child."

"No."

"Then he's unlikely to be the murderer."

"Those are two separate issues," Kendra pointed out, and bit into her sandwich. She chewed and swallowed. "If Lord Weston found out that his mistress was using their *love shack* to meet another man, he probably wouldn't have been happy."

Alec's lips twitched at *love shack*, but he said only, "Weston couldn't have expected exclusivity from Cordelia. He was aware of our involvement."

"Madame Gaudet thinks that since you were involved with Lady Dover first, Weston wouldn't have felt betrayed. Personally, I think the Countess fits the classic narcissistic personality disorder."

Sam asked, "What's that, Miss?"

"She had feelings of entitlement, the need for constant attention, admiration, adulation. She was exploitative and lacked empathy for others."

Rebecca gave a laugh. "That describes most of the Ton, Miss Donovan."

"My point being that her new lover could have been an impulse, one that she only later used to make Weston jealous. Or maybe that had been her plan all along. Either way, the new lover might not have anything to do with her murder, but we need to find out who he is to make that determination." Kendra finished her sandwich, and wiped her hands on the cloth napkin.

"His Grace told us that Mr. Roberts has a collection of knives," said the Bow Street Runner. "You think the villain took one of the daggers during the ball, Miss, and used it on Lady Dover?"

"I think it's too much of a coincidence that Lady Dover was murdered by a stiletto, and there just happens to be a collection of stilettos in the house that Weston and his family were at on the night of the murder," she replied. "The collection is arranged in such a way that I don't think anyone would have noticed if something was taken."

"The timing wouldn't be an issue," Aldridge put in. "Miss Donovan and I walked from the Roberts' household on Mount Street to Grosvenor Square. It took less than ten minutes."

"And we weren't even hurrying," Kendra added. She picked up her coffee cup. "The unsub could've made it in half that time. It was night, with a full moon." Sipping her coffee, she pictured it in her mind.

Sam shook his head. "Not here in London Town. There were clouds—no moon. And the fog had set in something fierce."

Kendra mentally revised the picture forming in her head. Pitch-black, with only oil lamps burning in the doorways. "That certainly makes it easier to hide. If the unsub walked fast or ran, he could've committed the murder and been back at the party in half an hour or forty-five minutes."

"In a crowded ballroom, it would be easy enough to lose sight of someone," murmured Alec.

Rebecca pushed her empty plate away. "'Tis difficult to imagine he could have murdered a woman and then returned to the ball. To *dance*. He's a monster. Has he no remorse?"

Kendra thought of Lady Dover's mutilated face. "No, I don't think he suffers from remorse. Or he knows how to compartmentalize his feelings pretty well—if he feels remorse, he does so only when he's alone and has a chance to think about what he did. Otherwise, I think he pushes it to the back of his mind and goes on with his life."

Rebecca looked troubled. "Is that possible?"

"We all do it to some extent, otherwise we would be overwhelmed with emotion. Grief from the death of a loved one, fear after a traumatic event . . ." *Shock at being stranded in the nineteenth century.*

Kendra rose and moved to the slate board. "The killer has to have a connection to Roberts. He had to know about the collection of knives. This is not a crime of opportunity. He knew he would have access to the murder weapon on the night of the ball."

"That would narrow it down to everyone in London who has called upon Lady Frances and her husband," Alec scoffed.

Aldridge added, "The net needs to be cast even wider. The weapons belong to Mr. Roberts's grandfather, and have been in the residence for at least thirty years. I'd say everyone in London who has ever crossed the threshold would know about the collection."

Kendra glanced at him. "But not everyone in London would want to murder Lady Dover."

"Just the wives," Rebecca muttered, then held up a hand. "Forgive me, I don't mean to be facetious. Again, I will point out the obvious—Lord Weston is the most likely suspect. The real question is how do we prove that he murdered his mistress?"

Kendra shook her head. "We can't operate with that kind of cognitive bias." She'd been involved in too many murder investigations where the local police had already formed their opinion on who the unsub was, and every piece of evidence that supported their theory was considered, while anything that disproved their initial determination was discarded. It was dangerous. "I agree that Lord Weston is the most likely suspect, but he's not the *sole* suspect."

She paused, then said, "Madame Gaudet said that Lady Louisa and Lady Isabella both expressed a desire to see Lady Dover dead."

"People say all sorts of things in anger," Rebecca said.

"I have difficulty imagining either young lady killing Lady Dover in such a horrific manner," admitted Aldridge.

Kendra thought of the biases of this era, one that would automatically eliminate the so-called fairer sex from any investigation. It made her wonder how many wives were poisoning their husbands and getting away with it.

"I'm not ruling anyone out," she said firmly. "Weston became agitated when his son's name was brought up. Was that because he's worried that his son will be dragged into the investigation—or because he fears his son is guilty?"

"We do know that Viscount Dawson became angry at Lady Dover after the incident with the necklace," Aldridge said, nodding. "And when he attempted to retrieve it, she laughed at him. That would hurt any young buck's pride."

"How much angrier would he become if he found out his father's mistress was pregnant?" Kendra wondered.

"The pregnancy would have caused gossip, but it would not have threatened Dawson's line of succession," Alec pointed out. "It's not uncommon to have by-blows, Miss Donovan. Half the royal family have sired children outside of wedlock. Even if Weston would have been so foolish as to divorce his wife and marry Cordelia, Dawson remains Weston's heir by primogeniture. The estate and title are entailed."

"Yes, but, as Lady St. James informed us, the estate is impoverished," Rebecca reminded them. "Dawson may be in need of an heiress. Even a merchant might think twice about marrying his daughter into a family tainted by divorce, or involved in the kind of scandal-broth that Lady Dover had been making."

Kendra finished her coffee and set the cup on the Duke's desk. "It sounds like the Viscount has a lot to lose, even without his title on the line. I think it's time I spoke with him. Who wants to arrange the introduction?"

26

As it turned out, Kendra didn't need an introduction—at least not a formal one. The Duke had received word that it was the Viscount's habit to spend his Saturday evenings at the house of one Mrs. Allen.

Kendra was resigned to spending an evening bored silly, while young ladies took turns playing the pianoforte. Lady Atwood corrected her misconception by informing her, with a curl of her lip that marked her condescension, that Mrs. Allen actually ran a gambling hell—though the Duke insisted that it was a gambling *establishment*. Apparently gambling hells were frequented by men, and if there were any women present, they were not ladies. Gaming establishments, on the other hand, had the veneer of respectability, where even gently bred ladies could try their luck at a game of chance. Regardless, the difference seemed to be lost on Lady Atwood, who decided to seek her evening's entertainment elsewhere.

Kendra tried not to smile. An evening without the Countess was already a plus in Kendra's book. And Mrs. Allen's establishment sounded a lot less dull than attending another rout.

Mrs. Allen had transformed her drawing room into what looked like an upscale gambling room on par with those at Caesars Palace, the kind reserved for whales who dropped $10,000 to $1 million a bet, far away from the shrill *ding-ding-ding* of slot machines. Men outnumbered women two to one, though the women at the tables tended to be older. Mrs. Allen's establishment might be considered respectable, but Kendra doubted whether any parent would allow their young debutantes to come through the doors.

A low murmur of conversation could be heard through the room, broken by quick bursts of laughter here and there. Yet beneath the genteel façade, Kendra sensed an intensity, a sour note of desperation that rose up to mingle with the flowery perfume, spicier cologne, smoke, and sweat in the air.

Mrs. Allen herself stood in one of the room's corners. She was an older woman wearing a brilliant green satin gown and a matching turban that sported no less than five curling ostrich feathers. Both gown and turban shimmered in the light given off by the numerous candles around the room. She wore what looked like a benevolent smile on her face, but even from a distance Kendra saw her sharp eyes constantly in motion, scanning the more than a dozen green baize-covered tables and their occupants, playing cards or rolling dice.

"She supposedly sleeps with a blunderbuss under her pillow and her money in her mattress," Alec murmured. He stood on one side of her, the Duke on the other. They'd tried to discourage him from accompanying them to the gaming house, but Alec had made it clear that he was done with sitting at home. His battered face had caused a few teasing comments from acquaintances as they'd threaded their way through the tables, but Alec either ignored them or offered a dry quip to fend off further inquiries.

"Five years ago, Mr. Allen put a pistol in his mouth when he couldn't pay off his gambling debts," Aldridge said quietly. "His widow turned this house into a gambling establishment to pay off the loan sharks, and has prospered ever since. Now she has become the loan shark."

"Pretty inventive." Kendra's gaze returned to the woman, unsure whether to be impressed or appalled.

They found Viscount Dawson at the third table. He resembled his middle sister, with the same beak nose and weak chin, this feature not helped by the elaborate cravat he wore, high enough to brush his earlobes. His hair was a dingy brown and, despite his being only in his mid-twenties, already receding, which gave him an excessively high forehead. Kendra observed the sweat that made the high forehead gleam. It was warm in the room, but she suspected the Viscount's perspiration had more to do with the meager stack of chips in front of him, compared to those of his fellow card players.

"He's playing deep." Alec had his gaze fixed on the younger man.

"I thought he and his family were broke," Kendra whispered.

Alec gave an almost indolent roll to his shoulders. "Most of London operates on credit."

Not unlike the twenty-first century.

As they watched, Dawson's small pool of chips shrank steadily. By the time he lost his last chip, he'd been forced to wipe the sweat from his brow at least five times, leaving his handkerchief crumpled and soggy. Kendra noticed his hand wasn't quite steady when someone thrust a paper and quill at him to write an acknowledgment of his debt. In a huff of temper, he signed and threw both quill and paper on the table, then lurched to his feet and propelled himself toward the French doors that opened to a veranda that overlooked the back gardens.

When Kendra and her companions stepped out onto the veranda after him, Dawson glanced in their direction, his expression pensive. There'd been another downpour earlier, leaving the grounds drenched and smelling of wet earth and vegetation. It was too dark to see the gardens, but Kendra heard the leaves ruffling in the cold breeze. She was grateful for the Kashmir embroidered shawl that Miss Cooper had given her to match the velvet sapphire evening dress she wore.

"My lord?" Aldridge said. "I am the Duke of Aldridge. This is my ward, Miss Donovan, and my nephew, the Marquis of Sutcliffe. Could we have a moment of your time?"

Dawson's eyes were dark brown like his father's and there was no mistaking the wary glint in them even in the uncertain light. He executed a perfunctory bow. "Your Grace. Is this about Lady Dover's death? I know you've been making inquiries." His gaze drifted to Kendra, then back to the Duke. "I saw you leave my sister's house this morning."

That surprised Kendra. "You were at Lady Frances's?"

"I didn't kill the wretched woman," Dawson spat, ignoring her question. "That's what you are going to ask me, aren't you?"

"I hardly think you'd tell me the truth if you did kill her, would you?" Kendra replied coolly.

Dawson stared at her and said nothing.

"Why don't you tell me what happened when you went to see her after the incident at the theater," Kendra said. "We've heard a lot of rumors. I'd like to get your side."

"Nothing happened." His mouth flattened. He reached into his inside coat pocket and withdrew a delicate papier-mâché container that Kendra now recognized as a snuffbox, and his handkerchief. "I requested that she return the jewelry. She said no."

"That must have made you angry. The necklace belongs in your family, doesn't it?"

A flash of fury in his eyes was quickly suppressed. "Of course it does," he snapped. "That necklace has been in my family for five generations."

Alec regarded the younger man with cool green eyes. "And yet it was your father who gave her the necklace."

Dawson frowned. Instead of responding, he flicked open the lid of the snuffbox, releasing the scent of citrusy vanilla. "It was not meant as a gift," he said finally. He took a small pinch of snuff, placed it in both nostrils, and inhaled deeply. He whipped his damp handkerchief up to his nose to absorb the two sneezes that followed.

"I will allow that my father made a mistake," he continued, tucking the snuffbox and handkerchief back into his pocket. "He could not anticipate her outlandish behavior. But she entranced him."

"What about you?" Kendra asked. "Did she entrance you?"

His eyes widened. "What are you implying? Good God, she was my father's . . . *mistress.*" He dropped his voice to a hiss. "And she was old, at least thirty." He shot Alec a look. "*You* are the one they are whispering about, Sutcliffe. I was with my entire family the night of the ball, but where were you? Perhaps you were so enraged that my father held her affection that you murdered the woman."

Alec let out a laugh. "I've parted ways with other mistresses, you know, and never murdered any of them. I have given them a nice bauble for our time together, a token of my esteem. My liaison with Lady Dover had finished. But it would seem she was very much involved with your family before her death."

In the golden glow of the French doors, Dawson looked very young. And suddenly very furious. "Damn you, don't laugh at me. I should call you out for your slander against my family!"

The statement seemed to electrify the air around them. The Duke tensed. The smile vanished from Alec's face, and, with skin darkened by bruises, he looked dangerous.

"That can be arranged. Shall I name my second?" he asked in a low, lethal voice.

"My boy . . ." the Duke said uneasily. "This is not what we intended."

Dawson seemed like a man who'd stepped on ice, only to have it crack beneath his feet. He hesitated, uncertain. Then he turned toward the Duke. "I did not murder Lady Dover. Nor did my father. The very idea is preposterous. I have nothing more to say on the matter." He gave a stiff bow. "Good evening."

They said nothing as the Viscount slipped back through the French doors. He hurried past his fellow gamblers and Mrs. Allen, who, Kendra noticed, also tracked his progress across the room until he'd disappeared out the door.

"Shit." Kendra spun back to Alec, glaring. "Did you just challenge that kid to a duel?"

"Actually, he challenged me," he drawled. "I simply called him on it."

Kendra brought up her hands to scrub against her face. Her heart was still thumping erratically in her chest over the breathless seconds when the threat of a duel seemed real. *This* was why she didn't belong here, in an era where civilized men could end their argument with pistols. How insane was that?

She dropped her hands, and inhaled deeply. *Focus.* "He didn't like being laughed at, did he?"

"Yes, I noticed that," Alec said drily.

"He also lied," the Duke said slowly, an odd light in his eyes. "He was involved with Lady Dover, I think. His snuff—it's quite distinctive. I recognized it as the same blend that the housekeeper found under the bed in the cottage."

27

Sunday morning arrived with an icy snap in the air and ominous gray clouds that hinted at more rain to come. It sent the servants scurrying to light candles and fires to chase away the gloomy chill inside the house. At ten o'clock, Kendra certainly appreciated the crackling fire as she stood in the Duke's study, her backside positioned to absorb the warmth while she cupped the mug of hot coffee in both hands, her gaze on the slate board.

The room was quiet except for the rattle of the windows caused by sporadic winds and light domestic sounds—the tick of the clock, the happy hiss and pop from logs in the hearth. The entire house had a hushed quality, a stark contrast to only half an hour ago, when Lady Atwood had persuaded (or bullied, depending on one's perspective) her brother and nephew into accompanying her to church services. Alec had attempted to use his injuries as an excuse to avoid it, but his aunt reminded him that if he had been well enough to go to a gaming hell the previous evening, then he was well enough to go to the house of the Lord this morning. Score one for Lady Atwood.

Kendra hadn't been sure if she should have been relieved or insulted when the Countess merely glanced in her direction without issuing the same command. She'd since decided to take it as a victory. *Score one for me.*

After they'd departed, so did half the staff, dressed in their Sunday best. For Miss Cooper, that meant wearing the hand-me-down green cloak, her chest swelling with pride. The servants left behind had gathered in the dining room belowstairs for prayers. Kendra had taken the opportunity to steal the pot of coffee and a cup from the morning room's sideboard and escape to the Duke's study, where she'd updated the slate board.

Lord Dover's name was still on it, but he'd fallen to the bottom. The names of the entire Weston family were above him.

Now her gaze fell on the name she'd recently written: Viscount Dawson.

She knew better than to trust any denials during a murder investigation. But damn it, she'd been halfway to believing Dawson when he'd denied any involvement with Lady Dover. But the fact that he used the same brand of snuff as the tobacco found in the cottage was damning.

Unless he'd borrowed the snuff from his father.

This seemed more plausible. Dawson didn't seem to be Lady Dover's type. What would she have to gain by sleeping with the son of the man she was trying to marry?

Sipping her coffee, Kendra considered Lady Dover's profile. Power; position; prestige—these were the things that motivated Lady Dover. She'd clawed her way out of the gutter to marry an Earl, and then appeared to have set her sights on Weston.

So why sleep with the son—*if* that was what had happened? Did she think she could use Dawson as leverage against

Weston? If she could twist the son around her little finger, could she force the father into doing whatever she wanted?

Kendra frowned. Lady Dover and Dawson engaged in a romantic tryst just wasn't working for her. Her gut said no. But logically . . . hell, there were weirder pairings. Sonny and Cher, for one. And there was the temper that had flooded Dawson's face the previous evening. *Damn you, don't laugh at me.* He'd practically challenged Alec to a duel over this perceived slight.

Lady Dover had laughed at him as well. Even Kendra knew you couldn't challenge ladies to duels. Perhaps he'd punished her in a different way. It was something to think about.

Kendra's gaze dropped lower. *Lady Weston.* In this era—hell, any era—she probably had the most to lose: her husband, her reputation, her standing in society. She'd already been humiliated. And while her nineteenth-century counterparts might dismiss her because she was a woman—a *Lady*—Kendra believed in equal rights. Even in murder.

She swung around at a soft knock at the door. A young footman entered, carrying a note on a silver salver.

"Um . . . a lad brought this to the door for you, Miss."

"For me?"

"Yes, Miss."

Frowning, Kendra took the paper as the footman silently departed. There was no seal to break, so she only had to unfold the note to read the scrawled sentences written in an uneven hand. Four sentences only, but they had the power to send her pulse racing.

Meat me at the Crown tavern at Piccadilly. At eleven. Come a lone. I no about Lady Dover.

❖

"Ye want the barking irons?" Molly said at Kendra's pronouncement. She was one of the servants who'd stayed behind. Now she stared wide-eyed at Kendra, who'd come belowstairs.

"I need to meet someone at the Crown Tavern in Piccadilly." She glanced at the clock. "At eleven."

"But that's an hour away."

"I believe in being early."

"'Oo wants ter meet ye?"

"Someone who might have information about Lady Dover's murder."

Despite her youth, Molly's pale blue eyes narrowed with distrust. "Could be a trap, Miss."

"That's why I want the guns that I lifted from Bear's two associates. Do you know where Harding put the weapons?"

"Maybe ye should wait until the Duke returns."

"I'm not waiting. Do you want me to go defenseless?"

Molly gave her an uncertain look, then shook her head. "All right, Miss."

She led Kendra to the butler's quarters, a suite with a bedroom and small sitting room. Molly hovered in the doorway, not daring to enter, and pointed to an enormous steamer trunk against the far wall. "Oi know Mr. Harding puts valuables in there."

Kendra moved across the room. She tried to lift the lid, but it wouldn't budge.

"'Tis locked," Molly said unnecessarily.

"Yeah, I figured that out." Kendra squatted beside the trunk and removed a pin from her coiled hair. She blocked out the last time she'd been forced to pick a lock, when she'd been shackled and lying helpless a month ago, and concentrated instead on feeling the tumblers with the thin wire, applying the right amount of pressure . . .

"Ah." She expelled a sigh of satisfaction when she heard the distinctive click of the latch coming undone. She lifted the lid and peered inside. The two flintlocks were lying on top of an assortment of books and smaller boxes. Only when she grasped the heavy weapons did she realize that she had no idea if they were still loaded with the remaining three balls. Worse, she had absolutely no idea how to load the old-fashioned weapons if the butler had taken the precaution of emptying them.

"Shit."

"*Miss!*"

Kendra ignored Molly's shocked admonishment. "I need to make sure these are loaded."

Molly sought the assistance of the young footman who'd earlier brought Kendra the note. Initially, he refused to help them, but Kendra lied, telling him that they were acting on the Duke's orders. He still looked dubious, but finally went about the business of priming and loading the weapons. He seemed relieved to finally hand them over to Kendra.

"Oi 'ave to come with ye!" Molly cried, following Kendra up the stairs. "Miss, ye're a lady. Ye can't be goin' around London unattended!"

Kendra nearly dropped another curse, a lot worse than the one she'd said earlier in Molly's presence, but she bit her tongue in time. "I don't need a chaperone, Molly."

"Ye do!"

"No, I don't . . ." She looked around at Molly's stubborn face, and was struck by an idea.

"W'ot?"

"I don't need a chaperone if I'm a servant." Women in this society's lower tiers could move about the streets freely.

"But ye're not a servant. Not anymore."

"Yes, I am. I've just demoted myself. C'mon, Molly." She grabbed the tweeny's arm and steered her to the stairs. "You and I are going to change clothes."

"Nay, Miss!"

"Yes." She forced her into her bedchamber and turned around. "Come on, Molly, hurry. Unbutton me, then I'll unbutton you."

Molly reluctantly obeyed Kendra's commands. She helped Kendra into the simple blue dress and white apron but stubbornly refused to put on Kendra's gown, setting her jaw and shaking her head.

"'Ow are ye gonna get there, Miss?" Molly asked. "'Is Grace took 'is carriage to church."

Kendra was trying to figure out what to do with the flint-locks. Carrying them out in the open didn't seem like a good idea. "I'll hire a hackney," she said absently, but then it occurred to her that she had no money. "Goddamn it. How much will that cost?"

"Oi dunno, Miss. Oi've never 'ired an 'ackney before."

Kendra pinched the bridge of her nose in frustration. Why was everything in this era so damn difficult? She swiped Molly's mop cap off her head and left the near-naked tweeny to her own devices, retracing her footsteps to the servants' quarters. The remaining staff stared at her, but she managed to procure a wicker basket in which to hide the pistols and a handful of coins.

She hesitated on the stairs. The note could be a trap, as even Molly had noted. But what could possibly happen to her in the middle of Piccadilly, a thoroughfare as busy today as it was in her own time? Then again, she'd been kidnapped in broad daylight right off the streets of Grosvenor Square.

"Hey—you." She pointed at the young footman who'd assisted her with the guns.

He swallowed hard. "Yes, Miss?"

"Can you go to Bow Street and find Sam Kelly? Tell him to meet me at the Crown Tavern on Piccadilly?"

"You want me ter find the Runner and tell 'im ter meet you at the Crown on Piccadilly?"

"Yes."

"Is that all, Miss?"

"No. Tell him to hurry."

She looped her arm through the basket, picked up her skirts, and raced up the stairs.

28

Eva Cooper swept up the stairs of the Duke's palatial mansion, and just for a moment she allowed herself to imagine what it would be like to be a Lady. It wasn't all that difficult to weave a fantasy, not with the elegant green velvet cloak falling off her shoulders, swirling like green mist around her skirts. The fine fabric made her feel special. Regal, even.

She'd been a lady's maid now for more than a decade, having begun as an upstairs maid in a marquis's great household in Kent. She'd acted as a lady's maid when they'd needed extra hands during their house parties. But Miss Franks, the Marchioness's personal maid, wasn't going anywhere, Eva knew, so she'd ventured to London to hire herself out as a lady's maid. She'd done well, finding herself in the rarified circles of the Ton. Her current position in the Duke of Aldridge's household, working for someone like Lady Atwood, was her most auspicious employment yet.

As she crossed the foyer, she caught one of the footman's eyes on her. Her instinct was to admonish him for staring so rudely. But she was feeling uncommonly content, and so merely raised her eyebrows at him in a reproving gesture as she moved past to the grand staircase. She knew that Lady Atwood and the Duke were still at church, otherwise she would never have been so bold as to ascend this particular staircase. She was a lady's maid, which put her above most of the staff, except for the butler and housekeeper—though Eva really considered herself on the same level as Mrs. Danbury— but she was still required to use the servants' stairs.

Her good humor lasted until she entered Miss Donovan's bedchamber. There she stopped in shock, her gaze falling on the half-naked tweeny sitting in a chair. And her shock turned to fury when the girl explained that Miss Donovan had dressed in the tweeny's uniform to meet with some unknown person at a tavern in Piccadilly.

Eva glared at the girl, who reacted by shrinking away from her. "How could you let her go?"

"'Ow could Oi stop 'er?"

"By keeping your clothes on!" she snapped, and pressed a hand to her stomach. How could Miss Donovan do this to her? The Countess had warned her that the American was peculiar, and unpolished in the ways of the Ton. That was why Lady Atwood had hired her, to help rid her of her vulgar tendencies. But this behavior . . . it was too much. She had been mortified, utterly mortified, when the woman had run out of the house the other day like a common trollop. She'd never expected that a duke's ward would have no sense of propriety or decorum.

Eva swallowed hard. The Countess had blamed her for allowing Miss Donovan to behave in such a way, to be caught by the criminal underworld. Thank heaven the Duke's nephew had been on hand to rescue her.

But now Eva grew faint with horror at the thought of the Countess learning about the American's appalling behavior today. To be caught dressed like a tweeny . . . dear heaven, that could spell ruin for them all. Miss Donovan's disgrace would ripple out like the waters of the River Thames, destroying even Eva's reputation. Instead of the exclusive circles of society to which she'd grown accustomed, she would be cast off. She'd be fortunate enough to find herself employment as a lady's maid for the daughter of a *merchant*.

The very idea sent a shudder through her.

Eva straightened her spine. The Duke and his family still hadn't returned from their church services. There was time for her to rectify this matter. "Where did Miss Donovan go?"

"Oi already told ye! Piccadilly. The Crown Tavern. What're ye gonna do?"

But Eva was already out the door, the green cloak fluttering behind her.

29

Kendra was well aware that she was under scrutiny. As the only woman not showing copious amounts of cleavage inside the Crown Tavern, she stood out like a sore thumb. Still, despite her modest servant's attire, she'd been approached by no less than seven men who'd thought to charm her with their smiles, offering her something more than the coffee cooling in the cup in front of her. After ascertaining that none of the men had sent her the note, Kendra had rebuffed each one of them with a hard stare and little regard for their egos.

Except for one, they'd retreated back to their own tables, eyeing her with hostility. The one who didn't go peacefully had limped away nursing a sore foot after she'd ground the heel of her half boot onto his toes. She was glad she'd changed out of her soft-soled slippers.

Though the Crown Tavern's patrons appeared to be merchants and workers rather than members of the criminal class, Kendra kept her hand near the wicker basket, prepared to use the pistols tucked under the colorful blanket should anything go wrong.

"Ye want more coffee, or somethin' else?" the buxom barmaid asked as she came over with a pot.

Kendra was painfully aware of both the few coins she had left on her and her lack of knowledge regarding this era's monetary system. The hackney driver she'd hired seemed to sense her uncertainty and had demanded a price that she was fairly certain was exorbitant. But because she'd been pressed for time, she hadn't argued. She now had exactly three shillings left on her.

"No, thank you."

The barmaid didn't move away, but studied Kendra with curious, dark eyes. "Eh, who you're waitin' for, then?"

"I'm not sure."

"How d'you know he's not here?"

"I guess I don't."

"You're a strange one, ain't you? An American?"

"Yes—and yes," Kendra said with a ghost of a smile. She hesitated a moment, then decided to ask. "Have you heard about the murder at Grosvenor Square?"

The barmaid's eyes widened. "Aye, folks have been talkin'. Some lord did the deed, they say. Wagers are bein' placed on whether he'll get the silk rope or not."

"Silk rope?"

"Aye. Nobility that hang can buy a silk rope, not the hemp us common folk get."

"What are the odds that he'll hang?"

Bitterness flashed in the girl's eyes. "The gentry stick together, the lot of 'em; they'll let him off. But . . ." She seemed to catch herself.

"But?" Kendra prompted.

The barmaid hesitated, then leaned forward and dropped her voice. "There's also talk that the gentry mort had dealings with someone powerful in the rookeries and he's gonna slit the Lord's gullet."

Kendra eyed the smile that curled the barmaid's lips. "I guess you're not concerned if he slits the throat of an innocent man."

"Who's ta say the bloke is innocent, eh? Besides, why should I care?" Her face hardened. "Our betters don't care whether we starve in the street, now, do they? With corn prices the way they are? And the fancy complain about highwaymen, when they're the ones robbin' everyone blind, sendin' folks to the poorhouse."

She gave a loud sniff, and, with a swing of her hips, wandered back to the tap.

Kendra picked up her coffee cup and sipped the now-cold brew. She looked out the windows at the busy street and the steady streams of humanity. There were merchants and laborers going about their business, peddlers pitching their wares in singsong voices. On the street, fashionable carriages seemed to fight for dominance against hired hackneys, public coaches, and lumbering wagons.

Kendra glanced at the clock on the wall. Five minutes after eleven. She thought about waiting a few more minutes, but she knew in her gut that whoever had sent the note wasn't coming. It left her with an uneasy feeling, a prickle at the base of her spine. *Something's wrong.*

She pushed herself to her feet, looping her arm through the wicker basket, making sure her hand remained close to the pistols inside, and made her way to the door. Outside, she joined the throngs of people.

Someone shouted her name. She paused and turned, and in the distance she saw Sam Kelly hop down from a hired hackney.

"Miss Donovan!" he yelled again, and waved.

She started to lift her hand when it suddenly dawned on her that he wasn't looking at her, but further down the street. Frowning, she swung around.

A sharp cry cut the air, rising over the general noise of the street, and then a team of horses pulling a cart reared up, shrieking, sending the cart swerving dangerously into the pedestrians. The driver pulled desperately at the reins, but couldn't control the startled animals. The crowd seemed to surge forward like a single unit, then people began to break free, scattering in all directions. Screams, both human and horse, swelled.

Kendra was caught in a tidal wave of humanity, pushed and shoved backward. She clutched the wicker basket close to her chest and made a dash for safety as more panicked horses thundered past, close enough for her to feel the heat rise off their sweat-slicked hides. As the animals finally skittered to a stop, men rushed forward to grab their harnesses and bridles. The beasts shifted uneasily, their eyes rolling wildly in their head, their nostrils quivering as they snorted billowing puffs of steam into the air.

"Oh my God," Kendra breathed. The people around her were still shouting and screaming—and sobbing. Her heart pounded in her chest as she fought her way up the street.

"I didn't see her! I swear!" The ashen-faced driver stumbled down from his wagon perch. His eyes seemed as wild as the horses'. "I didn't see her!" he kept shouting at the crowd who'd gathered. "She came outta nowhere!"

A shrill whistle blew as several constables jogged through the press of bodies. "Move aside. Move aside, I say!"

Kendra barely heard them above the strange buzzing in her head. Her gaze fell on a crumpled figure on the ground. The pool of blood beneath the body spread outward, crimson trickles oozing between the cracks in the cobblestone. She took one step forward, then another.

Sam Kelly was already bending over the mangled body, its limbs distorted into unnatural angles.

"Sam . . . Mr. Kelly . . ." She had to push the words through the bile that rose up in her throat. She didn't think he heard her; he didn't move at all. His attention was fixed on the figure lying on the ground before him.

Sam had lifted his arm. Kendra saw that his outstretched hand was trembling. Then it wavered and dropped, and he twisted around suddenly. The golden eyes, blank with shock, locked on hers. Kendra didn't know how long they stared at each other, but she knew the exact moment recognition hit him, when he saw beyond the mop cap and servant's garb. A fierce emotion rippled across his face.

"Miss Donovan? Good God! 'Tis you? But who . . ." He twisted back to study the awkwardly sprawled figure. His face settled into grim lines and he reached out again, his hand curling around the dead woman's shoulder.

Kendra didn't need him to turn over the crumpled body to know that it was Miss Cooper. She was unrecognizable, the bones of her face crushed beneath the wheels of the wagon, her body broken. The only thing recognizable was the green velvet cloak, now torn and bloody, that Kendra had given the maid the day before.

30

Kendra's hand convulsed around the worn leather strap hanging near the door of the hired hackney. She felt queasy, but she wasn't sure if that was from seeing her lady's maid, dead in the street, or if it was from the rocking of the carriage as it wheeled through London's narrow, winding streets.

"I thought she was you," Sam said. He still looked badly shaken.

"I know."

Kendra didn't dare say that, for a moment, when she'd looked down on the twisted, bloody figure under the torn green velvet cloak—a cloak that she herself had worn only a day ago—she had seen herself as well.

"Are you all right, Miss? Do you want me ter take you home?"

"No," she said, and then, realizing that short answer could apply to both questions, she added, "No, I don't want you to take me home. I want answers."

Still, she had to take a moment to concentrate on her breathing—*inhale and exhale*—to stem the horror rising inside her.

She gave Sam a sidelong look. The Runner had proven himself remarkably efficient earlier, sending one of the many children standing nearby to Dr. Munroe's for a carriage to haul the body back to his autopsy school. Another kid had been dispatched to the Duke's. Then Sam had even begun to interview the gawkers who'd remained at the scene. After watching him for a moment, she'd put aside the shock and joined him.

The driver of the cart, a farmer who's normally ruddy complexion had turned a sickly gray, had repeated over and over again that she'd simply flung herself out in front of him, and he hadn't been able to stop his team from running her down. No one else had seen anything or anyone suspicious. One moment they were huddled together on the street corner, with the usual bit of impatient jostling, as everyone was eager to go about their errands, and the next they'd heard a cry and the madwoman had pitched herself onto the street. There'd been nothing to do but watch the poor lass be trampled to death by the horses and wheels of the farmer's cart, God preserve her.

Now Kendra shook her head and met Sam's worried gaze. "Why was she even there?" Not for a second did she believe it had been a coincidence.

"Do you think she followed you?"

"How? I was gone before she returned home."

Sam rubbed the side of his nose in his habitual gesture. "Exactly why *were* you there, if you don't mind me askin'? A footman summoned me and said I was ter meet you at the Crown at Piccadilly, but he didn't explain why."

"I got a note to meet someone who had information about Lady Dover's death at the Crown Tavern."

"I see. That's why you're dressed the way you are?"

"Yes."

"You were takin' a chance, Miss."

Kendra leaned back against the cracked leather seat cushion, exhausted. "I knew it could be a trap. That's why I didn't go unarmed." She pushed back the blanket in the wicker basket to reveal the pistols. "I can take care of myself, Mr. Kelly."

"Aye, that you can."

"I was wrong about the trap, though. I thought it would be in the Crown Tavern." She swallowed hard against the lump in her throat.

It was the only explanation. Whoever had sent her the note had been hiding in plain sight, blending in with the pedestrians along the congested sidewalk. Or maybe the assassin had been waiting for her in one of the many Tudor-style shops, taverns, or coffeehouses lining the street. But when she'd finally arrived, he hadn't recognized her in the servant garb that she wore. Instead, he'd recognized the green velvet cloak.

"I didn't consider someone lying in wait outside," Kendra said.

"You are about the same height, and have the same hair color," Sam agreed in a low voice, echoing her own thoughts.

"And it's a cold day, so Miss Cooper probably had the hood pulled up, which would have concealed her face." Kendra was pleased that her voice sounded calm, with none of the tremors that she felt rippling through her. "We both know what happened, Mr. Kelly. I should be the one dead."

"You're making someone anxious, Miss."

"Apparently. Unfortunately, I don't know who. Lord Weston? His son? Lord Dover?"

Her gaze drifted to the window. They passed buildings of stone, brick, and stucco. Kendra couldn't help but think of modern London, with its extensive network of CCTV cameras on almost every corner. Civil rights advocates called London the most spiedupon city in the world. Kendra herself had always been torn between a citizen's natural fear of having their privacy invaded, even eroded altogether, and her position in law enforcement, where she wanted to utilize every tool at her disposal to stop criminals.

Would I know the identity of Miss Cooper's killer in 2015? Or would the camera have been turned off, or pointed in a different direction at the time the murderer had pushed the maid into the busy traffic? Those glitches happened more often than people realized.

"Why'd she have your cloak anyway, Miss?"

Kendra brought her gaze back to Sam. "I received a new cloak, so I . . . I gave her the old one." Her throat tightened as she remembered the look of surprised pleasure on the other woman's face the day before.

Sam nodded. "'Tis a common enough practice, Miss. An act of kindness."

Kendra said nothing, but she knew when she met the Runner's shadowed gaze that he was probably wondering the same thing that she was: How could one act of kindness have gone so horribly wrong?

31

D r. Munroe's anatomy school seemed oddly deserted to Kendra, until Sam reminded her that it was Sunday. While the surgeon wasn't a particularly religious man himself, he was clever enough to realize that his standing in the community was fragile at best. He didn't need to increase the neighborhood's antipathy against his profession by chopping up dead bodies—some probably illegally obtained through resurrectionists—on the Sabbath.

Kendra found herself affected by the grim purpose of their visit and had to suppress a shiver as they made their way to the basement. Their footfalls rang out too loudly in the empty hallway. When they descended the shadowy stairs, the air that rose up to greet them was cold and dank, and carried with it the scent of the grave.

In the autopsy room, beneath the glowing lanterns, Dr. Munroe and his apprentice, Mr. Barts, were examining the nude, broken body of Eva Cooper. The shock of the sight made Kendra inhale sharply—a mistake, as here the air reeked of hot wax, burning oil, and decaying flesh. She had to swallow hard against the reflex to gag.

Munroe and Barts straightened at their entrance. The doctor's gray eyes, behind his spectacles, immediately zeroed in on her.

"Miss Donovan," Dr. Munroe said. "The boy told me that a woman would be accompanying Mr. Kelly. I suspected that it would be you—though I scarcely recognize you, dressed as you are."

The killer certainly didn't, she thought again.

The doctor hesitated, but when no one offered an explanation for her clothes, he made a gesture to the body on the table. "I assume you knew this poor woman. That is why you're here, is it not?"

Kendra forced herself to look at the corpse. "Yes. She was my lady's maid—Miss Cooper. Miss Eva Cooper."

"I'm sorry."

The lump that had formed in Kendra's throat was as unexpected as it was unwanted. She jerked her gaze away from the body and it fell instead on the pile of rags tossed on the table that ran along the wall. No, not rags—guilt slammed into her as she stared at the torn velvet cloak, shredded, muddy, and stained with blood.

"Mr. Barts and I have concluded the visual examination," Munroe said. "Nasty business, this."

"Murder usually is," Kendra said softly.

But Miss Cooper's murder had been particularly gruesome, she thought, as she turned back to the body. Miss Cooper had been quite literally pulverized by the horses hooves and wagon wheels. The maid's head was misshapen, her face crushed and caked liberally with mud and blood, grotesque. Her neck had been broken, twisted now at a peculiar angle. Her flesh had been torn asunder; her bones had snapped and pierced the skin.

Until now, Kendra had no idea what being trampled could do to the human body. Now, she knew, and she would never forget the horror.

"You are already aware we are dealing with murder?" Dr. Munroe asked, surprised.

"It's wasn't an accident, Doctor," Sam said.

Kendra was grateful to have a reason to look away from the maid's brutalized form. She turned to address the doctor. "We don't have an eyewitness, but we think someone pushed her into oncoming traffic." Again she heard the sharp cry before the team of horses had gone crazy. *Before.* "Is there any way you can confirm that she was pushed through the autopsy?"

"No."

"Oh. Well, then—"

"You misunderstand, Miss Donovan," he said, and his spectacles glinted as he turned his head to stare at the body. "This poor wretch may have been pushed into the traffic, and that undoubtedly contributed to her death. But there's something else."

"Something else?"

"The victim wasn't only trampled—she was stabbed."

Munroe and his apprentice turned the body over and the doctor retrieved a magnifying glass, which he handed to Kendra.

"She sustained considerable damage from being crushed, of course. Look—you can even see the imprint of a horseshoe here. But this injury . . ." He took a moment to find the spot, lost amid the other lacerations. "If you'll notice, it's dissimilar."

Kendra put aside her own horror that the thing lying on the table was the woman who had buttoned up her dress that morning and peered at the wound through the lens. She then took the time to compare it to the other slashes. "I see what you mean. The flesh around the wound is more uniform. A cut rather than a tear . . . no, a *puncture.*" She looked up at Munroe. "A stiletto?"

"I'd say so, but I would need to wait until after I've done the autopsy to give you a conclusive answer." He gave her a long look. "I know you are an extraordinary female when it comes to postmortem surgeries. But under the circumstances, I don't think you ought to attend this one."

Kendra wasn't entirely sure what her response would've been. She was prevented from having to give one when the door suddenly swung open and the Duke and Alec came hurrying into the room.

Aldridge went immediately to Kendra, taking her hands as he scanned her from head to foot. "My God, Miss Donovan . . . we got word there was an accident and you were here. How are you? Are you injured? What happened?"

Kendra was aware of Alec's intense scrutiny as well.

"I got a note claiming to have information about Lady Dover's death," she explained. "He wanted me to meet him at the Crown at Piccadilly."

A muscle ticked alongside Alec's jaw. "And you thought you'd oblige this unknown person—a person most likely responsible for Lady Dover's murder?"

"I didn't go unprepared. I was armed."

That startled the Duke. "You had a weapon with you?"

Aldridge caught the glance she gave the wicker basket on the ground. He let go of her hands, and bent to lift the blanket, revealing the two flintlocks tucked inside. "You are a remarkable woman, Miss Donovan," was all he said.

Alec wasn't appeased. "Devil take it, you went alone, didn't you? That is why you're dressed as you are! Have you no notion of the danger you were in?"

"I know . . ." Against her will, her eyes traveled to the figure on the autopsy table.

"The boy told us there was an accident, and Miss Donovan and Miss Cooper were involved," Aldridge said. Then, understanding, he stared in horror at the body on the table. "Dear God, is that Miss Cooper?"

"Aye," Sam said simply.

"I don't understand any of this," the Duke said. "If you went unchaperoned, how did Miss Cooper . . . become involved?"

Kendra drew in a deep breath. "She must have followed me."

"The lass was waiting ter cross the street," Sam added. "It looks like someone stabbed her with a stiletto and pushed her into the traffic. A team of horses and a wagon did the rest."

"But why?" Aldridge shook his head, his blue-gray eyes dazed. "Who had such vitriol against Miss Cooper?"

"Not her," Alec breathed, and Kendra saw that his gaze had locked on the velvet cloak. In two strides, he was across the room. His fingers brush the shredded material. When he turned back, his expression was rigid, his emotions held tightly in check. Yet the light that blazed in his green eyes was dangerous. "He mistook your maid for you."

Kendra forced herself to answer. "Yes. We think so. We're similar in build and coloring—if he got a glimpse of her hair. She probably had the hood up, so he might not have seen her face—"

"But he saw the cloak," Alec cut her off. "*Your* cloak."

Kendra said nothing.

Aldridge stared at her, then shot a glance at the maid on the table. "My God . . . somebody tried to kill you, Miss Donovan. He deliberately lured you out, laid in wait, and tried to kill you. Your disguise saved your life."

Kendra put a hand to her violently churning stomach. Yes, her disguise had saved her life—and cost Eva Cooper hers.

32

Rebecca arrived at the Duke's residence later that day to find the Duke, Alec, and Kendra in the study. Sam had left for Bow Street to gather more men with the intention of returning to Piccadilly to go through the businesses lining the street. The others had gathered around a table in the study, Kendra again holding the note she'd received earlier that day. Rebecca quickly learned the horrifying news that Dr. Munroe was at that moment conducting the postmortem on Miss Cooper.

"Someone tried to murder you," she managed, eyes wide with concern as she looked at Kendra. "But who? No, that's a stupid question. 'Tis obvious it was the same person who killed Lady Dover. But why?"

Kendra was staring at the names on the slate board, but shook her head. "I don't know. Perception is reality. The killer obviously believes I know something."

Rebecca hesitated. "I'm sorry about your maid."

Kendra's throat tightened and she managed a nod. "Everyone's upset."

In fact, the death of Eva Cooper had cast an unexpected shadow over the household. None of the staff had known her for very long, nor had they really liked her. Molly had confided in hushed tones earlier that the woman had never let anyone belowstairs forget that she was a London lady's maid, whereas they were all from the country. Her snobbish attitude had rubbed a lot of the staff the wrong way. But none of that mattered now. Kendra doubted if anyone would be donning black crepe for Miss Cooper, which was the mourning tradition, but the maid's shocking death had melted their enmity.

"Would you like a cup of tea, or a glass of wine?" the Duke asked his goddaughter. "It's a chilly day." As if on cue, the windowpanes behind him rattled with a gust of wind.

"Thank you. Madeira would be lovely." She stepped over to the table that they were standing around. Her eyes fell on the sheet of paper in Kendra's grasp. "What is that?

"The note that was sent here to lure Kendra to her death," Alec said, his tone clipped.

Kendra met his gaze, which was still hot with temper, and shrugged. She couldn't argue with the truth.

Rebecca plucked the note from Kendra's fingers and read aloud: *"Meat me at the Crown tavarn at Piccadilly. At eleven. Come a lone. I no about Lady Dover."*

"Obviously someone who took great pains to convey the impression that they were practically illiterate," said the Duke, handing Rebecca the Madeira.

"They tried a little too hard," Kendra said. "An uneducated person would have spelled the words phonetically. That's where the unsub made his mistake. 'Meat'—why throw in an *a*? Someone who didn't know how to spell would go with an *e* because they'd be sounding it out. And *come*? The *e* is silent. If you were sounding out the word, you wouldn't put it in."

Rebecca took a sip of the wine as she studied the note. "The handwriting has also been disguised. It looks to be a jumble."

Kendra nodded. "Half the letters slant to the left, half to the right. Some are full and round, others are smaller and more angular. Handwriting is like a fingerprints, they have distinctive patterns. This is too inconsistent to be natural."

Alec was in the process of replenishing his glass of sherry, but froze. Slowly, he put down the decanter and turned to face Kendra. "Are you saying that you *knew* this note was not authentic, and yet you still went to the Crown?"

She didn't have to say anything. He read the answer in her eyes, and gave a bitter laugh. "Dear God in heaven. I suppose this is where you tell me again how you can take care of yourself!"

She stood up straighter. "I took precautions. That's why I went early. I'm not an idiot."

"Hell and damnation, how do you protect yourself from someone sneaking up behind you and sticking a stiletto between your ribs before pushing you out in front of stampeding horses?"

Rebecca gasped. "Is that what happened to your maid?"

"Yes," Kendra admitted. "Miss Cooper came after me . . . wearing my old cloak."

Rebecca's lips parted in surprise. Then horror dawned on her features. Slowly, she set down her wineglass. "Then I am to blame for the death of your maid," she said, stricken. "I am the one who suggested you give her that cloak."

"Enough," the Duke said, his tone taking on the rare steel quality he so seldom used. "Neither one of you are responsible for Miss Cooper's death. Her blood is solely on the hands of the man who killed her. Do you understand?"

They understood, and the Duke was right, Kendra knew. But no logic could erase the guilt, the remorse, the wish that you could go back and have a do-over.

Rebecca cleared her throat. "There's something I don't understand. How did the villain know you would be home to receive the note, Miss Donovan? Everyone else was at church services."

Kendra stared at her for a long moment. How indeed?

Abruptly, she shoved away from the table, crossing the room to the window. Outside, the sky had darkened with potbelly gray clouds hanging low, hinting at another deluge in the not too distant future.

"I think I have an idea."

❖

Alec refused to let her go alone, so they went together. But first she insisted on detouring to the kitchens. The Marquis of Sutcliffe's presence belowstairs sent the entire staff into a mad scramble into formation, as if he were a military general come to inspect the troops. It had been several weeks since Kendra had had to deal with Mrs. Danbury, but she recognized in the housekeeper's frosty regard that she was holding Kendra responsible for Alec's unprecedented descent to the servants' quarters.

After Kendra had received a package from belowstairs, they returned upstairs. Harding raced ahead to open the door for them. Outside, the cold wind stung her cheeks. She hunched against it, dashing across the street into the park.

They found Snake in his usual spot, huddled against the thick tree trunk for protection against the wind. He was wearing the same threadbare coat, a grubby scarf wound around his thin neck. He straightened when he saw them coming, his eyes darting suspiciously to the brown paper package she held.

"W'ot's that?"

"A ham and cheese on rye. Watching the house constantly must make you hungry." She thrust the package at him. "Take it," she urged when he hesitated.

His eyes, beneath the brim of his wool cap, were bright with hunger. He resisted for a full second before his small hand flashed out, and with a speed that made her blink, the brown package disappeared into his coat.

"W'ot d'ye want?" he demanded.

"You're welcome," Kendra replied drily. "You've been keeping the Duke's house under surveillance."

Snake frowned, perplexed. "Under what?"

"You're spying," Alec said abruptly. "Why?"

Snake gave him a cocky look. "Why'dya think? Bear wants ter make sure ye don't disappear ter the colonies with yer bit o' muslin 'ere."

Alec's jaw tightened. "Miss Donovan is the Duke's ward. You'd do well to remember that, boy."

Snake grinned, unabashed. "An' when does a lofty gent like a duke 'ave his ward go about looking like a servin' wench, eh?"

"You saw that, did you?" Kendra fixed her gaze on his freckled face. He was ten going on forty.

"Aye."

"What else did you see?"

He frowned. "W'ot d'ye mean?"

"Have you seen anyone else around, spying on the Duke's house? Like you."

"Why d'ye want ter know?"

Kendra showed him the gold guinea she'd palmed and watched his eyes go wide. "I want information, and am willing to trade you this coin to get it. Have you seen anyone else spying on the Duke's house?"

Snake licked his lips, transfixed by the coin in her palm. "Aye, for a couple of days."

"Who?"

"Oi dunno. 'E kept 'is distance, 'e did."

"What did he look like?"

"Yellow hair." Snake screwed up his face as he thought. "'Bout me size, maybe shorter."

"*Your* size? You mean a child?" Kendra wasn't sure why she was surprised. She'd been in London long enough now to realize that children like Snake swarmed the city, doing whatever they could to survive. Acting as a messenger or spy was more benign than other things they might be forced to do.

Kendra wished that she could view this child, and the thousands like him, as archaic pieces of history. But one of her first jobs at the Bureau had been tracking down Internet pedophiles. Western civilization in the twenty-first century might have laws on the books regarding a child's welfare, but she couldn't feel superior to her nineteenth-century counterparts. No generation, no society offered a safety zone for its most vulnerable members.

"Oi would've run 'im off if'n 'e gave me any trouble," Snake was saying. "Oi saw 'im today goin' up an' ringing the bell. 'E 'anded the stiff-rumped fancy a note an' ran off."

Stiff-rumped fancy. Kendra realized he was talking about the footman.

Snake's expression turned sly. "Next thing Oi knows, it gets peculiar-like. Ye're comin' out dressed like a wench. Oi would've followed ye, but Bear wanted me ter stay for the Lord 'ere ter get back from the parson's place."

"How do you know I went to church?" Alec demanded.

"Oi got bleeding peepers, don't Oi?" Snake looked indignant. "Oi waited until ye came back, and followed ye when ye and the old gent came peelin' out. Ye went ter the sawbones' place. Then Oi followed ye back 'ere. That's all Oi can tell ye."

Kendra pressed the coin in the boy's palm, but grabbed his wrist to prevent him from flying off with his prize. "Snake, I have a proposition for you."

He narrowed his eyes. "Eh?"

"She's offering you a deal," Alec supplied.

His brow cleared. "Why din't ye say so? W'ot deal?"

"I need to find the child who delivered the note. Do you think you can help me?"

"'W'ot for?"

"For you, it could mean several more guineas."

Snake's eyes brightened, but then he glared at her. "Are ye tellin' me a bouncer?"

"No. Will you do it?"

He considered it, then nodded. "Aye."

"It has to be the correct child," Alec put in drily. "We'll know if you try to substitute one of your friends."

Snake scowled at him, but Kendra thought the addendum had been smart. She could see that was exactly what the little con artist had planned to do.

She asked, "Do we have a deal?"

"Oi can't leave 'ere until Ned comes, or Bear'll skin me alive."

Kendra let his wrist go. "That's fine. Find the child and bring him to me—or take me to him. I promise to make it worth your while. Do you understand?"

"Aye."

Alec cupped her elbow as they hurried back to the house. They were forced to wait on the side of the road as a large carriage barreled past them, and Kendra suppressed a shiver, remembering all too well what had only just happened to Miss Cooper.

Alec gave her a sidelong glance when they finally hurried across the street. "That was a clever strategy, Miss Donovan—assuming, of course, that Snake will be able to find the right urchin in a city filled with wretched, towheaded children. And assuming that the child will be able to identify the man who gave him the note."

"I think Snake is enterprising. And I just gave him a lot of incentive."

"He's not the only one with incentive," Alec said as they jogged up the front steps. Harding was already opening the door, which nearly sailed out of his hands when a puff of wind caught it.

Kendra stopped in the middle of the foyer. The butler wrestled the door closed, but not before an icy draft swept inside, making the candle flames dance wildly and shifting the gloomy shadows.

"What do you mean?" But she thought she knew, and fear whispered down her spine.

"I mean, if a small, towheaded child was the only thing that stood between you and being exposed as a murderer . . . what would you do?"

33

What would you do?

The question kept her tossing and turning all night, until horrific visions drove her from her bed at six A.M. Jesus Christ, she didn't think she could take another death on her conscience.

She managed to put on a loose-fitting morning dress without anyone's help—how strange that should be an accomplishment—and made her way to the study. The servants were moving belowstairs, but the house had that hushed, early morning quality that under normal circumstances Kendra would have found relaxing.

Instead, she was disturbed, her mind on the nameless, faceless, blond-haired boy who'd delivered the note. He was out there, somewhere in London's vast sea of tattered children who scurried about the streets, scratching out a feeble existence by begging, hawking their fruits and posies, or performing dangerous, demanding work as chimney or cross sweeps. Some resorted to criminal enterprises, like Snake.

Maybe it hadn't occurred to the murderer that the child could identify him—*yet*. Kendra could only hope that Snake found the messenger before that happened. Or that they would identify the murderer first.

She used the bell-pull to alert the kitchen to send a footman to the study, and ordered a pot of coffee when he arrived. The caffeine probably wouldn't help the headache that had begun to throb between her eyes but, that didn't stop her from pouring a cup when the pot was delivered. Taking appreciative sips, she wandered to the window.

The promised rain had come last night, leaving the streets outside gleaming and marked with puddles, the park dripping with moisture. The night had also brought fog. In the country, Kendra had always found the mist enchanting. But here in the city, with its million-plus inhabitants, the fog was an oily gray or brown. It was now receding into slimy wisps close to the ground, writhing like serpents.

An ox-drawn wagon, its bed stacked with wooden barrels, broke through the haze, moving slowly up the street. Several young maids, bundled against the stiff breeze that was blowing in from the North Sea, were hurrying back from market, carrying baskets filled with fresh vegetables, meat, and fish, which would make their way into the day's meals for their household. The world outside woke up long before the masters and mistresses of the household would.

She took a seat on the sofa and again thought of the child who'd been hired to spy on the Duke's household. A couple of days—that's how long Snake had said the kid had been around. A couple of days ago, she'd begun interviewing the Weston family. But she didn't know anything then. Hell, she *still* didn't know anything solid. She only had theories, shadowy and shapeless things rolling around in her mind.

So why had the unsub felt the need to send the kid to watch her? What did he think she'd learned that had made him try to kill her yesterday? *What do I know?*

"You've risen early."

Kendra glanced around as the Duke entered the room. "So have you."

He smiled, but it quickly faded. "I suspect what woke me is what woke you."

"Yeah." She expelled a sigh, closing her eyes and tilting her head back against the cushions. "I've been trying to figure out why the unsub views me as a threat." She opened her eyes to find the Duke regarding her with concern.

"You cannot go anywhere alone, Miss Donovan, until the fiend is caught."

"You're starting to sound like Alec."

"My nephew is right in this regard."

Kendra decided not to argue the point. She wasn't about to let anything stop her from doing her job, not even the best intentions of the Duke of Aldridge. Instead, she said, "At least we know that we're on the right track. And it definitely puts the spotlight on the Westons."

"The spotlight was already on the Westons . . . I think. What exactly is a spotlight?"

Kendra gave a small laugh. "The focus of attention."

"That is what I assumed you meant," he said and then yanked on the bell-pull. "Lord Weston remains the most likely suspect. Of course, the fact that his son uses the same snuff that was found at the cottage is damning."

"It opens up a host of possibilities," she agreed. "If Weston had found out that his mistress had slept with his son, he could have killed her in a fit of rage. On the other hand, Dawson could have killed her if she threatened to tell his father about the affair. It's like a bad soap opera."

"I am not even going to ask."

Kendra pushed herself to her feet. "I can't quite wrap my head around Lady Dover having an affair with Dawson. She'd have more to lose than gain from it. And I think Lady Dover was all about gaining."

"I have an easier time imagining Dawson being a murderer than his mother. Or his sisters, for that matter." The Duke paused when a footman came to the door in answer to his summons, and he ordered a tray of tea and chocolate and toast.

After the footman left, Kendra said, "You're not going to tell me that females are weak and helpless, and could never resort to murder, are you? Women can kill. Women *do* kill. I'm a woman and I've killed."

"There were extenuating circumstances."

"Jealousy, hatred, and fear can create extenuating circumstances, given the right mindset. I'd say that Lady Weston had all of those going on."

The Duke looked like he wanted to say something else, maybe argue the point more, but the door opened and Alec came in. He was dressed for riding, in a dark olive green greatcoat with two capes that stretched across his broad shoulders, a simply tied white cravat, buckskin breeches, and gleaming Hessian boots. Despite the bruises on his face, which had faded to a yellowish green, he was still one of the best-looking men Kendra had ever seen—regardless of century.

She ignored the flutter in her stomach that his presence always brought. "Are you sure you should go riding?" she asked. "How are your ribs?"

He gave a soft laugh. "You are the only woman of my acquaintance who would ask about my ribs."

She scowled. "Your ribs were cracked. I'm hardly going to ask about your big toe."

He grinned at her. "You are a marvel, Miss Donovan. My ribs, toes, and every other part of my anatomy have recovered, thank you. I need to exercise Chance. The poor animal has been cooped up since my introduction to Bear."

"You could send a groom or stable boy to do that," Aldridge argued, eyeing his nephew with concern. "Are you quite up for it, my boy?"

"I need the exercise as much as my Arabian. Being an invalid is maddening. And I have an errand to run." He went to the sideboard for a cup of coffee. He looked at Kendra over the rim as he sipped. "You shall not be going anywhere alone."

"You're the one who has a man named Bear after you."

"And you are the one who was targeted only yesterday," he shot back. "Have you forgotten?"

"A woman died because of me," she said grimly. "I'm not likely to forget it."

In the small, tense silence that followed her statement, Kendra surged to her feet. "Remember when I talked about the ability to compartmentalize? That's what we need to do now. We can't afford distractions. The unsub is still out there, and he—or she—is obviously willing to kill again."

She set down her coffee cup and moved to the slate board, staring at the names that she'd written until her vision became blurry. She blinked and shook her head to clear it.

"The Viscount seemed pretty desperate the other night when he was gambling," she murmured, mostly thinking aloud.

Alec took a swallow of coffee and shrugged. "Unfortunately, that sort of desperation is not aberrant. Too many fools lose their fortunes in such places."

"But Dawson doesn't have a fortune," she pointed out.

"I told you, London runs on credit."

"Yes, but credit eventually runs out," said Aldridge. He looked at Kendra. "What do Dawson's finances have to do with Lady Dover's murder?"

"I left out one thing when we talked about extenuating circumstances that can lead to murder: greed. How much would the Weston necklace go for if it was sold?"

Aldridge lifted his eyebrows. "Does it matter? The necklace was stolen by the ruffians who broke into the Countess's residence."

"Was it? We won't know that until the goods are recovered. It could have been stolen by the killer—a killer who might need it to sell for money to pay off his gambling debts."

The Duke seemed unconvinced. "One only sells one's family heirlooms as a last resort."

Kendra shrugged. "Where I come from, one sells their family heirlooms before their kneecaps are broken. I can't believe it's that much different here."

"It is an interesting theory," Aldridge said slowly. "But what was done to Lady Dover . . . that was not because of greed."

"No," Kendra had to concede. "But if Dawson went to retrieve the necklace and she laughed at him again—I don't know. He seems to have a temper."

"And the mutilation?"

"I'm still working on that one."

"Well, while you do . . ." Alec drained his coffee cup. "I happen to know someone who ought to be able to tell me just how deep Dawson is playing, and if the merchants have begun to cut off his credit. That would certainly make him desperate." He looked at Kendra. "What is your plan today?"

"We need to interview everyone about their whereabouts yesterday." Kendra's gaze fell on the snuffbox on the Duke's desk. "We can do that when we return Lord Weston's property to him."

Alec followed her gaze. "And if it isn't his? If it's his son's?"

Kendra smiled. "Then, I think, things are going to get interesting."

34

They had to wait until after eleven to call on Lord Weston; anything earlier was uncivilized. When they were finally escorted into the study, Weston stood behind his desk. His eyes were guarded and his overall expression tight, in a way that revealed his unhappiness at their appearance.

"Your Grace, Miss Donovan." He didn't invite them to sit down. "I had hoped we were finished with this business. I have told you all that I know."

Kendra watched him carefully as she set the silver-and-enamel snuffbox on his desk. The metal striking wood sounded loud in the silence of the room.

Weston glanced at it, his eyes narrowing. He made no move to pick it up. "What's this?"

"Mrs. Frost—you remember her, don't you?" Kendra said, innocently enough. "She's the housekeeper hired to clean the cottage. She found it there, under the bed. I thought you might want it back. It's yours, isn't it?"

Kendra tried to read the emotions that flitted across his face like quicksilver. Shock and anger, she thought. But then he turned and clasped his hands behind the straight line of his back, and stepped over to the window, staring outside. The action, she guessed, was to buy him time to consider what he'd say next.

"I never denied renting the cottage," he finally said in a low voice.

"You didn't exactly admit to it, either," Kendra countered.

He gave a jerky shrug, and then pivoted back to look at them. He'd regained his composure, his expression smoothed into impassivity. "Touché, Miss Donovan. I shall confess to it right now, then. I bought the cottage in an effort to have more privacy with Lady Dover without putting her reputation at risk."

"You did all that, and yet she wore the necklace to the theater."

Weston's mouth tightened, but he said nothing.

"Why do you think she did that?"

After a long silence, he expelled a sigh. "We have already discussed this, Miss Donovan. I cannot fathom what was in Cordelia's mind to perform such an outrageous stunt."

"Maybe it was desperation." *Or recklessness.* She fixed her gaze on his, and made the decision to lay another card on the table. "You knew she was pregnant, didn't you?"

The breath that he sucked in was harsh. His hands curled into fists at his side.

"Were you the father?"

"You go too far, Miss Donovan! Sir—" He wheeled around to look at the Duke. "This is unacceptable."

"No." Kendra took a step closer, forcing him to look at her. "What's unacceptable is that Lady Dover is dead and no one wants to speak the truth. Were you the father?"

"How the bloody hell would I know that?"

"Did she tell you?"

He ran agitated fingers through his hair. "Even if she had, what does that prove? I knew of her relationship with Lord Sutcliffe." He shot Aldridge a brittle look. "Everyone in the Beau Monde knew she had ambitions to become a duchess one day. Your nephew could have been the father of the child."

"It would take more than Lady Dover's accusation to bring Sutcliffe to heel," Aldridge said coolly. "When he ended their relationship, she may have gone in search of easier prey."

Weston's eyes widened. "I would hardly consider myself easy prey, sir. I'm married. You know that divorce is not so easily done."

"'Tis an onerous procedure, I'll grant you that," conceded the Duke. "But it can be done, and has been—especially if one is motivated."

Weston said nothing. Kendra waited a beat, then asked, "Where were you yesterday morning until noon?"

Weston's eyebrows snapped together, obviously confused by the change of topic. "Why?"

"I'm curious."

"Curiosity is an unattractive quality in a female, Miss Donovan."

"Really? I happen to think it's laudable. Can you answer the question?"

"I went riding." He hesitated. "I stopped to watch a cricket match for a bit."

"Did you talk to anyone?" Kendra asked. "Can anyone verify your presence there?"

"It was an impulse to stop and watch the match. I spoke to several bystanders. We remarked upon the fact that the bowler was dreadfully incompetent."

"No one was familiar to you?" Aldridge wondered.

"No."

"What about your family? Where were they?" Kendra paused. "Your son?"

Weston's jaw tightened. "My son—my entire family was most likely in bed until noon."

Kendra was ready to point out that if he wasn't around his family, he couldn't verify their alibi. But before she could throw that at him, the door behind them swung open.

"Papa, I have—" Lady Frances came to an abrupt halt. "Oh, I didn't realize you had company." If she sensed the tension hanging thick in the air, she pretended not to notice, offering them a dimpled smile. "Your Grace, Miss Donovan. This is an unexpected surprise."

Kendra didn't believe her for a second. The butler would have alerted her to their presence the moment she set foot in the foyer.

"Lady Frances, you look charming." Aldridge summoned a polite smile.

She executed a perfect curtsy. "Thank you, sir."

Weston seemed to make an effort to pull himself out of the fierce temper that had darkened his face only a moment ago. "Yes, my dear," he said, forcing a smile. "You are in particularly fine looks today."

"Ah, but you are prejudiced, Papa." Lady Frances beamed, obviously comfortable with flattery. And why wouldn't she be? She was a beautiful woman, particularly striking today in a carriage dress of navy and white pinstripes.

She did her best to monopolize the attention of those around her. Lady Frances may have said that about Lady Dover, but it occurred to Kendra that she could have just as easily been describing herself. For the first time, Kendra wondered just how deep the rivalry between the two women went.

"This is rather early for a social call." Lady Frances glanced at Kendra. "Are you continuing your game of Bow Street Runner, Miss Donovan?"

"I don't consider it a game."

"Well, you must confess that it is certainly unusual. Tell me, have you learned anything new?"

Kendra eyed the other woman. Innocent inquiry, or something more? "There have been a few new developments. Tell me, Lady Frances, where were you and your husband yesterday morning?"

"Good heavens. Morning, you say?" Her skirts belled out as she advanced, tugging off the kid gloves she wore. "'Tis barbarous to rise before noon on Sunday."

"Can anyone confirm it?"

"No one disturbed me, if that is what you are asking. Pray tell, what happened yesterday?"

"We're not at liberty to say right now," Kendra said.

"Oh, my. This all sounds very mysterious." Her eyes gleamed with amusement. "Was someone else murdered?"

The comment appeared offhanded, said in that teasing way Lady Frances had. But was it really? Kendra didn't know.

"Yes," Kendra said, keeping her gaze locked on the other woman to gauge her reaction. "Someone was murdered."

"Indeed? Who?" Lady Frances's eyes widened in apparent surprise, but Kendra found herself not trusting it.

"My lady's maid," Kendra said. She studied Lady Frances and her father, but could see nothing beyond their politely expressed horror. It could be sincere, but this was an era where the upper classes applied all their skill to keeping up appearances.

"Why in heaven's name would anyone want to murder your maid?" asked Lady Frances.

Kendra hesitated. There were times when a smoothly told lie could drill past a suspect's fabrications and get to the truth. And there were times when honesty could accomplish the same thing by shocking a suspect into the truth. She decided to shock.

"Miss Cooper was in the wrong place at the wrong time and someone mistook her for me," she said. "I guess someone doesn't like me asking questions."

"Oh." Lady Frances put a hand to her throat and said nothing else for a moment. Then she added, "Well, I can think of a solution. Perhaps you ought to stop asking these questions."

"I don't think I can do that."

Aldridge frowned. "The maid's death is not something we are taking lightly, Lady Frances."

"I apologize most sincerely, Your Grace. I had not meant to jest. Truly." She moved to her father's desk, tossing her gloves onto the smooth surface. Then she gave a short exclamation, leaning forward to snatch up the snuffbox that Kendra had set down earlier.

"Mr. Roberts will be most pleased. He's been searching everywhere for this. Wherever did you find it, Papa?"

35

Kendra felt like someone had smacked her between the eyes with a nine iron.

"This is your snuffbox, Lady Frances?" She flicked a quick glance at the Duke and saw that he was just as stunned as she. Then Kendra shifted her gaze to Weston, who looked vaguely ill, and wouldn't meet her eyes.

Because you knew. As soon as you saw the snuffbox, you knew it belonged to your son-in-law.

"Of course it's not *mine*," Lady Frances said with a laugh. "It's my husband's. Mr. Roberts shall be relieved that it's been found. It's actually quite dear to him."

"You are absolutely certain this is your husband's snuffbox?" Kendra asked again. It was an effort, but she managed to keep her voice low and steady, even as her blood hummed with excitement. This revelation shifted the puzzle pieces on the board and generated an interesting new picture. "You haven't made a mistake?"

"A mistake? Certainly not." Lady Frances tapped the bucolic landscape painted on the enamel. "The case belonged to his grandfather. This is a specially commissioned rendering of his family's estate near Yorkshire." She clicked the lid open with her thumbnail, releasing the scent of oranges and vanilla. "This is Mr. Roberts's blend. It's quite distinctive."

Staring at Weston, Aldridge murmured, "Yes, it is."

Lady Frances seemed to finally become aware of the note of dissonance in the room. She narrowed her eyes at Kendra. "Why are you asking me these questions about Mr. Roberts's snuffbox?"

"I noticed that your brother uses the same blend," Kendra said carefully.

"Possibly. I know Arthur has borrowed some of Mr. Roberts's supply. 'Tis a special tobacco blend made specifically for my husband by Wilcox on Bond Street." She gave Kendra an arch look. "I do hope that your curiosity on this subject is not because you have any desire to indulge yourself, Miss Donovan. I am aware that Marie Antoinette had taken up the habit, but it is rather disgusting for our sex."

Kendra refused to rise to the bait. Instead, she pointed out, "You never did say where your husband was yesterday morning."

"Didn't I? But then *I* was in bed, if you remember. You shall have to quiz Mr. Roberts on his whereabouts, if you want to know where he was. But I rather doubt he was out murdering your maid."

"Do you know your husband's current whereabouts?" Aldridge asked.

Lady Frances turned back to the desk, her eyes scanning the surface before very carefully setting the snuffbox down. Kendra got the impression that she wanted to give herself a moment to weigh her words. "He mentioned going to Weston's, Your Grace, and then Tattersall's."

Kendra asked, "Weston's? A relative of yours?"

That brought Lady Frances's gaze around, torn between amusement and outrage. "Dear heavens, *no*! I realize you are an American, Miss Donovan, but surely you know that John Weston is a tailor, the best tailor in London—though the man is still in *trade*."

It was one of those bizarre rules of the aristocracy, where the Ton abhorred anything that gave the whiff of commerce. They could invest in manufacturing and land, but to actually roll up their sleeves to do any work was considered obscene. Kendra had a feeling that their snobbery was an attempt to retain some semblance of control over the burgeoning bourgeoisie class that the Industrial Revolution had created. A wealthy manufacturer could buy an impoverished lord's estates and dress as a noble, but he could never buy blue-blooded prestige. That could only be obtained through marriage.

Marriage, she was beginning to realize, was the biggest business around.

The Duke said simply, "Thank you, my lady." He then glanced at the Earl, who remained frozen by his desk. "My lord. We shall see ourselves out."

Weston's throat worked, and when it finally came, his voice sounded too harsh. "Good day, Your Grace. Miss Donovan."

They retraced their footsteps to the foyer. The butler materialized to hand them their coat and cloak. Kendra waited until they were out of the house and nearing their carriage before she looked at the Duke. "That changes a few things."

"Lady Dover and Mr. Roberts . . . 'tis difficult to credit."

"I'm pretty sure Lord Weston didn't know."

"I believe you're correct." Aldridge paused to give his coachman directions. Then they climbed into the carriage.

"The Honorable Cecil Roberts wasn't so honorable," Kendra murmured.

Aldridge smiled wryly. "It brings to mind a certain quote. 'Oh what a tangled web we weave, when we first practice to deceive.'"

"Sir Walter Scott was—*is*"—God, it was hard to remember that many of the notables she'd studied were still alive—"an excellent writer and poet."

"*Sir* Walter Scott?" Aldridge looked intrigued. "The poet will be knighted?"

Damn, damn, damn. And when would she learn that the history that she took for granted was still being made? "He was—will be—made a baronet. Now please forget I told you that."

Kendra steered the conversation back toward the investigation at hand. "I wonder if Lady Frances knew about her husband's affair with Lady Dover? I had heard she'd given her the cut direct, but I assumed that was because of Lady Dover's relationship with her father."

"From what little I know of Lady Frances, I do not think she is the type of woman who would turn a blind eye to the affair. I think if she discovered Mr. Roberts's infidelity, she would have been enraged."

"I think so too." Kendra nodded slowly. "The question is: would she have been angry enough to kill?"

❖

They decided to put aside the question of Lady Frances and concentrate instead on her husband.

They drove to John Weston's drapery shop on Old Bond Street. The tailor had built his reputation on the superior cut of his coat, which had garnered him the patronage of the Prince Regent and Beau Brummell. The shop was currently filled with at least half a dozen dandies; Roberts was not one of them. An assistant at the shop revealed that Mr. Roberts had left the establishment forty-five minutes ago to make his way to Tattersall's, a prestigious horse market located at Hyde Park Corner.

They returned to the carriage for the short ride, and once they'd arrived, Kendra looked over the area that was both familiar and not. One day, this section of London would become one of the most congested in the city, with a preponderance of memorials and monuments to honor Britain's most notable figures. Even though Hyde Park Corner was as busy in the nineteenth century as it would become in the future, there were no monuments yet. In their places were buildings and an enormous stable built around a vast cobblestone courtyard that was currently clogged with carriages and horses—and people. With some surprise, Kendra scanned the figures of both commoners and noblemen. The horse market appeared to be the one place in England where the classes could mix freely.

Aldridge said, "Tattersall's offers the best bloodstock in Europe. You really ought to learn how to ride. Or drive."

Oh, God. That was something else she didn't want to think about. But if she remained stranded here, she'd have to consider it.

Kendra's gaze drifted over the horses that were either being led around by stable boys or standing still while men went about the business of inspecting their fetlocks, hooves, and teeth. They were beautiful creatures, their hides gleaming like they'd just been freshly oiled, their tails flicking at flies, their long ears twitching.

The image of Eva Cooper's trampled body rose up in her mind. It was no different than the horrific injuries a person could sustain in an automobile accident. And yet the thought of actually getting on one of those beasts scared the hell out of Kendra.

"I'll think about it," she said evasively, and prayed she'd never have to do it. "Let's go find Roberts."

Except for the few women hawking pastries and fruit, the crowd consisted of men. Kendra was aware of heads turning in surprise as she walked beside the Duke. She ignored them as they traced the Honorable Cecil Roberts to a corner stable, running his hand down the flank of a beautiful chestnut thoroughbred. The air smelled strongly of manure, hay, and leather.

"Mr. Roberts," the Duke said. "That's a prime bit of blood. Are you thinking of buying?"

Roberts glanced around, eyebrows lifting. "Your Grace, Miss Donovan." He gave her a curious look, but was too polite to comment on her presence at the horse market. "I'm considering it. My stables are in need of fresh blood. Are you in the market, as well?"

"Not at the moment, no. Do you mind if we have a moment of your time, sir?"

Roberts stared at them for a long moment, then gave the horse's rump a light slap. "Certainly, sir." He pushed himself away from the beast and stable boy, and began walking. "What's this about?" He shot Kendra another look. "Tattersall's is not the usual destination for ladies."

Aldridge said, "We're not here to exchange civil whiskers with you, Mr. Roberts."

He frowned. "Is this about Lady Dover's murder?"

"Yes," Kendra said bluntly.

"We have already discussed this. I really have nothing more to say."

They were walking toward the street, where the throng of people thinned. The air was also a bit fresher.

Kendra fixed her eyes on Roberts when they finally drew to a halt. "You failed to mention that you and Lady Dover were intimate. Of course, I can see how that would've been a bit awkward, with your wife right there in the room."

He stiffened, his eyes widening. "That is a ridiculous thing to say! Whoever told you that bouncer, I ought to call him out!"

"Your snuffbox was found in a cottage bedroom in St. Margaret's," Kendra told him. "Lord Weston and your wife recognized it as yours."

He inhaled sharply and stared at her. "Are you saying . . . my God. Lord Weston knows?"

Lord Weston—not Lady Frances.

She told him, "He was shocked. But then it's probably pretty disturbing to realize that you were sharing your mistress with your daughter's husband."

Though Kendra had kept her voice low, Roberts let out an angry hiss, his eyes darting nervously around them for possible eavesdroppers. "*Please*. Can we walk?"

He began striding quickly toward the park. They followed, keeping pace easily enough.

"It was only once," he said as he came to an abrupt halt beneath a red oak, turning to face them again. "After the incident at the theater. I met Cordelia quite by accident while out riding. I expressed my displeasure over the humiliation she'd delivered . . ."

When he seemed suddenly at loss for words, Kendra asked, "How did she react to your reprimand?"

"She . . . she laughed, of course." His lips twisted, but there was a light in his eyes that made Kendra think his memory of their accidental meeting wasn't entirely unpleasant. "Cordelia was fearless in that way."

"What happened then?"

Roberts took off his black top hat and swept a hand over his reddish-blond locks, looking into the distance. "I asked her to return the necklace. She invited me to the house on St. Margaret's." Now he looked at them, his blue eyes wide and earnest. "I swear that I thought she was going to give me the necklace. That is the only reason I met her there!"

"And when she invited you into the bedroom, you . . . what? Thought she'd give you the necklace then?" Kendra asked wryly. "You are a very good son-in-law. The lengths that you were willing to go to, to fix Lord Weston's embarrassment."

He flushed a dull red. "I don't know how it happened. I truly do not."

"She entranced you."

"Yes!"

"And this was after the theater incident?"

"Yes."

"Except we have a witness who saw you with Lady Dover a couple of weeks before that," Kendra lied smoothly. She waited, watching. The red flush ebbed, leaving him pale. "How do you explain that?"

"I . . ." His eyes dropped to the hat in his hands. His fingers were splayed on the brim, holding it tight enough to make indentations. "All right," he finally said. "I did meet her while riding, quite by chance—I did not tell you a falsehood. But it was before the incident at the theater, and . . . I do not know how to explain it. That much is true. Lady Dover is—*was* a diamond of the first water, but she had more than beauty. She was a fascinating creature."

"You ended up at the cottage."

"I am not proud of myself, Miss Donovan . . . Your Grace. It was madness. I was aware before the theater incident that Weston and Cordelia were involved. I respect my father-in-law. I regret that he knows about the relationship."

"What about your wife?" asked Kendra. "Do you regret that she now knows about the affair?"

He gave her a cool look. "My wife has my name and is under my protection."

Kendra stared at him. "So she's fine with you jumping into another woman's bed?"

"You are being crude. I do not know what my relationship with Cordelia has to do with her death. I did not kill her. Devil take it, I was in the middle of a ball, with an entire roomful of people who can attest to that!"

"What about yesterday morning? Do you have a roomful of people who can give you an alibi?"

"Yesterday?" He frowned at the sudden change of topic. "What the devil happened yesterday?"

"Someone tried to kill me; they murdered my maid instead. So I'd like to know your whereabouts, Mr. Roberts."

He glared at her and muttered, "This is absurd. I didn't kill your maid, and I certainly didn't try to kill you, Miss Donovan."

"You haven't answered my question."

His jaw tightened. "I woke late and decided to walk to my club for a late breakfast."

"What club do you belong to, Mr. Roberts?" asked Aldridge.

"White's." He slammed his hat back on his head. "Now I think I am done answering these ridiculous questions, sir. I hope that I have your word as a gentleman not to spread the rumor about me and Lady Dover."

It's not a rumor if it's true, Kendra thought, but didn't say anything.

"This is a discreet inquiry," the Duke murmured.

Roberts had to be satisfied with that. After a moment, he gave a nod and a bow, and spun around to head back to Tattersall's.

They watched him go in silence. Then Kendra shot a glance up at Aldridge. "London is quite the den of iniquity."

"That is not exactly news, my dear."

"He didn't seem concerned about his wife knowing about his affair. I wonder if it's because she already knew?"

"It's possible, I suppose." The Duke offered Kendra his elbow, and they began walking back toward his parked carriage. "What I found most interesting is that Mr. Roberts said he went to his club yesterday morning."

"What's so interesting about that? Clubs seem to play an important part in the life of gentlemen."

"That they do." Aldridge smiled. "The interesting part is where White's happens to be located. St. James's Street—which runs into Piccadilly."

Kendra sucked in a quick breath. *And Piccadilly was where Eva Cooper was murdered.*

36

Alec kept Chance to a sedate walk along the pathways of Hyde Park, even though he could sense the Arabian's impatience to run. He would've liked nothing better than to give the beast its head, to fly across the gently sloping landscape. Unfortunately, galloping in the park was frowned upon by polite society. With the murder of Cordelia already casting a dark shadow across his reputation, Alec knew he couldn't afford any further censure from his peers. In little over a week, the House of Lords would be meeting to discuss his fate.

They'd either order a trial or let him go free. But even if his peers chose to look the other way, Alec knew he would never be free. He'd seen the way people had stared at him when he'd put in that appearance at Mrs. Allen's. It wasn't just the bruises marring his face. The taint of Cordelia's murder followed him like a sour stench. He didn't expect that to go away.

And then, of course, there was Bear. That hulking brute had promised to come after him, and Alec believed that, in this, the crime lord would be a man of his word.

The very thought of another confrontation with the ruffian made Alec wince. His ribs still ached like the very devil, despite the assurances he'd given Kendra.

Another reason not to gallop, but to keep a tight rein on Chance and alternate between a walk and a quick trot along Rotten Row. This was a wide bridle path originally created more than a century ago by King William III so he could travel safely between Kensington Palace and Whitehall. More than three hundred oil lamps used to dangle from the trees, lighting the way for the king and discouraging footpads and thieves. When later royals had decided to build other roads to travel upon, the Beau Monde had quickly seized Rotten Row for their own use, to exercise their horses—or, rather, to be *seen* exercising one's horses.

Alec's lips twisted. There was no shortage of vanity—or ridiculousness—in the Ton. Little wonder Kendra wanted to leave.

Frowning, he twitched the reins, guiding Chance around a fallen branch in the middle of the path. Kendra Donovan was stubbornly silent when pressed about her own era. There were times, though, when he thought he could detect a secret amusement glowing in those dark eyes. Like after the time she'd read an account in the newspaper about the latest foibles of the Prince Regent and his (allegedly) secret wife, Mrs. Fitzherbert. She'd shaken her head and muttered under her breath, "The Kardashians." What in hell, he wondered, was a Kardashian? Whatever it was, he got the impression that the world hadn't changed that much after all. It was still foolish.

And it was still violent. Kendra's own profession proved that.

The FBI, that's what she called it. Or the Bureau. He'd been a little surprised that America had managed to organize itself enough to create a police force. Despite its high-minded principles, he'd always regarded the new nation as wild and undisciplined. But, then again, so were the Scottish. And yet Glasgow, of all places, had persuaded its clutch-fisted citizenry (and, really, there was no one more close-fisted than a Scot) to loosen their purse strings and pay for eight permanent law enforcement officers on staff. *Eight.* It was remarkable, really.

London had failed to do such a thing, despite the relentless crimes committed in the city. Of course, there was talk. There was always talk. But Londoners were leery of spending capital on such a venture. They liked even less the idea of delivering such power into the hands of only a few men.

A light breeze, warmer than the recent days, stirred the trees lining the path, carrying a hint of lilac and lavender to him. It reminded him of Kendra—though nearly every damn thing these days reminded him of Kendra. She was becoming an obsession.

A soft laugh escaped him. There was rich irony in that. He'd spent his life avoiding matchmaking mamas and their dewy-faced daughters. He'd known that one day he'd be forced to set up his nursery. His lineage demanded it of him. And, at thirty-one, he was also aware that marriage was no longer a far-off notion. It had never once occurred to him that he'd have a difficult time securing a match with the woman of his choice. Such security wasn't vanity, but practicality. He was the Duke of Aldridge's heir, with estates that were far from impoverished. What woman would say no?

Kendra Donovan, that was who—the one woman in all of England who cared naught for her standing in society or Alec's titles, who seemed to view the very things that women in this world coveted with complete contempt.

No, contempt was too strong a word. *Disinterest.* In fact, the only thing she seemed to be interested in was returning to her own timeline.

And catching the killer.

His hands involuntarily tensed on the reins, causing Chance to pull up sharply and dance to the side. Alec expelled a breath and forced himself to relax. He lightly clicked his heels, propelling the horse to continue forward again.

Her courage awed him and terrified him. She wasn't the only brave woman he'd known, but she was the only woman he knew who could calmly stare down a crime lord and a crowd of angry men with four lead balls—*three*, he amended, since she'd fired a warning shot—knowing that if her bluff didn't work, she'd be torn to pieces.

His blood turned cold when he thought of how close he'd come to losing her. Not just to Bear and his mob, but also to that damn vortex. He still didn't understand the concept of a wormhole, a passageway between two time periods. He only knew that Kendra Donovan could disappear from his life as quickly as she'd arrived—if she didn't get herself killed first.

His mind returned to yesterday, when he'd stepped into Dr. Munroe's autopsy room. *Bloody hell*. He'd nearly fallen to his knees, the strength in his legs deserting him when his gaze had fallen on that damn cloak. Even now he could feel the rage and terror rise up inside him, just as they had when he'd realized that the woman lying torn and broken on Dr. Munroe's table could easily have been Kendra.

She was meant to be Kendra.

He'd had a small role in the war waged against Napoleon. As the Marquis of Sutcliffe and the Duke's heir, he was supposed to stay safely in England, protecting his blood rather than spilling it on the battlefield. But Napoleon's forces had occupied his mother's native Italy, and the War Department had viewed him as an asset to slip behind enemy lines. The work had been exhilarating and dangerous—and grinding. He'd witnesses atrocities that still had the power to sneak into his dreams and steal his peace of mind. Yet for everything he'd seen and done during the war, he'd never felt so helpless as he had yesterday morning, when his gaze had landed on the green cloak and he'd understood what it had meant.

How can you protect a woman who refuses to be protected?

Two horseback riders were trotting around the curve in the road. Alec wheeled Chance around so quickly that the Arabian kicked up gravel on the road and earned censorious scowls from the other gentlemen. He didn't care. Enough with this brown study. It was time he found out about Dawson's finances.

Luckily, he knew where to begin.

❖

The Red Devil was a gaming hell in Pall Mall. Alec supposed that the appellation had something to do with its hideous scarlet décor. Even the traditional green baize on the tables had been replaced with a crimson material. But a darker part of him wondered if the name might have been derived from the blood that had been spilled by the punters who had frequented the establishment. It was not unheard of for young bucks to kill themselves after losing their inheritances at the gaming tables.

Unlike the thin veneer of respectability that Mrs. Allen's gambling establishment boasted, drawing in men and women from the Ton, the Red Devil was a serious hell. Men of all ages were hunched around the tables or playing games of chance. Without a lady's presence, alcohol could be freely dispensed and the men were able to blow a cloud, creating a grayish haze that hung in the room like fog on the Thames. The atmosphere was hushed. The only noise was the soft shuffle and slap of cards as they were dealt and discarded. Even the tossing of chips or dice was muted by the material covering the tables.

Heavy red velvet, gold-tasseled curtains were drawn tight cross the windows, forcing candles and oil lamps to be lit and constantly replenished by the servants. It was an unexpected extravagance—the cost of candles, especially with the hefty tax, could add up. However, Alec knew from experience that it was more important for the proprietor of the hell to create an illusion of timelessness. Nothing ruined the mood more than the morning sun hitting a gambler in the eyes, reminding him of the world beyond these four walls.

Alec saw the man he was searching for immediately. Captain Craig Lawlor, formerly of the Fifth Cavalry Brigade and current proprietor of the Red Devil, was leaning with his shoulder against the doorjamb at the far end of the room. He was tall, with a head of curly dark hair and an attractive countenance. As Alec approached, Lawlor straightened and offered a crooked half smile.

"Sutcliffe. It's been a while since you've graced the Devil with your presence."

"Unfortunately, I'm not here to play, Captain. May we speak in private?"

Lawlor raised bushy black eyebrows, his dark blue eyes assessing the other man. Then he gestured toward the room behind him with his right hand. It was the only one he had. His left was gone, shredded by shrapnel and taken off by an army sawbones on the Continent. Lawlor had pinned his sleeve up rather than let it dangle empty.

"Of course," he said. "Come into my office. Would you like a whiskey?"

"No, thank you."

"You don't mind if I have one, do you?" He shut the door, and sauntered over to a sideboard to splash whiskey into a stout glass.

"How are you doing?" Alec asked. He'd known the captain before he'd lost his arm, when their lives had intersected on the Continent during the war. Afterward, the captain, disabled and discharged, had opened the Red Devil. Alec knew Lawlor was making a fortune from the enterprise, but he couldn't help but wonder if there was something more involved here, since the majority of Lawlor's customers were wealthy aristocrats who'd spent the war years arguing in Parliament about strategy, never setting foot on the battlefield.

Now the captain shrugged. "Plummy, for a one-finned fellow, I suppose." He tossed back the whiskey. "But it's the damnedest thing. There are times when I could swear my fingers on my left hand were itching like the very devil."

"I've heard of the phenomenon." Alec waited until the other man settled into the chair behind his desk, before coming right to it. "Arthur Weston, the Viscount Dawson—is he under the hatches?"

"Dawson . . ." Lawlor eyed Alec across the desk. "Has this anything to do with Lady Dover's murder?"

"Why do you ask?"

Lawlor looked amused. "I'm missing an arm, Sutcliffe, not my brain—or my ears. Men are no different than women when it comes to gossip. Mayhap even worse, since their mouths become unhinged so easily when they're foxed. There has been talk that the House of Lords is considering charging you for the lady's murder."

"I did not—"

"You don't have to convince me, Sutcliffe. During war, one becomes adept at reading characters." He paused, and then gave another one of his sardonic smiles. "And in a gaming hell."

"I can imagine."

The smile vanished. "I've heard what was done to Lady Dover," Lawlor said. "I do not believe you are responsible."

Alec inclined his head. "Well, thank you for that."

"Unfortunately, I don't know if your fellow noblemen will see it the same way."

"Which is why I'm being forced to investigate on my own."

"You and the Duke of Aldridge. And his ward . . . an American. A woman."

Alec stared at the other man. "What have you heard about Miss Donovan?"

The captain smiled again, this time slyly. "As I said, men gossip. They say she could be a pretty thing, but too much of a bluestocking and too outspoken and too damned odd. Then again most of the rakes who haunt the hells won't care if she's touched in the head. As the Duke's ward, they may have expectations of a fortune."

Alec scowled. "Men have been talking about marrying her?"

Lawlor cocked his head and regarded the Marquis with interest. "Do you have expectations there yourself, my lord? It would certainly be clever to keep the Duke's fortune in the family."

"I'm not here to gossip about Miss Donovan."

"Of course not. You want to gossip about Viscount Dawson." He lifted the glass to his lips and took another sip. "As to that, yes. The foolish pup has found himself with his pockets to let. I've heard the entire family is dipping their toe into River Tick. Weston has had some bad investments lately. Not impoverished, mind you. But their country estate is undoubtedly looking a tad shabby these days. They married off two of their daughters and continue to dangle the last daughter in front of Lord Ludlow, but I fear the scandal regarding the Weston family necklace has frightened the fellow off. He's a straitlaced old sod."

"If the family is in financial difficulties, what is Dawson using for credit?"

"He had a small inheritance from his maternal grandmother, which he's undoubtedly blown through by now. The fool plays deep, hoping to recoup his losses, and—"

"And ends up losing more," Alec supplied. It was all too common in the Ton, like a sickness they couldn't control.

"I think he may have sold a few family heirlooms to get the blunt to use at the tables. Mayhap that's why he was in such a dither about his father giving the Weston necklace to Lady Dover."

"Why hasn't Weston stopped him?"

"Weston's been a bit preoccupied," Lawlor remarked with a cynical glint in his eyes. "I believe the plan is for his son to marry well."

"An heiress."

"It's what polite society does. Unfortunately, Dawson has become tainted goods because of his father's rather public association with Lady Dover. I'd heard he was in a temper about the whole thing, even said some unflattering things about the lady in question. He was well into his cups, but I believe he wished her to Jericho."

Alec gazed at the other man. "It's one thing to talk. It's another thing to do what was done to the Countess."

The captain dropped his eyes and contemplated the glass he was holding. "Dawson is spoiled and immature and he has a violent temper when pressed—or when he's had a run of bad luck," he finally said, and looked back to Alec. "I think he can be a nasty piece of work, in the right circumstance. But I also think he's the kind to sneak up on you in a dark alley."

Or attack a defenseless woman in her home? Alec wondered, but kept that to himself.

"I've had Lord Weston in here as well, you know," Lawlor said suddenly. "I can see where the son gets his temper."

"Weston can be violent?"

"He accused a man of cheating and planted him a facer right at the card table. I think he would've done a hell of a lot more if two of my lads hadn't stopped him."

"Was the man that Weston went after a Captain Sharp?"

Lawlor shrugged. "Possibly."

"If the man was cheating him, one can hardly blame the Earl for being provoked into violence."

"What is more interesting is that I'd heard the gambler was attacked several days later in one of the more unsavory neighborhoods in London. Beaten pretty badly."

Alec silently absorbed the unspoken implication. Then he said, "You believe Weston did it?"

"Maybe. Or hired someone. I don't know. I don't care for the man myself." He gave another shrug, this one slightly embarrassed. "He appears the gentleman, but there's bad blood there, I think. I can't explain it."

"Do you think he could have killed Lady Dover?"

Lawlor drained the rest of his whiskey before answering. "Possibly. You and I have both seen men—even gentlemen—do things that are hard to credence. Vicious, vile things."

"In the lust of war," Alec countered, but something inside him tightened.

"Not always. Sometimes people do ugly things when they feel threatened or cornered. Sometimes they commit violence because they feel wronged, and they want revenge. I think you know all these things, milord."

Alec said nothing for a moment. Then he pushed himself to his feet. "Thank you, Captain. You're insight is invaluable."

Lawlor got to his feet as well and walked him to the door. There, Alec paused. "The father or the son—who do you think could have killed Lady Dover?"

Lawlor didn't hesitate. "If I had to bet, my money would be on Weston." He cocked his head and smiled at Alec. "Keep in mind that I'm the owner of a gaming hell, my lord—and the house usually wins."

37

L ater on, they'd all gathered in the Duke's study around a table laden with tea and a tray of fruit, wedges of Lancashire cheese, and small rum cakes. Sam's gaze fell on the delicate teacup that Lady Rebecca had thrust into his hand earlier. He'd read the advertisements touting the benefits of tea drinking, that the brew had the ability to invigorate the body and alleviate the twinges of old age, but Sam couldn't stop himself from casting a longing glance at the decanters on the sideboard, one which he knew was filled with a well-aged whiskey.

He'd been looking forward to a drink, a small bit of comfort after he'd come up empty in finding witnesses in the businesses along Piccadilly. Unfortunately, the intersection was one of the most crowded in London Town. Sam had learned that only last week, a crosswalk sweeper had been run over by some fancy's carriage. There was still discontented rumblings about that one, because the carriage had barely stopped—the baron inside had been late for an appointment and angry about the delay. As far as Sam was concerned, it just added another layer of bitterness to folks who were plenty hostile already toward their betters.

"Lady Dover's behavior seems highly erratic and irrational, to take up with the son-in-law of the man you had designs to run away with," Rebecca stated, bringing them all back to the investigation. "Why would she risk it?"

"Risk is part of Lady Dover's personality profile," Kendra said. "She did it with her masquerade, which netted her an Earl. It probably added to her excitement. It can be like a drug. To an outsider, her behavior may seem crazy. But to her, it was probably intoxicating—especially when she won."

Sam hadn't known the lass, but he remembered the portrait in the drawing room. Eve in the Garden of Eden; that had been his first thought. It would appear the artist hadn't been fanciful with his brush after all.

"For Lady Dover, sex was a tool," Kendra continued. "She used it to get ahead."

Sam nodded. "Me men have been making inquiries in Cheapside about the lass. Appears Lady Dover was born Cordelia Baker. Her pa was a butcher in the area but was shipped to Botany Bay after he was charged with being a knight of the road—a highwayman," he added, when he saw Kendra's quick frown. "Without her husband's support, Mrs. Baker couldn't pay her bills and was eventually sent ter debtors' prison. She died not long after, leaving Lady Dover and her brothers and sisters ter fend for themselves."

Rebecca looked at him. "Lady Dover had siblings?"

"Aye, three brothers and two sisters. Lady Dover was the youngest—ten by the time her ma had stuck her spoon in the wall. Folks said she was a fetching thing even then. Could charm a miser into giving up his gold." Sam paused to take a quick gulp of tea and tried not to think about the whiskey across the room.

"The folks said that the children got lucky, ended up in a Quaker orphanage, where they were taught ter read and write. The oldest lass was the first ter leave, when she married. No one knows what came of Lady Dover's other sister. The brothers were impressed ter serve in the Royal Navy. No one's heard from them since. Lady Dover ran away from the Quakers when she was fourteen and took up with Guy Ackerman—Bear—not long after. He was a couple years older, but already a mean son of a b—er, well-known in the criminal underworld."

"He protected her," Kendra said.

"From what me men learned, he doted on her something fierce. She wanted ter be an actress." Sam supposed she'd achieved that goal, in her own way.

Alec stirred in his seat. "She would have been celebrated by all of London if she'd taken to the stage."

"I guess even back then Lady Dover wanted something more," Kendra said. "Definitely more than what Bear could offer her."

Rebecca frowned. "I'm surprised he let her go."

"He loved her," Kendra said simply. "And if she could charm a miser into parting with his gold, I think she could have convinced Bear to let her go. He wanted her to be happy, and sometimes that means letting somebody go."

Sam wondered at the look the American and Lord Sutcliffe exchanged. But then Kendra continued, "As I mentioned, Lady Dover used sex to get ahead. But I think that she also used it as a weapon."

"A weapon?" Sam found himself leaning forward. "How?"

"I've been giving this some thought, and . . . well, I don't think her affair with Roberts just happened. I think she deliberately seduced him after Lady Frances embarrassed her in public by giving her the cut direct."

Sam was no innocent when it came to the ways of the Ton and their debauchery, but such antics were usually found among the young bucks, not ladies. Even knowing what he did about Lady

Dover, he found the idea shocking. "She began an affair with Mr. Roberts just ter get back at his wife?"

"I think it's possible." She shifted her gaze to Alec. "You knew her best. Is this behavior typical of Lady Dover?"

A faint tinge of color touched the Marquis's high cheekbones. He scowled, but Sam sensed it was from embarrassment, not anger. "I did not see a vindictive side to Cordelia such as you're describing," he said stiffly.

Aldridge said, his tone mild, "You wouldn't have, would you, my boy? She had set out to charm you."

"'Tis cold-blooded of her, but I believe the creature was more than capable of such a thing," Rebecca said, lifting her teacup and regarding them over its rim. "And I've seen Mr. Roberts. Seducing him would not be a great hardship."

Everyone looked at her, startled.

"I'm speaking of Lady Dover," she added hurriedly, "of course."

Sam had to suppress a smile. Miss Donovan wasn't the only interesting female in the room. He turned his attention from Rebecca back to Kendra. "So you think it's a possibility that Mr. Roberts killed her because she threatened ter peach on their affair ter his wife?"

The American surprised him by shaking her head. "No. I don't think Lady Dover threatened Mr. Roberts at all. This wasn't about blackmail. This was about retaliation. I think she told Lady Frances about the affair herself."

Sam stared at her. It was sordid, but it made sense. It was only retaliation if your rival knew about it. He frowned, trying to sort through the tangled threads. "So Mr. Roberts killed her because she told his wife?"

Again Kendra shook her head. "He didn't seem too concerned that his wife knew about it now."

Rebecca pursed her lips, setting down her teacup with a snap against the china saucer. "Well, why would he? What could she have done about it? She has no rights, and no

301

access to money or property, even if it was hers before the marriage."

Kendra nodded and said, "You make my point. Roberts might not like people knowing that he'd slept with Lady Dover—especially not his father-in-law, who was sleeping with her, too—but I don't think that would be enough for him to murder her. If he did do it, it would be for another reason, something we haven't considered yet."

Sam suddenly understood what she was implying. "God's teeth, you think Lady Frances murdered her because Lady Dover told her that she'd bedded her husband?"

"I think that would give her a pretty strong motivation, yes. And she has no alibi for the time Miss Cooper was murdered yesterday."

"But she *does* have an alibi for the time Lady Dover was murdered," Rebecca reminded Kendra. "In fact, she has the best alibi. She was hosting a ball. It's not like being a guest, Miss Donovan. There, you might be able to slip away unnoticed for half an hour. But it would have been much more difficult for the hostess."

"Aye, I don't see how she could've pulled it off," Sam agreed. His gaze went to the timeline on the slate board. "The murder had ter have happened between eight and eleven. Lady Frances's ball began at nine . . . it just don't seem likely. Seems ter me that this is another strike against Lord Weston. He wouldn't like his mistress makin' him out ter be a fool—assumin' he knew."

"He appeared surprised when he realized Mr. Roberts's snuffbox had been found at the cottage," said Aldridge. "Although I will allow that could have been an act."

Alec reached over for the teapot, replenishing his cup. "The man I spoke with earlier said Weston has a vile temper when provoked."

"This would've provoked him, I'd think," murmured Sam.

Alec continued, "He also told me that Viscount has lost his fortune at the gaming tables. Yet when pressed, he still believed that Lord Weston was the one who murdered Cordelia."

Kendra looked at Sam. "Have you made any progress on finding what was stolen from Lady Dover's house?"

He frowned, a little puzzled by her insistence on the subject. He wanted to find the thieves, certainly, but that was a matter of principle. "Nay. And if'n you don't mind me askin', what does it matter, Miss? The housebreaking was done *after* the murder. How could it help in findin' the murderer?"

"I still want to know if the Weston family necklace is among the stolen items or if Lady Dover was wearing it that night."

"She wasn't wearing it. The only thing she'd been wearing was a fancy comb . . ." The explanation was so simple that Sam was annoyed with himself for not thinking of it before. "If it's not with the stolen goods, then the killer took it."

Kendra nodded. "And there are only a handful of people who would have felt compelled to take the necklace after they'd murdered her."

"The entire Weston family," Aldridge offered.

Kendra smiled. "Yes."

"But we are already focused on them." Rebecca frowned, puzzled. "How does this help?"

"We only have theory and conjecture. This would be something more concrete. It also has the potential to eliminate both sons-in-law from the pool of suspects."

"Why would it eliminate them?" asked Alec.

Kendra shrugged. "What's in it for them?"

Rebecca said, "The necklace would never go to their wives. It would go to Dawson, to give to his wife when he marries. That certainly takes away the motivation to steal the necklace."

"But if it's just lying there, they'd leave it? Seems like an expensive trinket ter leave behind," said the Bow Street Runner.

Kendra looked at Alec. "That's a point to pursue—the finances of Mr. Roberts and Mr. Sedwick. But again, Lady Dover's death wasn't a robbery. If the necklace was stolen by the killer, it's because he or she has a personal connection to it. If Roberts or Sedwick stole it, what then? It's not like they could return it to the family without having the Westons wonder how the necklace had come into their hands."

"And if they are badly dipped and stole the necklace— secondary to the murder—they'd have to fence it," Alec pointed out.

"I'll have me men on the lookout—assumin', that is, it's not in with the rest of Lady Dover's stolen goods."

"You realize there is actually a very simple way to find out if Lady Dover wore the necklace that night," Rebecca said, and shook her head when she looked around the table at their perplexed faces. "Miss Marat, of course. Lady Dover's lady's maid helped dress her before they left. She would know."

38

"You want to know if Lady Dover wore a necklace the night she was killed?"

Miss Marat sat across from Kendra and Rebecca in the drawing room. Kendra realized she was tapping her foot with impatience and forced herself to stop. But, damn it, she felt like she was ready to jump out of her skin. They'd dispatched the note to Miss Marat two hours ago. It had taken that long for the footman to track down the lady's maid and bring her back to the Duke's residence.

Sam had left for Bow Street. The Duke had an appointment at the Royal Society, an organization advocating science and natural philosophy that Sir Isaac Newton himself had once governed. Alec had left to deal with correspondence at his own residence. Rebecca had stayed, occupying herself with a book while Kendra had updated the slate board, drank coffee, and paced. The nervous energy had forced Rebecca to depart for the more tranquil setting of the library until Harding announced Miss Marat's arrival.

"You said that Lady Dover had paid particular attention on how she dressed that night."

"She always paid attention, Lady Dover did. But, aye, she was set on wearing the blue frock."

"It occurred to me that she might also have been particularly interested in wearing a certain necklace."

The extra-long blond lashes fluttered. "Now that you mention it, Miss, she did seem to be in a peculiar excitement about the bauble."

"Can you describe it to me?"

The maid scrunched her face in concentration. "It was pretty. There were sparklers—diamonds, that is—and pearls."

"Can you be a little more precise?"

"How am Oi to do that, Miss?"

"How many strands of pearls?"

Miss Marat closed her eyes and counted her fingers. "Five, it were." She opened her eyes and smiled at Kendra. "And Oi remember those diamonds. Funny they were, because they were pink. Her ladyship was fond of pink, she was."

Kendra kept her expression neutral as she asked, "And the last time you saw this particular necklace?"

"Around Lady Dover's neck, it was. Oi put it there myself."

⁂

After Miss Marat had been dismissed, Rebecca and Kendra remained in the drawing room. "This new information definitely eliminates Lord Dover," said Rebecca. "He would have no reason to steal the necklace."

Kendra had already all but eliminated the man, but it still gave her a sense of satisfaction to wet a rag and erase his name completely from the slate board. She looked at Rebecca, and grinned. "And now there are eight."

"Seven, if you eliminate Lady Frances."

Kendra shook her head. "For now, she stays. Roberts and Sedwick drop down the list, for the reasons I've stated. Unless something pops with their finances, there's no reason for them to have taken the necklace. I want to take another run at Dawson over his whereabouts yesterday when Miss Cooper was murdered, and press Lady Isabella and Lady Louisa about what they were doing yesterday."

"I cannot imagine either one of those women killing Lady Dover. Or murdering Miss Cooper in the middle of Piccadilly. How would they manage it with their maids within walking distance?"

"The same way that I managed to go there without a maid. I wore a maid's uniform and blended in. It was actually surprisingly easy." *And freeing*, she thought, but kept that to herself. "I'd say all the women involved have the intelligence to know to don such a disguise."

"I suppose," Rebecca agreed grudgingly. "Still, it's hard to credit."

Kendra eyed the other woman. "Why? Each one has motive, and possibly opportunity. Even Lady Weston. The night of Lady Dover's murder, she was supposedly in her bedchamber in an opium-induced coma with a 'Do Not Disturb' sign on the door."

Rebecca frowned. "I had not heard about the sign."

"I'm speaking figuratively. My point is, she was left alone to sleep. But what was she really doing?"

"Do you honestly think she was sneaking out of her residence to murder her husband's mistress?"

"Stranger things have happened," Kendra said with a shrug. "I know of an Italian matron who drugged and chopped up three women, then used their bodies to make teacakes and soap, which she served to her neighbors and ate herself."

Rebecca's eyes widened in revulsion. "That can't be true!"

"Oh, it is." Leonarda Cianciulli—otherwise known as the Soap-Maker of Correggio. The woman would commit her hideous crime in the early 1940s, but Kendra could hardly tell Rebecca that. "Never underestimate the ingenuity of a woman."

Rebecca gave a shudder. "I never do—but that isn't ingenuity. That's madness."

"Sometimes, it's one and the same."

39

Based on the number of balls, soirees, and galas held every night in London, Kendra could only conclude that the city's upper class had an anathema to staying home in the evening. At least the social whirlwind gave her the opportunity to continue to interview the Weston family. They couldn't toss her out on her ass in the middle of a ball. She didn't think so, anyway.

Tonight, they were attending an event at the home of the Benson family, who were considered both commoners and landed gentry in the British class system. Mr. Benson, Rebecca informed Kendra, boasted a bloodline that could be traced back to Robert I, Duke of Normandy—although it was a branch of the Duke's family begun with one of his mistresses, not his wife. Apparently, a couple of centuries had the power to wash away the stain of illegitimacy, considering the number of London elite circulating through the Benson home.

Kendra wanted to interview Lady Isabella and her husband, Mr. Sedwick, both of whom she had yet to press about their whereabouts. However, the couple was on the dance floor, engaged in a quadrille.

Her gaze fell on Lady Louisa, who was once again blending into the curtains framing the large arching windows at the back of the ballroom, a perpetual wallflower. Her dark hair had been swept up into a sophisticated updo with two deep sapphire blue feathers tucked into the top knot. The hue matched the elegant gown she wore. The square neckline revealed a modest décolletage and filmy blue oversleeves allowed a glimpse of pale arms beneath the scrunched cap sleeves. The skirt, which dropped from an empire waist, had four decorative ruffles tiered along the hemline. She was elegant. And unnoticed.

Lady Louisa's eyes were fixed on the dancers. The longing expression on her plain face was almost painful to see, and again Kendra felt a twinge of sympathy. She knew what it was like to always be the outsider, the freak. For her, it had been her unconventional background that had set her apart from her peers. For Lady Louisa, it was her marital status—her lack of a husband made her an oddity.

Kendra slowly became aware of the stares and whispers behind fans as she entered the ballroom. At first she thought she was the focus of their attention—her life had always been under some kind of microscope—but then she realized that their attention was actually on Alec. In little over a week, the House of Lords would request his presence to stand before them, but the gossip had already begun.

"Perhaps I should distance myself from you," he murmured, his gaze meeting hers before turning to the Duke and Rebecca. "I would not wish to cause you any embarrassment, Your Grace."

"Don't be stupid, Sutcliffe," Rebecca said, but kept her voice low. "I expect you to take me out on the dance floor before the evening is over."

He grinned. "It would be a pleasure, my lady." He then cocked a brow at Kendra. "And what of you, Miss Donovan? Shall I put my name on your dance card?"

"Then I would be causing *you* embarrassment," she said with a smile. "Lady Louisa looks like she could use some company."

They threaded their way through the clusters of people to approach Lady Louisa. Her gaze washed over them, moved on, then jerked back. Color seeped from her plain face and she tossed a wild glance about the room, as if seeking an escape route. But then it was too late to politely run away. Rebecca called out a greeting that left Lady Louisa with little choice but to respond, unless she was prepared to give them the cut direct.

"Lady Louisa, good evening. You know Miss Donovan, of course. May I introduce His Grace, the Duke of Aldridge, and Lord Sutcliffe?"

Lady Louisa gave a nervous curtsy. "Your Grace, my lord . . ." Her expression turned guarded. "Miss Donovan."

The Duke smiled at her. "'Tis a crush. The Bensons ought to be pleased."

"Yes, sir."

"Alec, why don't we go and find refreshments for the ladies? What shall we bring you?"

Kendra caught the Duke's eye and silently applauded his tactic. The introverted Lady Louisa might talk more freely without male attention.

"Lady Louisa, do you have a preference?" asked Alec with a devastating smile in her direction.

She blushed and fluttered her fan. If it had been anyone else, Kendra would have suspected the action was an attempt to be coquettish. But for Lady Louisa, it looked like a genuine effort to cool her flushed cheeks. Alec might be under suspicion for murder, but he was still the best-looking guy in the room.

"Oh, a lemonade. Thank you, sir."

Kendra and Rebecca also requested lemonade. Alec and the Duke melted back into the crowd.

Kendra was surprised when Lady Louisa asked, "Is there any news about Lady Dover's death? Of course, I am cognizant that you are making inquiries of my family."

Kendra said carefully, "We're making progress. We've got some good leads."

Lady Louisa averted her gaze to the dance floor, but addressed Kendra. "Pray tell, what have you found out?"

"I'm not at liberty to say at this time."

She gave her a sideways look. "I do not know what I can tell you, Miss Donovan. You are already aware that I was at my sister's ball on the night of the murder, as was my entire family."

"Not your entire family," Kendra corrected, just to ruffle the other woman's composure a bit. "Your mother wasn't there."

Lady Louisa stiffened. "She was indisposed."

"Because of what happened at the theater?"

Lady Louisa sucked in a furious breath, but didn't deny it. She said in a low voice, "Lady Dover's behavior was despicable."

Rebecca touched the other woman's arm, her eyes filled with sympathy. "Lady Dover could be cruel."

Lady Louisa worked her fan harder, sending the feathers in her hair swaying back and forth. "Why can't men see women like her for what they really are? Vile, evil creatures."

"Men are too easily led astray by beauty," Rebecca agreed softly.

Lady Louisa hesitated, her gaze roving over Rebecca's pock-marked face. "They never see what lies beyond." She turned back to Kendra. "I confess that I wished Lady Dover to Jericho, Miss Donovan, but I hardly slipped away from my sister's ball to murder her."

Kendra gave a nod; she hadn't expected any other response. "What about yesterday morning? Where were you?"

Lady Louisa's eyes narrowed. "I heard about your maid, Miss Donovan. It would seem you have her blood on your hands."

It was Kendra's turn to suck in her breath at the verbal sucker punch—from a wallflower, no less.

"Lady Louisa, I understand that you are overwrought, but Miss Donovan is simply attempting to get to the truth," Rebecca gently chided. "Mayhap you should look at the situation from a different angle. If you explain your whereabouts, it could eliminate any suspicion against you."

Lady Louisa said nothing. The music and conversation flowed around them, filling the silence. The scent of flowers and bay rum cologne pressed around them, almost stifling.

Then Lady Louisa sighed. "I spent the morning in my room, writing letters to my cousins who reside in the country. My maid brought me a tray. Afterward, I went riding. It wasn't a fashionable hour, but it is a particular pleasure of mine."

"Mine as well." Rebecca smiled at the other woman. "We should make an appointment to ride one day soon."

Lady Louisa looked at Kendra. "Do you ride, Miss Donovan?"

"No."

She seemed to relax. "I should like that very much, Lady Rebecca."

Kendra gave a wry smile, aware that she'd just been dissed. "Did you ride with your father yesterday?"

"No. My groom accompanied me."

"What time?"

"Half past twelve, I think."

"And before that you were in your room?"

"Yes."

"What time did you get dressed?"

"Pardon?"

"I'm assuming your lady's maid helped you dress. What time?"

"Nine, I suppose. I don't recollect exactly."

"Then you stayed in your room, writing?"

"Yes."

"Did anyone see you, after your maid brought you a tray?"

"I . . . no. I was left alone."

"What about your mother and brother? Where were they yesterday morning?"

"I'm certain they were about."

"But you don't know?"

Lady Louisa began to look hunted. "I told you, I was in my room. If I was in my room, I don't see how I could know where anyone else was." She picked up her skirts. "Forgive me, I see an old acquaintance and I must pay my respects. Good evening, Lady Rebecca, Miss Donovan."

Kendra watched the other woman flee into the throngs of people. "An old acquaintance my as—eye."

Rebecca lifted a brow. "You do have an unfortunate habit of chasing people away, Miss Donovan."

"Yeah. Sorry."

Rebecca heaved a sigh. "I must confess, I feel sorry for Lady Louisa. She seems terribly alone."

"Is that why you asked her to go riding?"

"I suppose. Although I do enjoy it."

"She doesn't have much of an alibi for Sunday morning. Her house isn't far from Piccadilly and she could have stolen a maid's uniform from her household."

"You don't really suspect Lady Louisa, do you? She's so . . . retiring."

"Always standing on the sidelines."

"Exactly. You can scarcely blame the poor thing if her dance card is not filled." Rebecca shook her head, pensive. "Few gentlemen will take pity on her, I'm afraid. In a way, she's become a social pariah."

"Yes, but who would notice if she slipped away from the sidelines for half an hour or so?"

Rebecca frowned, obviously disturbed. "I agree that she is not a person who draws attention. But I can hardly credit her with murdering Lady Dover. She is not a bold person."

Kendra thought about the unexpected blow that Lady Louisa had delivered. *It would seem you have her blood on your hands.*

Lady Louisa was right; Miss Cooper's blood was on her hands. It made her sick to think about it. But to have Lady Louisa actually say it . . .

Apparently she wasn't quite the retiring wallflower she would have everyone believe.

40

The Duke persuaded Rebecca to join him in a reel forming on the dance floor, while Alec and Kendra found Lady Isabella and her husband in the morning room. The Bensons had transformed the room into a sugar fiend's paradise. The chairs had been removed, leaving only the massive oak table to groan under the weight of platters and serving bowls holding a vast array of desserts: lemon creams, baked custards, lavender rum cakes, glazed tartlets, and bread-and-butter pudding dotted with dark currants. The scent of warm cakes mingled with a touch of honey from the beeswax candles that flickered around the room.

Lady Isabella brandished a tiny spoon, scooping out baked custard from the bowl she held with obvious enjoyment. Kendra knew the second the other woman became aware of their presence—the spoon froze halfway to Lady Isabella's mouth and her hazel eyes narrowed. Then the spoon continued its trajectory.

She'd swallowed the dessert by the time they came to a halt in front of her.

"Lady Isabella, Mr. Sedwick, good evening." Alec offered them a faint smile. "I believe you have already been introduced to Miss Donovan."

"Yes. But Mr. Sedwick and I were preparing to leave," Lady Isabella said abruptly.

Sedwick glanced at his wife in surprise. Kendra couldn't be sure whether he was taken aback by Lady Isabella's discourtesy, or the fact that he still had half a glazed tartlet on his plate.

"This will only take a moment of your time," Kendra said.

"Certainly," Sedwick replied. He appeared a little less . . . *damp* than he had at the Digby Ball, Kendra thought, but his practiced, politician smile remained the same. "How can we be of assistance?"

"I am aware that you attended Lady Frances's ball, but could you tell me when you arrived and when you left that evening?"

Sedwick lifted his eyebrows. "Why is that important?"

"It was the night of Lady Dover's murder," Kendra reminded him.

Lady Isabella put her bowl and spoon down on a nearby shelf with a rattle. "Please do keep your voice down, Miss Donovan," she hissed, and her gaze flicked to the other small groups clustered in the morning room, sampling desserts. Nobody seemed to be paying them any attention, but that didn't stop Lady Isabella from leveling a glare at Kendra. "You can't possibly mean to quiz us here in the middle of Mrs. Benson's ball."

"My dear, calm yourself," her husband admonished lightly. "Lord Sutcliffe is the Duke of Aldridge's nephew. Certainly we shall speak to you." Sedwick dumped his plate with the half-eaten tartlet next to his wife's bowl, and then he looked at Kendra and Alec with a smile. "Perhaps we ought to step outside for this discussion?"

Kendra and Alec followed them to the French doors that led out to a wide veranda. The night was cool enough to keep everyone else indoors, with the exception of what appeared to be an amorous couple in one of the darker spots. At their arrival, the two broke apart and, with a furtive glance thrown in their direction, hurried back into the mansion.

Kendra clenched her hands against the chill. The paper-thin gown she wore offered no protection against the night's temperature. Lady Isabella wore a similar evening dress, in dark mauve silk beneath an organza overskirt, which matched the amethysts in her hair. But she didn't seem to be affected by the outside temperature.

Maybe her anger is keeping her warm, Kendra reflected wryly. In the faint glow from the candles burning inside the ballroom, Kendra had no trouble reading the hostility in the other woman's gaze.

In contrast to his wife's vehemence, Sedwick appeared relaxed. But Kendra wondered if the pose was genuine. He was a politician, after all. They all knew how to project the image they wanted to project, and to lie with ease.

"Now . . ." Sedwick said with a smile. "What is this matter of Lady Dover's murder?"

Lady Isabella looked at her husband. "I told you, Mr. Sedwick. Miss Donovan has a rather unnatural curiosity regarding the woman's death."

Kendra ignored that. "When did you arrive at Lady Frances's ball?"

"'Tis of no concern—"

Sedwick laid a hand on his wife's shoulder. "My dear, we have nothing to hide." He turned back to regard Kendra. "Lady Frances's event was important, but we did have a prior commitment. My wife and I were required to put in an appearance at Carlton House—a royal summons from the Prince, as it were."

As he talked, Sedwick reached into his coat and brought out a lacquered cherrywood snuffbox and used his fingernail to flick open the lid. Kendra was close enough to catch the scent of spearmint. He took a small pinch of the tobacco flakes between his index finger and thumb, placing the snuff into each nostril. He gave a delicate sniff, then snapped the snuffbox closed. "We did not arrive at Lady Frances's until well past ten o'clock. Is that not correct, Lady Isabella?"

"That is correct, Mr. Sedwick," his wife said stiffly.

"Can you be more specific than *well past*?" asked Kendra.

"Closer to eleven, I believe," Sedwick supplied.

"I see. And your presence at Carlton House can be corroborated by others in attendance?" Kendra felt foolish asking, because she knew that Carlton House was the Prince Regent's private residence. But she had to know.

Sedwick regarded her with amusement. "By all means, quiz Prinny. He shall verify my account."

Alec said, "Lord Shipley is an acquaintance of mine who often dines at Carlton House. Was he in attendance?"

"I believe he was, my lord."

"Then I shall ask him."

"Please, do."

Kendra asked, "When did you arrive at Carlton House, and when did you leave?"

"Half past seven. We departed a little after ten."

"It took you almost an hour to get to Lady Frances's ball?" Kendra frowned.

"The traffic was ungodly. Again, that can be easily verified. Ask my driver."

He sounded sincere, but Kendra still felt obligated to ask the next question. "What about yesterday morning, between nine and one?"

Sedwick frowned. "What happened yesterday morning?"

Kendra thought he appeared genuinely puzzled. Lady Isabella, on the other hand, was staring into the pitch-dark backyard, her profile haughty and distant.

"Another murder," Kendra said softly.

"Good God. London's criminal element grows more bold. Parliament really does need to put more laws into place. I believe it's the émigré population—I shall bring up the subject with Lord Sidmouth."

"Can you tell me where you were yesterday morning?" Kendra repeated.

Sedwick looked at her for a moment, then gave a slight shrug. "Naturally, my wife and I attended church services at St. Paul's. Then I was called to Whitehall to assist Lord Sidmouth in a delicate matter of state." His thin frame puffed up a bit, obviously proud of his position. "I spent most of the day in the office. Lord Sidmouth himself can verify my presence, as well as several clerks and assistants."

Kendra shifted her gaze to his wife. "And what did you do after church services, Lady Isabella?"

Lady Isabella glared at her. "I spent those hours at home. And I find your suspicion against my family insulting, Miss Donovan."

"I find murder insulting."

Sedwick lifted a placating hand. "Miss Donovan, you must concede that your inquiries are putting us in an uncomfortable position."

"Being under suspicion for murder *is* uncomfortable," murmured Alec. The light from the ballroom limned his chiseled features and played across the fading bruises. "Still, the truth must be sought."

Lady Isabella tilted her chin toward him, a challenge. "Is it the truth you are seeking, my lord? Or do you wish to divert attention from your own association with Lady Dover? Everyone in town knows that she was your mistress."

Alec's gaze was cool. "Not, I think, after the theater incident."

The statement was so quietly said that it took a moment to register. Then Lady Isabella inhaled sharply. For once, she seemed at loss for words.

Sedwick said, "I cannot deny that my father-in-law's indiscretion has caused considerable . . . embarrassment. However, Isabella and I have never been involved in it."

Kendra eyed him curiously. "You work for the government, Mr. Sedwick. Maybe you're worried that Lord Weston's involvement with Lady Dover could hurt your career?"

It was certainly plausible in the twenty-first century, she thought. But by Sedwick's reaction, apparently not so much in the nineteenth. He laughed out loud.

"Miss Donovan, that is rich! Whitehall has managed to survive the scandals of the Prince Regent and the royal family—including a mad king—for decades, if not centuries. My father-in-law's carelessness is hardly cause for concern, certainly not enough for me to resort to something as ugly as murder." He offered his arm to his wife, who immediately took it. "The night air grows cold . . ."

Still, he lingered. He cocked his head as he regarded Kendra. "You are an unusual female, Miss Donovan." She didn't think he meant it as a compliment.

Sedwick bowed low. "Good evening, Miss Donovan, Lord Sutcliffe."

Alec responded with a slight bow of his own. "Good evening, Mr. Sedwick, Lady Isabella."

They watched as the couple hurried back through the French doors, then Alec looked at Kendra. "He's right, you know. Lord Weston's affair with Cordelia may have been embarrassing, but it would hardly have curtailed his career as a civil servant."

"I'd still like to have their alibi for last Monday confirmed. If they were at Carlton House"—*with the freaking Prince Regent, the future King of England*—"we can cross them off the list. There's no way either of them could have gone to Lady Dover's and murdered her without getting caught by the maid."

"Housekeeper."

"Whatever."

He smiled. "I shall make inquiries. It oughtn't be too difficult."

321

"Good. Our pool of suspects is shrinking."

She started to smile, but stiffened when she felt a familiar prickling sensation between her shoulder blades.

She glanced over her shoulder and her gaze fell on the figure on the other side of the French doors. The candlelight was behind him, leaving him little more than a silhouette, almost insubstantial. It was too dark to see his face, but she recognized the shape of his head, the brown hair slowly turning silver. Shadows dug pits for his eyes, but Kendra thought she still could detect a furious glitter.

Lord Weston.

Alec put a hand on her arm, making her jump. "You are cold," he murmured. "Let's go inside, Miss Donovan."

She said nothing. But when she swung her gaze back to the French doors, Lord Weston was gone.

41

Edmund Sedwick escorted his wife back into the ball-room and wasn't surprised when she suggested that they depart the festivities.

"'Tis not even midnight," he said gently, and regarded Lady Isabella's tense face. "Do not look so blue-deviled, my sweet. People will talk."

"I am feeling unwell."

"I have not had a chance to speak with Carlsbad yet," Sedwick pressed. "That is why we are here, if you will remember. Lord Sidmouth desires Carlsbad's support against the growing radical elements in this country. He fears the monarchy is being threatened with the tensions in the north, with the Luddites terrorizing the citizens."

He paused, and inclined his head in a nod of polite acknowledgment as they passed a particular lord who belonged to the radical Whig party. "The Duke of Aldridge would be a useful ally," he continued. "We cannot alienate him."

His wife sniffed. "His Grace prefers to keep to his country estate rather than take advantage of Town life."

"Clearly he has given up his country pursuits." He steered her toward the stairs.

"We know why he has abandoned the country," Lady Isabella shot back.

Sedwick gave his wife a look. "It appears that Lady Dover is almost as much trouble dead as when she was alive. Your father was foolish to take up with her."

Lady Isabella's mouth tightened. "She was a trollop well used to seducing men."

"Softly, my dear," he advised. Usually his wife was much more astute than to let her emotions run away with her. It was one of the traits for which he had married her.

Like his superior, Henry Addington, the first Viscount Sidmouth, Sedwick had trained for the law and practiced as a barrister. And like the Home Secretary, he'd always had an eye on politics. His match to Lady Isabella hadn't been financially lucrative—she had only brought a miserly dowry—but in her he'd recognized the perfect politician's wife, with the manners and upbringing both to be a hostess or to accompany him to the many dinners he was required to attend. She was attentive to his political ambitions without being political herself—and thank God for that. He couldn't abide an interfering female, like the Countess Von Lieven, the wife of the Russian ambassador. While some believed the fashionable Countess advanced her husband's cause with her shrewd advice, Sedwick had to suppress a shudder at the thought of having a woman hold so much power.

"Forgive me," Lady Isabella now said, her voice low and stilted. "If you'll excuse me, Mr. Sedwick, I shall go to the withdrawing room. Mayhap a maid there will have some powder for my headache."

He smiled, since he'd spotted the man that he wanted to speak with. He didn't want his wife to witness the conversation. "Very good, my dear."

He watched her glide down the hall, then veered off to catch up with his father-in-law.

"My lord?" He kept his smile in place when Weston glanced around. "A moment in private, if I may?"

Weston frowned. "What is it?"

Sedwick had no great feelings for his father-in-law one way or the other. They got on well enough, although Sedwick was often aggrieved by Weston's refusal to throw in wholeheartedly with Lord Sidmouth's leadership of the Tory party. Weston had even made disconcerting remarks, suggesting he favored some of the views expressed by the opinionated—and often hated—George Canning. The statesman claimed to be a Tory, but given his previous Whig leanings, Sedwick thought he was still secretly the latter, especially after he argued in favor of Catholic emancipation in the House of Commons. Then again, what else could one expect of a man whose mother had been an actress?

"I have had the most interesting conversation with Miss Donovan and Lord Sutcliffe," Sedwick murmured. "She is a most peculiar female, is she not?"

Weston glanced around them. "Shall we walk, sir?"

The younger man inclined his head, and they ambled down the corridor to an alcove that, except for the footmen and maids scurrying by in their duties, offered some privacy.

"What did they wish to speak to you and Isabella about?" asked Weston.

Sedwick smiled. "I thought I noticed you inside. You should have made your presence known. I dare say Miss Donovan would like to quiz you as well."

"She has done that already."

"Ah." Sedwick retrieved his snuffbox. He eyed his father-in-law as he opened the case and took a pinch. "Miss Donovan appears to be fixated on Lady Dover's murder."

"What did she want to know?" Weston asked again.

Sedwick inhaled the snuff and suppressed the need to sneeze. Being able to control one's bodily functions when taking snuff was an art form. "Have you heard about the factory in Manchester that the Luddites demolished?" he asked, as he slipped the snuffbox back into his coat pocket.

Weston frowned at the non sequitur. "What has that to do with anything?"

"Lord Sidmouth is quite concerned with the unrest in our country. There are rumblings of revolution."

"There are always rumblings of revolution," the Earl snapped. "'T'would be unnatural if England managed a score of years without becoming involved in some ridiculous war." He took a breath. "Shall we return to the subject at hand? What did Miss Donovan say to you?"

"She pointed out that Lady Dover was murdered during the evening of your daughter's ball. She wanted to know when we had arrived. Thankfully, Lady Isabella and I arrived late, having attended a function at Carlton House. Miss Donovan feels the need to verify this." He waved his hand in a languid manner. "As it is the truth, I believe Miss Donovan will be satisfied that I didn't sneak out of your daughter's ball to dispatch Lady Dover."

Weston said nothing.

"Of course," Sedwick continued, "I had no reason to murder Lady Dover. The awkwardness over the necklace had nothing to do with me."

"Yes, well." Weston's gaze slid away. "If that is all—"

"I recall that evening very well, you know," Sedwick cut in easily. "The Prince does tend to overindulge with his dinner courses. The food and wine are excellent, but one's stomach is always uncomfortably full when one leaves Carlton House."

Weston stood still, his eyes locked on his son-in-law, wary. He might not know why Sedwick was sharing this particular memory, but he seemed to understand that there would be a point.

"When we arrived at Lady Frances's, we paid our respects to our hostess and her husband," Sedwick said. "Afterward, I thought to step out in the gardens to walk a bit—the food and wine from Carlton House, you understand. I remember the night was cold and damp, but I wanted to clear my head a bit. I had paused near the arbor to take out my snuffbox . . . when I saw you, my lord."

Weston said nothing.

"You were not stepping outside. You were walking down the path from the street. It must have been near eleven o'clock, as we'd just arrived."

Weston appeared frozen. When he finally spoke, he sounded hoarse. "I did not see you."

"I was in the shadows of the arbor and you appeared quite preoccupied. I had not thought to interrupt your reverie. But I now find myself curious—Miss Donovan's inquiries into our whereabouts has me wondering about *your* whereabouts, sir."

His father-in-law stared at him for several moments. Then he said, "Like you, I had thought to clear my head with a stroll."

Sedwick pursed his lips. "London is a dangerous place to stroll at night in the fog. 'Tis why I stayed in the gardens." He paused. "Though London appears to be a dangerous place indoors, as well, given Lady Dover's shocking end."

Sedwick allowed the sentence to hang, watching countless emotions flit across Weston's face. He offered a smile.

"Do not fear, sir. This is a family matter, after all; I shan't say a word. Miss Donovan appears to be a persistent female, but I am busy with matters of state. Lord Sidmouth and I are working on a bill to suppress the Luddite movement, as well as the more radical elements that have begun forming in this country. There are those in government who are even sympathetic to returning rights to the Catholics. Can you imagine? 'Tis unthinkable."

Sedwick looked at his father-in-law. "I would hope that Lord Sidmouth and I have your support."

Weston's eyes sparked briefly with rage. "I don't suppose you would listen to me if I told you that I did not murder Cordelia?"

"If you did or did not, it has nothing to do with me, sir. I am simply a civil servant. My concern is for England's survival. Do we understand each other?"

Weston's lips twisted as he met his son-in-law's implacable gaze. "Yes, I believe we do."

42

Lord Reginald Shipley was an avid sport enthusiast. When he was in London, he could often be found at cricket and tennis matches, cockfighting pits, or boxing rings. On Tuesday morning, Alec located His Lordship at a fencing academy in Soho, where Shipley was engaged in a vigorous match. He and his opponent seemed to dance back and forth, their skinny foils glinting in the sunshine that poured through the high Palladian windows that lined one wall.

Once the match was finished, Shipley bowed to his opponent, tucked his sword under his arm, and came jogging toward Alec with a jovial greeting. "Sutty!"

Shipley was a man of medium height and build. His round face, surrounded by golden curls, remained as cherubic as it had been when they'd attended Eton together.

"Ship," Alec returned with a smile. While he hadn't shared his friend's mad passion for all things sport, he'd liked him well enough to stay in touch, and whenever Alec ventured to Town, they'd often met at one of their clubs to share dinner and a bottle of port.

Alec said, "Excellent form, by the way."

"Thank you." Shipley used his sleeve to wipe the sweat from his brow. "Do you want to give it a go?"

"Not today, thank you. I came to inquire whether you dined at Carlton House last Monday evening."

"Last Monday, you say?" He frowned as he thought it over. "I believe so. Prinny has been out of sorts since his falling out with Brummell, you know. He's trying to keep up his spirits by throwing lavish dinner parties."

Alec couldn't remember a time when the royal hadn't enjoyed lavish dinner parties, but decided not to say anything against the increasingly corpulent Prince Regent. "It was the night of Lady Dover's murder."

"Good God, that is madness, eh?" Shipley shook his head. "A Lady! London's cutthroats will murder us in our beds if we're not careful. I have now required my butler to carry a blunderbuss in the evenings." He regarded Alec steadily. "I heard that you've come under suspicion for the woman's killing, Sutty. 'Tis absurd."

"Thank you for that. Not everyone agrees with you."

"I know that the House of Lords will be convening in a week to discuss the matter. They won't charge you. Never fret about that, old boy!"

"Why? Because they know I'm innocent?"

Shipley laughed like Alec had just told a joke. "What has that got to do with anything? No, you can't go about hanging the aristocracy. What kind of society would we live in then?"

A fair one, Alec reflected, and remembered Kendra's appalled reaction when she'd learned how England's justice system was structured, where he could only be charged by his peers. Bloody hell, the woman was changing him. He'd never once considered the matter but now felt a strange sense of disquiet.

"The nobles won't do it," emphasized Shipley. "They're too afraid of what happened in France. Common folk turning against their betters and chopping off their heads. Gave my father nightmares, it did. And what came out of it? Democracy? Napoleon declared himself emperor!"

"Well, Napoleon has now been banished and a new France is rising. But I didn't come here to speak to you about international politics, Ship."

"Thank God. I never cared much for politics of any stripe. What did you come here to speak to me about, then?"

"The guest list at Carlton House on Monday night. Do you remember if Mr. Sedwick and his wife, Lady Isabella, were among the guests?"

"Sedwick? Most likely. He's Sidmouth's lapdog, isn't he?" Shipley rolled his eyes. "I swear, if I took this foil and cut his arm, he would bleed Tory. He has government on the brain, you know."

Alec laughed. "Why do you go to Carlton House, Ship? You know politics is a prerequisite."

"My father orders it, threatens to cut off my allowance if I don't. But it's not too ghastly. Prinny and I share similar interests in sport, you know. The Prince was actually an accomplished rider until he . . ."

"Became so fat," Alec finished drily.

"Robust," Shipley corrected with a twinkle in his eye. "I don't want to be ostracized like Brummell."

"The *on dit* was that he asked Lord Byron who his 'fat friend' was."

"Yes, but the fat friend in question *was* the Prince Regent. Stupid man—Beau, not the Prince. Heard he's drowning in the River Tick, and without his alliance with the Prince, creditors have begun demanding their due. He'll soon take a French leave, mark my words."

Alec was sure that was true, but circled back to the subject that had brought him here. "Do you recall when Sedwick and his wife left Carlton House?"

"Can't say that I do."

"Did they stay until the dinner was finished?"

"Yes. That much I do know. But more because no one would have left *before* the Prince. Very ill-mannered to do so."

"When did the Prince Regent leave the dinner?"

"Ten o'clock? Half past? I'm uncertain."

"Could it have been nine?"

"No. I didn't return home until well after midnight. But there was dreadful traffic on the road, you know. Damned nuisance."

"You are certain that Sedwick and his wife left *after* ten o'clock?"

"Yes, definitely later in the evening. Does that help you, Sutty?"

Alec smiled. "As a matter of fact, it does."

※

"And now there are six," Kendra murmured, wetting the rag and wiping Sedwick and Lady Isabella's names off the slate board.

Alec had arrived ten minutes ago with confirmation that Sedwick and Lady Isabella had been at Carlton House until at least ten o'clock on the evening of the murder. Unless they'd flown, there was no way they could have arrived at Lady Frances's ball, snuck away to Grosvenor Square to stab Lady Dover and carve up her face, and return. Not without being caught by Mrs. Pierson— Lady Dover's housekeeper—along the way.

"We're making progress," Aldridge said from his position behind his desk.

Slow progress, Kendra thought. True, even in the twenty-first century, investigations could happen at a painfully slow pace. If they ground to a halt, they ended up pushed to the side, and eventually in the cold-case file. Here, though, she felt hampered by the lack of forensic tools and frustrated by the proprieties that prevented her from yanking the entire Weston family into interview. She'd hoped to put some pressure on Dawson last night, but he'd never shown up at the Bensons' soiree. And by the time she'd sought out Lord and Lady Weston, they'd already left.

She sighed heavily and went to pour herself another cup of coffee from the tray they'd brought into the study after breakfast. She was exhausted, with another headache stabbing behind her eyes. She attributed it to the sleepless night she'd had, thanks to a nightmare about a small, blond-haired child being chased through the streets of London while she watched, helpless. She'd woken with a start just as a hand holding a stiletto had swung down with the intent of impaling the boy.

Suppressing a shudder at the memory, she said, "We need a break in the case right now. Unfortunately, our best lead is Snake finding the boy who delivered the message. If he can identify the killer . . ."

She swung around when the door opened, and Harding announced Sam Kelly's arrival. The Bow Street Runner came into the room at a more rapid pace than usual. "Good morning," he greeted them.

He had a cop's face, schooled into impassivity. Yet there was something in his golden brown eyes that made Kendra straighten, a curious excitement rushing through her. "You've found something."

"Me men have found the ruffians that broke into Lady Dover's house. And the goods are still there." He grinned as the Duke and Alec surged to their feet. "I thought you might want ter take a look."

43

They traveled at least twenty minutes into the outskirts of London, by the time the carriage finally came to a rocking stop, the door opened, the steps unfolded, and Kendra was able to step down onto the ground. She was grateful that she'd donned a spencer jacket before she left the Duke's residence when a stiff, cold breeze suddenly buffeted her and stirred the trees in the heavily wooded area around the clearing.

In a few weeks, it would be October. And then what? Christmas? Spring? Her stomach squeezed as she thought of the months that loomed ahead—in the nineteenth century. These little moments of awareness came at the damnedest times. She couldn't, *wouldn't*, think about it.

She turned her attention to the house. It wasn't a mansion by any means, or even the size of one of the smaller London terraces, but it was still larger than one of the tiny cottages that dotted the English countryside. Made of stone, it was painted white and topped with a thatched roof, the straw gray with age and layered with moss and lichen. Three small square windows, winged with shutters, were cut into the stone.

It would have been considered quaint if not for its dilapidated condition. Large sections of the thatch were missing from the roof, which sagged in the middle; the stone itself was chipped in places and crumbling to dust in others. The shutters had at one time been painted blue, but most of the paint had faded to gray or chipped off altogether. Still, Kendra knew that Americans in the twenty-first century would probably happily fork over a fortune just to spend the night in this place, and consider the experience to be authentically English.

About five men were sitting on crates and the stump of a tree outside the cottage. Four of them jumped to attention when Sam walked toward them. Kendra suspected they were his men, fellow Bow Street Runners. The fifth man, his muscular frame clothed in a grubby, homespun smock and wool trousers, remained sitting on the tree stump, his curly brown head hanging low. But at Sam's approach, he raised his head with a snarl. If he hadn't been shackled, Kendra thought he might try to leap at the Bow Street Runner. Instead, he simply glared at Sam, not an easy task as one eye was swollen shut. His lip was also split, and his face a patchwork of bruises.

Kendra stopped to stare. "What happened to him?"

"He took exception ter our arrival," said Sam.

In her time, the thief would be shouting police brutality, calling for his lawyer to file a million-dollar lawsuit against the city.

"Ye focking—oof!"

One of the standing men slammed the butt of his rifle into the ruffian's stomach, causing him to gasp and double over, his head bent to his knees.

"Hey." She frowned at the guard, her own temper rising at the needless violence against a man who couldn't fight back. "Try to keep his teeth in his mouth. I might want to talk to him, you know." She moved past the group of men and through the low door of the cottage. Alec, Sam, and the Duke followed.

Just inside the door, Kendra came to a halt. "Wow."

There was a long oak table and chairs, and every surface was filled with items that clearly didn't belong in the ramshackle thatched cottage. Even though the light was dim inside the room, Kendra could see in the jumble silver candleholders, cutlery, gold-edged and monogrammed plates, and crystal decanters and glasses. It looked like a Black Friday sale at Macy's.

"Shit. Is this all from Lady Dover's house?" she asked, staring in amazement.

"Aye."

"How did the rogues manage to get all of this from Grosvenor Square to here?" wondered the Duke, clearly as astonished by the massive haul as she was.

"There's a lot of incentive here, sir," remarked the Bow Street Runner. "We got the lad outside, but he'll lead us ter his gang, I suspect."

The "lad" was probably a few years younger than Sam, Kelly thought with a flash of amusement. And she wasn't entirely sure he'd give up his fellow thieves.

As her gaze swept the table, she caught the glimmer of jewels and perked up. She hurried to that side of the table, her hand delving into the tangle, sorting through it.

"Lady Dover had been wearing that hair frippery," Sam said, coming up next to her and pointing at the Spanish comb that winked with rubies and moonstones. He reached past to pick up another item. "And here's her fan."

The gold- and pale-blue-painted fan flopped limply in his hand, its delicate spokes broken. Why would the thieves take a broken fan? It was made of ivory, so maybe it could be fixed, or reassembled into something new?

She didn't have time to ponder the thieves' motives further, as the door to the cottage was yanked open to reveal a man almost vibrating with rage. She would have recognized his black top hat and lion-headed walking stick anywhere.

"Put that down, sir!" Lord Dover ordered as he came into the room. "That is mine! Everything in this room is mine!"

"It's evidence in a criminal investigation," snapped Kendra.

"Who told you about this, sir?" asked Sam, but he set down the broken fan, as ordered.

The arctic blue eyes narrowed in the lean greyhound face. "I am not without resources. I hired several Runners to investigate, with the hope of retrieving the stolen goods. I was contacted an hour ago and hired a carriage to bring me here."

Sam looked like he wanted to let loose a few choice words. His face turned red. "We are investigating Lady Dover's murder," he finally said. "We need ter go through everything here."

"I told you before, whatever Lady Dover owned is now *my* possession." He looked down his nose at Sam. "My servants ought to be arriving shortly to pack everything up and return it to my townhouse at Grosvenor Square."

Kendra raised her eyebrows. "*Your* townhouse?"

He shifted his cold eyes to her. "We have already discussed this, Miss Donovan. I am the rightful heir to that house."

Kendra had crossed his name of the list herself. Still, she asked, "Why didn't you tell us that you argued with your stepmother after she wore the Weston necklace to the theater?"

He stiffened. "I can scarcely recall the event. My stepmother and I had many disagreements."

"This disagreement was loud enough to be heard all the way down to the kitchens."

"I was appalled by Cordelia's conduct, and thought a reprimand was in order."

That annoyed Kendra. She might not have liked Lady Dover, but who the hell was Lord Dover to scold her like she was a two-year-old? "I'm sure that went over well," she commented drily.

"She'd embarrassed the Dover name. Her behavior at the theater was utterly without decorum. When I spoke with her about the incident, I was overcome with emotion. Cordelia tended to shout like a fishwife. No doubt the staff heard her."

"I think they heard both of you."

He drew himself up. "I do not need to explain myself to you. And as I've said, I did not kill Cordelia. I was at my club."

"Have you ever used a stiletto?"

Lord Dover's mouth dropped open. But he snapped it shut and replied, "Of course not." He paused. "Is that how Cordelia was murdered?"

"You don't seem too upset by the thought," Kendra observed with narrowed eyes.

"I . . . I have made no secret over my feelings for the woman who married my father," he said finally. "She was an ill-mannered baggage from questionable origins. Now, I ask you to leave. The servants will be here shortly to pack up my items."

"You can't take anything—it's evidence," Kendra repeated, irritated. She glanced at Sam, who frowned. *Oh, shit.* "He can't just take it . . . *can he?*"

"Well, Miss . . . ah, you see . . ."

"Oh, for Christ's sake. Your Grace?" She whipped around, taking her appeal to Aldridge. "We need to make absolutely certain that the necklace isn't here. It's important."

"The necklace? What necklace?" Lord Dover asked sharply.

"The Weston necklace," she shot back. "Or are you going to try to claim that, as well?"

He went quiet, but the expression that came into his eyes made Kendra think he was contemplating it. *Greedy bastard.*

Aldridge spoke up at last. "Your Lordship, surely you are concerned about justice? It is in our best interests to keep society— polite society—safe from the fiends who walk our streets. You must allow us to search through the stolen items before you take them."

Lord Dover gave Alec a quick sideways glance. Most likely he believed the other man was one of the fiends that walked the streets.

"Our search shan't take long," Aldridge pressed.

It wasn't easy to argue against someone like the Duke of Aldridge. Lord Dover seemed to recognize that, and pressed his thin lips together. "I suppose I can give your ward permission to look through the lot," he said grudgingly. He narrowed his eyes as his gaze went to Kendra. "You must be careful, though. I do not want anything broken by careless hands."

Kendra tightened her jaw and bit back a snide retort. *Asshole.* She returned to the glittery tangle of jewelry, and slowly picked her way through the necklaces, bracelets, broaches, and earrings. It was like sifting through pirate booty. She'd never bothered much with jewelry herself, but found herself enchanted by the icy brilliance of the diamonds, the way the sapphires seemed to glow in the dim room, the odd luminance of the pearls, the silk glide of the gold chains.

But there was no necklace with five strands of pearls interspersed with pink diamonds.

She moved on to the other items. The Duke and Alec joined her in inspecting boxes that held silverware and peering into vases. Lord Dover watched them with an air of condescension. She would have loved to find the necklace, just to wipe that arrogant look off his greyhound face, but after forty-five minutes, she had to concede that particular piece of jewelry was not among the items taken from Lady Dover's house.

"The necklace is not here." The Duke was the one to state the obvious. He straightened from a wooden chest he'd been checking. His eyes met hers across the table piled high with the stolen goods. "Now we know the murderer took the necklace."

"Now we know."

44

She knew. But Kendra wanted to be absolutely certain.

Outside, she walked over to the prisoner, still sitting on the stump surrounded by Runners, and, by what she could determine of his expression, still obstinately against informing anyone of the identities of his fellow robbers.

"Oi ain't gonna peach on me lads," he snarled, and spat with pretty good accuracy at her toes. Luckily, she was faster, and stepped back before the spittle could hit its mark.

"I don't give a rat's ass about your partners," she told him. The eye that wasn't swollen shut widened in surprise as he looked at her with renewed interest. Feeling safe for the moment, she stepped forward again, squatting down to be eye level with him. "How did you know to rob that particular residence on that particular night?"

He hesitated, then shrugged his muscular shoulders. "Word got around, didn't it, 'bout the gentry mort gettin' 'er gullet slit. We 'eard the 'ouse was empty. What for yer askin'?"

"So you went inside and robbed the place?"

"Aye. 'Twasn't easy neither, not with the thief-takers walkin' the street. But Bart—ah, Oi figured it out, Oi did. Were finished in three 'ours. Right smooth job, it was."

"Bully for you."

"W'ot?"

"Did you or your partners sell anything from the house?"

"Oi told them," he said, and tipped his head back to glare at the men standing around him, "we were layin' low ter sell the lot. Seemed like the thing ter do with all of bleeding Bow Street out lookin' fer the goods."

"So you didn't take a necklace—five strands of pearls with pink diamonds—and sell it?"

"Oi jest told ye, we didn't. Are ye deaf, woman?"

One of the men slapped the thief on the side of his head. "Watch yer tongue, ye cur! Ye're talkin' ter a lady!"

The thief was unrepentant, his eyes bright with anger as he swung his gaze toward the Bow Street Runner. "Is that so? Well, it bloody well seems like Oi'm talkin' ter a thief-taker wearin' skirts!"

The Runner looked like he was going to backhand the robber again, but Kendra put up her hand. "I got what I wanted. Thank you." She pushed herself to her feet, then hesitated. She looked at Sam. "Have you thought of making a deal with him? Lessen his prison time if he tells you who his accomplices are?"

"Prison time?" One of the other Bow Street Runners laughed. "His stay in Newgate is gonna be quick. Then he'll be facing Jack Ketch, he will."

"Jack Ketch is slang for death, or the hangman," the Duke said when he saw her frown.

Kendra fell silent, chilled. Like most people in law enforcement, she believed in law and order, and justice. As far as she was concerned, the death penalty was warranted for certain killers. She'd sat across from too many victims' families, their eyes red and swollen from sleepless nights and tears over the often grisly fate that had befallen their loved ones. She'd sat across from too many serial killers, too, as they took perverse pleasure in recounting the details of their gruesome crimes, reliving each murder in their minds. She'd seen too many killers walk free, escape, or adjust so well to prison life that they even managed to marry and have children. Hanging a man for robbing an empty house struck her as barbaric.

This is why I don't belong, she thought, as she turned away from the doomed prisoner and began walking back to the carriage. Alec and the Duke fell into step beside her. Sam caught up to them at the carriage, as the coachman opened the door.

"I'm gonna stay here, make sure the prisoner gets transferred ter Newgate, and help Lord Dover with everything."

Kendra gave him a wry look. "Good luck with that."

Sam grinned at her. "Aye." He stepped back, allowing them to climb into the carriage.

Kendra settled into the seat, looking at Alec and the Duke. "Okay, now we really do know that the necklace was taken by Lady Dover's killer."

"You are meticulous in your methods, Miss Donovan," the Duke said approvingly. "If you hadn't sought employment at your Federal Bureau of Investigation, you would be an excellent natural philosopher."

Kendra gave an involuntarily grimace. "A scientist."

Aldridge regarded her with surprise. "You do not oppose science. You, more than anyone, are cognizant of its importance."

"It's not that." Kendra hesitated. What to say? She wasn't afraid that she could change the future by revealing her own past. But thinking about that period of her life still had the power to send her stomach churning.

Finally, she simply shrugged. Maybe it was time they knew about her bizarre background. "My parents were scientists," she said. "My mother is a quantum physicist and my father is a scientist in genome research."

Aldridge looked puzzled. Neither of those words held any meaning for a man of science in the early nineteenth century. "Admirable occupations, I am certain."

"Oh, yes." Kendra laughed, but it sounded hollow. "They're the best at what they do. They married with the intention of having a child who would be the best, the brightest, because that child would be a combination of both of their genes. It was a deliberate decision on their part—carefully weighed and measured, I'm sure, before they acted."

Her gaze fell to her hands, and she realized her fingers were twisting the material on her skirt. She forced herself to stop, aware of her companions' gazes on her. "I was an experiment. To prove that if two individuals of superior intelligence had offspring, the offspring would have equal or greater intelligence."

The Duke smiled. "It would seem that they achieved their ambition. You are the best and the brightest, Miss Donovan."

Kendra shook her head. "If you knew my parents, you'd realize that it didn't work. Or, at least, not the way that they'd wanted. They expected me to follow them into their professions, or at least something equally prestigious."

"And you wanted to join the Federal Bureau of Investigation," Alec said.

"Yes. Although not immediately. That came later."

"I don't understand." Alec frowned. "Isn't the Federal Bureau of Investigation prestigious?"

"For many, it would be. But not for my parents." Her throat felt tight, and she forced herself to swallow. "Our estrangement came long before that, though, when I told them that I wanted to decide for myself what I wanted to do with my life."

The Duke asked gently, "What happened, my dear?"

Kendra licked her dry lips and looked out the window of the carriage, not seeing the squalid buildings they rolled past as they entered into London. She didn't know why it mattered, really. It had happened so long ago. "They left. I never saw them again."

"Your parents abandoned you?" Aldridge looked shocked. Something seemed to shift in his eyes. Kendra realized that he was probably thinking about his own daughter, lost at sea.

"They had other priorities. I saw my father once after that . . ." She shook her head. They didn't need to know about her time in the hospital, recovering from a deadly mission. "Let's just say that the word *scientist* doesn't bring back pleasant memories."

"No, of course not. They left you." The Duke still appeared to have trouble absorbing that revelation.

"It's not just that." Christ, why didn't she just drop the subject? It was as if she'd opened her own personal Pandora's box, and all her troubles were spilling out. "It was before . . . I was a product of their crazy experiment into positive eugenics."

They stared at her.

"Now you know," she concluded very softly, feeling vaguely ill. "I've always been a freak."

She saw Alec exchange a look with the Duke and felt even sicker. Damn it, why couldn't she keep her mouth shut? She was already considered strange here.

"In the twenty-first century, this is not normal," Alec said slowly.

"It's not normal at all."

"No, you misunderstand. Your background is not normal in the twenty-first century."

Kendra frowned.

"I believe what my nephew is trying to say is that what you are describing is actually quite normal here."

"What are you talking about?"

"Miss Donovan, what do you think the Ton does?" Alec said, sounding exasperated. "Bloody hell, they scrutinize potential mates like they were prized horseflesh at Tattersall's! 'Tis why we have assemblies and routs and house parties, to match those mates—but only the appropriate mates for the desirable bloodline."

"Poets may write about love, but the Beau Monde has never attached much confidence to such fanciful notions," agreed the Duke. "Marriage and bloodlines are serious business. They call it good breeding, Miss Donovan, for a reason."

"Or coming from good stock. There are no shortage of cattle terms," said Alec, his lips twisting in wry humor. "The Quality does not want to dilute their blood with their social inferiors. There are times when a lord runs off with an actress, of course, but he is ostracized by society for it. Or sometimes money forces us to marry outside our social sphere. God help those children, because society's matrons shall watch them like hawks when they come of age. If they deviate from what society considers acceptable, they're bad Ton—never mind that those with the purest, bluest blood also drink too much, gamble too much, and behave in an atrocious manner. The Prince Regent could be counted among them."

The Duke smiled wryly. "Alec is correct. What your parents did, it's not uncommon here, my dear. We call it having the right blood, whereas you call it genes. But it's the same concept."

Kendra didn't know what to say. She'd spent her entire life ashamed of her odd background. It had set her apart, made her different. What her parents had done wasn't quite the same as marrying for status or prestige, but perhaps they—she, Alec, the Duke—had all been experiments, in their own way.

Alec settled back on the seat. He seemed to recognize the tumult in her emotions. His mouth curled into a satisfied smile. "You dwell on our differences, Miss Donovan. Perhaps it is time that you consider our similarities."

It was disconcerting for Kendra to have her entire viewpoint shifted in a matter of minutes. The circumstances surrounding her birth had always been a source of deep embarrassment. It made her different, when she'd only ever wanted to fit in. To realize that she was actually normal in this timeline, more than two hundred years before her own birth, was strange, to say the least.

Well, calling herself *normal* in this era might be going a bit too far. Everything was upside down. Her background made her different in the twenty-first century, but was a fairly accepted practice here. Meanwhile, no one in 2015 would blink an eye at an independent woman working in law enforcement, but that was viewed as a peculiarity here.

Maybe I'll never really fit in.

She should've been too old to still have that desire, but she knew that the need to conform, the longing to fit into a larger group, was genetically coded into mankind. Biologically, humans were social animals, like wolves and their packs or whales and their pods. It was why peer pressure could compel people to do stupid things. It was why a college student might express his individualism with a tattoo or a radical haircut or his wardrobe, but still subject himself to hazing to fit into a fraternity.

But damn it, she couldn't think about mankind's foibles right now. She needed to think about only one person—the killer.

Two hours later, she was in front of the slate board with Alec sprawled out in one of the chairs behind her, reading the *Times*. They'd returned to a light meal, and then Lady Atwood had managed to pressure her brother into accompanying her on a few morning calls. They'd have to be social acquaintances, since it was still early in the afternoon. Later afternoon was reserved for intimate connections, like Lady St. James.

How scary was it that she was beginning to recognize 1815's complex rules of social etiquette?

"Perhaps I can take you for a drive around the park," Alec murmured, apparently feeling her anxiety. "It may relax you."

"If I want to relax, I'll do yoga."

"I don't even know what that means, but I'd suggest you do it. You've been tense since we returned home."

"I'm not tense. I want to focus on the investigation." She paused, then did just that. "Roberts would have no reason to steal the necklace. I think I can safely eliminate him from our pool of suspects." She found the damp cloth, hesitated for a second, then wiped his name off the slate board. It felt right.

"And then there were five," she murmured. She glanced around at Alec. "Could you find out where Roberts will be this afternoon? I'd like to talk to him again."

Alec frowned. "Why? You only just erased his name from the list of suspects."

"Yeah, but he doesn't know that. And when I talk to him next, I won't have to focus on him. I might be able to play him against his in-laws."

"Does that work in the FBI—playing people against each other?"

She gave a roguish smile. "More often than you realize."

45

Roberts was at White's. Because women were not allowed to cross the threshold of the gentleman's club, Alec went inside to persuade the future Earl to venture out. Kendra waited in the carriage, drumming her fingers on her knee and cursing the circumstances.

She wasn't sure how long she waited, but it felt too damn long before the door finally opened, and Alec and Roberts climbed inside. Alec rapped his knuckles against the trap, and the carriage jerked forward.

Roberts didn't bother to conceal his irritation. "Now what do you wish of me, Miss Donovan? Haven't you caused enough mayhem in my life?"

"How have I done that?"

"My wife's ill temper has forced me out of my own home and into my club."

"Infidelity can put anyone in a bad mood, I suppose."

He glared at her. "Your attempt at humor is appalling."

"I wasn't trying to be funny." *Maybe a little sarcastic, but not funny.* "You want us to believe that you didn't kill Lady Dover—"

"I did not kill her!"

"Then who do you think did?"

He stared at her. "I have not a notion."

"Come on, you must have some suspicions. This is your moment to give us someone else to focus on, because I've gotta say, you look pretty good as a suspect, Mr. Roberts."

"You're daft."

"You were having an affair with Lady Dover." She raised her hand and began to tick the points off with her finger. "You didn't want your father-in-law to find out, because he might not have been into sharing. She threatened to tell Weston—"

"She did not!"

Kendra studied him. "Lady Dover was mercurial. You couldn't be sure that she wouldn't tell him. You killed her to make sure she never would."

"That's preposterous."

"A magistrate on Bow Street doesn't think so."

"You've discussed this with Bow Street?"

"Of course," she lied, and leaned forward, fixing him with her gaze. "You're looking good for the murder, Mr. Roberts, unless you can give me another name. If it wasn't you, it had to be someone in the Weston family. Lady Isabella and her husband are in the clear. They have an alibi—"

"So do I. I was at the ball."

"Sorry, not good enough. Your house is a ten-minute walk from Lady Dover's. It would be easy to slip out of your house during a crowded ball. So what about Lady Weston? She wasn't there."

Roberts's eyes widened. "Are you bloody serious? *Lady* Weston—you *are* daft!"

"Because she's a woman? Or because she was supposedly home in bed?"

"Yes—both!" He looked at Alec. "Your Lordship, this is utter madness. Miss Donovan may be the Duke's ward, but she belongs in Bedlam."

"Miss Donovan's methods may shock you, but she has a way at getting to the truth," Alec said. "I would suggest you answer her questions."

Roberts looked at him like he was insane too.

"How do you know Lady Weston was really indisposed that night?" Kendra pressed. "It's the perfect alibi. She tells everyone that she's not feeling well and supposedly locks herself in her room until morning, but instead of sleeping, she goes over to Lady Dover's house. Maybe she only wanted to scare her into leaving her husband, but things got out of hand. It happens."

"Such things may happen in America—but not in England."

"Really? Because someone here in merry old England stabbed Lady Dover to death."

Alec held up a hand. "Let's not quibble about geography. Mr. Roberts, how can you know that Lady Weston was in her bedchamber the evening Cor—Lady Dover was murdered?"

Roberts was silent for a long moment. Then he gave a disgruntled shrug. "After the incident at the theater, the woman was overwrought and took to her bed. Lady Frances was concerned and spoke with Lady Weston's lady's maid. She reported Lady Weston's habit of lacing her tea at night with laudanum in order to sleep."

"Lady Weston seems to have recovered remarkably well after Lady Dover's death," remarked Kendra.

Another shrug. "I cannot tell you what goes through a woman's mind. If you want confirmation that Lady Weston was in bed as she claimed, I suggest you speak to the maid—Miss Aubert. She supplied Her Ladyship with the tea."

Kendra kept her eyes on his. "What about Weston, or his son?"

"Lord Weston . . . in truth, I have no idea. He does have a temper, and what Cordelia did would enrage any man. But . . . I don't know."

"Dawson?"

Roberts shook his head. "He's a young pup. I can't imagine him doing anything more than sulk."

"He seems to frequent the gaming hells, and rarely wins," said Alec. "Gossip is he's being crushed with debt."

Roberts didn't look surprised. "I am aware that he has played foolishly at the tables. But what young buck has not?"

Kendra said, "If he has money problems because of his gambling addiction, that can put a great deal of stress on a person. Lady Dover's actions would mean more stress."

Roberts frowned. "What are you implying, Miss Donovan? That Dawson lashed out at Cordelia because he was in dun territory? It seems unlikely. Besides, he was at the ball. Everyone was at the ball. You appear determined to forget that fact."

"Did you have your eye on him the whole time?" Kendra asked.

"Well, no, of course not—"

"What about Lord Weston?"

"No."

"And Lady Louisa?"

Again his eyes widened in disbelief. "Good God, you can't be serious? Lady Louisa is the most timid of creatures."

"Sometimes it's the quiet ones who most surprise us." How often had she heard that during her own investigations? *But he was such a nice young man, so quiet . . .*

Roberts shook his head. "The very notion is preposterous."

"She tends to be in the background. You wouldn't have noticed if she snuck out of your ball for half an hour or so."

"No, but . . . No, I cannot imagine it. 'Tis stupid to even consider such a thing."

Kendra regarded him closely. "What about your wife? Did you keep her in your line of sight that evening?"

His eyes flashed. "Devil take it, that is as laughable as Lady Louisa! She was hosting the ball. *Everyone* had her in her line of sight! Now, I'm done with these ridiculous questions. Bring me back to my club, or let me out and I shall summon a hackney."

"We'll bring you back," Alec said, and knocked again on the ceiling's trap.

Kendra kept her gaze locked on Roberts. "You don't think Lady Frances has it in her to kill a possible rival?" she asked softly.

Something flickered in his eyes.

"This is an outlandish discussion and I shall have no further part on it."

Roberts settled back in the seat and stared out the window at the passing buildings as the carriage drove around the square to loop back to White's. He refused to say anything more during the remainder of the journey.

But Kendra barely noticed the oppressive silence. She was busy wondering if what she'd seen in his eyes was fear, or if it had just been her imagination.

46

Kendra wasn't entirely sure Lady Weston's maid, Miss Aubert, would meet with her, but she dispatched the note anyway. She was pleasantly surprised when she received an acceptance note, along with a time and a place to meet. That required her to send the poor footman back to the Westons' with a note of agreement. Not as easy as making an appointment via cell phone, but it did the job.

Of course, Alec insisted on accompanying her. And to protect her reputation against being seen alone with a gentleman, Molly was enlisted to come along as her maid and to act as a chaperone. This only made Kendra sigh. Never before had she had to have an entourage when interviewing people.

Miss Aubert selected the lake at St. James Park as the place to meet. The day had grown increasingly cold and blustery, the wind strong enough to whip the lake into frothy whitecaps. The weather kept attendance in the park to only a scattering of people. Two men Kendra now recognized as merchants by their style of dress walked along a footpath, winding their way beneath fluttering leaves of black mulberry trees and scarlet oaks. A handful of ragged children played along the sloping hillside, their whoops and hollers carried away by the blowing wind, their antics watched by an old woman wrapped in a black shawl.

There was only a single figure standing in front of the lake, but Kendra thought she would have recognized Miss Aubert even if the park had been filled with people. She'd never met the woman, but she was coming to recognize the *look* of a lady's maid—subdued hairstyle and dark conservative clothing, so as to avoid overshadowing the mistress of the house, while still projecting an aura of competence.

Kendra looked pointedly at Alec. Molly was trailing at a discreet distance behind them, like any good lady's maid. "Miss Aubert might be more comfortable talking to me alone."

Alec said, "You may conduct the interview alone, Miss Donovan, but you shall be in my line of sight."

"I doubt Miss Aubert is going to attack me."

He gave her a crooked smile. "I have learned to expect the unusual where you are concerned." He lifted his hand to capture a tendril of hair that had escaped the tight coil that Molly had styled Kendra's hair into, and held her gaze as he tucked it behind her ear. "I will wait for you over there."

Kendra expelled a low breath when he jammed his hands into his greatcoat pockets and sauntered off to the side, ostensibly to watch the ducks. Yet he positioned himself to keep his eye on her.

She shook her head, her feelings, as always, ambivalent when it came to the Marquis. He wanted to protect her, not because she was a member of the team, a valuable colleague, but because he cared for her on a personal level. Because he loved her. She'd been in exactly two relationships—a shockingly low number for someone in their mid-twenties in the twenty-first century, she knew—but love had never been on the table. And eventually, both relationships had fallen under the grinding heel of her career, ending in a flurry of canceled dinner reservations and recriminations as she raced to the airport to fly to her next case.

She'd never had anyone love her before and she didn't know how to handle it. She especially didn't know how to handle her own baffling feelings.

She became aware that Miss Aubert had turned away from viewing the choppy water, and was now regarding her, waiting.

Kendra stifled another sigh. This was another reason why she'd never wanted to open herself up to love—it made you stupid. When she should have had her entire attention focused on Miss Aubert, she'd been standing with her head in the clouds, thinking about Alec.

Striding forward, Kendra said, "Miss Aubert? I'm Kendra Donovan."

Miss Aubert was wearing a long, dark navy pelisse that was briefly flipped open by the wind. Hands, encased in kid gloves, jerked the garment closed. Her dark blond hair, nearly hidden beneath an unadorned bonnet that matched her coat, was neatly plaited, framing a face that could best be described as elegant rather than pretty. She was probably thirty. The gray eyes that met Kendra's held an intelligent gleam.

"Thank you for seeing me." Kendra offered a smile.

The maid nodded. "This is about Lady Dover's murder?"

Kendra detected a slight French accent, which sounded genuine. There were a lot of fake French lady's maids in London, but apparently Lady Weston had hired the real thing.

"It is. How long have you worked for Lady Weston?"

"Five years."

"And how is Lady Weston to work for? Is she demanding? Difficult? Kind? Generous?"

"She is neither difficult nor particularly kind."

"That's not much of an answer."

"It's an honest one."

"Fair enough. I take it that you two aren't especially close?"

"She is my mistress, not my mother." The woman gave a ghost of a smile. "Still, I do not wish to gossip about Lady Weston."

"I don't want to gossip, either. I want to get some sense of what Lady Weston—and the Weston household—is like."

The maid gave her a look. "There is much talk about how you and the Duke of Aldridge are making inquiries into the murder. It is very curious. This is not customary for a lady to do—even for an American lady."

"Is that why you answered my note? You wanted to satisfy your curiosity?"

Another small smile. "Perhaps." Then, she sobered. "And to tell you that Lady Weston was in her bedchamber the night of the murder."

Kendra eyed her. "How do I know you're telling the truth, Miss Aubert? You could be covering for your employer, protecting your own job."

The maid looked a little nonplussed at having her statement questioned. Then she shrugged. "I do not know how to convince you, Miss Donovan, but I am telling you the truth. And I do not need to protect my position. I am from France and I am very good at fulfilling my duties. Skillful French lady's maids are always in demand among the aristocracy of England."

"I've noticed that."

"The French have always had a great deal of influence in this country." Miss Aubert gestured to the lake and the sloping hillside. "Did you know this royal park was actually designed by a Frenchman? England's King Charles II commissioned André Mollet to redesign it to reflect the parks at Versailles. The King opened it to the public, but also used it to entertain his guests—and his many mistresses."

"It's beautiful," said Kendra, but she wasn't here to discuss landscaping. "Speaking of mistresses . . . tell me what happened that night at the theater when Lady Dover wore the Weston necklace."

Miss Aubert looked surprised. "The night at the theater?"

"Yes. That's when this first started."

"I suppose that is true." Her gaze shifted back to the lake thoughtfully. "Naturally, I waited for Her Ladyship to return from the theater, in order to prepare her for bed. The family returned earlier than expected and my lady was quite distraught."

"Was she crying, or angry? Did she throw things around?"

Miss Aubert let out a laugh, but then caught herself. "She was in a temper, yes. But she is not the kind of person to throw around her perfume bottles. I was once employed by a lady who displayed such fury. She threw a jewelry box at me, hit me right here." She lifted a gloved hand to rub her shoulder, as though the hurt was still fresh.

"What did you do?"

"I handed in my notice and was hired by Lady Weston."

"Okay, so you knew Lady Weston was upset. Did she tell you why?"

"No. She said she had a headache, and wanted to retire. She asked for laudanum to help her sleep."

"What did the rest of the family do? This isn't gossip, Miss Aubert," Kendra added when the maid hesitated. "I'm trying to find a murderer."

Miss Aubert frowned. "Everyone was terribly distressed. Lord Weston and the Viscount sequestered themselves in His Lordship's study. I believe they argued—this is what some of the other staff have said. Lady Louisa was . . . disturbed as well. She has hopes of marrying Lord Ludlow, but he was at the theater, too—I do not think she will be marrying Lord Ludlow."

"I suspect you're right," Kendra said. "What about the next day? What was the mood like in the house?"

"Lady Weston remained in her bedchamber. She was unwell. Lord Weston and the Viscount departed shortly after breakfast. Lady Louisa, I do not know. As I said, she was very upset."

"Do you know where Lord Weston or his son went?"

"No."

"And Lady Weston stayed in bed?"

"In her bedchamber. Lady Isabella and Lady Frances joined her."

"How did they seem?"

The maid gave her a look. "To be expected—disturbed, agitated. Lady Frances, now she is one who will throw things, I think. She was in a fury. When she was leaving, she said . . ." Miss Aubert hesitated, then finished her thought. "She said that Lady Dover was a strumpet. She loathed her and said Lady Dover ought to be taught a lesson. These were just words, you understand, said in the heat of anger."

"I understand." Still, Kendra knew that anger that began as words could end in action—violent action. "Did things eventually calm down?"

Miss Aubert's gaze drifted back to the lake and she let out a sigh. "It is not a happy household. There has been much strife and it has infected the staff. The groom accused one of the stable boys of stealing his coat, and they quarreled. The boy's mother is the cook, so the groom now has accused her of deliberately burning his dinner. You see how a family's mood can affect everyone? How the cycle continues below stairs? This melancholy is not good for a person's nerves."

"No, I wouldn't think it would be."

"I am considering seeking a new position." Miss Aubert opened her pelisse to check the small watch she had attached to the bodice of her gown. "I must go. My duties have been reduced considerably since Lady Weston has become unwell, but my services are still required."

"Just a couple more questions, Miss Aubert. What happened on the night of Lady Frances's party?"

"Lady Weston remained in her bedchamber; she could not face the Beau Monde. She requested laudanum . . ." Miss Aubert shrugged. "I gave it to her in her tea."

"Did you watch her drink it?"

"I waited for her to drink the tea so I could return the cup to the kitchen," Miss Aubert replied. "Later, when I looked into the room, she was sleeping."

"What time did you check on her?"

"This I do not remember."

"But you don't think she left and killed Lady Dover?"

"No. I absolutely do not."

"Thank you, Miss Aubert. You've been very helpful."

The maid looked at her for a long moment. "You are a very unusual woman, Miss Donovan. This I do not mean as an insult."

"Ah . . . thanks."

Kendra watched the lady's maid as she walked away. When she was swallowed up by the trees, Kendra turned and crossed the grass back toward Alec.

"What did Miss Aubert say?" he asked at her approach.

"She said that Lady Weston was in bed at the time Lady Dover was being murdered."

"So not the scorned wife."

"No." She smiled slightly. "Now there are four."

47

Rebecca leaned low, her nose practically touching the mane of the horse, as she raced her mare across the heath of Putney. It was only six miles from central London, but she felt like she was back in the country again. Her blood rushed through her veins. The wind was cold, but she barely felt it between the heat of the beast rising beneath her and her own exhilaration. *This* was what she missed most when in London—this heady sense of freedom when riding without restraint.

Five hundred yards ahead of her, Lady Louisa was a bright streak in her scarlet riding habit. As Rebecca watched, Lady Louisa's thoroughbred stretched and flew in a graceful arc, clearing a hedgerow easily. Rebecca felt her mare's muscles bunch and held her breath as the beast's hooves left the ground, and braced herself for the impact as they came down on the other side of the hedgerow. She pulled up on the reins and gave a loud laugh—also something frowned on in London society—when the horse finally came to a halt next to Lady Louisa.

"This is wonderful! You are a brilliant horsewoman, Lady Louisa!"

She grinned at the other woman. She had to admit that Lady Louisa had surprised her. When she'd invited Rebecca to gallop on the outskirts of London, Rebecca's expectations had been low. She'd anticipated Lady Louisa riding a gentle mare, their excursion more a canter than a gallop. Yet Lady Louisa had shown up sitting on a hot-blooded thoroughbred stallion, more temperamental than Rebecca's own warm-blooded Hanoverian mare. Even now, Lady Louisa had to keep a tight rein on the beast as it sidled to the side, its head twitching impatiently, clearly anxious to keep moving.

Beneath the black hat she wore, Lady Louisa's cheeks were ruddy from the wind. The added color, Rebecca thought, suited her.

"Thank you, Lady Rebecca. 'Tis a passion of mine. And poor Caspian needed a run. He was becoming quite bad-tempered."

"London is ill-suited to a horse of Caspian's temperament. My Sophia here has a calmer spirit, and yet I know she longs to be back in the country." She leaned forward and stroked her mare's sweaty neck. "Did you name your horse after the Caspian Sea?"

"The name was chosen before my father bought him," Lady Louisa said as she guided the horse to walk alongside Rebecca's mare. "And you? Was Sophia your choice?"

Rebecca smiled. "Yes. I named her after Princess Sophia. My mother urged me to reconsider, thinking it was an insult to the Princess. As there was little chance of the Princess ever hearing about it, my father allowed me to keep the name."

Louisa bit her lip and gave her a sideways glance. "Do you believe the rumors that the Princess gave birth to a bastard child?" asked Louisa. "They say that is why she never married."

"From what I've heard, the reason she and most of her sisters have never wed was because of Queen Charlotte's uncommon fondness to keep them near her. I believe Princess Sophia, as well as the other princesses, had very much hoped to find husbands and set up their own households."

"That is a great desire."

Rebecca immediately regretted her words. She'd forgotten Lady Louisa's own unwed state. "I did not mean to bring up an unpleasant subject," she said.

"Do not concern yourself, Lady Rebecca. My circumstance is well-known, I think." She gave a sad smile. "I fear I have lost the affections of Lord Ludlow."

Rebecca doubted that she'd ever had the Earl's affections. Most likely, she'd only had his interest because the old man had lost the sons he'd sired by his first wife and wanted to set up another nursery. But she could hardly say that, so she instead turned in her saddle to look at the stretch of country behind them. "We appear to have lost your groom in our last race. Shall we wait for him, or continue?"

"Let us thoroughly confuse him." Lady Louisa gave a surprisingly impish grin and lifted her reins, a signal that sent Caspian trotting toward the coppice spread out before them.

They had to slow down once they were in the forest. It was like a different world here, Rebecca thought, quieter without the wind buffeting them. The only sounds were the twigs snapping under the horses' hooves, the branches whispering overhead, and the tweeting calls made by the various birds. Rebecca breathed in the woodsy smells of loam and vegetation.

The trees thinned a moment later and they emerged in another clearing. A crumbling stone ruin, once a Norman keep, had been built on the embankment overlooking the churning dark water of the Thames.

Rebecca smiled in delight. "Oh, 'tis a pretty area."

"I've always loved it. I believe the fortress and lands were once owned by Lord Fairchild, but it now belongs to Putney. My family would often come here to picnic when I was a child, as it's not far from Town." She pulled up on the reins of the stallion. "My brother and sisters would climb the ruins looking for treasure."

"Did you find any?"

"We found a Roman coin once." She smiled. "Frances claimed it."

"Somehow that does not surprise me."

Lady Louisa slipped off her saddle to the ground. "Those were happier times." She glanced at Rebecca as she climbed down "These are not happy times. Miss Donovan continues to quiz my family."

Rebecca hesitated, wondering if this had been the real purpose behind Lady Louisa's invitation. "Miss Donovan is assisting the Duke in his inquiries," she said carefully.

"You said that Miss Donovan has an exceptional skill at finding murderers," Lady Louisa reminded her, glancing over her shoulder at Rebecca as she tied Caspian's reins to tree branch. She gathered her long skirt in her arms as she walked toward the river.

Rebecca let Sophia's reins go, knowing the more gently bred horse would graze rather than bolt, and followed Lady Louisa up the stone embankment that had been built at one time to protect the area from flooding. Now it was covered in spots of green lichen. A few wildflowers poked through the stones, offering bright splashes of color against the gray and green. Lady Louisa paused long enough to pluck one of the flowers.

"'Tis an odd skill to have," murmured Lady Louisa. "She is a very strange woman to occupy her time in such a manner. Why does she do it?"

"I believe it is a passion of hers, much like riding is for you." Rebecca could hear a note of defensiveness creep into her voice. She didn't like to hear Kendra described as strange, even though she herself found much about the American strange. But she meant strange in a *good* way—not as an oddity, as Lady Louisa was clearly regarding her.

"She feels very strongly about justice," she added primly.

Lady Louisa's lip curled. "For Lady Dover?"

She understood the woman's hostility toward the Countess, but couldn't find herself placating her, even for politeness sake. "For anyone," she said.

Lady Louisa said nothing for a moment, her gaze dropping to the flower she twirled. She tossed the wildflower and they both watched as the wind caught it and spun it a little farther out over the black rushing water. Then it fell into the Thames, turning for a moment before rapidly sinking.

"She believes my father murdered her, doesn't she?" Lady Louisa asked suddenly.

"Miss Donovan is considering many suspects," Rebecca said, lifting her gaze from the submerged flower. She didn't know what else to say. It was clear to her that the other woman was miserable, but she felt helpless to soothe her pain.

"Why did he do it?"

Rebecca's breath caught, and she wondered if Lady Louisa was about to incriminate her father. "Do what?" she asked, pleased that her voice was steady.

Lady Louisa's head snapped around and she fixed her gaze on Rebecca. "Why did he have to have an affair with *her*? I realize that gentlemen often take mistresses. But why did he choose *her*? She was utterly vicious."

Rebecca saw the pain shimmering in Lady Louisa's eyes and could imagine just how vicious Lady Dover had been to this plain, awkward woman, who would most likely end her days as a spinster. Rebecca faced a similar future, but not with the same despair. "I'm sorry," she said softly, feeling completely inadequate.

Lady Louisa pressed the palms of her hands to her hot face and shook her head. "We were happy until she destroyed my family."

Lord Weston had something to do with the destruction of his family, as well, Rebecca thought, but kept quiet.

"I can feel everyone's stares when we go out," Lady Louisa whispered. They were silent for a moment, then Lady Louisa gave a bitter laugh. "Dear heaven, I'm turning positively maudlin. I do apologize, Lady Rebecca. This excursion was meant to be pleasant."

And for you to pry into Kendra's investigation, Rebecca thought, but she forced a smile. "I am quite enjoying myself. But perhaps we should return to the heath. Your groom may be getting worried."

Lady Louisa waved that away. "Oh, he knows where we are. I always come here when I exercise Caspian. Though you are right; we should return. We still have a half-hour ride back to London."

They slung their long trains over their arms and walked down the embankment toward the horses. At the bottom, Lady Louisa turned to look at Rebecca. "You are Miss Donovan's friend. Can you not persuade her that nothing can be served by her investigation into Lady Dover's death?"

"My lady, you are forgetting that Lord Sutcliffe is under suspicion for the murder. The House of Lords will be convening soon to discuss the matter."

"He will not be charged. He is a marquis and the Duke of Aldridge's heir."

Rebecca thought about the crime lord named Bear. "There are extenuating factors. But that is not the point."

"What is the point?"

"Justice, of course. Miss Donovan is not alone in her desire to bring the murderer to justice." She hesitated, her gaze on the other woman's. "If you know who killed Lady Dover—"

"I do not!" Lady Louisa spun away, but not before Rebecca saw the fear that leaped into her eyes.

"Your father—"

"Is innocent!" she snapped.

"Or your brother."

"Arthur? The very notion is absurd."

Lady Lousia was untying Caspian's reins when her groom emerged from the forest on his aging dappled gray.

"Lady Louisa, ye shouldn't run away from me." He raised an admonishing finger. "Beth here is old. Ye know she can't keep up with your stallion."

He dismounted and hurried over to them, lacing his fingers together to create a mounting block for them to get back on their horses. Rebecca hooked her leg over the pommel and rearranged her skirts to drape across the saddle in a ladylike manner. Lady Louisa was already trotting toward the forest. Picking up her reins, Rebecca made to follow, but she hesitated, her gaze traveling over the glen with its tumbling ruin and the waters of the Thames as a picturesque backdrop. This would be a lovely place for a family to picnic—in happier times.

She remembered the fear that had flashed in Lady Louisa's eyes when she'd asked if she knew who had killed Lady Dover. It had been an adamant denial. And, Rebecca thought, almost certainly a lie.

48

They were at yet another ball that Wednesday night, this one hosted by Lord and Lady Ogilvy, who were close friends of Lady Atwood. That meant the evening was mandatory, at least for the Duke. Kendra had a feeling that the Countess would have preferred if she'd stayed home with a good book. But since there was a chance that Viscount Dawson would be in attendance, Kendra had dressed in an emerald silk evening gown and accompanied them to the mansion at Hanover Square. Rebecca had arrived with her parents ten minutes ago and Alec five minutes later, and Kendra stood with them in one corner of the ballroom.

So far Dawson was a no-show, along with the rest of his family. She wondered if there was any significance in their absence.

"I think she is sad," Rebecca said, telling Kendra about her afternoon with Lady Louisa. "She brought me to an old ruin in Putney, where her family once picnicked. She said that they were happy once. It was really quite awful."

Kendra regarded Lady Rebecca, then asked, "Did she say anything about Lady Dover?"

"She didn't say anything that we didn't already know." Rebecca shrugged. "She despised the woman. It's certainly understandable that she wished her dead."

Their conversation about murder should have struck an odd note against the merriment surrounding them, with the orchestra playing a lively piece and couples dancing. But as they often discussed such a grim topic in assorted ballrooms, it now seemed normal.

"She actually said that she wished her dead?" Kendra pressed.

Rebecca frowned. "No, of course not—at least, not in so many words. She blamed Lady Dover for her father's affair, but I sensed that her loathing may have been more personal. Lady Dover was not kind to her own sex."

"Cordelia was hardly alone in such behavior," Alec said in a low voice.

Kendra suspected Alec was right. She allowed her gaze to travel over the glittery assembly, lingering on a trio of young women across the room. Debutantes, by the look of them, wearing simple flowing white dresses, their hair pulled up and decorated with matching ribbons, as well as daisies, pearls, or diamonds. They may be innocent maids, cultivating their virginal look with their appearance—and how *that* would change in her era, Kendra thought, where virginity had become almost an anathema among young girls in western cultures—but they operated their fans like seasoned courtesans, using them to flirt with the young bucks standing across from them. *The games people play.*

"I'm not interested in anyone else. I'm interested in the woman who ended up with forty-three stab wounds in her chest. If she bullied Lady Louisa, we need to factor that in. She isn't like her sister—Lady Frances would give as good as she got." But did that include figuring out how to sneak out of her own ball to murder her rival?

"Lady Louisa would have remained silent, unable to respond to Lady Dover's insults," she continued. "That kind of thing festers. The hostility builds, until it explodes. It just needs a trigger." *Like Lady Dover wearing their family necklace to the theater.*

Rebecca shook her head. "I don't believe Lady Louisa killed Lady Dover."

Kendra said, "It's only a theory. We've got four suspects; Lady Louisa happens to be one of them. Lady Frances has the personality, but is the most unlikely because she was hosting the ball. Lady Louisa is barely noticed and could have slipped out pretty easily, but she's the most unlikely because of her personality. Weston works on all counts, I think."

"And Dawson?" asked Alec.

"Yeah, he rings every bell too." She paused. A sensation, whisper-soft, was beginning to tease the edges of her consciousness.

Rebecca eyed her. "Is something the matter, Miss Donovan? You have a most peculiar look on your face."

Kendra held her breath, trying to capture the elusive thought. But even as she reached for it, trying to identify the source of the disquiet, it vanished into the ether. She released her breath in a frustrated sigh.

"I'm fine. It's just . . ." She shook her head, annoyed with herself. "I feel like I'm missing something vital. I'm sure it will come to me."

"Mr. Kelly also continues to pursue his line of inquiry among the servants and stablehands," said Alec. "Unfortunately Lady Frances's staff has been remarkably reticent about the night of the ball."

"Or they did not witness anything unusual that night," Rebecca countered.

"Lord Sutcliffe, good evening. Lady Rebecca, Miss Donovan."

Kendra turned to find Lady St. James barreling toward them. She wore a bright cantaloupe-colored gown with five flounces that began in the vicinity of her knees, the last sweeping the floor. The bodice above the high-waisted gown glittered with sequins. She had hidden her graying brown hair beneath a matching turban adorned with a single white plume that resembled a giant question mark bobbing above her head.

Lady St. James was holding the elbow of an old woman dressed entirely in black, including the lace cap she wore over her thinning white hair. She was short, barely topping five feet, Kendra estimated, but made even shorter by her spine, which curved into a dowager's hump that left her head permanently thrust outward like a turtle. One of her clawlike hands was wrapped around a walking stick, which clicked rhythmically against the marble floor as the two ladies approached.

Alec executed a proper bow. "Good evening, my lady. Your Grace." He turned to Kendra. "You have already made the acquaintance of Lady St. James, but may I introduce you to the Dowager Duchess of Chatsworth?"

Nothing was more awkward to Kendra than the curtsy. Not because it was difficult to do, but because it wasn't something she'd ever had to do. But because it was expected of her, she bent her knees a little in a quick dip.

The Dowager Duchess fixed her small, nearly lashless eyes on Alec, thumping her cane on the floor. "You. What is this nonsense I've heard about you murdering Lady Dover?"

Kendra gave Lady St. James a sideways glance. She had a feeling she knew where the Dowager Duchess had been hearing the nonsense.

"I can assure you that I'm innocent, madam," Alec drawled.

"Of course you are. I pride myself on being a keen observer of my fellow man—and woman. Lady Dover . . ." The woman drew back her lips to reveal teeth stained from tobacco and tea. "Coquettish piece of baggage. Met her when Lord Dover brought her to one of the assemblies at the time. Dover, he'd always been a fool. So was Martha—his first wife.

"Now Cordelia, she wasn't a fool. But the chit was a mushroom, to be sure. And scandalous. Wearing the Weston necklace out in public like she did—*very* bad Ton."

Kendra asked, "Who do you think killed her, Your Grace?"

The old lady slewed her gaze at Kendra. "You are the Duke of Aldridge's ward. Odd, I've known Bertie since he was in short pants. But I don't recall any mention of this friendship he had with your father. What's his name again?"

Kendra immediately regretted bringing attention to herself. "Mr. Donovan," she said calmly.

The old woman gave a snort, her beady eyes gleaming with amusement. "You must pay me a morning call, when we can converse more freely."

God, no. In fact, the Dowager Duchess, with her sharp little eyes, was someone Kendra was going to most definitely avoid.

"I'd imagine most wives aren't too troubled that the woman stuck her spoon in the wall," the old lady continued. "Not to mention any of the debutantes who failed to capture the attention of the young swains because Cordelia was around. They were all blinded by her." She turned back to Alec. "Even you. Thought you had better sense, my boy."

Alec gave her a wry smile, but wisely kept silent.

She made a harrumphing sound. "Cordelia was ill-bred, but I will allow there can be no denying her beauty. You certainly weren't the first fool entranced by her."

"Thank you," murmured Alec.

"Lord Weston—now that's who should be looked at. Stupid fellow. If I were Lady Weston, I'd have poisoned the chit. But I don't see her doing that. Doesn't have enough gumption." She gave a sharp bark of laughter. "Have I shocked you, Miss Donovan?"

"More like terrified me."

She gave another crackling laugh. "I like you, girl, even if you are one of those damned colonists. Lost a son fighting in your war for independence."

Holy shit. Kendra didn't know what to say.

"A younger son, not in line for the dukedom. But I still rather liked the boy," she said gruffly, turning her gaze to the dance floor.

"I've heard that you've been making inquiries, Miss Donovan," said Lady St. James, giving Kendra a measured look. "Who do you think murdered the creature?"

"The investigation is ongoing."

The Dowager Duchess turned back at this and she issued another one of her barking laughs. "Put you in your place, Anne." Thoughtfully, she added, "I ought to take a look at Lord Weston's head the next time I see him."

"His *head*?" Rebecca frowned in confusion.

"Yes, his head. Are you deaf, girl?" The Dowager Duchess turned to peer up at Alec. "You appear to have a nicely shaped head, although it's not easy to tell because of all that hair. Come down here, boy."

Alec gave her a dubious look, but complied, bending low so the old woman could drive her talon-like fingers through his thick, dark brown hair. "Yes, yes. A most excellent head. Sutcliffe here is not the murderer."

"Thank you, madam," the Marquis said when he straightened.

Rebecca smiled. "I see you are an admirer of Franz Joseph Gall, Your Grace." She glanced at Kendra, and explained, "Mr. Gall is an advocate of cranioscopy."

"I believe they are now calling it phrenology," corrected Lady St. James.

The Dowager Duchess thumped her cane for their attention. "Cranioscopy or phrenology—whatever it is called, it is an infallible measurement to determine one's character. I have begun to study the science extensively and Sutcliffe here has a very well-shaped head with no overdeveloped bumps that would indicate a murderous nature."

Kendra stared at the old woman. She didn't look gullible. But then the pseudoscience was just gaining in popularity. Even

Thomas Edison would become a believer before phrenology would eventually be debunked.

Alec said, "I don't suppose you could speak on my behalf at the House of Lords, madam?"

The Dowager Duchess gave a sharp smile. "I may just do that, boy. Someone has to bring those popinjays into the future. You can't stop progress."

Kendra bit her tongue. It wasn't as if she hadn't heard some crazy theories in her own time. She thought Rebecca looked ready to respond to the old woman's words, but a buzzing noise distracted her. Kendra recognized the sound as gasps and an electrified murmuring from the crowd around them.

She turned to look at what might be causing the commotion when Lady St. James breathed, "Dear heaven. Can it be . . . ?"

"The waltz," the Dowager Duchess intoned. "Lady Ogilvy is allowing the waltz. Clever puss. This was a deadly dull affair; now it will be the most talked about ball tomorrow morning. Come, Anne, I need to see this. Good evening." The old woman gave them a distracted nod and grasped Lady St. James's arm for support as they pushed themselves through the circling eddies of people, getting a better position to watch the scandalous dance.

Rebecca gave a laugh. "Not everyone will be happy about this development."

"Lady Atwood won't," agreed Kendra.

"I think the Countess may change her mind when she only considers what this means." Rebecca looked at Alec. "You will no longer be the topic in London most gossiped about, Sutcliffe. That is a form of progress, too, is it not, Miss Donovan?"

But Kendra wasn't listening. Her gaze traveled over the ballroom and the dancers that had begun twirling around the floor, colorful skirts belling against pantaloons. The odd sensation was back again, a quiet dread knotting her stomach, telling her she was overlooking something important, a piece to the puzzle that could change everything.

49

Kendra couldn't sleep. She stared up at the canopy over her bed, the silk just a gleam in the heavy shadows that had invaded the bedchamber. It was sometime after two A.M. and the fire in the hearth was more cold ash than burning embers. She tried rolling onto her side. When that didn't do anything, she switched positions. She was exhausted. And yet her mind continued to race in a series of disjointed thoughts.

After another ten minutes, she gave up. She fought her way out of the blankets twisted around her legs and put on the velvet robe that Molly left draped across a chair every night. Tying the sash, she found the slippers under the chair and was grateful for their small bit of warmth when she pushed her feet into them. Back in her Virginia apartment, she'd never worn slippers. If she got up in the middle of the night to sift through files, she'd pad around barefoot. But then, even in the dead of winter, her apartment had central heating. She didn't exactly know when that would be invented, and until it was, fires from coal and wood just didn't cut it.

Moving back to the bedside table, she found the box containing the flint. It took her about seven minutes to light the candle, which actually wasn't too bad for a woman who'd grown up with light switches and remotes (or so she told herself). She took the candle with its feeble light toward the door. In the hallway, she hesitated, the floorboards creaking under her weight, sounding unnaturally loud in the silence of the house. One candle flame barely penetrated the inky darkness of the hallway.

She continued down the corridor and eased open the door to the study. Inside, she spent the next several minutes lighting the brace of candles on the table and desk. The footmen had shuttered the windows, but she could still hear the windowpanes rattling with the wind. She considered building a fire, but she didn't think she was up for that. Instead, she crossed the room to where the decanters were and yanked the stopper from the brandy. She splashed a small amount of alcohol into the glass, replaced the stopper, and lifted the glass to her lips.

"Do you do this often—sneak in here in the dead of night to accost Duke's spirits?"

She nearly dropped the glass as she spun around and put her hand over her pounding heart. "Jesus Christ. *Alec.* Do you want to give me a heart attack?"

"I apologize."

He closed the door and advanced into the room with the easy stride of an athlete. Like her, he'd put on a robe, dark green patterned silk, over what appeared to be silky black trousers. Kendra had the oddest desire to rake her fingers through his tousled hair, much like the Dowager Duchess had done earlier that evening.

"What are you doing awake?" he asked. "Aside from drinking?"

"I'm not . . ." She stared at the glass in her hand. "It's damn cold in here. I couldn't shut off my mind, so I thought I'd look over my notes. Sometimes that helps. Something pops out; you see something from a fresh perspective."

Alec went to the fireplace, squatting down to gather kindling from the box next to the grate. With quick efficiency that Kendra could only marvel at, he started a small fire that crackled and popped as the flames quickly devoured the kindling, then tossed a few logs on top. For a moment, Kendra thought he'd extinguished it, but then the flames caught the denser wood and the small fire was suddenly transformed into a blaze.

"You're quite the Boy Scout," she said, coming over to take advantage of the warmth.

He gave her a crooked smile, still squatting. "I'm not certain I should even ask."

She smiled back, and again had to resist the urge to run her fingers through his hair. She knew from personal experience that it would be cool and silky to touch. Her smile faded as their eyes locked. For a long moment, the only sounds in the study were the fire and the rattle of windowpanes. Then Alec slowly rose and put one arm around her. He took the glass from her suddenly nerveless fingers and set it down on a nearby table.

"Alec . . ." She didn't know what she was going to say, could barely hear the whisper above the hammering of her heart.

"We never had our waltz," he murmured, drawing her nearer. "You said it is a dance that you are familiar with."

With the first step, she stepped on his toes and let out a low, hoarse laugh. "I didn't say I was any good at it."

"Just relax," he whispered, and guided her in slow circles around the room.

"What will happen if the House of Lords decides to charge you?" she asked, unable to set the investigation aside for long.

"A warrant for my arrest will be issued. They may try to put me in Newgate until the trial, but the Duke will use his influence to see that doesn't happen."

"And if he doesn't succeed?"

"He will."

"But if he doesn't?" she persisted.

"Life will not be comfortable."

It would be more than uncomfortable, she knew. The prison itself could be a death sentence. Not only because of the harsh living conditions, the lice and fleas spreading typhus, but because someone like Bear could easily get to Alec inside. Kendra shivered.

"Are you cold?" he asked, misinterpreting.

"No." But she allowed him to gather her closer against his warmth as they spun around the room to phantom music.

It suddenly occurred to Kendra that she could lose him. She'd accepted that if she found a way back to her own timeline, she would be leaving him. But now she realized that she could be stranded in this era and still lose him to death or disease or prison.

Their dance slowed. Their bodies pressed together, swaying as though moved by a gentle breeze. Kendra dropped her head to his chest. She could hear his heartbeat, strong and sure, against her ear. How had this man come to matter so much?

"I don't think this is the waltz," she whispered.

He hesitated, and his arms tightened around her. "I should go."

Kendra lifted her eyes to meet his gaze, recognizing the blaze of desire she saw there because it matched her own. It would be a mistake to become more involved with him, she knew. She couldn't just abandon hope of returning to her own timeline. Maybe there were a few slivers of her life that could fit in this era, but she still didn't belong. She'd never be comfortable here, with this rigid class system and the restrictions on women. And if she tried to fit in, how long would that last? If she gave up searching for a way to return to her own era, how long before she began to resent him?

She didn't realize that she hadn't responded, hadn't even moved, until Alec dropped his arms from around her and stepped back. His gaze traveled over her for one heart-stopping moment, then he offered her a faint smile. "Don't forget to blow out the candles when you leave."

"Alec . . ." she whispered.

But he was already gone.

✣

Alec stacked his hands behind his head and stared, unseeing, at the coffered ceiling. It had been the hardest thing he'd ever done, leaving Kendra standing in the study, looking soft and rumpled and, to his mind at least, ready to be ravished. Yet he sensed a rare vulnerability in her, and couldn't in good conscience take advantage of that.

He thought he understood her a little better now, after she'd shared the details of her upbringing. He'd dismissed her revelation about her parents' arrangements; it was her disclosure about her relationship with her parents that had struck a chord inside of him, and given him new insight. She'd been put on a preordained path, much like his with his family. Her parents had expected her to honor it, much as he was expected to honor his lineage. And she'd essentially been abandoned. He understood that terrible desolation. His parents hadn't walked away from him—his mother had died and his father had then married a woman who thoroughly detested him. His stepmother had hidden it while his father was alive, but once he'd followed his first wife to the grave not many years later, Alec's stepmother had essentially ignored his existence, leaving him in school and pouring all her attention on her son, Alec's half brother, Gabriel.

That had been disastrous, but he hadn't known it at the time. He'd only known the same sense of abandonment that Kendra had felt. They may have been from different times, but they had more in common than Kendra knew. It would be up to him to convince her.

He'd just decided that when his door opened and closed quietly. He sat up and silently cursed that he'd let the fire go out, leaving the room in almost total darkness. But he didn't need to see her face to know who it was. He could sense the uniqueness that was Kendra, and smell the faint lavender scent of her as she drew near.

"Alec?"

"Yes?" His heart was in his throat, damn near strangling him. He was surprised that he managed to say anything.

"I've been thinking . . . there may be no tomorrow. There's only now. Today."

He heard her breathing, light but quick, as she advanced. It occurred to him that she might have as much trouble seeing in the dark as he was. But then she was there. He felt the feather mattress sink under her weight, and her hands, soft and smooth, reach out to touch him.

"I want to enjoy this moment," she breathed. "Here. Now. With you."

"Kendra." He summoned the strength to reach out and grab her shoulders, to hold her still. "I don't want to take advantage of you."

She hesitated. "Do you want me?"

"God, yes."

"Good." She lifted the blankets and crawled in beside him. "Then I'll take advantage of you."

❖

Alec cradled her in his arms, his fingers sliding through the heavy silken strands of her hair. "I shall get a special license and we can be married immediately."

The hand that had been stroking his chest paused. "No."

He said nothing for a moment. Then he expelled a sigh. He'd known this would be her response. Any other woman in the world—in *his* world—would be terrified that marriage would not be offered. But not Kendra Donovan.

Almost of its own volition, his hand caressed the satin skin of her shoulder, feeling the puckered scar she carried there, like the others she carried in other places on her body. They were a reminder that this woman was not ordinary. She was both the most foolish and the most brave woman he'd ever met.

"Would it be so very awful to be married to me?" he finally asked.

She shifted in his arms. Despite their intimacy, it was still so dark that it was impossible to see her expression. Still, he sensed her eyes on his. "You know that's not what this is about."

"You may never return home, Kendra. Do you really want to spend the rest of your life here as a spinster, with no husband or children of your own?"

"An ape leader?" She sounded amused.

"Yes." The word came out more harshly than he'd intended. But damn, the woman was frustrating. Deliberately, he slid his hand down to her flat stomach. "You could be carrying my child at this moment."

She was silent. He thought she was considering the possibility, but there was something in the quality of the silence that made him tense.

"That might not be possible," she said. He felt her fingers curl around his wrist, moving the hand he'd splayed across her stomach to touch the thin ridge of scar tissue on the side of her abdomen. "This injury reduced the chances of me ever having children."

He stopped breathing. "But you don't know, not for certain . . ."

"No. But the odds aren't in my favor."

He didn't know what to say. This was another thing that he'd always taken for granted, along with a grateful—yes, *grateful*—bride. He liked children well enough, but he'd never given too much thought to setting up his nursery. His progeny would simply *be* there someday, a requirement in his world, to carry on the family name.

How in God's name had he fallen in love with a woman who had no wish to be a wife, who might not be able to produce children?

"I guess this changes things, doesn't it?" He could hear the wry note in her voice, could sense her withdrawal even before she began to shift away from him.

Instinctively, he brought his arms around her. "I'll get the license—"

"Alec, I'm not stupid. You might not be required to marry an heiress, or even someone with a title. But children . . . that is the one thing you *do* require in a wife, isn't it? I can't guarantee you that."

"I love you."

She said nothing for a long moment. Then she lifted a hand and stroked his cheek, a featherlight touch that made him stir again. "You know it's not that simple."

He was silent. She was right; it was bloody complicated. His duty to his lineage had been drummed into him since he was a boy. He wasn't so selfish as to simply toss all those years, all those expectations away. He *owed* his family something. And yet . . .

His earlier thought drifted back to him. She'd been abandoned by her family, so she expected to be abandoned by everyone—by him.

"I'm not giving up," he said slowly. "Let's not think about tomorrow. There's only—"

"Here. Now." She slid her hands up his chest. He could feel her lips curve in a smile against his neck. "Yes. If there's nothing else, that is something we can both agree on, my lord."

50

They stayed in each other's arms until the sky began to lighten. By the way the windowpanes rattled in the fitful gusts outside, the weather would remain temperamental. The servants would soon be stirring, the scullery maids stifling yawns as they made their way down to start the coal fires in the kitchens and began scouring and black-leading the mammoth cast-iron stove, filling the enormous tubs with water that would be brought to boiling.

Kendra sat up, then shivered when she felt Alec trace his finger down the indention of her spine.

"You have been thoroughly compromised, Miss Donovan," he murmured softly.

The quick bubble of laughter took her by surprise. She twisted around to look at him. Then she leaned down to capture his face in her hands and gave him a long, toe-curling kiss. Lifting her head, she smiled. "I think I've done a pretty good job of compromising you, too, Lord Sutcliffe. Now I have to go."

She dressed in silence, while Alec threw on his robe. When he began to follow her out of the room, she smiled at him and said, "You don't need to show me to my door."

"I will do the honorable thing, you know."

"You mean make an honest woman out of me? Thanks, but I'm as honest as I want to be."

"Kendra—"

She raised herself on her toes and kissed him briefly. Then she sank back down, keeping her eyes locked on his. "Nothing has changed, Alec. So no regrets, okay?"

He said nothing for a long moment, and she could tell he was conflicted, his sensibilities at war against her more modern viewpoint. Finally, he sighed. "No regrets," he agreed.

He opened the door to make sure the hallway was empty. Then, despite her protest, he accompanied her to her door, like a boy escorting his prom date home. She wasn't used to such solicitous gestures, so she found herself sucking in her breath when he lifted his hand, brushing her cheek in a gesture that struck her as unbearably sweet. Then he was gone.

She closed the door softly and sagged against the panel. *Nothing has changed.* She'd meant it. She just didn't know if it was true.

�֍

Kendra opened her eyes when the door opened. The bedchamber was soft with shadows. She flopped around and saw Molly standing on the threshold.

"Good morning," she said, and covered her mouth to capture a yawn.

"Good morning—ye're awake then?"

"I hope so. What time is it?"

"Half past ten."

"Christ! Are you kidding me?" She bolted upright, glancing at the clock for confirmation.

Molly crossed the room to push back the drapes, allowing the gray light of day to invade the room. "Are ye feelin' ill, Miss? Ye never sleep this late."

"Why didn't you wake me?"

Molly seemed perplexed by the question. "W'ot for?"

"Because . . ." What for indeed? It's not like she had an office to go to. "Because like you said, I never sleep this late."

"'Tis normal for the gentry to stay in bed 'til noon, Miss."

"I'm not gentry."

Another questioning look. "If ye're not gentry, w'ot are ye, Miss?"

What am I? Who am I? Who am I—here? She didn't know. "I'm not up for a philosophical debate right now." She raked fingers through her hair. "God, I'd love a bath."

"I'll have one fetched, Miss."

"Oh, I didn't mean . . ." She bit her lip—she actually *would* love a bath—and tried not to feel guilty when Molly went in search for half a dozen servants to make it happen. Two footmen hauled a large copper tub into the adjacent dressing room and three maids brought buckets of hot water from the kitchen. Twenty minutes later, Kendra eased herself into the steaming water, feeling quite decadent. It was eleven in the morning and she was soaking in a hot bath. She rested her head against the rounded lip of the tub and closed her eyes.

"Do ye want me ter bring ye breakfast?" asked Molly.

"That would be nice," she said, and smiled.

Molly hesitated, giving her a puzzled look. "Are ye all right, Miss? Ye seem a bit different."

Nothing has changed. Her words now seemed to mock her. She straightened abruptly, the water sloshing dangerously close to the edge. "Why? What do you mean?"

"Nothin', Oi suppose. Ye just seem . . . happy."

Oh, God, she was acting like some giddy, lovestruck teenager. "I'm—" Shit, what could she say? That Molly was mistaken, that she *wasn't* happy?

"I'm starving, Molly. I'd love something to eat. Thanks."

She reached for the cloth and the lump of lavender-scented soap that the tweeny had left on the stool next to the tub, and focused on lathering her arm. She was aware of Molly regarding her closely, and expelled a relieved breath when the maid finally left.

By the time Molly returned with a tray, Kendra had finished bathing and was pulling on her chemise. She poured herself a cup of coffee from the pot and, surveying the plate of eggs and plump sausage, broiled tomato, and sautéed mushrooms, she realized that she really was starving. She slipped into her robe and tried not to think about the last time she'd worn it—or what had happened when it had come off—and dug into breakfast like she hadn't eaten for a week.

She was finishing the last bit of eggs when there was a knock at the door. Molly went to answer it, only opening it a crack so Kendra couldn't see who was on the other side. There was a quick murmur, then Molly closed the door and spun around, excitement making her eyes sparkle.

"Yer clothes from the Countess's Frenchie mantua-maker has come, Miss! They'll be bringing the boxes in a bit. Do ye want ter wait ter see w'ot's there before ye dress?"

"Ah, sure," Kendra said, but more so to avoid disappointing the tweeny. She pushed herself to her feet and replenished her coffee cup, and another knock a short time later sent Molly racing back to the door. Three footman came in, loaded down with boxes that they set carefully on the bed. Molly was already ripping off the lids, pulling out gowns, and oohing and ahhing when the servants marched out.

"Would ye look 'ere! 'Tis lovely, this is!" She held up an ivory gown decorated with intricate beadwork on the high bodice.

Kendra had to smile at the girl's enthusiasm, and wondered what the tweeny would think if she had the chance to go to any one of the shopping malls that dotted the landscape near where she lived in Virginia. She *was* only fifteen, Kendra reminded herself. She'd probably be like any twenty-first-century teenage girl who found utopia scouring the clothing racks and trying on new fashions.

"Miss, look 'ere. Ye'd look beautiful in this gown."

She brought out a sea green, sequin-embroidered evening dress. When Molly whirled around with it clutched to her breast, the skirt flared out in a dazzling display. "Oi could do up yer hair with those green sparklers, Miss. Ooh, Oi 'ope ye're going ter another ball soon!"

"This is London—there's always another ball, Molly. Tonight there's the musical recital . . ." Kendra stopped abruptly, and felt like she'd just run headlong into a brick wall. Now she knew what had been bothering her. *Holy crap* . . .

"Miss?" Molly eyed her with concern. "Are ye all right? Ye're lookin' peculiar again."

"I just realized . . . my God, I've been so *stupid*. It was right there in front of my eyes. Lady Dover . . ."

Molly's eyes widened. She gave a gasp. "Ye know the fiend that killed 'er?"

"Almost. I know who *didn't* kill her."

51

The theory was taking shape in Kendra's mind, but she didn't want to talk about it yet. She wanted to review her notes in the study first.

She was actually opening the door to do that when Molly reminded her that she was still in her robe. Biting back an impatient oath, Kendra closed the door and moved back into the bedchamber. She managed not to snap at Molly when she was slow in selecting a gown, finally settling on the glazed cambric morning dress in a dusky lilac hue, designed with a modest square neckline and long sleeves that were trimmed at the wrist with a narrow band of lace. She even kept her toe-tapping to a minimum when the tweeny pinned her hair in a coil and added a few complimentary ribbons.

As soon as Molly had finished and stepped back, Kendra shot to her feet and was out the door, racing down the hall. The footman and maid who were talking near the stairs stopped to stare, wide-eyed, as she bolted past them. She didn't care.

She yanked open the door to the study, only then coming to a stop when she saw that the Duke was behind his desk, his head bent, his brow furrowed, reading a letter. Alec was sprawled in a chair, still wearing riding clothes, his nose buried in the *Times*. At her entrance, they both looked up. Kendra couldn't stop her gaze from going to Alec, who pushed himself to his feet.

The Duke rose, as well, holding the letter aloft with obvious interest. "Miss Donovan, good day. I am reading the most remarkable letter by a fellow philosopher—or, as you like to say, scientist." The word was still new enough to the Duke that he pronounced each syllable. giving it an almost exotic sound. "Monsieur Niépce appears to be experimenting with an advanced form of lithography. His results have been sporadic, but he believes he is close to inventing a process that may record a scene like a painting. He calls it heliography."

This gave Kendra pause. "Niépce. You mean Joseph Nicéphore Niépce? The French inventor?"

"Before the war, we corresponded frequently. Unfortunately, the war—and the fact that Monsieur Niépce was an officer in Napoleon's army for a time—made that quite difficult." Aldridge smiled. "You know of Niépce, then? Am I correct in assuming that he is the inventor of your moving pictures?"

"I think you could say he contributed to the eventual development of movies," Kendra said slowly, and once again her head swam with the knowledge that the Duke was actually writing letters to the man who would create the world's first photograph. Not for a while, though—whatever he was experimenting with now, it would take at least another decade before he achieved success and shared it with the world.

Aldridge looked at her with the kind of bright curiosity that always made her feel a little twitchy. *Because I know he's going to push for information that I shouldn't tell anyone,* she thought.

"Monsieur Niépce is becoming discouraged over his lack of success," he said. "Can I not write anything that may give him hope?"

"Tell him that you have faith in him, and you are confident that one day he will have great success." Kendra thought of what she'd read about the Frenchman, and decided to keep to herself that the man would eventually die penniless.

She drew in a deep breath and got back on track. "That's not why I came in here, anyway. Look, I realized—"

She broke off, annoyed, when the door swung open. Harding came into the room, followed closely by Sam. "Mr. Kelly," the butler announced, then frowned at the Bow Street Runner as he departed, clearly displeased that Sam hadn't waited in the hall until he could be announced.

There was something in Sam's face that made the Duke eye him intently. "Mr. Kelly, is something amiss?"

"Aye—I mean, nay . . ." His golden eyes gleamed as his gaze washed over each one of them. "We found the necklace."

Alec raised his eyebrows. "The Weston family necklace?"

"Aye, I just got word. A pawnbroker has it. I thought you'd like ter go and see him."

"Miss Donovan?" The Duke glanced at her. "Did you have something to say?"

Kendra hesitated, then decided, "It can keep. Let's go talk to the pawnbroker."

52

Alger and Blackwood was located on Brick Lane in the East London area, within walking distance of Whitechapel, which would become notorious in another seventy-three years when Jack the Ripper began terrorizing the city. The shop itself was a narrow, medieval-looking brick structure, wedged between a haberdashery and an apothecary shop. A small wooden sign painted with three spheres suspended by a bar—the ancient symbol for a pawnbroker hung over a hunter-green door.

The interior of the shop was remarkably similar to its twenty-first century counterparts, Kendra thought, as she scanned the shelves, tables, and glass cabinets that displayed everything from gold pocket watches to silver candlesticks to dainty silk handkerchiefs. It wasn't just the look of the store that struck her as familiar; it was also the faintly melancholy aura. Kendra could almost smell the fear and desperation of those individuals who'd been forced to part with their beloved heirlooms.

Assuming, of course, that everything displayed had been procured honestly. By the way Sam studied a few of the items, Kendra suspected the Bow Street Runner might have a few doubts on that count.

But they hadn't come there to find stolen goods—or rather, they only were concerned with one stolen item: the Weston necklace.

A small, round man wearing a rather gaudy red-and-black-striped coat over a yellow embroidered waistcoat and black trousers was standing behind the counter. He had brushed his thinning gray hair forward, and grew whiskers on the side of his face. The whole affect gave him a rather jovial appearance, but Kendra noticed the shrewd, hard gleam in his eyes. She wasn't surprised. This was a tough profession. Anyone who profited from the broken dreams of others couldn't be taken in by a sob story.

There was a young man and woman perusing a case that held an assortment of snuffboxes. Otherwise, the shop was empty. The proprietor watched as they approached. He dismissed Sam, his eyes calculating the cost of the Duke's and Alec's clothes and zeroing in on them as Quality. As a woman, Kendra supposed, she didn't count.

"Gentlemen, what can I do for you?"

Sam brought out his baton and dropped it on the counter with a *thunk*. "You can show us the necklace that one of me men said you had here. And then you can answer some questions."

"Ah, you are the thief-taker."

"Bow Street Runner," corrected Sam coldly.

Kendra asked, "And you are Alger or Blackwood?"

The pawnbroker's eyes swiveled in her direction and gave her a quick up-and-down. Kendra thought that if there'd been a scale there, he'd have asked her to hop on, so thoroughly did he weigh and measure her with that glance.

"Blackwood," he replied. His eyes moved to Alec and the Duke. "And who are you, if I may be so bold?"

"I am the Duke of Aldridge and this is my nephew, the Marquis of Sutcliffe. And my ward, Miss Donovan."

That made the little man straighten up, as if he could puff himself up to the five-foot-four mark. "I can assure you, Your Grace, the necklace was acquired by honest means. The man who brought me the jewels was no thief."

Kendra said, "We need to see the necklace."

"Of course. If you will wait, I won't be but a moment."

He hurried into the backroom. The young couple left the shop with only one curious glance tossed in their direction, then Blackwood returned, carrying a velvet pouch. He unrolled the pouch on the counter, exposing a vintage-looking necklace. The milky pearls that made up the five strands appeared to glow against the velvet cloth. Pink diamonds twinkled on the strands, as well, one diamond for every four pearls.

"It matches the description." Kendra glanced at the Duke and Alec. "Did you ever see the Weston necklace?"

They both shook their heads. Alec said, "We should have brought Lady Atwood with us."

Aldridge's mouth curved in a wry smile. "My sister in a pawn-shop? I shudder to imagine it."

Blackwood bristled. "This is a respectable establishment."

"No insult meant, sir. Can you tell us about the man who brought this in? What did he look like?"

"He looked like you—by that, I mean he was obviously gentry. His cravat was excellently tied with the barrel knot." He touched his own cravat and eyed Alec's neck cloth enviously. "I'm partial to the waterfall knot myself, like yourself, my lord. However, I can never quite get the look. I suppose you have a manservant?"

"I have a valet. I believe he's partial to using a considerable amount of starch."

"Ah, yes."

Kendra leaned forward and tapped the glass with her finger to capture the pawnbroker's attention. "If you could describe the man who pawned the necklace?"

His eyes narrowed, his eyebrows lowering as he considered the matter. "Well, as I said, he was Quality. Cut a dashing figure. Not as tall as you." Again he looked at Alec. "And much older."

"Brown hair, turning gray?" Kendra prompted, then bit her lip. The proper procedure was to let a witness take their time in giving a description. Offering suggestions could influence their memories. Most people had no idea how easily their thoughts could be distorted. She'd once observed a witness who swore on his mother's grave that an unsub had held up a liquor store wearing a blue down vest jacket, only to have him falter and then change his story completely after hearing another witness, equally adamant, insist that the robber had been wearing a yellow wool peacoat.

"That's right," Blackwood said with a nod.

"What color were his eyes?"

"I don't recall."

"How old, exactly?"

Blackwood rubbed his lower lip with his index finger thoughtfully. "Like I said, older than His Lordship . . . late forties?"

Kendra straightened up and glanced at the Duke. She was a little shocked; this news was blowing her earlier theory to hell and back. She didn't like it, but she pushed aside her unease and stated the obvious: "Weston."

53

As they approached the front door of the Westons' Georgian townhouse, the calling card ritual having been abandoned for this trip, Kendra was reminded of the first time they'd called on the Earl. The sky had been gray then, too, the clouds swollen and hanging low over chimney stacks and roof peaks. Weston had invited them inside with a pleasant smile, assuming their call was a social one. By their second visit, he'd known better and hadn't even offered them a seat—an unusual rebuff given the Duke's presence. The steady decline in hospitality and the escalation of hostility was the price to be paid for anyone leading a murder investigation. She was used to it. But she snuck a sideways look at the Duke and Alec and wondered if any of this made them uncomfortable. She also wondered what kind of reception this third call would bring.

By the surprised-then-guarded look that immediately closed over the butler's face after their knock, they wouldn't be getting a warm welcome. Still, the servant made his way up the stairs to see whether the Earl was "at home" to his unexpected visitors. Kendra considered their course of action if Weston sent the butler back down with a negative response. Thankfully, when he returned, it was to escort them up the stairs to the study.

Weston eyed them as they filed into the room, his gaze lingering on Sam. Though Sam was law enforcement, it was one of the oddities in this era that the Runner would need more than his gold-tipped baton to make it across the threshold of a peer of the realm.

"Thank you for seeing us, my lord," Kendra said.

Weston turned his gaze to her. "My daughter is playing at a musical recital soon. I don't have much time for"—he lifted his arm and made an abstract gesture with his hand—"whatever this is."

"This shouldn't take long." She brought up her reticule and opened the strings, then brought out the velvet pouch within and rolled it open on the desk, much like the pawnbroker had on his counter. "As you can see, we retrieved the necklace that you brought to Alger and Blackwood."

Weston said nothing as he stared at the family heirloom, his face leaching all color.

"You did a pretty good job at cleaning the blood off of it."

The Earl flinched and jerked his eyes up to meet her gaze. "I don't . . . I didn't . . ."

"Don't lie," she snapped. The time for finesse had ended. "Mr. Blackwood described you. But if there's any doubts, we can make sure you two meet. Will he identify you, Lord Weston?"

Weston swallowed hard but said nothing.

Aldridge said quietly, "I believe it is time for you to explain yourself, sir."

"We know that Lady Dover wore this necklace on the night of her murder. Did you take it before you mutilated her face, or after?"

"No!" Weston crumbled, suddenly sinking into the chair behind his desk like his knees had gone out on him. Revulsion and horror crossed his face before he brought his hands up to hide his expression. "No, I didn't kill her!"

"This suggests otherwise," Alec said. A muscle ticked in his cheek. "You killed and mutilated her."

Weston shuddered, as though remembering the gruesome injury inflicted on the woman who'd been his mistress. Then he dropped his hands and looked up at them, his brown eyes dark with fear. "I swear to you, I didn't kill her—she was dead already. *Murdered.* Dear God . . . do you think I could have done *that* to her? What kind of monster do you think I am?" He swiveled his head to shoot the Duke a beseeching glance. "Sir, please, you must know that I could never do that!"

Kendra kept her gaze locked on Weston. "Tell me about that night," she said more softly, "and how you came to pawn your family's necklace."

He drew in a breath, then let it out in a raggedy huff. "I attended my daughter's ball, just as I told you. However . . . Cordelia had requested that I visit her that night as well."

"So you were the one she dressed up for," Kendra said quietly.

He hesitated, but gave a nod. "I believe so."

"You *son of a bitch.*" Alec made a move forward, but the Duke put a hand on his arm to restrain him. "You knew I was under suspicion, and yet you said nothing. The House of Lords is planning to convene on Monday to decide whether to have me arrested. You'd have let me hang."

"No." But Weston couldn't meet Alec's eyes. "I don't believe they would have charged you. There was no evidence but the housekeeper's suspicions. 'Tis unlikely they would have put much weight on the woman's word. Not against a Marquis—the heir of a Duke."

"Damn you! Even if they never charged me, it's a black mark against my character. There will always be whispers." Alec's green eyes blazed at the other man. "You're a fucking coward, Weston. Why shouldn't I believe that someone like you wouldn't have killed Cordelia? If she threatened to tell the world that you were the father of her child, you could have easily murdered her."

"I would never . . . I *loved* her!" Anguish twisted Weston's face. "I would never have harmed her. I was even—God help me—considering leaving my wife to be with her."

That seemed to stun everyone. Watching Weston closely, Kendra asked, "What about the affair she'd started with your son-in-law, Mr. Roberts?"

"Good God, I didn't know about that until you set the snuffbox on my desk." He glared at her and scrubbed his palms against his face. In the gray light streaming in from the windows, he looked old, exhaustion and fear carving new lines on his face. "She likely did it in retaliation. Cordelia was pressuring me to divorce my wife and marry her, but it is not an easy thing to walk away from your family."

"But you were ready to do that?"

He swallowed again, looking vaguely ill. "Yes . . . no! I don't know. I loved her."

"You attended Lady Frances's ball. And you slipped away . . ."

"There was a crush. I waited until after ten—"

"How much after?" Kendra asked.

"I don't know—not much after. I left through the back garden. It wasn't far. I knocked . . . I remember knocking. No one answered. Christ, I almost left then, you know. I wish that I had left then . . ."

He seemed to sink into a stupor, staring blindly in front of him.

"But you didn't," Kendra prompted. She walked over to the sideboard with the decanters and splashed a generous portion of whiskey into a glass. She brought it over to him, nudging his shoulder to get his attention.

He stirred, reaching for the glass and then tossing the entire contents back. He coughed lightly as the alcohol hit the back of his throat and wiped his mouth with the back of his hand. "No, I didn't," he continued hoarsely. "I tried the doorknob. I didn't think it would open, but it did. I went upstairs and saw the light in the drawing room. I went there . . ." He took another drink. "She was there, on the sofa. And her *face* . . . I could never do that. *Never.*"

"You didn't leave, though, did you?"

"I did. I was almost down the stairs when I thought about . . . about the necklace." The hand holding his glass shook, Kendra noticed. "I returned and retrieved it. The thing has been in my family for generations," he added, his tone taking on a defensive note.

"Why not leave it and claim it afterward?" wondered Kendra.

Weston lifted his shoulders. "It might not have been that easy. Lord Dover's cheeseparing ways are well-known. He could have fought me for it. It would be mortifying to be forced to petition the courts, another humiliation against my family." He shrugged. "I decided to make use of the opportunity. It seemed like the best course of action."

"So you took the necklace from around your dead mistress's neck. Sure, how can anyone fault you for that?"

"Damn you, I didn't know what else to do!" Weston glared at her. "Cordelia was already dead. It wasn't as though I could revive her. Yes, I took the necklace, but I bloody well didn't murder her. She was dead when I got there!"

Kendra thought about the door that had been open in the back of the townhouse. "Did you see anything or hear anybody?"

Weston set the empty glass on his desk and wearily rubbed his palms across his face. "No, I don't think so."

Sam spoke up. "Why'd you pawn your family's necklace, sir? After all that trouble, you were ready to let it go."

Weston hesitated, then gave a low, bitter laugh. "I had the necklace, but it occurred to me that it could not be seen again without implicating me in Cordelia's murder. Everyone in town knew Cordelia had it. My wife couldn't very well be seen in public with it around her neck, now could she? Not without questions."

"You could have locked it in a safe," Sam said with a puzzled frown.

"Never to be seen again? It's my family's necklace. My wife, my daughters have the *right* to wear it in public."

"You pawned it to put the necklace back into circulation," Alec guessed, staring at the other man with narrowed eyes. "You could then buy it back and tell everyone that the murderer had obviously pawned the necklace. Don't you think Blackwood would have recognized you when you came in for it?"

"I planned to send my son to purchase it, when the time was right."

"We'll need an official statement from you—in writing," Kendra said. She had no idea what the procedure was in this era, but she didn't think the extra precaution would hurt.

"Why? I told you, I didn't murder her!"

"The House of Lords will still convene on Monday. A written statement from you that explains you were the one that Lady Dover was to meet will confirm what Alec—Lord Sutcliffe—has been saying, that he had no plans to meet her that night."

Weston hesitated, clearly not liking the idea of putting into writing something that might incriminate him. But then he heaved a sigh and fished out some sheets of foolscap. It took him ten minutes of dipping quill in ink to scratch out his timeline on the night of Lady Dover's death. Then he sanded the paper, folded it, and handed it over to Kendra.

Meeting her gaze, his eyes burned with emotions: anger, guilt, remorse. "I swear to you, I did not kill her. I loved her."

Kendra said gently, "I believe you."

54

Once they were settled back into the carriage and barreling back toward the Duke's residence, Alec eyed Kendra curiously. "Do you really believe him?"

She thought about it, then said, "It's certainly plausible. It would explain why the murderer arrived at the front door but left by the back—Weston was already knocking at the front door."

Sam nodded. "I suppose we need ter put Mr. Roberts name back on the list of suspects, then. He was only taken off because he'd have no reason ter take the necklace."

But *why* had the murderer left the necklace? Kendra tried to imagine the evening: the rush of adrenaline and rage; the shocking violence; the madness, plain in the wielding of the stiletto to gouge Lady Dover's face. And afterward . . . what? Panic? Euphoria?

"I think we can still eliminate Roberts," she said slowly.

Sam regarded her curiously. "Why?"

"Because I have a new theory," she said, just as the carriage came to a stop outside the Duke's mansion. She hesitated, debating whether she should just tell them now or review her notes first. "I don't mean to sound mysterious, but it's something that only just occurred to me. If you don't mind, I'd like a little time to review my notes before I present it to you. Give me an hour."

Outside, the coachman had hopped off his seat and was coming around to unfold the steps and open the door. Aldridge smiled. "You sound like you are preparing to discuss a new scientific theory before the Royal Society."

"It's a little like that." *Especially when you know you'll encounter some resistance*, she added silently.

"Very well, Miss Donovan. One hour. I'm certain we can occupy our time until then."

They climbed down from the carriage.

Alec laid a detaining hand on Kendra's arm, sending a jolt of awareness through her, a reminder of the intimacy they'd shared the previous night. If he had similar thoughts, though, he kept them concealed.

"Do you really believe you know who murdered Cordelia?" he asked.

She hesitated. "Not exactly. I'm narrowing it down, though."

"Oh?"

"Now there are two."

❖

But which two?

At the moment, the killer was still just a misty figure. But that figure was emerging, if slowly, as she considered the two personalities. Again, she thought of the red-hazed rage that had compelled the murder to thrust the blade into Lady Dover forty-three times. In her mind, she envisioned the moment, the surprise on Lady Dover's face when the first blow was struck.

Then shock, falling back on the sofa, bringing up her arms to protect herself even as she felt her life slip away.

After sanity returned, the killer had hacked away at Lady Dover's face, destroying her beauty with brutally cold calculation. An impulse, yes, but also a message to be sent. A conversation was coming back to her . . .

A small knock interrupted her focus and Harding opened the door. He regarded her with his solemn, slightly disapproving face. "A . . . person is asking to see you, Miss."

"A person?"

"A *young* person. I believe he said his name was Snake."

Kendra felt a spurt of electricity zip down her spine. "Thank you. Show him up, please."

The butler cleared his throat. "Ah. As to that, he is requesting your presence in the park, Miss. He says that he's found what you want, and he wants his . . . *bread*." This was said with a curl to the lips.

"He means money."

"I'm aware of that, Miss. Lord Sutcliffe departed for a ride, but His Grace and Mr. Kelly are in the morning room. Shall I inform him of this young person's demand?"

"I can handle it." She pushed past the butler, but paused just outside the room. "Can you get some money for the kid? And some real bread, too? He looks like he could use both."

Harding frowned uncertainly. "Molly ought to accompany you."

But Kendra ignored him, racing to the stairs.

Outside, she saw Snake hovering near the entrance to the park. She darted across the wide street, seeing in her peripheral vision a sporty red phaeton being pulled around the corner by a pair of matching bays. Then she was on the other side of the street, her gaze locking on the small tow-headed child that Snake was grasping by the shoulder.

"Where's me bread like ye promised?" demanded Snake.

"You'll get it, don't worry." Kendra knelt down so she was eye level with the child. He was about seven. His face was pinched with hunger, his eyes wary and too old for his age.

"You're the one who delivered a note here last week?" she asked gently.

He knuckled the bridge of his snubbed nose. "Aye."

Kendra had to control the excitement beginning to rise inside her. "Okay. Good. Can you tell me who gave you the note? Describe the person?"

"Aye," he said, but his gaze slipped past her shoulder. His eyes widened.

Kendra's neck prickled and she twisted around just as the person came up behind her.

55

Y ou must stop her."

Rebecca gave Lady Louisa a sideways glance as they trotted across the Putney heath. It had been a mistake to agree to accompany the other woman for another ride, she now knew. But Lady Louisa had been agitated and Rebecca had thought a good gallop might be just the thing to calm her overwrought nerves. Unfortunately, it didn't seem to be working.

"I'm afraid I have very little control over Miss Donovan's actions," Rebecca said.

"She brought a Runner into our home! To question my father!"

"I'm terribly sorry that you are overset, but I'm certain Miss Donovan had good reason," she said carefully. "I have not spoken to her today, so I do not know about this latest development."

"It is insulting. A Bow Street Runner!" Lady Louisa whispered, obviously horrified. "Everyone in London will know about it."

Rebecca looked at Lady Louisa's face, tight with her anger, and sighed. "Miss Donovan does not mean any harm."

"But she does harm. She's destroying my family."

Rebecca twisted in her seat to see that Lady Louisa's groom had fallen some distance behind. "Shall we race again?" she suggested, turning back to Lady Louisa. There was no way her mare could beat Lady Louisa's stallion, but she wanted something to distract the woman from her melodrama about Kendra.

She thought Lady Louisa might object, so she spurred her horse, leaning low as Sophia flew over the heath toward the hedgerows. Out of the corner of her eye, she saw Lady Louisa whip past, sailing Caspian over the hedgerows as easily as she had the previous day.

Rebecca had thought to stop at the hedgerows, but now she pushed Sophia onward. Her heart pounded in her veins and the ground and hedges blurred for a moment as the horse leaped in a graceful arc, coming down on the other side with enough force to throw her hat over her eyes.

She pulled up on the reins in order to straighten her hat, and only then did she realize that Lady Louisa had continued on through the copse of trees. Rebecca lifted her reins to urge Sophia forward, to catch up with the other woman.

"You won," she said when she finally caught up.

Lady Louisa said nothing, and it became clear that the race hadn't been enough to distract her from her problems at home.

"Do you know why Miss Donovan and Mr. Kelly visited your father?" Rebecca asked finally. It seemed better to have the conversation out in the open than to continue to dance around it.

"Frances said that they'd found the necklace."

They'd come into the picturesque clearing. Lady Louisa pulled up on her reins, bringing her horse to a stop. She lifted her knee from around the pommel, and slid to the ground. She gathered up her riding habit's skirts over her arm and then walked the horse to the nearest tree, tying the reins.

"Lady Frances?" Rebecca dismounted.

Lady Louisa bit her lip, and tears glittered in her eyes. "She overheard them talking. She was furious. I'm almost afraid of what she will do."

❖

Kendra slowly pushed herself to her feet, angling herself in front of both boys when she faced the other woman. "Lady Frances."

She looked as beautiful as always, wearing a mauve carriage dress and a matching bonnet with feathers, rosettes, and ribbons. Yet her hazel eyes glittered dangerously and the hand holding her riding crop twitched, the crop snapping against her skirt violently.

"Miss Donovan." The woman's lips curved in a sharp, almost predatory smile. "I would like to speak with you. I've brought my phaeton. Shall we go for a ride?"

Kendra eyed the riding crop. "I don't think so."

Lady Frances dropped her smile. "Then I shall talk to you here. I do not care a fig if you are the Duke of Aldridge's ward, you have crossed a line. How dare you come to my family's home and accuse my father of murder. How dare you humiliate my family by bringing a common thief-taker into our home!"

"If you were humiliated by that, I can only imagine how you felt about Lady Dover."

"My God, you have nerve . . ." Rage contorted Lady Frances's features as she advanced. "I shall *destroy* you."

She raised the riding crop and brought it down with such force that Kendra had no doubt it would have flayed her flesh, leaving her face permanently scarred, if she hadn't dived to the side. After this initial attack, Kendra didn't hesitate. She darted forward and brought her elbow up, smashing it with a satisfying crack into Lady Frances's nose.

The other woman screamed and dropped the riding crop, bringing her gloved hands up to her nose, now gushing blood.

"Gor! Ye done drawn 'er cork!" Snake exclaimed and shot Kendra an admiring look.

Kendra pivoted back to the towheaded boy. "Was she the one who gave you the note?"

"Watch out!" Snake yelled.

Kendra twisted around again just as Lady Frances, blood smearing her face and dripping from her chin, came at her.

�֍

"What do you think your sister would do?" Rebecca asked.

"I don't know," Lady Louisa said quietly, and looked at Rebecca. "Do you see why it's imperative that you stop Miss Donovan from her inquiries?"

"I am not Miss Donovan's keeper. I cannot stop her, even if I wanted to. And I don't want to. Lady Dover deserves justice."

Lady Louisa's face twisted in pain. "How can you say such a thing? She was a trollop—a whore! She seduced my father and turned my mother into a laughingstock in the Ton."

Rebecca reacted to the despair she saw in the other woman's face, reaching out to touch her arm. "I'm so very sorry. But if this is why you invited me to ride, so I could be your conduit to Miss Donovan . . . I cannot help you."

"You *will not* help me. And for what? For a woman like Lady Dover?" She gave a hollow, bitter laugh.

"You are overwrought."

Lady Louisa jerked her arm away from Rebecca's touch, wiping at the tears that spilled down her cheeks. "I have every right to be. Lady Dover was a whore intent on destroying my family— wearing the necklace, my *mother's* jewels! And using her bastard child to convince my father to leave us. She was *evil*."

Rebecca stood very still, watching the other woman's features contort with her rage. "Lady Dover told you that she was pregnant?"

It wasn't exactly a fair fight, Kendra knew. But she wasn't feeling in the mood to make things fair. When Lady Frances came at her again, she met the attack with one of her own, grabbing Lady Frances's wrist and twisting her arm around in a quick maneuver that had the other woman on her knees in seconds, shrieking.

"Bleeding 'ell!" Snake declared, astonished.

Kendra looked at the fair-haired child who had delivered the note and realized that she didn't even know his name. "What's your name, kid?"

His eyes were as round as saucers as they darted between her and Lady Frances. "Luke."

"Okay, Luke. Was this the woman who gave you the note for me?"

Luke studied Lady Frances's face, now caked with blood beneath a swollen nose. "Nay, she ain't the one. This 'ere one's pretty—or she was before ye punched 'er. The gentry mort that gave me the note weren't 'alf as pretty. Face as plain as puddin', it was."

Kendra sucked in a harsh breath. *Lady Louisa.* She turned to Lady Frances and demanded, "Where's your sister?"

"Let me go!"

Kendra released the woman's arm. "Where is Lady Louisa? At home? Or at that musical recital?"

Lady Frances glared at her as she got to her feet. "Why should I tell you?" Her voice sounded nasal. Kendra made a move toward her and Lady Frances squealed, hastily backing up a step. "She could hardly go to a sodding musical recital! Not after your visit. She was distraught and invited Lady Rebecca out for a ride."

There was no reason to assume anything bad was going to happen, Kendra knew. But she still felt an icy frisson run down her spine. "Where'd they go?"

"Putney." Frances attempted to wipe the blood away with her glove. "Look at what you've done! You are a lunatic."

"Miss Donovan?" The Duke, joined by Alec and Sam, appeared at the entry to the park. "Harding said you—" Aldridge caught sight of Lady Frances, and gaped. "Good God, Lady Frances! What happened?"

Snake was nearly dancing with his excitement. "This 'ere mort planted the other one a facer!"

Kendra ignored them all and grabbed Lady Frances's arm. "Where did they go in Putney?"

Lady Frances stared at her in outrage. "Unhand me! I shall call the constable on you for striking me!"

"I'll do more than fucking strike you—"

"Miss Donovan!" The Duke was aghast.

Kendra looked at him. "Lady Louisa murdered Lady Dover."

Lady Frances gasped. "You're mad!"

"No." Kendra was trying to keep calm, but her sense of disquiet was growing. She leveled her gaze at Sam. "The hair comb you found under the sofa; you assumed it had fallen off in the struggle. You were right—but it didn't fall out of Lady Dover's hair."

The Bow Street Runner stared at her.

"The comb was decorated with rubies and moonstones," she continued. "Lady Dover was dressed in a light blue gown. She would never have worn rubies in her hair with that gown."

The Bow Street Runner still looked uncertain, as if he couldn't believe the answer to a murder investigation could hinge on something so frivolous as a hair ornament.

Kendra almost couldn't believe it either. "Damn it. I should have realized it as soon as I saw the comb. Madame Gaudet said Lady Dover was a woman of discerning tastes . . ." She turned back to Lady Frances and squeezed her arm. "Does your sister own a Spanish comb with rubies?" When she said nothing, Kendra ordered, "Answer me!"

"Yes! Yes—but this is absurd . . . Your Grace . . ." Lady Frances's gaze swung to Aldridge. "Your ward has gone insane. Look at what she did to me!"

Kendra let her go and fixed the Duke with her own look. "We need to find them. Now."

Aldridge turned to Lady Frances. "Do you have any information that would narrow down our search?"

"I . . . our family would picnic by the River Thames. It used to be the Fairchild estate."

"I know the site," Aldridge said. "I shall have my phaeton brought around."

"My horse is ready," Alec said, and began jogging toward the street.

Kendra caught up with him as he crossed, heading for the mews. "I'm going with you."

He glanced quickly at her. "I shall be riding horseback."

"I know."

56

I think we ought to return home," Rebecca said, feeling oddly breathless as she took a step toward where Sophia was grazing.

"She told me about the baby," Lady Louisa said, in such a quietly savage way that the hair on the back of Rebecca's neck rose.

Rebecca turned to face the other woman again. A memory floated up, both unexpected and amazingly clear. She recalled how her parents had brought her to London as a child and they'd toured the Exeter 'Change on the Strand. A leopard, its coat shiny and black as pitch, had prowled back and forth inside a cage, its tail swishing, its strange yellow eyes restless. Then, the creature's gaze had suddenly fixed on her and it had dropped into a crouch. The bars that separated them mattered naught. In that one terrifying instance, she'd known the difference between predator and prey. Her mother had broken the spell, grasping her hand and tugging her away from the leopard's cage. She'd never felt that way again.

Until now.

Rebecca's throat felt so tight it was difficult to get the words out. "That must have been difficult for you to hear," she said softly.

"She was a vile, despicable creature. A Haymarket ware."

"She didn't deserve to be murdered."

"Yes, she did."

In a move that took Rebecca by surprise, Lady Louisa darted forward. With a cry, Rebecca picked up her riding habit's heavy skirts and ran toward the woods. Only then did she realize that she hadn't been Lady Louisa's intended target. The other woman was launching herself at Sophia, slapping the mare's flank that sent her bolting toward the trees and field beyond.

❖

Kendra supposed that it was somewhat unusual for people to see a gentleman on a horse galloping through the streets of London with a woman riding astride behind him. But she didn't give a damn about the shocked faces that she saw as they rode past, her skirts hiked up to her knees, her arms clamped around Alec's waist.

Alec must have been thinking along similar lines. "You may have to marry me now. Your reputation is unlikely to survive this," he said, his voice flying back to her.

"I don't give a rat's ass about my reputation. Can you make this horse go any faster?"

"I don't want to tire Chance out too quickly. Even if Lady Louisa killed Cordelia, there is no reason to believe Becca is in danger. They've ridden before without consequence."

He was right. Except Kendra couldn't shake the terrible fear that was curdling her stomach. A month ago she hadn't antici-pated the danger . . .

"I'm not going to lose another friend," she whispered, and pressed her face into Alec's back. "Ride faster. *Please.*"

❊

The woods were densely packed with black alder, ash, oak, and hawthorn trees and bramble and blackberry bushes, leaving long, murky shadows crisscrossing the green oasis. The scent of earth and vegetation was heavy in the air. Fear tore Rebecca's breath from her lungs so that it came out in ragged pants as she darted around the trees and over twisted roots, moss-covered rocks, and creeping ivy.

"Lady Rebecca!"

Rebecca cast a wild glance behind her, but just as the forest shielded her from Lady Louisa's sight, it hid the madwoman from hers. She wanted to continue to run. Everything inside her propelled her into flight, the primordial instincts of a hunted animal. It took all her willpower to pause in her headlong rush and scan the woods with its tangle of bushes and twisting trees.

"I didn't mean to kill her, I swear to you!"

She still couldn't see Lady Louisa, but she sounded closer. Panic nearly made her bolt again, but then she saw it—the low-hanging branches of a hawthorn tree surrounded by a sprawling rosebush.

"It was an accident!"

Rebecca ran to the bush, dropping to her knees. The shrubbery was thick, the branches and thorns snagging at her clothes and hair, raking like hot needles against her unprotected face as she burrowed her way through. She could feel warm blood ooze from the scrapes, but she kept crawling until the rough bark of the hawthorn was at her back. Out of the corner of her eye, she saw a flash of brown fur as she displaced a creature—a mouse, rabbit, or rat, she wasn't sure—from its habitat.

"I went to see her that night to beg her to leave my family alone." Lady Louisa's voice was closer now, echoing in the unnaturally silent forest. It was as though all the woodland animals recognized something evil had invaded their domain and had hidden as well. The only sound was the leaves and brush blowing in the breeze and the tumble of water as the Thames's current rushed nearby.

Rebecca curled up as much as possible and raised a gloved hand to press against her mouth to stop herself from making any noise. From her position, she could see through the leafy mesh to the woods. Her heart jumped when she caught a glimpse of scarlet, as Lady Louisa threaded through the trees, searching for her. Rebecca was grateful that her own riding habit was a dark green, which helped camouflage her from the other woman's scanning eyes.

"I knew she was to meet my father that night. I found her note in his study. She only need call him and he went running! Even after she humiliated our family." Rage had seeped into Lady Louisa's voice. "She was a siren tempting a man to his doom."

With startling suddenness, Lady Louisa emerged from the trees. Rebecca dug her fingers into her jaw as her gaze dropped to the thick, heavy stick that the other woman was now carrying like a cudgel.

"She was surprised to see me," continued Lady Louisa. "But she invited me inside. I can see her, you know, if I close my eyes. So confident. So beautiful. So amused. With my family's jewels around her throat!"

Lady Louisa paused, cocking her head to the side as though listening. Rebecca held her breath, an unreasonable fear taking hold that the other woman might be able to hear the air passing through her lips.

"She poured herself a glass of whiskey," Lady Louisa continued, "as if I were there for a social visit." She gave a sharp peal of laughter and Rebecca flinched. The sound held a dark undertone of madness. "Can you imagine? I was pleading for my family's very existence!"

Lady Louisa began to move again, close enough that Rebecca could hear the snapping of twigs under her feet and the quiet slither of her riding habit's long train over grass. Rebecca began to shake, the cloying sweet scent of the rose blossoms making her ill.

"That's when she told me about her unborn bastard, a child that she would use to entrap my father. And she laughed at my horror. She laughed when I mentioned my association with Lord Ludlow. She said that I should resolve to becoming a spinster, that my—my looks could not overcome my lack of dowry. She was wicked, *evil* to taunt me so."

Lady Louisa was coming closer, her gaze seeming to strip away the leafy green vegetation around her. She was using the stick now to poke into shrubbery, like she was trying to flush out a hare.

"You understand what it's like, don't you, Lady Rebecca? You and I are alike on that score. Always watching men become entranced by a pretty face . . . to make fools out of themselves."

Rebecca pressed her hand tighter against her mouth. Through the leaves and rose blossoms, she saw the other woman slowly swivel in her direction.

And move closer.

57

Terror rose up inside Rebecca, her eyes fixed on the other woman as she approached the rosebush. Lady Louisa was looking directly at her, as if she could see her through the leaves and roses. Rebecca jerked her gaze away and belatedly dropped it to the grass, looking for anything she could use as a weapon. *Hell and damnation—nothing.*

Lady Louisa was still speaking. "I would have taken the necklace, but someone knocked at the door. I had to leave through the back entrance. I didn't realize until today that my father was the one who interrupted—" She broke off.

Rebecca lifted her gaze to see that Lady Louisa had stopped her advancement and was now spinning around to stare off to the left. Then Rebecca heard it, too, a shuffling movement in the undergrowth. Lady Louisa's mouth twisted into a sharp smile and she moved toward the noise, obviously mistaking a woodland creature for a panicked woman.

Rebecca kept her gloved hand clamped over her mouth as Lady Louisa disappeared into the trees. The other woman had begun speaking again, but Rebecca didn't pay any attention, too busy thinking about her next move. She couldn't stay here. As soon as Lady Louisa realized that she'd been hunting a rabbit or fox, she'd be back, her large stick attacking the bushes, and she'd find Rebecca's hiding place. She thought of Lady Louisa's horse, his reins tied to a tree near the embankment. If she could get to the animal, she'd be able to ride out for help.

It wasn't a bad strategy, Rebecca decided. But still she waited, counting the seconds while her eyes and ears strained to pick up any sounds or movement. As the seconds turned into minutes, Rebecca's nerves stretched taut. Finally, she could bear it no more and she crawled out of her self-made tunnel, the thorns from the surrounding rosebush once again raking across her tender flesh.

Rebecca emerged from the green tunnel and, gathering her skirts, raced through the dense woods. She came out near the ruins. About fifty feet away, Caspian was grazing. Rebecca paused, again listening, but couldn't hear above the Thames's rushing current on her right. She moved forward cautiously. The horse jerked its head up and made a nervous prancing motion to the side, his eyes wary at her approach.

"I'm not going to hurt you," she murmured. She had taken a few steps when she realized that the horse wasn't looking at her.

Rebecca pivoted just as Lady Louisa rushed forward, the stick held high. Rebecca stumbled back with a cry. At the last minute, she regained her footing, then spun and fled up the embankment.

❖

Kendra didn't know how long they'd ridden, but it seemed like forever, the stallion's hooves churning up the ground as they sped across the countryside. Throughout the ride, she kept her arms wrapped tightly around Alec's waist, terrified she'd fall off the beast and break her neck. She lifted her head to look around when Alec suddenly pulled up the reins on the horse, slowing down.

"What is it?" she asked, but she had already spotted the old man studying the fetlock of a pretty mare. Another dappled gray horse stood by his side, tail swishing against the flies.

Alec said, "That's Becca's horse."

He urged his horse over to the man, who dropped the fetlock to watch their approach.

"Where did you get that mare?" Alec demanded.

The old man pushed his cap up and scratched his head. "It came bolting out of woods," he said, pointing to the copse ahead. "She belongs to Lady Louisa's friend. Must've got away from them. Stumbled a bit, the poor dear. Ain't nothing that I can't fix up, just a little ligament—she'll be as right as rain soon enough."

Kendra asked, "Who are you?"

"Lady Louisa's groom. Liam's the name."

"Why aren't you with your mistress?"

Liam didn't seem to see anything odd in Alec's harsh question. "She likes to race her horse. Poor old Beth there can't keep up. We usually—" He paused, but then stared wide-eyed toward the road in the distance. "Is that a phaeton? Bleeding hell, is the driver actually getting *off* the road? He's gonna break his wheels!"

Kendra and Alec turned. It was too far away to see the occupants, but she suspected that the driver of that particular phaeton was the Duke, and his passenger Sam.

"Never mind them," said Kendra. "Where's Lady Louisa?"

"Same place this here mare came from." Again he lifted a finger to point to the trees. "In there."

※

Rebecca had miscalculated—badly. The stones of the embankment were more slippery than usual with the previous night's rain, slowing her down, and the woods now seemed too far away. On the right side of her was the Thames, the recent rain having raised its level, and on the left side—coming fast—was Lady Louisa.

"I'm sorry, I'm sorry, I'm sorry," the young woman was chanting, but her eyes, fixed on Rebecca, appeared almost feral.

Lady Louisa brandished the stick now like it was a sword, forcing Rebecca to step backward, further up the embankment, trying desperately to keep her balance. "Please, you don't have to do this." Rebecca was surprised the words even came out; her throat appeared to have closed into a tight knot. "Lady Louisa, I'm your friend."

Something flickered in the madwoman's eyes, a small bit of humanity. But then it was swallowed up by an unholy determination. "I need to protect my family," she said, and continued to advance.

Rebecca realized she'd committed another fatal error by going up the stones rather than trying to sidle toward the woods. She saw the flurry of crimson rushing toward her, the stick raised and then swinging down in a brutal arc. Rebecca tried to evade, but the stinging blow caught her on her arm. Lady Louisa brought the club up again, her face twisted in a murderous rage. Rebecca danced backward, but her feet got caught in the long train of her riding habit. With one arm hanging uselessly, she couldn't balance herself, and she screamed as she toppled backward and plunged into the icy, torrential waters of the Thames.

58

Rebecca felt the shock of the freezing black waters as the river engulfed her, invading her nose and mouth. She ignored the pain in her arm as she fought her way to the surface, desperate, her lungs burning. She broke through with a spluttering gasp. Unlike ladies of her acquaintance, Rebecca knew how to swim. But these was not the genteel laps she'd completed in the placid waters of the lake on her family's estate, when the sun was a burning in the sky. This was a life-and-death battle. The river was brutally cold, delving into the very marrow of her bones and sapping her strength. The current was strong, greedy, and grasping, spinning her around and pulling at her. The material of her skirts were like an anchor, weighing her down.

Her arm screamed in agony as she attempted to swim toward shore. She was caught again and dragged under by invisible chains. Just before she went under, she caught a glimpse of scarlet on the embankment and knew that Lady Louisa was watching her. Then the Thames closed over her.

She tried to kick to the surface, but her skirt had wrapped around her legs like a rope. In a burst of energy, she clawed her way back to the surface, her head breaking the surface. Lady Louisa had vanished. This was the time to swim toward shore—except her strength had been completely depleted. A strange sort of numbness crept over her and she sank for the third time.

❖

The scream brought Alec's, Kendra's, and the groom's eyes to the forest. The horses ears twitched.

"My God . . . *Becca*," Alec breathed. He yanked the reins to the side, which sent his horse wheeling around. Kendra clutched at his waist as they galloped toward the woods.

They were nearing the outside of the tree line when Lady Louisa exploded from the tangle of vegetation on the back of an enormous black stallion.

"Don't!" Kendra said sharply, when Alec pulled up on his reins, prepared to go after the fleeing woman. "Leave her. We need to find Rebecca."

Alec gave a quick nod to let her know that he'd heard, then sent his Arabian into the forest. There, they were forced to travel more carefully over the tangled roots and loose rocks, so as not to cripple the horse. The gray light of day was cut off here, leaving only dense shadows. The thick, almost syrupy scent of flora and fauna rose up around them.

Impatience thrummed in Kendra. She opened her mouth to suggest that it would be faster if she got off and ran the rest of the way on foot, when the trees suddenly thinned and they entered a large clearing. Here there was a stone embankment and the ruins of a castle, a place that would have been quaint on any other day.

As soon as Alec brought the horse to a stop, Kendra slid off the animal and cupped her hands around her mouth to amplify her voice. "Rebecca!"

A terrible foreboding, worse than before, struck her. She darted forward, calling Rebecca's name, only to be met with the woodsy sound of chirping birds and rustling grass and trees, and the muted roar of the River Thames as it twisted through the landscape.

"Becca!" Alec joined in with the calls. He dismounted and led the horse to a tree with a low-hanging branch near the embankment and tied him up. His gaze met Kendra's as she stalked the area. The fear she saw in his eyes echoed her own.

"She's got to be here," she said.

"Lady Louisa wouldn't have left Becca . . ."

Alive.

He didn't say it, but she knew that's what he meant. Alec pivoted, his long legs moving up the embankment as he called Rebecca's name.

"Becca! Becca! Bec— My God!"

"What is it?"

Kendra hurried toward him as he wrenched off his shoes and jacket. He had already dove into the water by the time she reached the spot where he'd been standing. She followed the trajectory of his swim, sweeping farther down the river until she spotted a hat riding the choppy waves of the Thames—*Rebecca's hat.* Her gaze continued to move, and in the blackish waters she thought she saw movement below.

Kendra realized she was holding her breath as Alec's strong arms slashed the water, swimming in fast strides toward the figure caught in its current, being swept inexorably downstream. She had been so transfixed by the scene in front of her that it took her a moment to realize that her name was being called from somewhere behind. She spun around to see the Duke, Sam, and, oddly, Snake, emerge from the forest.

She didn't bother to acknowledge them, but turned back to continue her vigil. Alec had finally caught up with his target and managed to flip Rebecca on her back, her face a pale cameo in the distance. He curved his arm around her head and towed her toward the nearest shore.

Kendra ran along the embankment, then hopped off the stones and sped through the tall grass and cattails along the shoreline. She reached the spot at the same time Alec came dripping out of the Thames, carrying Rebecca in his arms.

"Put her down. *Hurry!*"

Alec gently laid Rebecca on a carpet of grass. He brushed the dark auburn tresses out of her face, then he lifted his gaze to Kendra, the horror and pain in their depths so intense that for a moment, Kendra could have sworn that she was looking into the pits of hell.

His throat worked for a moment before the words came. "It's too late . . . Becca's dead."

59

N*o!*" The word ripped through Kendra like a gunshot blast. She dropped down beside Alec, shoving him away. Rebecca's lips had already turned blue, her face pinched. Kendra worked quickly, straightening Rebecca's body, checking for signs of life. Then she grabbed her chin with one hand, her forehead with the other, and tilted Rebecca's head back to open her airways.

"What's happening?" the Duke demanded, his voice rising. *"Rebecca . . ."*

Alec said in a husky whisper, his breath hitching, "She's gone . . . she's gone . . . "

"What's the mort doin'?" asked Snake.

Kendra leaned over, pressing her mouth to Rebecca's to administer two rescue breaths. She turned her head, feeling for a breath on her cheek, and gave two more breaths. She pulled back, locking her hands together and placing them over Rebecca's sternum to begin compressions. She pressed down no more than two inches, for fear of pushing Rebecca's organs into her spine.

One, two, three . . .

"What are you *doing*? Miss Donovan, stop it! Stop it, I say!" Panic made the Duke's voice unrecognizable.

. . . four, five, six . . .

Alec said helplessly, "I don't know . . . Kendra . . ."

She ignored them, concentrating on pumping up and down. She knew the chances of saving a drowning victim in this manner were slim—thirty percent. If this was the twenty-first century, she'd be able to administer an electric shock with an AED, which would bring Rebecca's chances of survival up to ninety percent.

. . . seven, eight, nine . . .

"You're hurting her! I order you to *stop*!" The Duke reached out to catch her by the shoulder. His reaction wasn't abnormal, she knew; panic turned people senseless. But she couldn't afford to deal with it. Without breaking her rhythm, she shot a furious glance at Alec.

"Keep him away from me! I know what I'm doing!"

. . . ten, eleven, twelve . . .

"Gor, she's beaten 'er!" Snake piped up.

"Miss Donovan . . ." Sam stepped forward, maybe to pull her away.

Suddenly, Rebecca jerked and issued a wet cough. Kendra quickly rolled her on her side, so she could vomit up the dark water of the Thames.

She heard the Duke's hoarse cries behind her, and was surprised to realize that there were tears in her own eyes. She blinked quickly and said, "We need to get her warm or she'll probably go into shock."

The Duke and Sam stripped off their coats and wrapped them around Rebecca, who continued to hack up river water until it turned into dry heaves.

"We had to leave the phaeton on the outside of the forest. There wasn't a path wide enough for it," Aldridge said. He raised a visibly shaking hand to wipe across his mouth. His eyes met Kendra's. "You . . . what you did . . . *thank you.*"

"She killed her . . ."

They looked down at Rebecca. Her eyes were open. Her face was still pinched and so white it looked bloodless, except for a web of painful-looking lacerations. But it no longer had that terrifying blue cast. Her teeth were chattering as she struggled with the words. "Lady Louisa . . ."

"We know," Kendra said, and looked at the Duke. "We need to get her home, into a hot bath, get some brandy in her . . ."

Snake withdrew from his grubby coat the small silver flask that she remembered from when she and Alec had been kidnapped. "It ain't brandy, but if'n ye wanna give it ter 'er."

Kendra frowned at the kid, but took the flask. "You know this could stunt your growth."

She uncorked the flask and nearly handed it back when her eyes watered from the scent of strong whiskey. But one look at Rebecca's shivering form changed her mind. Squatting down again, she tipped the flask to Rebecca's lips.

"Just a little," she cautioned, and pulled it away as soon as Rebecca began coughing. Still, she was satisfied to see the color that bloomed in the other woman's cheeks, chasing away the death pallor.

"Dear heaven, that's ghastly," choked Rebecca.

Snake scowled, snatching the flask away from Kendra. "Ain't neither. Oi knows a bloke 'oo knows the man 'oo makes it fer a flash 'ouse. The Blind Duck 'as the best whiskey in London Town."

60

When they emerged from the forest, they found Lady Louisa's groom, Liam, standing near the Duke's phaeton, holding the reins of both his horse and Lady Rebecca's mare, looking bewildered by the behavior of his betters.

Rebecca was obviously in no condition to ride her horse, so Alec carried her to the phaeton. It was only supposed to seat two people, but Snake was small enough to slide in between Rebecca and the Duke. Because of the mare's injury, they tied her to the back of the phaeton. Sam rode double with the groom, while Kendra hoisted herself up behind Alec again.

There was no way their little procession would make it to London in this fashion. Not only was it impractical, but night was falling rapidly, which would make traveling the short stretch of highway difficult and dangerous. Aldridge made the decision that they would ride into the village and stay at a traveling inn, while Liam rode back to London with instructions for Aldridge's staff to send his traveling carriage.

Kendra had to sigh. Why could nothing be simple in this era?

Their entrance into the village caught the attention of a shop-keeper locking up and the lamplighters—a man and a boy, the latter carrying a ladder to light the lanterns set on poles. *We probably look like a suspicious crew*, Kendra thought. Then it occurred to her that she was the one who probably earned the most looks, riding astride with her skirts rucked up to reveal a scandalous length of leg.

The Duke guided them to the Black Lion Inn, a sprawling Tudor that was built in the shape of an L that rose two stories. The stable was located on the other side of its cobblestone courtyard, and as soon as they arrived, several stable boys ran out to capture bridles and reins. Aldridge issued instructions, while Alec helped Kendra down, and then returned to carry Rebecca.

"I can walk," she grumbled, still wrapped in the Duke's and Sam's coats.

"After a swallow of that whiskey, I'm not so sure," Alec joked. He carried her into the inn and demanded a room with a hot bath. Once upstairs, Kendra helped Rebecca undress and scanned her friend for injuries—scratches on her face and an ugly bruise on her arm, which Rebecca held gingerly against her.

"You can move it, so I don't think it's broken," said Kendra, as she helped Rebecca into the copper hip bath. "But I'm not a doctor. We should send for one to look you over."

Rebecca eased into the water with a hissing sigh. "Don't be absurd. I'm fine. Just sore." She lifted a hand to her chest, which also sported a large black-and-blue mark from the chest compressions. "You saved me, Miss Donovan. I don't know how, exactly, but you saved my life."

Kendra was grateful for the knock at the door. She crossed the room and opened it a crack. The innkeeper's wife stood there, holding out a bundle of clothes. "They're a trifle big, but His

Grace gave me good coin for a frock for Her Ladyship, so she won't have to wear those wet things."

"Thank you," Kendra said, taking the bundle and then closing the door.

From the tub, Rebecca said softly, "I believe she is quite mad."

Kendra turned to face her. She knew to whom Rebecca was referring. "Maybe," she said, and shrugged. "Maybe not."

"She said it was an accident. She said that she went there to plead with Lady Dover to let her father go."

"Do you believe her?"

Rebecca was silent for a long moment. "She brought the stiletto," she said finally. "That wasn't an accident. But I don't understand why she did that to Lady Dover's face."

"I think she told us." Kendra went to stand before the coal fire, stretching out her hands toward the warmth. "Remember, she said, 'Why can't men see women like that for what they are?' And when you said that men are led too easily astray, she said she wished that men could see what was beneath their beauty."

"She cut Lady Dover's face to show us what was beneath her beauty?" Rebecca shook her head. "'Tis lunacy—which proves my point."

"Anger, resentment, passion, hatred, jealousy—they're all a form of lunacy, aren't they?"

Rebecca shuddered. "She turned into a different creature, right before my eyes. I was terrified. And yet, for a moment, I felt sorry for her. Lady Dover treated her terribly."

"Lady Dover treated a lot of people terribly. None of them tried to murder her."

"She said she did it for her family. She was afraid Lady Dover would entice her father into divorcing her mother."

"Lady Dover didn't deserve what was done to her, regardless of the provocation. And Miss Cooper certainly didn't deserve to be stabbed and pushed into oncoming traffic."

"Why did she do that to your maid? I know that she thought Miss Cooper was you, but *why* did she do it?"

"It's one of the questions that I'm going to ask her." Kendra turned around to look at Rebecca. "I suspect she thought I knew more than I did and panicked."

Rebecca nodded and agreed, "She panicked after she mentioned the baby, and I quizzed her about it. She could have told any number of lies, but . . . that's when she changed." She pressed her lips together in a tight, remorseful line. "Your maid . . . 'tis my fault. I nattered on about how bloody brilliant you are about solving murders. I think she must have panicked then as well."

Kendra said nothing—but it made sense, she supposed. She tilted her head and regarded Rebecca. "It sounds like you had quite a conversation with her."

"I was hiding . . ." She lifted her hand to the scratches on her face. "These came from one particularly vicious rosebush. She kept talking, trying to lure me out. I waited. I thought if I could get to her horse . . . unfortunately, she got to me first."

Rebecca's gaze fell on the cloth she was twisting in her hands. Then she glanced up. "How did you come here? You seemed to know that Lady Louisa was the monster even before I told you."

Kendra shrugged. "Would you put your hair up with a ruby comb if you were wearing a light blue evening gown?"

Rebecca frowned at the non sequitur, but answered anyway. "Of course not. My maid would have the vapors if I tried such a thing."

"Exactly. A woman like Lady Dover, renowned for her style, would never have done it, either. And yet a comb with rubies was found under the sofa. It had come off during the struggle." It was always details like these that could break an investigation wide-open.

"Mr. Kelly believed Lady Dover was meeting her lover, so he never considered a woman as the killer," she added. "He assumed the comb had been Lady Dover's. He never thought about it not matching the dress."

"Men rarely think of such things."

"Then it was stolen . . ." Kendra sighed. "I should have realized the significance when I saw it. There was something off, but I didn't connect the dots. If I would have figured it out earlier, none of this would have ever happened."

"You take on too much, Miss Donovan. Such self-recrimination is pointless, and misplaced."

Was it? Kendra wasn't so sure. It was difficult not to feel like she'd failed. And her failure had nearly gotten Rebecca killed.

"The rubies on the comb only proved that it was not Lady Dover's, though," Rebecca pointed out. "It didn't prove that it was Lady Louisa's."

"I've had Snake hunting for the kid who delivered the note to bring me to the Crown Tavern. He found him today."

"Snake—the boy who gave me his whiskey? His timing is most fortuitous. He identified Lady Louisa?"

"Yes—or rather, the pudding-faced mort."

Instead of smiling, Rebecca pursed her lips. "We're always reduced to our appearance, are we not?" She pulled herself out of the tub and reached for a towel. She caught Kendra's eye. "You saved my life, Miss Donovan; I am in your debt. I don't think there's anything I can do to repay it, but if you should need anything, you need only ask."

"There might be one thing . . ."

"Yes?"

Kendra smiled. "Maybe you can start calling me Kendra."

❄

They joined the men and Snake in a cozy room with low, beamed ceilings, darkly paneled walls, and an enormous brick fireplace with logs ablaze. Candles were lit around the room and the table was already set with platters of boiled potatoes and cabbage, thick brown bread, and a rib roast cooked on the bone. Kendra knew she was hungry when even the boiled cabbage made her mouth water. The too-large slippers that Rebecca wore slapped against the wooden floor as she hurried to sit down at the table.

The Duke eyed Rebecca carefully. "How are you doing, my dear?"

"I'm alive—thanks to . . . Kendra."

Kendra had to suppress a smile. This was such a funny era, with its penchant for formal address. Rebecca had agreed to call her by her first name in private and among close intimates—but not in public, because that would have been a sign of disrespect.

Aldridge glanced at Kendra. "I apologize for my behavior, Miss Donovan. I . . . I'm ashamed to say that I did not understand what you were doing, and I reacted badly."

She met his eyes. The Duke had lost a wife and child to drowning. Of course the experience had been traumatic for him. "Don't worry. People panic. It's been known to happen, even in . . . America."

Alec lifted the stopper on a bottle of sherry. "Would you ladies care for refreshments? We have sherry. Or I am told the innkeeper's wife makes an excellent plum wine."

Snake picked up a glass. "Oi'll 'ave a dram, gov'ner."

Kendra frowned. "You'll have milk."

The kid stared at her in horror. "Gor, Oi'm not a baby."

"Nevertheless."

A maid came in carrying a long-pronged fork and a carving knife, and began to work on the roast as they sat down at the table. Kendra caught the maid casting glances at the occupants at the table as she served, probably wondering how a Duke ended up sharing a meal with a Bow Street Runner and a young criminal.

"How long before your carriage arrives, Your Grace?" Kendra asked. She picked up her knife and fork to slice the cabbage into bite-sized sections.

Aldridge took a moment to peer at his pocket watch. "I expect them to be here in half an hour."

"Lady Louisa—" she began.

"I sent a note ter Bow Street." Sam looked across the table at her. "The magistrate will have a couple of constables go over to meet with Lord and Lady Weston."

"Will Lady Louisa be taken into custody?" In her era, the suspect would be brought in for questioning, and would then be formally charged. She had no idea how it worked here.

Sam frowned. "She'll likely stay in the house. I've ordered constables and the Watch ter stand guard, ter make sure she stays on the premises. She ain't goin' anywhere if'n that's what you're worried about, Miss Donovan."

Kendra wasn't entirely sure if that was what she was worried about. She only knew that instead of a sense of satisfaction, she had a strange sense of dread growing in the pit of her stomach.

61

The Duke's coachman didn't come alone. He brought four outriders carrying large blunderbusses to deter any highwayman unwise enough to attack the carriage. Snake, his stomach full of roast beef, cabbage, potatoes, and, yes, milk—Kendra had put her foot down on the matter; she'd never realized until now, but she had her own twenty-first century sensibilities—clamored into the carriage, his eyes going wide as he took in the luxury. Kendra suspected the closest he'd ever gotten to something like the Duke's carriage would've been holding it up at gunpoint with Bear.

"What will happen to Lady Louisa?" she wondered as they barreled toward London.

The Duke said, "It's likely that Lord Weston will argue for house arrest, if she faces trial at the Old Bailey."

Kendra felt another frisson of disquiet. "*If?* Why wouldn't she face trial? She murdered Lady Dover and Miss Cooper. For Christ's sake, she just attempted to kill Rebecca."

"I'm certain her family will use their influence to have her declared insane," said Alec.

Rebecca shifted in her seat, shivering a little beneath the carriage blanket that the Duke had given her. Kendra didn't think the shiver had anything to do with the chill in the carriage. "She *should* be placed in a madhouse."

Kendra considered what she knew about insane asylums in this era—grim, soulless places. As punishments went, she'd almost prefer the hangman's noose.

It took them twenty minutes to enter the sprawling outskirts of London. The carriage slowed to a jerky stop-and-go as they hit a traffic jam. The Beau Monde was out again, seeking their nightly entertainment.

Kendra gave a startled jolt when Alec took her hand. Only then did she realize that she'd been drumming her fingers impatiently on her knee.

"All will be well, Miss Donovan," he reassured her.

Her smile was forced. "I'm sure you're right."

And yet she couldn't shake the sense of urgency.

❖

They deposited Snake in Covent Garden near the Royal Opera House, at his request. Though she hadn't given much thought to where the kid spent his days or nights before, Kendra suddenly felt a little squeamish about letting him out in this unsavory section of town, filled with gin shops, bawd houses, and taverns. Again, those pesky twenty-first-century sensibilities—no one else seemed to give it a second thought when the kid hopped off and vanished into the crowds streaming out of the Royal Opera House.

Delivering Rebecca to her home at Half Moon Street proved more complicated. Before he'd left, the Duke had sent word to his sister about what was happening, and the Countess had gone to inform Lord and Lady Blackburn of the events. Rebecca's parents and Lady Atwood were sitting in the fire-lit drawing room, the trio having passed a tense evening, waiting for news.

Lady Blackburn began crying when they entered the drawing room, racing to hug Rebecca, while Lord Blackburn demanded answers. After they were given, including the unprecedented action Kendra had done to save Rebecca, Kendra was shocked to find herself caught in Lady Blackburn's strong embrace.

"Thank you, Miss Donovan." Rebecca's mother stepped back and wiped away tears. "Forgive me, but I am overcome . . . I cannot imagine life without my daughter. Will you not stay? Have a glass of wine?"

Rebecca, who was now being held in the circle of her father's arms, looked at Kendra. "I think Miss Donovan has another commitment, don't you?"

"Yes, we do."

Still, it was well after ten o'clock by the time they were able to extricate themselves. As they clamored back into the carriage, a dirty gray fog rolled in, adding to Kendra's sense of foreboding. It also lengthened the time it took for the coachman to maneuver his way through the streets to the Westons' Georgian house.

When they finally made it, the mist was wet against Kendra's face as she descended the carriage steps. Through the thick haze, she observed the blurry glow of light from several windows in the upper story. Two men wearing greatcoats materialized out of the grimy fog, approaching Sam.

"All's well?" asked the Bow Street Runner.

"Aye, not a peep outta them," the taller man said. "No one 'as left the premises since we delivered your message, sir."

"There are men guarding the back?"

"Aye, Gerald and Wallace."

Sam nodded, then looked to Kendra. "The guards will keep ter their post until tomorrow morning. Lady Louisa will then be escorted ter the Magistrates Court on Bow Street. She won't be leavin', Miss."

"I don't want to wait until morning," Kendra said. She'd spent too damn much time waiting as it was and she couldn't shake her unease. Lady Louisa had slipped away from the eyes of the Ton at her sister's ball to commit murder and she'd managed to leave her family home with no one being the wiser to kill Miss Cooper. Kendra didn't trust the constables standing guard on a foggy night to stop her from escaping, if that's what she planned to do.

The butler, more grim-faced than usual, answered their knock. His gaze rested on Sam and Kendra for a long moment, and Kendra had a feeling that he was considering turning them away. Then his gaze moved beyond them to where the Duke and Alec stood.

Sam spoke up. "We need ter speak to Lady Louisa."

The servant hesitated. "Lady Louisa is indisposed."

"Then we shall need a word with Lord and Lady Weston," said Aldridge.

The butler inclined his head but opened the door to allow them into the foyer. Only two wall sconces were lit, leaving the entrance hall draped in opaque shadows. "If you'll wait here, I shall let His Lordship know of your arrival, sir."

"That won't be necessary, Wilson." The voice of Lord Weston drifted down to them from the landing above. His face was barely discernible in the shadows as he leaned forward, his hands gripping the balustrade. "You may let them pass."

The Earl waited for them to ascend the stairs, his face as expressionless as that of the Sphinx. Then he turned on his heel and went through the open doorway of the drawing room. They followed him into the room, and though Kendra didn't know what to expect, this scene hadn't been it. Lady Weston was sitting on the sofa, working on her needlepoint; she didn't even glance up when they entered the room. Weston returned to the wingback chair, positioned to face the fire. Earlier, Kendra had thought that he looked older than his forty-eight years. Now, she thought he'd aged decades—his face had a sunken quality, the skin hanging loose in the jowls.

Weston finally broke the eerie silence. "Have you come to gloat about our misfortune?"

"I think you know that is not true," Aldridge said gently.

"I would like to speak to your daughter," Kendra said.

"Why?" Lady Weston looked up and her gaze went to the clock ticking on the shelf before focusing on Kendra. Her eyes were red and puffy, but otherwise she seemed oddly calm. Shock, Kendra guessed. "Can you not leave her in peace?"

"I'm sorry, but it's important."

Lady Weston studied her for a long moment. Then she glanced at the Duke. "My family is coming to terms with what has happened. We would prefer to do so in privacy, to avoid having our grief displayed to the word like some minstrel show."

"I am aware that this is a difficult time for you, madam . . ."

Her lips twisted into a bitter smile. "A difficult time is running out of port while hosting a dinner party. This is the destruction of my family, sir."

"Your daughter is responsible for murdering two women," Kendra felt the need to remind Lady Weston. "And nearly killing a third."

For a moment, Kendra caught the flash of rage in the other woman's eyes. Then it was gone, and she said coldly, "My daughter was not herself. Lady Dover's actions pushed her into madness."

"That will be determined at her trial," Aldridge said.

Lady Weston flinched. "Another public humiliation." The words were said in a low voice, but filled with accusation.

"I really need to talk to your daughter," Kendra insisted.

Sam nodded. "Aye, milady. I would have words with her as well."

Lady Weston's gaze slipped again to the clock. "Can this not wait until morning? The hour is late. What could you possibly learn from Louisa that you don't already know?"

"I would like to hear in her own words why she committed the crimes."

Lady Weston flicked a look at her husband's tense, haggard face. "I think we know who is at fault in this fiasco. One selfish act begot another selfish act. And my family will continue to suffer because of it."

Aldridge said, "We do not wish to see you suffer, madam. Miss Donovan and Mr. Kelly shall be quick about their business."

Lady Weston glanced at the clock a third time. *Something is wrong*, Kendra thought, a thrill of alarm darting through her. She gave Sam a sharp look. "Do you know if your constables outside actually saw Lady Louisa here? Or were they told that she was inside?"

The Bow Street Runner's eyes widened. By the look on his face, Kendra knew it was a possibility that his men had been guarding a house without a murder suspect within it. The constables probably wouldn't have questioned Lady Weston if she said that her daughter had taken to her bed, distraught. They certainly wouldn't have insisted on going into the bedchamber of a lady of the aristocracy to check on her.

Why hadn't Lord and Lady Weston been with their daughter? Knowing what confronted her in the morning, wouldn't they be with her right now?

"Where is Lady Louisa's room?" she snapped, turning back to the door. "If I have to search this entire house for her, I will."

"That won't be necessary." Lady Weston spoke in a measured tone. She slid another look at the clock as she pushed herself to her feet. "I tell you, she's asleep. She retired hours ago."

"Then I'll wake her up."

Lady Weston set aside her embroidery. "If you insist. I shall bring you to her, Miss Donovan." She looked to Aldridge, Alec, and Sam. "I realize this is an unusual circumstance, but I would not be comfortable having gentlemen enter my daughter's bedchamber while she is sleeping. You understand, I'm certain."

Kendra found Lady Weston's concerns bizarre, but no one else seemed particularly surprised.

Aldridge inclined his head. "We shall wait here, my lady."

Weston didn't even glance around from his position by the fireplace. It was as though he'd been hollowed out; the only thing remaining was the outer husk of a man.

The Countess picked up a single candle to light the way. Kendra glanced at her compatriots and saw some of her own tension reflected on their faces. She followed Lady Weston out of the room and her sense of wrongness intensified as they walked silently down the hall.

Lady Weston stopped outside a door and, for just an instant, Kendra saw her icy composure crack a little. Then the woman drew in a deep breath and reached out to turn the knob.

The door swung inward. The room beyond was absolutely silent, dark, and cold, with no fire in the hearth to offer light or warmth. Lady Weston advanced a step and light from the single candle touched on the bed. A shiver of uneasiness danced across Kendra's flesh.

Lady Weston took another step, slow, almost hesitant. The candle's glow now reached out to trace the outline of the occupant of the bed. Lady Louisa was lying there, eyes closed.

"I told you she was abed." Lady Weston's voice broke the silence, sounding strained and hoarse. "You can return tomorrow morning."

Kendra stared at the still figure. Then she grabbed the candlestick from Lady Weston.

"What are you doing . . . ?" the other woman demanded.

But Kendra wasn't listening. She hurried over, bringing the candle close so the light played over Lady Louisa's utterly still features. She didn't need to press her fingers against the carotid artery to confirm her suspicions, but she did it anyway, her breath catching in her throat. Lady Louisa was dead.

62

L audanum." The Duke infused the word with horror. They'd finally returned to the carriage, which was now making its way slowly through the thick soup of the fog that had invaded the city. Somewhere in that grayish mist a church bell clanged three times. "'Tis tragic, but I dare say, she couldn't accept the prospect of spending the rest of her life in a madhouse."

They'd stayed with the Westons until Dr. Munroe could be summoned to examine the body. It almost didn't seem necessary, given the empty laudanum bottle found next to the teacup on the bedside table. Regardless, Dr. Munroe had pronounced Lady Louisa's death an accident. Apparently it wasn't unheard of for ladies of the Ton to accidentally overdose themselves with the narcotic. Kendra had to wonder how many of those deaths, like Lady Louisa's, were actually suicides.

The lie didn't set well with Kendra, but the Duke informed her that since suicide was against the Canon Law of the Church of

England, Lady Louisa couldn't be buried on consecrated ground, nor could the Westons hold a funeral if it was determined that was what had actually happened. Besides, what did it matter whether Lady Louisa had accidentally taken too much of the drug, or if she'd deliberately killed herself?

So they'd left the body lying in the bedchamber in which she'd spent her life. Without the need for an autopsy to determine the cause of death, and since Lady Louisa wasn't actually a convicted criminal, she wouldn't end up in Dr. Munroe's autopsy school. *At least not right away*, Kendra amended silently. It could still end up there eventually. This was, after all, the era of resurrectionists.

"God have mercy on her soul," murmured the Duke.

"I wish I'd had the chance to question her," Kendra said.

Aldridge eyed her. "What purpose would that serve? Lady Louisa is a murderess. That is the question we came here to answer. What else is it you wish to know, Miss Donovan?"

"Why she killed Lady Dover, really. Why she killed Miss Cooper." She shrugged. "Rebecca said that Lady Louisa was afraid her father was planning to leave the family for Lady Dover. She claimed that she was trying to protect her family from further humiliation."

"You don't believe the claim?" asked Alec.

Kendra was silent as she thought of Lady Louisa, so desperate to marry, to avoid becoming a spinster. She'd probably thought Lord Ludlow was her one shot at stepping away from the sideline along which she'd always hovered, only to watch him slip away after Lady Dover had flaunted the Weston necklace that fateful night at the theater. Was that when she'd begun plotting the other woman's death?

"I don't know," she finally said, lifting her gaze to Alec's eyes. "But now I'll never find out."

Kendra woke up at seven the next morning, and, despite only having had a couple of hours of sleep, she felt clearheaded and ready to accomplish a certain mission—one that she didn't want the Duke or Alec finding out about, and trying to stop her. Unfortunately, she needed Molly's help.

The tweeny proved surprisingly stubborn about her request. It took at least half an hour to convince her. But afterward, dressed as a servant with a plain wool cloak over the maid's uniform and wearing a serviceable bonnet, Kendra managed to dodge the staff that were awake and sneak out the back door of the mansion. She wondered if Lady Louisa had used similar tactics to evade her household's servants when she'd murdered Miss Cooper.

The fog curled around her skirt as she hurried across the street into the park. The air was cold enough to make Kendra grateful that she had put on the wool cloak. She walked through the park, scanning the trees as she hurried through, not surprised to find it empty. When she exited the park on the other side of the square, she was forced to continue walking for another quarter of a mile before she found a hackney. The jarvey eyed her, but, disguised as she was as a servant, he didn't appear to find her appearance on the early-morning street all that unusual. He did, however, demand that she pay his fare upfront, before he agreed to bring her to her destination.

Kendra dropped the coins in his hand and climbed into a cabin that stunk of tobacco smoke, sweat, and tawdry perfume. She sat back in the old leather seat as he cracked the whip, and the two horses started out at a brisk pace. As they moved away from the affluent residential neighborhoods and into the working-class areas, the streets became more choked with wagons and cattle. Costermongers were already out, pushing their carts and yelling their wares.

The hackney stopped and Kendra clamored down, joining the queue of pedestrians flooding the street. She didn't know exactly where she'd find him, but she didn't think Bear would be all that difficult to locate in Cheapside.

It became clear that everyone knew where Bear was, but they weren't forthcoming with the information. It took a bit of cajoling—and giving a coin to a kid to deliver a message to the crime lord. When the kid finally came back, it was to bring her to a tavern, where she found Bear sitting at a worn wooden table in the corner of the smoky interior, aggressively cutting into a joint of lamb and swilling down a tankard of ale.

He didn't stop shoveling food into his mouth when she slid in the chair next to him. She chose the seat so she could have the grimy wall at her back, rather than the roughly dressed men who were hanging out in the tavern. She angled her body toward him.

"I've got a flintlock aimed at your balls, so don't do anything stupid," she said.

That got his attention. He paused with the tankard of ale halfway to his mouth. Slowly, he set it down, his mud-brown eyes fixed on hers. "Ye are the most peculiar wench I've ever met."

"Ah, now you've hurt my feelings. Alec didn't murder Lady Dover."

The giant grunted. "Aye, Snake told me a gentry mort did the deed." He picked up his fork and knife again, and continued eating.

"Good. I wanted to make sure we understand each other. We had a deal and I kept my end of it. I want to make sure you keep yours."

"I'll leave yer tulip alone," he said from around a mouthful of food. "Can't say what I'll do to the murderess of me Cordi."

Kendra said, "She's dead. The woman who killed your . . . Lady Dover is dead."

He picked up the tankard again and regarded her over the rim. "Ye kill her?"

"She killed herself."

He considered that news, then took a long drink. He set the tankard down with a loud sigh. "I guess dead is dead, whether the bitch got there by me hand or her own. And at least by her own, she'll be burnin' in hell." He paused and gave her a long look. "Ye're not gonna bring her back, are ye?"

"What?"

"The murderess? Ye're gonna leave her dead? Snake told me how some fancy cocked up her toes, but you brought her back and she began casting up her accounts. Ye're gonna leave the murderess dead, then?"

"Ah . . . sure. I'm gonna leave her dead."

Bear nodded, satisfied.

Feeling a bit bemused, Kendra pushed herself to her feet, but kept her hand on the flintlock that she'd pulled from her reticule. "I'm walking out of here, and I don't want anyone stopping me. Do I make myself clear?"

A glint of what might have been amusement came to Bear's eyes. "Ye've got lashings of courage. If ye ever get tired of yer tulip, ye come see Bear." He grinned at her.

I'd rather be given a lobotomy in one of the madhouses. Without further conversation, Kendra left the pub.

63

Kendra walked with Alec on the grassy knoll in St. James Park with Molly, beaming in her new role as lady's maid, keeping pace at a respectful distance behind. The fog that had blanketed the city earlier had lifted completely by the afternoon. Amazingly, the gray clouds had even begun to part, revealing the sun for the first time in days.

"The Duke is anxious to return home," Alec murmured.

Kendra had to smile. "Yes, I know. He says it's impossible to view the night sky here, and he's itching to get back to his telescope."

"How do you feel about it?"

"I miss the night sky too."

He smiled slightly. "I think you know what I'm asking."

She said nothing for a long moment. Then she sighed. "It's not like I have a choice in the matter, Alec."

She paused, letting her gaze travel across the landscape. There was an older woman walking with a companion, and two gentlemen conversing near the lake. Another man was strolling down the path, twirling his walking stick. A lone woman was standing with her back to them, her eyes on the lake.

She glanced at Alec. "Will you wait for me here?"

He held her gaze. "I'll wait for you."

Kendra forced herself to walk away, down to the woman standing in front of the lake. If Kendra happened to look a little flushed, Miss Aubert was too smart to comment on it. It was probably all those years working as a lady's maid.

Kendra said, "I got your note. Why did you want to see me?"

Miss Aubert turned to meet her eyes. Her own gaze was troubled. "Lady Louisa's funeral is tomorrow."

"I know."

"It is a terrible thing. The household . . . it is not a happy one."

"I imagine it wouldn't be," Kendra said slowly.

"Lady Weston most likely realizes that she should not have left a newly purchased bottle of laudanum on the tea tray that she brought her daughter."

Kendra couldn't control her swift intake of breath. "Lady Weston gave her daughter the laudanum?" she asked, careful to keep her voice neutral.

"Yes. I saw her go into Lady Louisa's room with the tray."

"And she left the laudanum for Lady Louisa?" Kendra suddenly felt chilled as she remembered how Lady Weston kept glancing at the clock. At the time, Kendra had thought she was buying time for her daughter to escape. Now she realized that maybe she was just making sure enough time had elapsed for the poison to work.

"I'm sure she will tell you that she only meant for her daughter to take a small dose, as ladies do to calm their nerves and sleep. But Lady Louisa was a fragile woman. There are such high expectations, you see. Lady Weston mourns her daughter, but, I think, there is a certain relief too. The Westons have endured so much humiliation lately. At least they will be spared a trial and sending Lady Louisa to the madhouse."

"Better to send her to the grave?"

Miss Aubert gave a light shrug. "For certain English families, yes. There will be rumors, but there are always rumors. The Ton has a short attention span. The Prince will do something next week, and everyone will be talking about him. The Westons will continue to receive their invitations to the balls and routs and assemblies. Viscount Dawson will have access to young heiresses."

"And if Lady Louisa had stood trial, and then sent to an asylum?"

The maid gave her a long look. "There would be no invitations. There would be no young heiresses waiting to marry an impoverished viscount."

Kendra fell silent and they both turned to stare at the lake. Today, it was placid, only the tiniest ripples across its mirror like surface.

"Why are you telling me this?" Kendra finally asked.

"You are the one who wanted answers, did you not?"

"I suppose so." Still, she felt a little sick that Lady Weston had most likely encouraged her obviously disturbed daughter to commit suicide.

Miss Aubert gave a sad smile. "Sometimes answers are not enough, are they?"

"No, they're not. Not when you can't prove anything."

"I will be handing in my notice after the funeral."

Kendra was surprised. "Where will you go?"

This time Miss Aubert's smile was jaunty. "I am French, Miss Donovan. And good with the needle. I can find another position as a lady's maid. Or perhaps I shall seek something new. It's not good to live your life in fear; I learned that from France's revolution. Maybe I shall book passage to your America and set up a dress shop. Life is what you make of it."

Kendra returned her smile. "I think you'll do well in America."

Miss Aubert flicked a glance toward Alec, in the distance. "I think your beau is waiting . . ."

"He's not my beau," said Kendra, but Miss Aubert was already walking away.

When Kendra joined him again, Alec asked, "What did she want to tell you?"

"Lady Weston supplied her daughter with the laudanum."

"What is she suggesting? That the woman wanted her daughter to die?"

"It would seem that way. Miss Aubert made a point of telling me that Lady Weston went in with a teacup and a full bottle of laudanum. There's no way we can prove it, of course. And even if we could, Lady Louisa is the one who took it of her own volition."

"Why did Miss Aubert confide in you, then?"

Kendra allowed her gaze to drift to the figure walking in the distance. "I'm not sure. Sometimes, when you have a secret, it's a little less of a burden to carry when you share it." She turned to look up Alec. "I'm glad I've been able to share my secret with you and the Duke." She tucked her hand inside the crook of Alec's arm—a gesture that was becoming more natural, she realized. "Someone just told me that life is what you make of it. I want to go home."

He drew in a breath. "To Aldridge Castle?"

She smiled as she met his eyes. "For now."

ACKNOWLEDGMENTS

I always imagined my first novel would be the most difficult to write. In fact, I believed that until I sat down to write *A Twist In Time* and discovered that there are just as many, if not more, nerve-racking moments. Taking an idea and shaping it into a book can be both exhilarating and terrifying—and an effort that is not done alone. Again, I have to thank the wonderful team at Pegasus, Claiborne Hancock, and my fabulous editors Katie McGuire and Maia Larson. Like expert diamond cutters, you know how to smooth out the rough edges and make everything sparkle. Derek Thornton of Faceout Studios deserves a special thanks for his talent in designing such lovely covers. As always, I am eternally grateful to my agent, Jill Grosjean. Without you, none of this would be possible. My gratitude extends to Karre Jacobs and Bonnie McCarthy, both gifted writers themselves who have never failed to champion my writing endeavors.

ACKNOWLEDGMENTS

I would also like to thank the librarians and their LibraryReads program for selecting my first novel, *A Murder in Time*, for its April book list in 2016, Overdrive for choosing it as their mystery to read last summer, and all the bloggers who took the time to spotlight it. I continue to be honored and humbled by your support.

Even though I'm writing fiction, I have tried to be as accurate as possible. I did take some creative license in describing the park at Grosvenor Square—based on the drawings that I've seen, the park wasn't quite as wild and woodsy as I've described—but I've made every attempt to ground my fiction in fact. This requires poring through books and blogs of the Regency period. When I ran into a brick wall over the customs of this period, I was lucky to be able to turn to Regency researcher extraordinaire Nancy Mayer, who never failed to answer the oddest of questions. Similarly, I have to give a big thanks to Tanya Hauf for her medical expertise; Dylan McCarthy, who guided me on the life-saving techniques of a drowning victim (may I never be in the position to have to do this in real life); and Alex Toutounji for being my French translator. Any errors are mine, and mine alone.